## Reginald Hill

Reginald Hill is a native of Cumbria and a former resident of Yorkshire, the setting for his novels featuring Superintendent Dalziel and DCI Pascoe. Their appearances have won him numerous awards including a CWA Gold Dagger and the Diamond Dagger for Lifetime Achievement. They have also been adapted into a hugely popular BBC TV series.

# By the same author

# REGINALD HILL

# THE ONLY GAME

*Harper*
An imprint of HarperCollins*Publishers*
77–85 Fulham Palace Road,
Hammersmith, London W6 8JB

www.harpercollins.co.uk

This paperback re-issue 2010
1

Previously published in paperback by
Grafton 1992

First published in Great Britain by
HarperCollins*Publishers* 1991
under the author's pseudonym Patrick Ruell

A catalogue record for this book is
available from the British Library

ISBN 978-0-00-733485-8

Set in Meridien by Palimpsest Book Production Ltd
Grangemouth, Stirlingshire

Printed and bound in Great Britain by
Clays Ltd, St Ives plc

**Mixed Sources**
Product group from well-managed
forests and other controlled sources
www.fsc.org  Cert no. SW-COC-001806
© 1996 Forest Stewardship Council

FSC is a non-profit international organisation established to promote the responsible
management of the world's forests. Products carrying the FSC label are independ-
ently certified to assure consumers that they come from forests that are managed to
meet the social, economic and ecological needs of present and future generations.

Find out more about HarperCollins and the environment at
**www.harpercollins.co.uk/green**

# Part One

'Life is either comedy, tragedy, or soap,' said Oliver Beck.

'All right. What are these two?'

A middle-aged couple strolled by them on the promenade deck.

'He's tragic, she's comic, together they're soap,' said Beck promptly.

She laughed out loud and for the next half hour they lounged in their deck chairs, categorizing passers-by and giggling together behind a glossy magazine.

The all-seeing purser intercepted her as she went down to the gymnasium.

'Miss Maguire,' he said grimly. 'I think you should remember you're a recreation officer on this ship, not a first-class passenger.'

'We could soon change that,' said Beck casually when she told him.

'For what?'

'For good maybe.'

She'd come to his cabin for a night cap, but she knew then she was going to stay.

It was her first time and she modestly turned aside as she slipped off her pants. His hand flapped her buttocks, more a caress than a slap, but she spun round, modesty forgotten, and blazed, 'Don't do that!'

*A small child being dragged unwillingly along a busy street, her mother pausing to lift the girl's skirt and administer a sharp slap to the upper leg. 'I'll really give you something to cry about, my girl, if that's what you want.' People passing by, indifferent.*

'Sorry,' he said. She saw a veil of wariness dim the bright desire in his eyes. I'm spoiling it, she thought desperately. A child again, but now a child wanting to please, she raised her right leg till it pointed straight in the air, then bent her knee and tucked her foot behind her head against the cascade of long red hair.

'Can you do that?' she challenged.

'Oh my God,' he said thickly. 'That's real crazy.'

If she amazed him with her double-jointed athleticism, she amazed herself even more with the depths of her sensuality. Afterwards they rolled apart, exhausted, and she examined his face. In the liner's public rooms he looked smooth, sophisticated, a successful businessman in his thirties, clearly at least ten years her senior. Now, his hair tousled, his face muscles relaxed with satisfied desire, he looked barely twenty.

'What are we?' she asked softly. 'Tragic, comic, or pure soap?'

He grinned and lost a couple more years.

'None of those, my crazy Jane,' he murmured. 'There's a special category for people like us. We're the ones who decide what the rest are. We switch them on and off. We're the Immortals, baby. We're the Gods.'

And lying there, lulled by the great seas streaming under the ship's bow and bathed in the afterglow of those ecstasies which had lifted her out of this time, this space, into a universe of their own creating, she almost believed him.

*The sea again, that same sea, picked up in handfuls and hurled like gravel against the storm windows of their house on Cape Cod. A ringing at the door bell. Two men in sou'westers.*

*'Mrs Beck?'*

*'Yes?'*

*'It's bad, I'm afraid, Mrs Beck. Your husband's boat. They've spotted some wreckage.'*

*'But that could be anything. In weather like this . . .'*

*'They found this too.'*

*An orange life preserver. Stencilled on it 'The Crazy Jane'.*
*Still she protests. 'But that doesn't mean . . .'*

*The second man, impatient of hope, cuts in. 'He was wearing*
*it, Mrs Beck. We'll need you for identification.'*

*She begins to sway, clutches the door frame for support.*
*Behind her, deep in the house, a child begins to cry.*

★　★　★

'So you're back,' said her mother. 'You could have given me a
bit more warning.'

'It was a snap decision.'

'Act in haste, repent at leisure, always your way. And he's dead?
Drowned, you said?'

'Yes.'

'Well, I'm sorry for your sake. I can't say more than that, never
having had the pleasure of meeting him. And this is the boy.'

'That's right.'

'Come over here, Oliver, and let's be taking a look at you.
What's up with the child? I'm your gran, Oliver. Though it's
maybe not so odd he's shy. Most kiddies know their gran before
they get to four.'

'He's a bit tired. And we . . . I call him Noll.'

'Noll? He'll not thank you for that. What's the point of
baptizing a child if you're going to start fiddling with his
name?'

'It's what I want to call him. And he's not baptized.'

'Holy Mary, Mother of God. How can you take such a risk?
We never know the moment when we'll be called. You should
know that better than most, you who've had both your da and
your man snatched away from you in their prime. Never mind.
We can soon put that to rights.'

'No!' she cried. 'I don't want him baptized, Mam. And it's no
use bringing in the Inquisition, I'll not talk to any priests,
especially not old Father Bleaney from St Mary's. He's half dotty
and he doesn't wash!'

'You're not wrong there, girl. He smells of more than sanctity,
there's no denying it. But he's a holy man for all that. And you'd

better understand this. I'm the one who says who'll come into this house, and you're the one who'll be polite to them while you're living here. God preserve us, if you'd come a half hour earlier you'd have met Father Blake. What would you have done then, my girl? Turned on your heel and flounced off like you used to do?'

'No. Of course not. Who's Father Blake anyway?'

'A colleague of your Uncle Patrick's, rest his soul. Do you not read my letters as well as not answer them? He comes across from time to time to inspect the Priory College where your uncle worked. He always calls to pay his respects and he brought me pictures of Patrick's grave. You'll meet him if you stay long enough. And you'd better be polite. How long are you staying, anyway?'

'Till I get settled, if that's all right.'

'All right? This is your home, whatever you may treat it as. What do you mean, settled?'

'Till I find a job.'

'Did he not leave you provided for? Typical Yank. All show. Any man rich enough to drown in his own boat ought to be able to leave his wife looked after. What'll you do? Try the teaching again?'

'No!'

*Mist on Ingleborough. Not yet thick but blowing in patches. A crocodile of teenagers descending, now visible along its length, now segmented.*

*Two girls crouching in the lee of a rock to light cigarettes.*

*'What are you two playing at? Didn't you hear Miss Marks tell you to keep close?'*

*'We'll be along in a minute, miss. We'll soon catch up with them wallies.'*

*'You'll get along now. Come on. Put those fags out and move yourselves.'*

*The girls exchange glances, neither wanting to show weakness.*

*'For heaven's sake, don't act so stupid. Don't you know how dangerous it can be out here in the mist?'*

*'We're almost down, aren't we? And who are you calling stupid?'*

*'Don't give me any of your cheek, Betty. I'm not asking you, I'm telling you. Move it.'*

*One girl rises, the other lowers her head sullenly, draws deep on her cigarette, mutters, 'Get stuffed, you smelly dyke.'*

*Mist on Ingleborough. An experienced teacher might play deaf, save it for later.*

*'What did you say, Betty?'*

*A glance at her friend. Too far for retreat. The cigarette dangling from the side of her magenta mouth. 'Everyone knows what old Ma Marks is like. Same with all PE teachers, I expect. Is that what the hurry is? Can't wait to get us in the showers?'*

*'You foul-mouthed slut! And put that cigarette out!'*

*A hand snakes out. Flesh cracks on flesh, the cigarette goes flying in a trail of sparks.*

*'You rotten slag! I'll get the law on you for this! My mum'll have your eyes out when I tell her.'*

*'Betty, come back. Not that way. Betty!'*

'No need to shout,' said Mrs Maguire. 'You always were too sensitive, even as a child. Stop dwelling on things. You'll never get anywhere if you're always lugging the past along with you. Oliver, that's not to play with. Oliver, put that down . . . There, now look what you've done. Are you not going to chastise him then? It's the only way he'll learn.'

'There'll be none of that, not with my son, Mam.'

'No? Well, it's your business, I suppose. And it'll be you who gets to suffer later. But I'll tell you this, my girl. I kept that ornament on that shelf all the time you were growing up, and it never got broken. So make what you like of that!'

\* \* \*

11

The streets of home, unchanged but measuring change, familiar sights that no longer include her, that make her a ghost.

Then suddenly a welcoming and welcome voice.

'Jane? Jane Maguire! I'd know that hair anywhere. I didn't know you were back in Northampton.'

'Jimmy. How are you? It's good to see you. Still running the club?'

'Such as it is. Tell you what, Jane, we could do with a few young prospects like you. Remember the Junior AA? By God, you shifted that day! I thought, another two, three years, next Olympics maybe . . . Anyway, what are you doing now? You went to PE college, didn't you?'

'That's right. But I didn't take to teaching. I worked as a recreation officer with a cruise firm for a while, but now I'm back on the market. Any ideas?'

A shrewd examination. 'Still in good shape? You look it. PE qualifications? Aerobics, physiotherapy, that kind of thing?'

'I did a bit on the liners. And I specialized in sports injuries at college. Why?'

'Chum of mine, George Granger, has started a health centre and I know he's looking for qualified staff. Trouble is, it's down in Romchurch, just outside London, so it won't be cheap living and I doubt if he'll be paying a fortune.'

'Romchurch in Essex? I did my training in Essex, near Basildon, not too far away . . .'

The returning ghost clings to the familiar . . .

'Jimmy, can you give me a number? Essex would suit me very well.'

'Going?' said Mrs Maguire. 'But you've been here no time at all.'

'Nearly a month. It's long enough.'

'This job. I thought you said you weren't starting till the beginning of September?'

'I've got things to do, arrangements to make.'

'About Oliver, you mean?'

'About Noll. Yes. And other things.'

'I don't see how you're going to be able to work and look after him. He'll be a tie. You're not settled inside yourself yet, I can see that. Why don't you leave him here till you see how things work out?'

'Leave him with you, you mean?'

'No need to sound so disbelieving. I've got used to him. He's a bit on the spoilt side, maybe, but that's the Yank way, and he's young enough not to have suffered any lasting damage. His old gran will soon lick him into shape . . .'

'No way!'

'Well, it's a fair offer and for the child's sake, I'll let it stand. Remember that when things start going wrong for you, as they surely will. It's not your fault, you take after your da, God rest his soul, and like him, you're proud and stubborn, never admitting you're in the wrong, always looking for someone else to blame . . .'

'How dare you! You of all people, after what you did to him and me . . .'

'There you go. What was it I just said? Well, blame me all you like, my girl, but remember, there'll be no excuse for blaming little Oliver, not when he's got a good home waiting for him here.'

She left the room, closing the door firmly behind her.

Jane stood for half a minute, perfectly still. She forced herself to relax, but when she looked down she saw that her hands were still tightly balled into fists. Slowly, finger by finger, she opened them wide.

Her power over me is finished, she told herself. The power of family, the power of priests. It's all in the past, everything is in the past, my mistakes, other people's mistakes. The future is mine to make it what I will. Mine and Noll's. Together.

Nothing will make me leave him here.

I'd rather . . .

*Nothing!*

# 2

It was still raining when Jane Maguire came out of the pub.

She'd had three gin-and-tonics and a packet of crisps which she'd only bought because the barman had said, 'You OK, darling?' as she ordered the third gin, as if buying something to eat changed her from a woman with a problem to a working girl on her lunch break.

Coatless, she ran across the car park, feeling as light and easy as when she'd been fourteen and one of the best sprint prospects in England. She hadn't bothered to lock the car. Once inside, only a madman would steal it. There were spoors of rain down the windows where the sealing had perished, and the carpet was soggy through the rust holes in the floor.

But at least it started first time. There was always something to be grateful for, as her mother used to say. Including presumably slaps across the leg.

She didn't want to think about that, not after this morning.

She drove steadily, blanking out past and future. Dead on three, she turned into Charnwood Grove. Perhaps once the narrow street *had* been lined with trees, but now only a few lamp posts rose between the twin terraces of big bayed Edwardian villas confronting each other so self-importantly, like wise guardians of the poor . . . where had that phrase popped up from? It was hardly apt, especially at this time of day. Until the arrival of her mobile rust bucket, there was little sign of poverty outside Number Twenty-nine which housed the Vestey Kindergarten. Mercs, BMWs and Audis gleamed and purred here, most of them newish and many, she guessed, second cars. Fathers sometimes figured in the morning drop, but the afternoon pick-up was entirely female.

As she went up the steps a couple of women, expensively

14

wrapped against the rain, looked at her strangely. Nearly three months of twice daily encounters hadn't got her past the nodding stage with any of them. She didn't blame them. People who drove cars like theirs steered clear of people who drove cars like hers – in every sense! She paused in the doorway to confirm their wisdom by shaking the raindrops out of her hair, then stepped inside.

Mrs Vestey did her best with beeswax polish and ozone-friendly aerosols, but on a wet day it was beyond even her powers to stop the school from smelling like a school. As usual she was standing by the entrance to the cloakroom, in which a melee of staff and mothers were preparing the youngsters for the perilous passage from front door to kerb. She was a tall, dark woman with a slightly hooked nose and long white teeth which she flashed in a welcoming smile as she said, 'Hello, Mrs Maguire. No problems, I hope?'

'No,' said Jane harshly.

'Oh, good. I feared that you might be going to tell me that the little upset had turned into something communicable. It's a constant nightmare as I'm sure you can imagine. So, what can I do for you?'

'Nothing,' said Jane. 'I'll just pick up Noll and be on my way.'

She pushed past the headmistress into the cloakroom and stood there a minute looking at the children.

Then she turned and said quietly to Mrs Vestey, 'Where's Noll?'

The woman gave her another long-toothed smile, this time not of welcome but incomprehension. At the same time her nostrils flared as though catching a worrying scent.

And Jane knew that the moment was close, the moment when fear became fact. But there were still lines to speak.

'Please, Mrs Vestey,' she said, 'has something happened? Has he been taken ill?'

'Yes, yes . . . at least I understood so . . .' said the woman uncertainly. 'But you yourself . . .'

She paused, took a deep breath, and when she spoke again, it was in the assertive tone of someone who needs to get basic facts established in a welter of uncertainty.

'Noll is not here, Mrs Maguire,' she said.

'Not here? Where is he then? Has he been taken to hospital? Why wasn't I . . .'

'No! Mrs Maguire,' interrupted Mrs Vestey, 'I mean Noll has never been here today. You yourself rang to say he was ill . . .'

'I rang? What do you mean? Why should I . . .'

'Someone rang,' said Mrs Vestey firmly. 'But if it wasn't you, then why didn't you bring Noll to school as usual?'

'I did!' cried Jane, her voice rising now and attracting the attention of other parents. 'I did!'

'You brought him yourself? And brought him inside?'

'No,' admitted Jane. 'Not inside. I was going to, but I was very late, so I left him on the steps with Miss Gosling . . .'

'I'm sorry? With whom?'

'Miss Gosling. For God's sake, what kind of school is this where you don't know your own staff?'

'I know my staff very well,' said Mrs Vestey. 'And I assure you, I employ no one called Gosling.'

'So I've got the name wrong!' cried Jane in a voice of rising panic. 'She's the new one. She started last week. I want to see her, where is she? What's she done with Noll?'

And now a little compassion crept into Mrs Vestey's voice as she produced her clinching argument.

'Perhaps you'd better sit down, Mrs Maguire. I can assure you I have appointed no new member of staff for over a year now, so whoever you left your son with had no connection with this establishment. Mrs Maguire, are you all right? Mrs Maguire!'

But Jane was swaying away from her. This was worse than her worst imaginings. Her body was no longer her own. She heard a voice say, 'It's all my fault. I shouldn't have hit him.' The room turned and a carousel of anxious faces undulated round her. But she could see beneath their surface concern to the grinning skulls, and the wintry light was flickering at the edges as though cast by flame.

It was time to fall into that flame and let it consume her.

# 3

Dog Cicero dropped a few threads of cheap Italian tobacco into a paper, rolled it between finger and thumb, lit it, and puffed a jet of smoke at the NO SMOKING sign.

A nurse came out of the door in front of him and said, 'Can't you read?'

He said, 'Best five card stud man my Uncle Endo ever played couldn't read a word.'

She looked at him blankly. He tossed the cigarette into a fire bucket. It had given him what he wanted, the tobacco smell to remind him of his father living and mask the hospital smell, which reminded him of his father dying.

The nurse said, 'You can go in now.'

He went through the door and looked down at the woman in the bed.

He saw a pair of dark green eyes, huge in an ashen face framed in a sunburst of red hair which almost concealed the pillow.

The green eyes saw a face out of an old Italian painting, lean, sallow, with a long nose, a jagged fringe of black hair, and deep watchful eyes. It was a mobile and humorous face. At least the right side was. The left was stiff with a shiny scar running like a frozen river from the ear across the cheek to the point of the jaw. Her gaze slipped away from it. He was wearing a light blue denim jacket, damp around the shoulders.

She said, 'Is it still raining?'

Her voice was soft, with a whisper of a brogue in it so distant he might have missed it if the hair and the eyes hadn't sensitized his ears.

He half turned his head so the frozen side faced her and said, as if she'd asked several other questions, 'You're in hospital, Mrs Maguire. It's three-fifty. When you fainted, you banged your head.'

17

She sat up, felt pain spark through her skull, ignored it.

She said, 'Noll,' and began to cry.

He said, 'I'm Detective Inspector Cicero of Romchurch CID. We've put out an alert but we need more details.'

'I can't stay here,' she said urgently. 'If there's any contact . . .'

'I've sent a man to your flat,' he interrupted. 'We borrowed your key. Look, the doctors want to X-ray your head, treat you for shock, give you sedatives, but I said you'd want to talk first.'

'Yes.'

The tears had stopped. It wasn't control, just a break in the weather.

He said, 'We've got the photo from the kindergarten files. But we need to know what he was wearing.'

She said, 'Black shoes, grey trousers, blue sweater over a white short-sleeved shirt, blue quilted anorak with a hood.'

He said, 'Get that out, Scott.' For the first time she realized there was a uniformed woman constable at the other side of the bed, taking notes. Their eyes met. The policewoman, a pretty girl of about nineteen, smiled uncertainly, decided smiles were inappropriate, flushed and hurried out.

'Right, Mrs Maguire,' said Dog Cicero. 'We're doing everything we can to get your son back, believe me. I just need to ask a few questions to make sure we're not missing anything. OK?'

She looked at him dully and he nodded as if acknowledging her agreement.

'Your full name is Jane Maguire? And from the form you filled in for the kindergarten, I gather you're a widow?'

She nodded. Once.

'Could I ask how long it is since Mr Maguire . . .'

'Beck.' She interrupted his search for a euphemism. 'His name is . . . was Beck. I started using my own name again when I came back.'

'From where?'

'America. He was American. He died eight months ago. In

18

a boating accident. He drowned.'

'I'm sorry,' said Dog formally. 'Now, we've got your address. Do you live alone, by the way?'

He dropped it in casually. Johnson, the DC dispatched to Maguire's flat, would have checked it out by now, but he wanted to see the woman's reaction.

She said, 'I live with Noll. My son. No boy friend, if that's what you mean.'

'No live-in boy friend, or no boy friend period?'

'No boy friend, no lover, no one, period!' she said harshly.

It was a strong reaction. Worth pressing? Not yet, he decided. First get the facts. Or at least, get her story.

He said, 'OK. Now, in your own time, tell me what happened. Start when you left your flat this morning.'

She closed her eyes as though in pain. The silence stretched till it became a barrier. The door opened and WPC Scott slipped back in.

'Mrs Maguire,' said Dog.

She sighed deeply and began to speak.

'It was raining,' she said. 'It had been raining all night. Perhaps that's why the car wouldn't start. But I was late already. Noll hadn't been too well over the weekend and he was still a bit fractious when I got up. Usually he's keen to get to the kindergarten, and I know he'd been particularly looking forward . . . it's the last week before they break up, you see, and they were doing all kinds of Christmassy things . . .'

Her voice faded then picked up again before he could frame a consolation.

'Anyway, he announced this morning he didn't want to go. I suppose he sensed I was in a hurry and just decided to be bloody minded. They can be like that, you know, kids. *Don't want to, don't want to,* over and over . . . and you try to be reasonable like you were taught, and time's passing, you can hear it ticking away . . .'

'Did it matter so much if Noll was late for school?' wondered Dog.

'No, of course not. But I've got an aerobics class at nine-thirty on Mondays . . .'

'You take it, you mean? That's your job?'

A hesitation. A decision?

'Yes. I work at the Family Fun Health Centre in Shell Street. It's about thirty minutes' drive through the morning traffic, so I've really got to be on my way by nine.'

'But this morning the car wouldn't start?'

'No,' she said. 'I kept on trying the starter, then I got worried about the battery. So I got out and looked under the bonnet.'

'And you found the trouble?'

'No. I'm not mechanically minded. I suppose I was just trying to advertise that there was a helpless little woman in trouble. It didn't work at first. Seems those macho know-it-alls don't function so well in the wet either.'

It sounded like a bitter joke, but he got the feeling it was also a delaying tactic. This was painful, but the greatest pain was yet to come.

'So in the end you managed yourself?' he asked.

'No. There was this man, a boy really, you know, leather jacket and jeans, he stuck his head under the bonnet, fiddled around for a few seconds, said, "There you go," and went on his way. I thought he was joking, or maybe just walking off fast rather than admit it was beyond him. Men do that, don't they? Walk away rather than admit defeat? But when I tried it again, the engine started straightaway. So did Noll. I'd strapped him in his chair in the back and he'd sat there, happy as Larry, all the time I couldn't get the thing going. But now he started up again. You wonder where they get the lung power from. All the way to Charnwood Grove he kept it up without a break. And the rain was still coming down, and the windows were all misted up, and all I could think of was that Mr Granger would be furious . . .'

'Mr Granger?'

'George Granger. He owns the Health Centre.'

'Where you work from nine-thirty till . . ?'

20

'Till two-thirty.'

'Odd hours.'

'They suit. Housewives in the morning fighting the flab. Businessmen pumping iron, over their lunch hours.'

She spoke with something close to contempt, noticed him noticing and went on in a neutral tone, 'Then it's fairly quiet till evening. I go in four nights a week, seven to ten.'

'Leaving Noll with a baby sitter?'

'Yes. Naturally. Do you think I'd leave him alone?' she flashed.

'*Naturally*, no. What do you do for lunch, Mrs Maguire?'

The question surprised her, quenched her anger. Made her wary.

'Nothing really. There's a coffee machine. I usually don't bother till I get home. Then Noll and I have tea together . . .'

Tears brimmed again. He preferred anger to tears. He said brusquely, 'Is there a bar at the Centre?'

'No,' she said. She watched him, saw his nose twitch, remembered Vestey's nostrils flaring. He'd smelt the gin, or that cow had told him she'd smelt it. She waited for the question. If asked, she'd tell him. But he had to ask. She had no strength to tell what she wasn't asked.

But he was set in his method. The diversion was over. He was back on the old rails.

'So you finally arrived in Charnwood Grove. At what time?'

'Nine-fifteen. Nine-twenty. I parked the car and got Noll out. He didn't want to come and I almost had to drag him out. And then Miss Gosling came along . . .'

She halted. It was close now. The moment when she described seeing Noll for the last time. The last time . . .

She had to move. She thrust back the sheet and swung her legs over the side of the bed. There was a moment of dizziness but her body was so well tuned it carried her easily through it. Then she was on her feet. Cicero drew in his breath. All impression of frailty was dispelled. Not even the shapeless hospital gown could disguise her grace as, long-legged and full-bosomed, she moved around the room with the frustrated energy of a circus cat

21

exploring the limits of its cage.

'Who's Miss Gosling?'

'One of the teachers . . . at least I thought . . . She was walking along with her head down into the rain. Noll ran into her. She almost knocked him over.'

She seemed to have got past a sticking point and was now talking fast and fluently.

'She stooped down and steadied him and she said, "Hello. It's Noll, isn't it? You must be in a hurry to get into school. Is it those Christmas decorations you're so keen to finish off?" And Noll said, "Yes." All that grizzling about not going to school and here he was saying yes to a stranger . . .'

'Stranger?' interrupted Dog. 'I thought you said this Miss Gosling was a member of staff.'

'She was!' insisted the woman. 'She knew all about Noll's class making Christmas decorations. He'd told me about them on Friday. And she was wearing the uniform, well, not exactly uniform, but Mrs Vestey likes her staff to wear these brown skirts and cream blouses . . .'

'And you could see this? You mean she wasn't wearing a coat, even though it was raining cats and dogs?' said Cicero, gently puzzled.

Jane thought, then said, 'Yes, she was wearing an anorak, a blue anorak with the hood up.'

'Like Noll's. That was what you said Noll was wearing, wasn't it?'

'That's right. They matched. It was the same blue, I remember. And she was walking along with the anorak unfastened but with her hands in her pockets to clasp it tight across her body as she walked. But when she bumped into Noll she took her hands out to steady him and the anorak fell open.'

She stood in front of him and looked down at him almost triumphantly. A problem posed, a problem solved. But was it a problem of memory or a problem of explanation?

'And what happened then?' he asked.

'She said she'd take Noll into the kindergarten, and I got in the car and drove away,' she said.

'What? You left your child with this stranger? All right, so she said she was a teacher at the kindergarten, but you only had her word for it, didn't you? And didn't it occur to you to wonder, if *you* were so late, what was this so-called teacher doing wandering around outside at that time too?'

'No,' she said. 'I didn't think of that. Not then.'

She sat down on the edge of the bed and regarded him earnestly.

'But I wouldn't have left Noll if I hadn't been certain, no matter how much of a hurry I was in. I knew she was a teacher because I'd met her in the school. On Friday afternoon when I picked Noll up. She was there. In the school. She talked to me about Noll. She said she'd just started and was trying to get to know all the mothers.'

'But Mrs Vestey says . . .'

'She's a liar!' cried Maguire, jumping up once more. 'She's the one you should be questioning. That bitch. She's a liar, a liar, a liar!'

She was moving round the room again. But now the cat-like grace had gone, to be replaced by something much more spasmodic, angular, almost manic.

WPC Scott was looking at him anxiously. He nodded and she rose and slipped quietly out.

He said, 'When you fainted, Mrs Maguire, the last words you said were, I quote: *it's all my fault; I shouldn't have hit him.* What do you think you meant by that?'

She came to a sudden halt, freezing to complete stillness like a child playing statues.

'It was me who said that?' she asked, though it was only marginally a question.

'So I am informed.'

'I must have meant . . . I suppose I meant . . . it was when I was getting him out of the car. That's it. He was yelling his head off and flailing out with his hands and legs. He kicked me on the shin. It was an accident. When I looked down, I saw he'd torn my tights and I swore. I said, "Oh shit!" and he took it up. You know what little boys are like with naughty words. He just stood there shouting, "Shit! Shit! Shit!" and I hit him. I didn't think about it. I just slapped his leg very hard like my mother used to do to me. He didn't cry or anything. In fact he went completely silent. I'd never hit him before, you see. Then his face began to crumple up and he turned to run away, and that's when he ran into Miss Gosling. Perhaps if I hadn't hit him . . . And we never made up . . .'

Her body was racked with huge sobs, each one of which visibly drained her reserves of strength. She seemed to be collapsing in on herself and she had started rocking to and fro like a tower in an earthquake, when the door opened and a nurse and a doctor hurried in, with Scott close behind.

They caught her and lifted her towards the bed.

'Do you mind?' said the nurse angrily, as she found Cicero in her way. The doctor scowled at him with unconcealed distaste and even WPC Scott couldn't hide her disapproval.

Dog Cicero didn't seem to register any of this, but watched pensively as they laid Jane Maguire on the bed. The doctor said, 'I think you'd better go now, Inspector. We can't delay this X-ray any longer.'

'Yes, of course. Excuse me.'

He leaned over the bed before they could draw the sheet up and looked at the woman's shins. Then he went across to the tall locker against the wall, opened it, reached in, and emerged with a pair of tights. He held them up to the light, and stretched them out.

They were perfect.

'Let us know as soon as she's fit to talk to us again, won't you?' he said pleasantly.

He went out. The young constable followed. In the corridor he said to her, 'You stay here, Scott. By the bedside. Whatever she says, waking or sleeping, you make a note. Get me?'

'Sir, what do you think . . ? The child, will he be all right?'

'Is he still alive, you mean?' He regarded her steadily. 'If you can get even money, take it, Scott.'

He walked away. She watched him go, then with a sick heart went back into the room.

# 4

The sign was brash and new: FAMILY FUN HEALTH CENTRE in big black letters on a white ground strewn with cameos of families having fun on exercise bikes, in a sauna, under sun lamps.

Dog Cicero had been here before. He knew if you removed the sign above the entrance you would find chiselled in the granite lintel: SHELL STREET YOUTH CLUB, OPENED MAY 1921 BY ALDERMAN CALDER DSO JP.

Last time he had stepped through these doors, he'd been fifteen, and memory programmed him to expect peeling olive green paint, worn linoleum, bare bulbs, a smell of damp wood, the stridency of punk guitars.

Instead he found pastel shades, carpet tiling, strip lighting, an odour of embrocation oil and the bounce of James Last.

Someone had turned Shell Street Youth Club into a place fit to get fit in.

Not that the woman sitting at a small reception desk looked much of an advertisement for the service. If fat was still a feminist issue, here was a profound political statement.

'I'm looking for Granger,' said Dog.

'He's in the gym. Can I help? I'm Mrs Granger. Was it one of our courses you're interested in?'

'No.' He produced his warrant card. 'Just an enquiry.'

She didn't look surprised. Or worried.

'Come with me,' she said.

She led him through a door into a corridor. A willowy blonde looking like the *after* to the older woman's *before* came towards them. Mrs Granger said, 'Suzie, watch the desk for a minute, will you?'

There had been something euphemistically called a gym in

the youth club. This too had changed; sprung floor, white pine, and enough gleaming implements to delight an Inquisitor's heart. A couple of youths were pushing and pulling at steel levers, watched by a burly middle-aged man who came to the door in response to a gesture from Mrs Granger.

'George, this is Inspector Cicero,' she said. 'My husband, Inspector.'

'Cicero? There was a chippie called Cicero's.'

'My father's. Mr Granger, if you can spare a moment, I'd like to ask about a member of your staff. A Mrs Maguire. Mrs Jane Maguire.'

The Grangers exchanged glances.

'So what's she been saying?' demanded the woman.

'Is there somewhere we can talk? If you're not too busy.' He glanced into the quiet gym.

'We fill up later on,' said Granger defensively. Dog looked at his watch. Ten to five. He recalled what Maguire had said.

Granger led the way to a small office. Three was very much a crowd in here, especially when two were built like the Grangers. He had clearly eaten at the same table as his wife even if he had been rather more successful in preserving the fat–muscle ratio.

'Right, Mr Cicero, let's hear it.'

There was an edge of something there. Aggression? Anger? Defiance? Endo said, just keep dealing the cards, son, and sooner or later they'll tell you what they're at.

He asked, 'What time did Mrs Maguire get to work this morning?'

Another exchange of glances, this time puzzled. Then the woman said with remembered indignation, 'Ten to ten. I had to start her aerobics class.'

Dog thought of Maguire's lithe athletic figure and nodded gravely.

'And did she leave at her usual time? That's two-thirty, I believe.'

'*No!*' exploded Granger. 'She did not!'

'You mean she left early? Why was that?'

'She left early because I fired her! That's why she left. What's she been saying, Inspector?'

'You fired her?' said Dog. 'For being late?'

Again he got the bewildered reaction.

The woman said, 'I think you'd better tell us why you're asking these questions, Inspector.'

'No,' said Dog equably. 'I think you'd better tell me why you're giving these answers. Why did you dismiss Mrs Maguire, Mr Granger?'

He looked at his wife. She nodded permission. He said, 'I sacked her because there was a complaint. I'd asked her to give one of our regular clients a massage. It was about midday. Some little time later I heard her voice raised in the treatment room and then she came out. I went in to see what was the matter and the client made a very serious complaint which left me no alternative but to sack her.'

'What exactly was this complaint?'

Granger said hesitantly, 'Well, he, the client, accused Mrs Maguire of . . . making an indecent suggestion.'

'I'm sorry?' said Dog.

'For heaven's sake, George,' interrupted Mrs Granger impatiently. 'She offered to jerk him off. For twenty-five pounds, Inspector!'

She sounded more indignant at the price than the proposal.

'And what did Mrs Maguire say when you put this to her?' said Dog to the man.

'She told me it was *her* business. She said she was only offering what these men really wanted. And when I told her she was fired, she became very abusive and said if it was the Centre's good name I was worried about, I'd better forget it, because by the time she was finished with me, it would stink.'

'And then she assaulted him,' said Mrs Granger.

'What?'

Granger looked embarrassed.

'It wasn't anything.'

28

'She punched you in the stomach,' retorted his wife. 'He was doubled up with pain. I wanted him to call the police. If it had been a man he would have done, and in my book a violent woman's just as dangerous as a violent man.'

'It would have made me look silly and not done the Centre's reputation any good,' said Granger. 'The same about the other thing. Sacking her and letting the whole thing drop seemed the best course.'

'And your client went along with this?' said Dog.

'Oh yes,' said the woman. 'He'd got a name to protect too. Mud sticks.'

'And what is this name he's protecting?' asked Dog.

The man said, 'I daresay you'll know it, Inspector. It's Jacobs. Councillor Jacobs. So you see, Mrs Maguire picked the wrong man when she picked on him!'

They were right. Councillor Jacobs was the amplifier through which the still small voice of God was heard plain in Romchurch. The scourge of corruption, the trimmer of budgets, the guardian of the public purse and, as chairman of the Police Liaison Committee, the answer to the Chief Constable's prayers.

He asked a few more questions then left. On his way past the desk, he paused and smiled at the skinny blonde. She looked about twenty and had a cheerful, open face. He said, 'Do you know Mrs Maguire?'

Her expression lost its openness.

'Who's asking?' she said guardedly.

He told her and she said, 'Is it about her getting the boot?'

'That's right,' he lied easily. 'Were you around?'

'No. I had to go out at lunchtime. I had a dentist's appointment.'

She opened her mouth as though inviting him to check. He looked in and she ran her moist pink tongue along her upper teeth and grinned as he looked away.

'Is it right she belted old George in the gut?' she asked.

'Did you know her well?'

'No. Hardly at all. She was a bit stuck up, know what I mean?

29

But she'll be OK, won't she?'

Dog said, 'Any reason she shouldn't be OK?'

'No!' she asserted strongly. 'Not as if she hasn't got someone to take care of her, is it?'

'A boy friend, you mean? I thought you said you didn't know her socially.'

'That's right, but I know a dreamboat when I see one. I could have eaten him for supper, numb gums and all.'

'What are you talking about?' demanded Dog.

'Her boy friend, of course! He was looking to meet her after work this afternoon, only he wasn't to know she'd got the heave, was he? So he came in when she didn't come out at half two like she usually does, and asked where she was.'

'And what did you tell him?'

'Nothing at first. I just played him along to see how well attached he was. We were getting on fine till I told him she'd left early, then he took off pretty smart so it must be serious, worse luck.'

'Describe him.'

'Well, like I say, he was gorgeous.' Seeing from Dog's face that more was required, she went on, 'Like Tom Cruise, know what I mean? Only really blond. And he had this sexy accent, Scotch or maybe Irish, they all sound the same, don't they? And his name was Billy.'

That was it, but it was enough. In a lot of child abuse cases there was a boy friend on the scene, not the child's father. Maguire had denied having a man in her life. Another question mark. Sometimes you couldn't see the answers for the questions.

Sometimes you didn't want to see the answer.

He walked twice round his car, got in, set off back to the station. The evening traffic was building up, smearing light along the wet roads. He got stuck at the roundabout outside Holy Trinity. They'd got the Christmas lanterns up in the old yew tree by the porch. He leaned across to peer at them. This church and the Shell Street Youth Club had been the poles of

30

his boyhood world and the next turn left would take him past its centre, the old shop.

He wouldn't make the turn. Church, club, shop, they belonged to another country, another time. Another person.

The person he was now had only one concern. What had happened to young Oliver Maguire? What odds would he recommend to WPC Scott now?

His radio crackled into life with his call sign. He responded and the metallic voice said, 'Message from WPC Scott at City General Hospital. Maguire has absconded. Repeat, Maguire has absconded.'

'Shit,' said Dog. The traffic started to move. A gap opened in the outside lane. Engine snarling in protest, he forced his way into it, got one wheel on the central reservation, crowded the van ahead of him over to the nearside and swept round the front of the line onto the roundabout with emergency lights flashing.

Behind him, pressed back against the oak door in the shadowy porch of Holy Trinity Church, Jane Maguire watched him drive away.

# 5

Fear heightens perception.

Jane Maguire had spotted Dog Cicero the instant she stepped through the church door. One car in a line of traffic, one silhouette in a gallery of portraits, but her eyes had fixed on it. Then it had turned full face towards her and she'd been certain the magnetism was two-way.

Next moment, however, he'd spoken into a mike and driven away like a madman. She knew beyond guesswork what he'd been told and she almost felt a pang of sympathy for the young policewoman. Not that it had been her fault any more than it had been Jane's plan. As she'd been wheeled down to X-ray, she'd heard the girl ask, 'How long?'

'Thirty minutes at least,' had been the answer. In the event she'd been through in five, back in her room in ten. And she was alone, except for the almost tangible after-image of Cicero's distrust. She saw again those coldly assessing eyes in the half-frozen face and she knew she'd made a mistake, not in lying, but in lying about things he could check. He would be back and she couldn't keep fainting her way out of confrontation for ever.

It was time to go. Her body had made the decision before her mind and she was already out of bed and pulling on her clothes.

No one challenged her as she walked along the corridor to Reception and out into the chill night air. It was still raining. She felt it would never stop. Momentarily she got entangled in a small queue of mainly old people climbing into an ambulance. Instead of passing through, she let herself be taken up with them. Soon afterwards when the first passenger was dropped near Holy Trinity roundabout, she got down too. Every day she passed the church on her way to the Health Centre. If she noticed it at all, it was with a sense of relief that she'd shed that particular delusion. Now she went inside, rationalizing that she needed somewhere quiet to sit and think. But as the door closed hollowly behind her, the smell, the light, the sense of echoing space sent her reeling back to her childhood and she felt her controlling will assailed by a fearful longing for the cleansing darkness of the confessional.

A priest came down the aisle. Sensing her uncertainty, he asked courteously, 'Can I be of any assistance?' He was an old man with a kind face but his accent was straight out of O'Connell Street.

'No, thank you,' she said harshly, and turned on her heel and left.

Flight or victory? Would any other accent have had her on her knees?

Then she had seen Cicero and for one superstitious moment felt that perhaps God was laying her options unambiguously in view.

Now she watched his car out of sight before hurrying down the side of the church, following a gravel path that continued between mossy headstones till it reached a graffiti'd lych-gate which opened onto a quiet side street.

Here she paused, sheltering from the rain under the gate's small roof, and summoning reason back to control. Where should she go? Not her flat. Cicero had told her he'd got someone waiting there. Run home to mother? That's what she'd done last time, with mixed results. But she couldn't do it this time, not with the news she would have to bear. Besides, Cicero of the unblinking brown eyes would soon ferret her mam out.

No, there was only one place to go, one person to turn to. No matter if angry words lay between them. There and only there lay her hope of welcoming arms, of a sympathetic hearing, of lasting refuge.

Putting her head down against the pelting rain, she began to walk swiftly towards the town centre.

# 6

Dog Cicero parked his car obliquely across two spaces and ran up the steps into the station. A small man wearing oily overalls and a ragged moustache blocked his way.

'Call that parking?' he said. 'You're not in bloody Napoli now, Dog.'

'I hate a racist Yid,' said Dog. 'You done that car yet, Marty?'

'Report's on your desk.'

'What's it say?'

'Given up the adult literacy course, have we? All right, car's a rust bucket but not a death trap. Should scrape through its MOT.'

'How's the engine? Poor starter?'

'No. Fine. In fact in very good nick, considering. It's the upholstery, not the mechanics, should be interesting you, though.'

'Why's that, Marty?'

'Some nice stains on the back seat round the kiddie's chair. That black poof from the lab's looking at them now. Hey, doesn't anyone say thank you any more?'

'I'll give you a ring next time I feel grateful,' Dog called over his shoulder.

As he ran up the stairs to his office a youngish man in a shantung shirt and dangerously tight jeans intercepted him.

'You've got a visitor,' he said.

'No time for visitors, Charley. Can you raise me Johnson at Maguire's flat?'

'No-can-do,' said Detective Sergeant Charley Lunn, with a built-in cheerfulness some found irritating. 'There's no phone there and it's a radio dead area. Shall I send someone round?'

Dog thought, then said, 'No, I'll go myself. You get anything

34

for me on Maguire, Charley?'

He'd instructed his sergeant to run the usual checks, not with much hope.

But Lunn said, 'As a matter of fact, I did. Maguire's her real name, by the way, not her married name . . .'

'I know that,' said Dog impatiently, leading the way into his office.

' . . . and she's twenty-seven years old, born Londonderry, Northern Ireland, but brought up since she was nine in Northampton where her widowed mother still lives . . .'

'You got an address?'

'Surely. Here it is. To continue, our Maguire trained as a teacher at the South Essex College of Physical Education, qualified, and got a job at a Sheffield secondary school, but quit in her probationary year . . .'

'Is any of this relevant?' interrupted Dog. 'And where the hell did you dig it up anyway?'

'Obvious place,' said Lunn modestly. 'I punched her into the central computer and out it all came.'

'Good God. What's she doing in there? Has she got some kind of record?'

'Indirectly. It's a bit odd really. Seems that during this teaching year, she went with a school party on a walking tour up on Ingleborough in Yorkshire. There was some kind of row which ended with her hitting a girl who took off into the mist and fell down a pothole. The place is honeycombed with them, I gather. The girl was seriously injured and the family tried to bring a private prosecution against Maguire for assault but it never got off the ground.'

'Then why the hell is it on the computer? And what did she do after she resigned from teaching?'

'Don't know. That was it. Any use?'

'The address might be,' said Dog. 'Charley, get a general call out for Maguire, will you? Nothing heavy. Just to bring her in for her own good.'

'It shall be done. You won't forget your visitor, will you?'

'I'll do my best. Who the hell is it anyway?'

'Not just any old visitor,' grinned Lunn. 'A real VIP. Very Indignant Person. It's Councillor Jacobs. He's making do with the super till you get back.'

'They were made for each other,' grunted Dog. 'He can wait a bit longer.'

As Lunn left, he picked up the phone and dialled.

'Dog, my man! Knew it was you. Recognize that ring anywhere, as the actor said to the bishop. It's the stains in the car, right?'

'Right. Got anything yet?'

'Natch. Can't hang around when it's a job for Generalissimo Cicero, can we? It's blood and it's Group B. How does that grab you?'

He looked at the copy of Oliver Maguire's record he had taken from the kindergarten. Blood Group B.

'Where it hurts,' he said and replaced the receiver. The phone rang instantly.

'Dog, could you pop along to see me? I've got Councillor Jacobs here and he's keen to meet you.'

Detective Superintendent Eddie Parslow had been a high flier till his late thirties when the heat of a peptic ulcer had melted his wings. Since his return to work, his sole aim had been to achieve maximum pension with minimum stress. A foxy face and lips permanently flecked with the white froth of antacid tablets gave him the look of a rabid dog, but none need fear his bite who did not disturb the even tenor of his ways.

Jacobs was a stout, florid man who needed no padding when he played Father Christmas at the council's children-in-care party. He was clearly not in a ho-ho-ho-ing mood.

'I gather this Maguire woman's been stirring things up,' he growled. 'I thought I'd make sure you'd got the record straight.'

Dog glanced at Parslow and received a little shake of the head. He took this to mean that nothing had been said to the councillor about the real reason for their interest in Maguire.

'That's what we like,' he said equably. 'Straight records. So what happened, Councillor?'

'She was massaging my back,' said Jacobs. 'When I turned over, she pulled my towel off and said, "Fancy a bit of relief? It'll only cost a pony." '

'And what did you take this to mean?'

'I took it to mean she was offering to masturbate me for twenty-five pounds,' said Jacobs sharply. 'What the hell else could it mean?'

'Hard to say,' said Dog. 'Were you erect, by the way?'

'What?'

'Erect. Excited. It'd be natural. Pretty girl rubbing your body . . .'

'No, I was not erect,' snarled Jacobs. 'What the hell is this? I have a massage at least once a week. I don't care if it's a pretty girl or Granger himself, as long as it helps my back. God, I knew I should have had her arrested straight off and not given her the chance to pour her poison out . . .'

'Why didn't you?' asked Dog. 'Call us straightaway, I mean. A man in your position with your reputation can't be too careful.'

'Don't you think I know it? Mud sticks. I thought, better to forget it perhaps. Also George Granger's by way of being a friend. I didn't want to get his centre into the papers.'

'Very commendable,' said Dog. 'So you decided very altruistically to keep stumm, till your mate Granger rang you up to say I'd been round?'

'I don't like your tone of voice,' said Jacobs softly. 'As it happens I didn't keep stumm. As it happens I was chairing a meeting of the Liaison Committee this afternoon and Jim Tredmill, your Chief Constable, was there, and after the meeting I had a word with him, asked his advice. He said I'd probably done the right thing, no witnesses, hard to prove, but he'd see his men kept their eyes open for this tart. Clearly he hasn't had time to ask you yet, Inspector. But never fear. I'll make sure he knows just how ignorant his senior officers are!'

The door banged behind him with a force which set the coffee cups on Parslow's desk vibrating.

'Now I'd say you handled that really well, Dog,' said the superintendent mildly.

Dog shrugged.

'You've got to play 'em as you see 'em,' he said.

'One of your famous Uncle Endo's gems, is it?' enquired Parslow. 'All right, fill me in.'

He listened, sucking reflectively on a tablet.

'Sounds like it could turn out nasty,' he said unhappily. 'Maguire. Is she Irish?'

'Born in Londonderry, brought up in Northampton.'

'Is that a problem for you, Dog?'

'No,' he said emphatically. Too emphatically? But Parslow just wanted formal reassurance.

'Good. It's an odd tale she tells, certainly. Over-ingenious, you reckon? Or odd enough to be true?'

It dawned on Dog that Parslow did not yet know that Maguire had walked out of the hospital.

He said, 'Hardly matters, does it? One way the kid's dead, the other, he's likely to be in danger of his life.'

He saw Parslow register glumly that hassle awaited them in all directions, then tossed in his poison pill.

'One more thing,' he said. 'I've just heard from Scott at the General that Maguire's had it away on her toes.'

A spasm of pain crossed Parslow's face, mental now but with its physical echoes not far behind. He should go, thought Dog. To hell with hanging on till he topped twenty-five years, which was Parslow's avowed aim. But who the hell was he to give advice? Another month would see his ten years up, and for the past eighteen months he'd been promising himself that the decade was enough, he'd have done whatever he set out to do by joining. Only, his motives were now so distant, he couldn't recall whether he'd achieved them or not.

Parslow said, 'Have the press got a sniff yet?'

'No. And I'd prefer to keep it low key till we know which way we're going,' said Dog.

'Fine,' said Parslow. 'I suppose I'd better have a word with

Mr Tredmill.'

He didn't sound as if he relished the prospect. Everyone knew that the Chief Constable was keen for him to go and didn't much mind if it was in an ambulance.

'I'm going round to Maguire's flat,' said Dog.

'You think she might show up there?' said Parslow hopefully.

'Only if she's mad,' said Dog.

Parslow popped another tablet into his mouth.

'What makes you think she isn't?' he asked, sucking furiously. 'And if she is mad, and she's killed one kid, you'd better find her pretty damn quick, Dog, before she gets the urge to kill another!'

# 7

Jane Maguire's head was aching. She wondered what the result of the X-ray had been. Most shops were already staying open late as Christmas approached and she went into a chemist's and bought some aspirin. The shop was packaged for the festivities with golden angels dangling from the ceiling and carols booming out of the P.A. Noll was to have been an angel in the school nativity play on the last day of term this coming Thursday . . .

She had to get out of this perfumed brightness. Clutching her aspirins, she started to push through the thronging shoppers towards the door. Behind her someone called, 'Excuse me . . .' A woman said, 'I think they want . . .' but she thrust her rudely aside and did not pause till she was outside on the glistening pavement dragging in litres of the cold damp air.

A hand grasped her arm. She pulled it free, turned, only fear preventing her from screaming abuse. A girl in a blue overall looked at her strangely and said, 'You forgot your change.'

She took the money and managed to croak a thank you. Despite the chill rain she felt hot and weak. Across the road was a pub. Oblivious of traffic she made her way towards it. Only when she reached the bar did she realize it was the same pub she'd been in this lunchtime. It seemed light years ago. Would the barman remember her? What if he did? There was hardly time for her face to have appeared in the papers.

She ordered a brandy. She didn't like it, but her mother had always insisted on its medicinal qualities. Her mother . . . She took a sip and pulled a face. The barman said, 'All right, is it?' She said, 'Yes. Sorry. It's just the taste . . . I mean, I'm starting a cold . . .'

It was a productive lie. He said, 'What you really need is

something hot. We do coffee.' And as he poured her a cup in response to her nod, she was able to take a couple of aspirin without him calling the drug squad.

She sipped the coffee and felt a little better. It occurred to her that the last time she had eaten had been in this place several hours ago, and that hadn't been much. There were some corpse-pale pies in a plastic display cabinet. She asked for one. The barman put it in a microwave and a few moments later handed it to her, piping hot but still pale as death. She bit into it. The meat was stringy, the gravy slimy, but it tasted delicious. So. Forget the soul, forget the intellect. Animal pleasure was still possible even after . . .

She pushed the thought away as she ate the pie. Then she ordered another. No pleasure now, but a simple refuelling, an anticipation that she would need all her resources.

Finished, she went to the cloakroom. The mirror showed her a face as pallid as the pies. Her long red hair, usually electric with life, hung straight and lank and darkened almost to blackness by its exposure to the rain. It was, she guessed, a good enough disguise, but it was not how she cared to see herself. She stooped to get her head under the hand drier and combed her hair dry in the hot blast. Then she washed her face, rubbed it vigorously with a paper towel and applied a little make-up to her skin, which was glowing with friction.

Once more she inspected herself. It was better, this shell she had to present to the world. Little sign there of the hollow darkness beneath, empty of everything but the echo of a child crying . . .

Her clothing was very damp. She took off her linen jacket and dried it as best she could under the hand drier. Then she thought, 'What the hell am I doing?' It was these damp clothes that the fearsome Cicero would have a description of. Out there was the High Street full of shops desperate to take her money, no matter how tainted it might be.

She left the pub without re-entering the bar and half an hour later she had solved both the problems of damp and disguise. In

41

black trainer-type shoes, loose slacks, tee shirt, and a chunky sweater, topped by a thigh-length waxed jacket with her hair tucked beneath its wired hood, she felt herself anonymous and warm. Her headache had gone and though she felt her body to be far from the high muscle tone she had enjoyed since her early teens, she was walking with some of her old long-limbed athleticism as she approached the bus station.

Despite the weather and the hour there were still plenty of people about, seduced by the lights and the music and the glittering prizes on offer in the late-closing stores. A couple in front of her turned aside abruptly to peer into a toy-shop window and in the gap created she glimpsed, twenty yards ahead at the bus station entrance, the tall helmets of a pair of policemen.

Immediately, without thinking, she too halted and turned towards the display of toy space ships, ray guns, spacemen helmets, all the TV-age artefacts designed to delight the heart of a little boy. Her brain refused to register them. Instead her head kept turning till she was looking back down the street. It felt like slow motion, but it all happened quickly enough for her to catch a man's eyes before he too paused and looked aside into a shop window. That was all it took. He was an ordinary-looking man from what she could see of him under a narrow-brimmed tweed hat and a buttoned-up riding mac. But that brief eye contact was enough, even if the shop window he was peering into with such interest hadn't been a ladies' heel repair bar.

She glanced the other way. The helmets were moving towards her.

She peered into the toy-shop window. The toys presented no problem now. She couldn't see them, only the street behind her reflected in the glass. The tall helmets like ships' prows came alongside. They didn't pause, but sailed on by. She didn't wait to see what would happen when they reached the man outside the heel bar but strode out along the pavement, leg muscles tensing and untensing, almost trembling in their anticipation of being called upon to explode into a sprint. But she mustn't draw attention to herself. Then, as she reached the station entrance, she saw at the far side the bus she wanted, the last couple of passengers stepping aboard.

Now she had her excuse. The legs stretched and she floated across the intervening fifty yards with the balanced grace of a ballet dancer.

The engine was running, the automatic doors closing. The driver saw her, decided it was near enough to Christmas for charity, and pressed the button to reopen the doors. She scrambled aboard.

The bus pulled out of the station with that minimal acknowledgement of the presence of other traffic which distinguishes the bus driver the whole world over.

Jane Maguire flopped into a seat and looked out of the window.

For the second time her eyes met those of the man in the tweed hat.

Then he was falling away behind her. She relaxed, or rather felt her body go weak. She tried to set her thoughts in order but found her mind had lost its strength too. The bus moved on through the garishly lit streets, then out of the town into the sealing darkness of the countryside, and Jane sat still, feeling herself more part of the country's dark than the bus's light, with little sense of either presence or progress, and unable even to tell whether she was hiding or seeking, chasing or chased.

# 8

Dog Cicero stood outside Maguire's apartment block and felt his unhappiness grow. It was a modern three-storey building, purpose built, in a good residential area less than ten minutes' drive from the kindergarten. Renting or buying, these flats would cost. Add the kindergarten fees . . . he had forgotten to check out her salary at the Health Centre but doubted if it would be enough to cover flat, school *and* food, clothing etc.

Maguire's apartment was Number Seventeen on the top floor. He rang the bell, felt himself observed through the peephole, then DC Johnson opened the door.

'Any action?' asked Dog.

'Nothing. There's no phone, and you'd need to be a pretty thick kidnapper to knock at the door with a ransom note, wouldn't you? Thousand to one it's a weirdo anyway.'

Always interested in odds, Dog said, 'Reason?'

'I've had a poke around. Jackie Onassis she ain't.'

Dog glanced round the room. It was clean, tidy and comfortable, but hardly suggestive of wealth worth extorting.

He said, 'It may be neither. Take a stroll around the neighbours. Keep it low key but find out what they know about Maguire, when they last saw her and the kid, especially if anyone noticed her having trouble with her car this morning.'

Johnson, a plump, comfortable-looking man whose sleepy exterior belied a sharp mind, looked shrewdly at Dog and said, 'She's in the frame herself, is she, guv?'

'Could be. One thing – she's on the loose. I doubt if she'll come back here, but keep your eyes skinned.'

He closed the door behind the plump DC and began to search the flat.

Johnson hadn't poked deep enough. The clothes in the

44

wardrobe might not be designer originals but the pegs they came off weren't cheap. They all had American labels. The same went for most of the kid's toys, expensive and made in the USA. Her lingerie was of the same quality. He looked without success for anything that might be professionally kinky. Nor did he find anything in the way of contraceptive medication or stocks of condoms to suggest a commercial sex life. Not even a domestic one. He searched diligently for drugs, both prescribed and proscribed, anything which would suggest nerves stretched close to breaking point, but found nothing more than a bottle of paracetamol and a child's cough mixture. There was flour in the flour jar, tea in the tea caddy, talc in the talc tin, and nothing at all on top of the wardrobe, in the lavatory cistern or under the kitchen sink. There was no alcohol in the flat nor any tobacco. She had a small portable television set and a radio tuned to Radio Two. Her small tape collection was mainly soul and folk. There were quite a lot of books, mostly paperbacks. Her taste in fiction was for chunky historical romances, though he did find a couple of Booker nominees which she was either still reading or, on the evidence of the hairpin bookmarks, had abandoned at page seventeen and page thirty-two respectively. There were two PE manuals, one on athletics coaching, the other on sports injuries, both inscribed *Jane Maguire, South Essex College of Physical Education*. There was also a beautifully bound edition of Blake's *Songs of Innocence and Experience*. It was inscribed, *To Jane, going out into the world, with love and best wishes, Maddy*. He opened it at random and found himself looking at a poem called 'The Little Boy Lost'.

> 'Father, father! where are you going?
> O do not walk so fast.
> Speak, father, speak to your little boy,
> Or else I shall be lost.'

> The night was dark, no father was there

45

He closed the book abruptly and sat down in an old armchair which creaked comfortably, and tried to think like a copper. He had found nothing remarkable, nothing incriminatory. The only oddness was an absence, not a presence.

There was no mail except the usual junk addressed to the occupier which he'd found in the kitchen pedal bin. But there was nothing to suggest that anything either official or personal had ever come addressed to Mrs Jane Maguire.

And there was nothing either which referred to her dead husband, Oliver Beck.

He closed his eyes and played through what he had got, but it came out blurred and distorted with too much interference from other channels.

He'd told Parslow that Maguire's Irish background was no problem, and he'd meant it. But then his eyes had been wide open and he'd been able to blot out the mental image of a tall, graceful woman with huge green eyes and hair aflame like a comet's tail . . .

He opened his eyes abruptly and found to his surprise that he had rolled and lit one of his capillary cigarettes.

There were no ashtrays. Maguire didn't smoke, probably didn't like the smell of tobacco in her home. He experienced an absurd guilt, told himself she wasn't going to be back here soon enough to notice, and felt guiltier still.

He went into the kitchen and flushed the butt down the sink. Then he put the kettle on and made a cup of very strong coffee.

As he drank it Johnson returned.

'You've been quick,' said Dog.

'I've not been on house to house,' said the constable defensively. 'Just the other flats, and at half of them I got no answer, and as good as none at a lot of the rest. I only managed to raise three who admitted ever having noticed Maguire. First was an old lady called Ashley who is more or less confined to the flat beneath. Didn't know Maguire by name but says that she's heard a child crying in the flat above on several occasions and the mother shouting angrily, after which the crying died

46

to a whimper. She says she got so concerned last week that she rang the council's Social Service department and reported it.'

'Any action?' asked Dog.

'She says someone came round on Saturday morning but couldn't get any answer from Maguire's flat. But later she claims she saw Maguire putting the child into her car and driving away.'

'I thought she didn't get out of her flat?'

'Her window overlooks the front. She spends a lot of time there.'

'What about this morning?'

'She didn't get up till half past nine.'

'Pity. OK, what else?'

'Number Fourteen, Nigel Bellingham, would-be yuppie, driving a Sierra until he can afford a Porsche . . .'

'For Christ's sake!'

'Sorry, guv, but it's relevant, sort of. He doesn't notice people, this joker, but he notices cars. It's all resident-permit street parking round here, and those with regular habits usually end up at about the same spot. Maguire was very regular, and her car hasn't been in its usual spot since Saturday morning.'

'Why should he notice her car in particular?'

'Cars equal pecking order in his tiny mind. Maguire's banger was right at the bottom of his league table.'

Dog considered this, nodded, and said, 'OK. I'll buy that. What about the third witness?'

'That's Mary Streeter, Number Six. She's got a little girl, takes her to that park across the shopping precinct most Sundays to feed the ducks and usually sees Maguire there with her boy. They're not friends. I got the impression Mrs Streeter wouldn't have minded being closer but Maguire wasn't having any. Anyway, she says Maguire definitely missed the park this Sunday, and it was a fine afternoon.'

'So she was away for the weekend,' said Dog.

'So she went away after the social worker called and she didn't answer the door,' corrected Johnson unnecessarily.

'So what?' said Cicero. 'Would you let a social worker into

your house?'

The door bell rang.

The two men exchanged glances. It wasn't likely to be either Maguire or the alleged kidnapper. On the other hand it was silly to take risks.

Dog moved quietly to the front door and squinted through the peephole.

Nothing.

Motioning Johnson to one side, he gently turned the handle of the Yale lock. Then he dragged the door open and leapt out into the corridor.

An arm like a steel bar caught him round the throat, his right wrist was seized and his hand forced high up between his shoulder blades, while his left shoulder was thrust with such force against the wall that he screamed out in pain and felt his left arm hang paralysed. He tried to lash back with his heel but his assailant was ready for that and he kicked feebly into air while the pressure on his neck redoubled.

Then a voice said, 'Tommy, what are you playing at? Put him down at once. This is my old mate, Dog Cicero. Dog, how've you been, old son? Long time no see. We've got ever such a lot to talk about.'

# 9

'Funny old thing, life,' said Superintendent Toby Tench.

Dog Cicero said, 'Can't argue with that,' leaving the sentence hanging uncertainly over *Toby* or *sir*.

Tench had never lost his stoutness. At nine it had given him the bulk to back up his claim to be pack leader in the school yard. A rival had started picking on the slight, sallow, silent Italian kid and Tench had taken him under his wing to affirm his primacy. Then puberty, the great equalizer, had got to work, turning Dog into a darkly attractive young man, academically able and athletically outstanding, while it marooned Tench in a podgy, spotty, undistinguished adolescence. Their ways seemed to have parted forever when Tench left to become a police cadet and Dog stayed on to qualify for entrance to Sandhurst.

He recalled their last encounter. He'd just come from saying goodbye to Father Power at Holy Trinity. Tench, looking like the stout constable of the comic books, was walking past the church yard gate.

'Hello, Dog,' he'd said with surface affability. 'Off to officer training, I hear. You'll need to watch it on that drill square.'

'Will I?' he'd asked foolishly. 'Why's that, Toby?'

'Come on, Dog! Everyone knows when you Itis hear the order, *Forward March!* you automatically start running backwards!'

He'd almost hit him, but had had control enough to know that assaulting a policeman would probably stop his army career before it began.

Now it felt like a chance missed.

But perhaps it was going to be offered again.

The podginess had turned into a solid bulk, no less menacing for being gift-wrapped in a Pickwickian waistcoat and topped with a matching smile. The two men were sitting in the armchairs in the living room of Maguire's flat. Tench's companion was searching the bedroom. Introduced as Sergeant Stott, he had the features of a Narcissus, and if his Cartier watch and Jean-Paul Gaultier jacket stretched across pumping-iron shoulders reflected the inner man, there was no shortage of self-love here either.

From the sound of it, the body-beautiful muscles were being exercised just now in tearing the bedroom apart. Johnson's face appeared in the doorway with an expression of shocked interrogation, but Dog motioned him back inside. He had no idea what the newcomers were after, but if they found it, he wanted a witness.

'Heard you joined the local boys after your spot of bother with the mad Micks,' said Tench. 'Surprised me, that did. Thought you'd have had enough of uniforms, especially when it meant dropping down to plod level.'

'Can't recall what I felt,' said Dog evenly. 'It was ten years ago.'

'Long as that? Well, I never. And this is the first time our paths have crossed.'

'Us plods don't have much to do with the Branch,' said Dog.

He didn't add that one thing he'd done before joining the Romchurch force was check out Tench's whereabouts. He might have been confused, but not so confused as to take the risk of finding himself in the fat boy's gang again. But now here Tench was, and clearly enjoying the ambiguities of the situation hugely.

Time to clear the official ground at least.

'What's the score, Toby?' he said. 'What's the Branch's interest in Maguire?'

'No real *interest*, Dog,' said Tench with mock solemnity. 'Nothing that I'd call an *interest*. Just that she's on a little list of ours. People with a fine thread tied to their tails. Touch 'em and there's a little tinkle in the guardroom, know what I mean?'

'The computer?' said Dog. 'I wondered why that entry was there. Anyone asking questions jerks the trip wire, right?'

'Clever boy,' said Tench. 'So tell me all you know.'

Briefly, Dog outlined his investigation so far.

Tench produced a notebook, not to make notes in but to examine.

'Well done,' he said at the end of the outline. 'Missed out nothing.'

'You've spoken to Parslow? You knew all this! What the hell are you playing at? Checking up on me or what?'

'Hold your horses, my son,' said Tench earnestly. 'Not you. Old Eddie Parslow, he's the one we need to double check. He's so demob happy, he's stopped taking bribes.'

The muscular boy came out of the bedroom. In his hand was a foolscap-size buff envelope.

'Found this in the mattress cover, guv,' he said, handing it over.

'Well done, my son,' said Tench, smiling fondly.

'You want I should organize a real search, guv?' asked Stott.

Dog Cicero had no doubt what a real search meant. He'd supervised enough in scruffy Belfast terraces and lonely country farms, watching as floorboards were ripped up, tiles stripped, walls probed, while all around women wailed their woe or screamed abuse, and men stood still as stone, their faces set in silent hate.

Tench shook his head.

'Early days, Tommy. Just carry on poking around.'

Tommy went into the kitchen. A second later what sounded like the contents of a cutlery drawer hit the tiled floor.

Tench was peering into the envelope.

'What's in it?' asked Dog.

'Not a lot. Hello. Must be saving for a rainy day. Well, the poor cow's got her rain. Bet she'd like to get her hands on her savings!'

He tossed a smaller envelope across to Dog. He opened it. It was full of bank notes, large denomination dollar bills and sterling in equal quantities, at least a couple of thousand pounds' worth.

'Can see what you're thinking, Dog. That's a lot of relief

massage. Maybe she upped her prices for more demanding punters. Any complaints about queues forming on the stairs?'

He looked at Dog with his head cocked to one side, like a jolly uncle encouraging a favourite nephew.

'No,' he said. 'Nothing like that. Not so far.'

The last phrase was an attempt to compensate for what had come out as a rather over-emphatic denial.

Tench caught the nuance, said, 'You don't think she gives the full service then? Just the odd hand job for pocket money?'

'I don't know. I just don't like running too far ahead of the evidence, that's all.'

'Oh yeah? Of course, she's Irish, isn't she?'

'What's that got to do with anything?'

'Quite a lot, as it happens, my son. But in your case, it could mean you're so desperate to put the slag away that you're falling over backwards to be fair. You never were much good at thumping people just because you didn't like them, Dog. Always had to find a reason! You'll not admit it, but what you'd really like is solid evidence that she's topped her little bastard, then you can go after her full pelt! Well, you can relax, my boy. Uncle Toby is here to tell you it's going to be all right. It doesn't matter if she's cut his throat or she's the loveliest mum since the Virgin Mary. You're allowed to hate her guts either way!'

Dog was half out of his chair. One part of his mind was telling him to sit down and laugh at this provocation. The other was wondering how much damage he could inflict before Tommy, the gorgeous hulk, broke him in two.

Tench wasn't smiling now.

'Down, Dog. Down. If you don't like a joke, you shouldn't have joined. Man who's not in charge of himself ain't fit to be in charge of anything.'

Slowly Dog relaxed, sank back into the armchair.

'That's better. Godalmighty, just think, if you'd stayed in the Army, you'd have had your own company by now, maybe your own battalion. You'd have been sending men out where the flak was flying. Few more like you, and I reckon we'd have lost the

Falklands. Still, not to worry, just think of the money we'd have saved!'

Dog said steadily, 'Don't you think it's time you put me in the picture, *sir*. You called the boy a bastard. I presume you were being literal rather than figurative.'

'I love it when you talk nice, Dog. Shows all that time in the officers' mess wasn't wasted. But yes, you're dead right. Bastard he is, or was. One thing we know for sure, Maguire never got married. How do we know? Well, Oliver Beck was never divorced, was he? Let me fill you in, old son. After she jacked in the teaching, our Jane got herself a job with a shipping line, recreational officer they called it. On one Atlantic crossing she came in contact with an American passenger, Mr Oliver Beck. On the massage table, I shouldn't wonder! Anyway, he was so impressed with her technique, he set her up in his house on Cape Cod. Oliver was living apart from his wife, natch.'

'So it was more than just a bit on the side for him?' interrupted Dog.

'Why do you say that?'

'He took her into his home. They had a child.'

'Rather than setting her up in a flat and having an abortion? You could be right, Dog. Or maybe he just wanted a son and heir and didn't much mind who the brood mare was. We don't know just how close they really were, and it's of the essence as you'll see if you sit stumm for a few minutes. They certainly stuck together for the next five years. On the other hand he was away a lot and a live-in fanny probably comes as cheap as a live-in nanny. To cut a short story shorter, last April Oliver Beck snuffed it. He was a sailing freak, always shouting off he could've done the round-the-world-single-handed if he'd only had the time. This time he didn't get out of Cape Cod Bay before a storm tipped him over, and put the Atlantic where his mouth was. Now came crunch time for our Janey. Who'd inherit?'

He paused dramatically. Dog said, 'I thought this was the short version.'

'Satire, is it?' twinkled Tench. 'All right. Well, it certainly

53

wasn't Maguire. There was no will and in less time than it takes to say conjugal rights, the real Mrs Beck came swanning in to claim everything. At least she wanted to, only at just about the same time, the Internal Revenue boys turned up too, and *they* were claiming everything times ten for unpaid taxes. Our Janey summed up the situation pretty well. There was nothing in it for her, so she upped sticks and headed for home, taking with her every cent she could lay her hands on plus everything portable in terms of jewellery, *objets d'art* et cetera. Only thing was, none of it belonged to her officially, and if she shows her face again back in Massachusetts she'll find a warrant for her arrest waiting.'

He looked at Dog as though inviting a comment.

'She was in a tough situation,' he said. 'She was entitled to something, surely.'

'You reckon? Still falling backwards to be fair, are we, Dog? Even though this lady has an undeniable tendency to violence, an undeniable tendency to help herself to what ain't hers, and an undeniable tendency to pull men's plonkers for pocket money? Jesus, Dog, it's the priesthood you should have turned to, not the police!'

'You still haven't said what your interest is, *sir*,' said Dog.

'Haven't I? Neither I have! The thing is this, Dog. It wasn't just the IRS who were keeping a friendly eye on Oliver Beck. It was the FBI. You see – this'll slay you, Dog – it appears that one of the many shady ways that Beck earned his crust was by acting as a bagman for Noraid. I knew you'd like it! Now no one knows how much Janey was involved but one thing's sure, she can't have been ignorant. So now you can really let all that nasty bubbling hate go free, my son. You see, the money that kept that slag in silk knickers, maybe even those nice crisp folders you've got in your hand, all came from his commission moving the cash which bought the Semtex that cut your shaving bills in half for the rest of your natural life!'

# 10

Jane Maguire stood in a telephone kiosk in Basildon town centre. She could have been anywhere. One of the new towns built after the war to ease the pressure on London, its designers probably comforted themselves with the thought that a couple of hundred years would give it the feel of a real place. But in the decades that followed, up and down the country they had ripped the guts out of towns and implanted pedestrian precincts lined with exactly the same shops that she was looking at here. Why let the new grow old gracefully when you can make the old grow young grotesquely?

The thought wasn't hers but standing here brought it back to mind, and the dry amused voice that spoke it. She longed to hear it now at the end of the phone, but the ringing went on and on. Abruptly she replaced the receiver.

It was time to move. The journey, though not long, had dulled the impression of the man in the tweed hat. Was he watching her or was it just her terror and guilt which needed some visible object to slacken the pressure within? No matter. Her mind had gone beyond rationality. Almost beyond pain. She needed a safe place to curl up in till she was able to plan the future – and feel the agony – once more.

She started walking away from the commercial lights. She could have got a taxi where the bus had dropped her but she had felt a need for movement without confinement. The rain had grown finer till at last its threads wove themselves together into a silky mist which clung just as dampeningly but at least did not lash the exposed skin. She found herself walking faster and faster till suddenly, without conscious decision, she was running. Her newly bought clothing constrained her, particularly the waxed coat, and she felt an urge to pull it off, to pull everything off, and run with no restraint, as sometimes secretly she had done in the past when her cross-country training had taken her on a safe, secluded route.

But here even a fully clothed woman running was going to attract notice. In fact in these conditions a woman walking, once she left the lights of the town behind, was likely to draw attention, both friendly and unfriendly. She slowed to a steady walk, pulled her hood up over her head, and tried to swing her shoulders with the aggressive rhythm of a man.

A car passed, slowed, picked up speed. A lorry thundered by, almost upending her with its blast. A van drew alongside, matching her pace. A window was wound down and a voice said, 'Like a lift, mate?'

She shook her head, or rather her hood, vigorously and grunted a *no* in the lowest register she could manage.

'Please yourself,' said the voice, and the van drew away.

She reached a crossroads, turned left on a narrower minor road, and after a traffic-free half a mile, she climbed over a gate into a field. By daylight she was sure she could have walked this path with her eyes closed. But with the pressing damp darkness closing her eyes against her will, things were very different. Her feet were slipping and slithering in the muddy ground and eventually she felt one of them sink in so deeply that the cold mud oozed over her new footwear.

But her memory had not failed her. In mid-stride she hit the high wire fence, and clung on to it to stop herself falling as she bounced back.

Slowly she moved to the left till she reached a metal support post. She let her hand run down it to three feet from the bottom. Then she reached through the mesh.

For a moment she thought it was the wrong post. Then she found the loose staple and slipped it out. In a changing world some things didn't change. She tried to think of another, failed, slid through the gap she was able to force in the fence, refixed it behind her, and set off now with perfect confidence at a forty-five-degree diagonal.

There was a light ahead, the dim glow of a curtained window. She made for it, feeling a great sense of relief. The unanswered phone had been a worry. Even though she had a key, she would have felt uneasy about using it uninvited after the bitter words she'd flung over her shoulder last time she'd departed from here.

Now there was concrete underfoot once more. She moved forward swiftly and as she passed the curtained window, she gave it the double rap with which she usually presaged her arrival.

Inside there was movement and as she approached the door, it opened.

There was no light on in the hallway and for a second she hesitated, unable clearly to make out the dimly silhouetted figure that awaited her there.

Then it moved forward, and the dark was light enough for her to recognize the stubbly blond hair, the bright blue eyes, the slightly crooked and very attractive smile as he reached out his arms and said, 'Hello, Jane. I've been expecting you.'

# 11

It was a lousy night for driving. Traffic was heavy and the rain had thinned to a glutinous mist which speeding juggernauts layered across his windscreen. It felt like a pointless journey. Far simpler would have been to ask the local force to talk with Mrs Maguire and keep an eye on her house in case her daughter returned. Instead here he was letting himself be carried along at eighty in the outside lane on the doubtful grounds that if he got involved in a pile-up, he'd prefer it to be fatal.

So why was he doing it? Possibly to escape from Tench. Or, more accurately, to escape from what he feared Tench might provoke him to. To be fair to the man, he had laid it on the line.

'The way I see it, Dog, it's likely I'm wasting my time. Could be she's just got so strung out taking care of the brat that she hit him too hard, and he snuffed it. Happens more and more, especially with a boy friend around. Could be she's telling the truth, even though there's no witnesses, and some weirdo's snatched the kid. Could be that none of this has got the slightest to do with the late Ollie Beck and his Irish connections. In which case, I'll be more than happy to say, over to you, Mr Plod, and get back to the bright lights. But until I do, you'd better understand this is my case, my son, and you don't do nothing that hasn't been agreed with me first. OK?'

Parslow, when consulted, had said, 'Can't argue with the Branch, Dog. National Security, and all that.'

'More like National Socialism,' Dog had retorted but the superintendent had preferred not to hear.

So, he had announced challengingly that he was going to drive up to Northampton and interview the mother.

Tench had considered, smiled, and said, 'Good thinking, Dog. You do that. One thing though. Keep a low profile. Don't give the local plods any details. Don't want them muddying the waters, do we? Above all, I don't want anyone getting a sniff that the Branch is interested, not till I'm good and ready. So, mum's the word. And watch out for Indians north of Watford!'

Tench's agreement as much as anything had convinced him he was probably wasting his time.

It was his first visit to Northampton, so when the traffic on the approach road slowed to a crawl he had no local knowledge to make a diversion. The problem turned out to be a roundabout next to which some planning genius had built a superstore whose car park spilled a steady stream of late shoppers into the carriageway. On the other side, bright and compelling as a wise man's star, beamed a sign: CLAREVIEW MOTEL: *Accommodation, Fuel, Cafeteria, Toilets.* Feeling the need for a pee, a coffee and a map of the city, preferably in that order, Dog turned in.

Five minutes later, all his needs satisfied, he sat in the cafeteria smoking a roll-up and studied the map. The Maguire house was in a suburb quite close on the ring road, but it wouldn't do to head straight there. Courtesy, and also common sense, required a visit to the local nick to reveal his presence and check out any local knowledge.

He got lost twice in a one-way system before he made it to Police HQ. There he was passed on to a grizzled chief inspector called Denver. Dog outlined the situation, following Tench's instruction to keep things as low key as possible. Without actually lying, he gave the impression that Noll Maguire had probably just wandered off and his mother had gone looking for him and possibly one or both of them might fetch up at the grandmother's house. He anticipated some probing questions. Instead Denver's face lit up when he heard the name Maguire.

'Janey Maguire! She was at school with my girl. Lovely lass, and by God she could move! I mean *move*. National standard, international maybe. Sprints, hurdles, cross-country, they were all one to her. If you could run it or jump it, she was your girl. And when it came to throwing things, she was no slouch either.

Modern pentathlon, that's what she should have done. But you need encouragement at home to buckle down to that kind of training.'

'Which she didn't get?'

'No, more's the pity. From all accounts she didn't get much encouragement to do anything. Mrs Maguire sounds like a real throwback. Type who thinks decent Catholic girls don't need educating for anything but keeping house, getting married and having babies. As for athletics, that was carnal display! Their parish priest backed her up. He was out of the Middle Ages. You a Catholic, Inspector? Name like Cicero . . .'

'Was,' said Dog.

'Then you'll know what I mean. Fortunately, her uncle, old Mrs Maguire's brother, was a priest too, taught at the Priory College, Catholic boarding school, just a few miles out of town. All boys, naturally. But at least he was able to put his vote in for education so Janey didn't leave school after "O" levels like her mam wanted but went on into the sixth form. She still did her athletics, but never lived up to her promise. Some said she lost her edge because she filled up too much up top. Me, I don't think so. There's been plenty of world beaters with big knockers. I think she was just so worried about not making the grade that she spent more time on her books than she needed to. It was her escape route, see? Get away to college, then get a qualification that'd get her a job anywhere.'

'You're very well informed,' commented Dog.

'My daughter. She was a little bit younger and she thought the sun shone out of Janey's bum! I used to get Janey Maguire night and day and, of course, she was always round at our house.'

Another line of enquiry? Dog said, 'Is your daughter living locally?'

'No.' The man's face saddened. 'Melbourne. We're going out to see them when I retire next year. But she'd not be able to help even if she still lived here. They kept in touch through college, but after that they lost touch. More Janey than my girl.

60

She had a bit of bother in her first job. After that, she seemed to cut contact with all her old mates.'

'She never came back here?'

'Not that I know of,' said Denver. 'My girl heard she'd married some Yank and settled down over there. Then she got married herself and next thing, Australia. They say the world's getting smaller. It doesn't feel like it! Now if you'll excuse me, I've got work to do. I hope you get things sorted out, Inspector. She was a nice kid and I'd hate to think of any harm coming to her. You'll keep me posted? I like to know exactly what's going on on my patch, preferably before it happens.'

There was a warning in his voice. He's no fool, thought Dog. He's wondering why the hell I've come up here personally when a phone call would have done. Sod Toby Tench! It's my case and Denver ought to be told that there's a possibility his daughter's nice school friend's on the run from a charge of child-killing.

He was on the point of saying something when the phone rang. Denver picked it up, listened, covered the mouthpiece and said, 'Sorry, this'll take a bit of time. Are we done?'

'Yes,' said Dog. 'I'll be in touch.'

And left, feeling both relieved and guilty.

He found Mrs Maguire's house without any difficulty. It was a thirties semi, narrow and single fronted. There was an old Ford Popular parked in front of it. He drew up behind, locked his car and went through a wrought-iron gate and up a scrubbed concrete path alongside a tiny garden so compulsively neat, it seemed to owe more to needlework than horticulture. The doorstep was an unblemished red, the letter box glinted like a Guard's cuirass, and Dog found himself touching the bell push gingerly for fear of leaving a print.

The small middle-aged woman who opened the door looked a fit custodian for such a temple of neatness. Her hair was tightly permed like a chain-mail skull cap, her lips were like a crack in the pavement, and her eyes regarded him with fierce suspicion through spectacles polished to a lensless clarity. She bore such little resemblance to her daughter that Dog's 'Mrs Maguire?' was tentative to the point of apology.

'And who wants to know?'

The brogue was there, strong and unmistakable as poteen.

He produced his warrant card, certain that proof was going to be needed before he got over this step.

She examined it and said, 'Cicero. That's not an English name.'

'It is now. I mean, I'm English and it's my name.'

She nodded sharply as if the logic satisfied her sense of tidiness, and motioned him to enter. He followed her into a chill and cheerless sitting room where a bearded man in a dark suit and clerical collar sat on the edge of an unyielding armchair, a cup of tea in his hand.

'Father Blake, this is Inspector Cicero, he calls himself, come to see me, I don't know why. Now there's no need for you to go with your tea still hot.'

The priest had risen with an expression of alarm. He was a tallish man in early middle age, his beard beginning to be flecked with grey. He looked at Dog anxiously through heavy horn-rimmed glasses and said in a low, unaccented voice, 'I hope there's no bad news, officer.'

'Just some help with an enquiry,' said Dog vaguely, not wanting to encourage a disruptive third party to witness his interview with the woman.

'Fine,' said the priest. 'In that case, I will be running along. Thanks for the tea, Mrs Maguire. I'll call again soon. I'll see myself out.'

He gabbled a blessing and made for the door.

Dog said, 'Oh, Father, is that your car outside? I may have blocked you in. Better have a look.'

He followed the priest into the hallway and at the front door he said in a low voice, 'Look, there is some news, potentially bad. I need to talk to her alone but if you could come back in twenty minutes, say?'

Father Blake said, 'Could you give me some idea . . . I'm not her parish priest you see, more a friend of the family.'

62

'You'll know her daughter then?'

'Jane? No. I've never met her but naturally we've talked about her. Why? Is there something wrong? There hasn't been an accident?'

His voice had risen and Dog glanced warningly towards the sitting room door.

'Nothing like that,' said Dog. 'I'm sure Mrs Maguire will tell you all about it. Twenty minutes?'

He didn't give Blake time to reply but urged him out of the front door and closed it behind him. Then he returned to the sitting room where Mrs Maguire was sitting by the empty fireplace. She motioned him to the chair Father Blake had occupied, which proved as hard as Dog had suspected.

'Sorry to chase the Father away,' he said. 'He's not your parish priest?'

'No. He'd not be coming to my house in a suit if he was at St Mary's, I tell you,' she said scornfully. 'He's from the Priory College, if it's any business of yours. A friend of my brother Patrick's, God rest his soul.'

She glanced at a photo on the mantelpiece of a man in a soutane standing in front of a gloomy Gothic pile. It was her pride in having had a priest in the family which had made her uncharacteristically forthcoming, Dog guessed. Now, as if in reaction, she snapped, 'What have you done with your face?'

The question took him by surprise. He was used to the curious side-glance or the carefully averted gaze, but direct questioning was a rarity.

'A car accident,' he said dismissively.

'Oh yes. The drink was it?' she said.

'Yes. The drink played a part,' he said softly.

*Sitting in the bar, wanting another, hardly able to rise and go for it. The barman setting a pint of Guinness and a chaser before him. 'Compliments.' Nodding across the room to where a man stands, face beneath his old tweed hat unmemorable enough to be a forgotten acquaintance. A faint smile, a glass half raised, then the unmemorable blocked out by the unforgettable, a woman, her face candle-pale with emotion, her hair a flame that never burnt on any mere candle. 'What the hell are you doing here, Dog? After what happened you must be mad! Let's get you home.'*

'Men,' said Mrs Maguire contemptuously. 'If it's not the fancy women, it's the booze.'

*Coming out of the bar, his arm across her shoulders. Light and the sound of laughter behind them; ahead, darkness and a rising wind with a caress of soft Irish rain. Her face turned up to his as he staggered on the uneven surface of the car park. 'Darling, are you all right for the driving?' His own voice slurred and angry. 'Why not? No one asks me if I'm all right for the killing, do they?'*

'You're so right, Mrs Maguire,' he said. 'It's usually one or the other.'

She looked at him sharply, suspicious of irony. Then, surprised at detecting none, she folded her arms and said, 'All right, Mr Cicero, what's your business with me?'

He brought himself back to the present and said, 'It's about your daughter.'

'Has there been an accident?' she asked in alarm. He examined the alarm, found it genuine. Why not? Love was not a prerogative of the attractive.

He said, 'Not an accident. An incident. As far as we know your daughter is fine.'

It was an evasion, also an economy with the truth, but he wanted as many answers as possible before the direction of his questions hit her.

'When did you last see Jane?' he asked.

Use of the Christian name seemed to reassure her.

'At the weekend. Saturday,' she replied.

So she *had* come here when she fled the social worker's knock.

64

'Were you expecting her?' he asked.

'No, I wasn't. They came right out of the blue,' she said in an aggrieved tone. 'I had nothing ready, I might have been out or anything.'

He noted *they* but didn't comment. He guessed that the moment she got wind he was interested in the boy, there would be no progress till she learned what was going on.

He said, 'How long did Jane stay?'

'Not long.' A barrier had come down.

He said, 'Overnight?'

'No. She could have done. The room was there like it always has been.'

'But she decided to leave?'

'Yes.'

'You quarrelled,' he said flatly.

She hesitated then said, 'What goes on between my daughter and myself is our business. What's this all about, mister? You said she was all right . . .' Then her face went stiff as if she at last felt the chilly north in his questions. 'It's not the boy, is it? Nothing's happened to Oliver?'

There was nothing for it but another fragment of truth.

He said, 'I'm sorry to say that your grandson is missing.'

Her hands seized the hem of her apron and threw it up to cover the lower part of her face beneath her fear-rounded eyes. It was a gesture he'd only ever seen in films, but there was nothing theatrical about it here in this cold front parlour.

'Believe me, there's probably nothing to worry about,' he urged, justifying his lie with his need to get coherent answers from this woman who might turn out to be one of the last to see the boy alive. 'Children go missing all the time. Most of them turn up fit and well.'

Slowly the apron was lowered. She didn't believe him but her wish to be reassured was still stronger than her disbelief.

He went on quickly, 'Tell me about the visit on Saturday. It might help.'

'Has he run away, is that it?'

He didn't answer but smiled encouragingly and felt a pang of shame as she took this for agreement.

'And you're wondering if he's come up here.'

'Do you think he would come back here?' he asked. His intention was simple evasion, but he provoked an indignant response.

'And why wouldn't he? We get on all right, me and Oliver. But he's only a baby, how'd he find his way up here? And do you think I'd not let her know straight off though that'd not be easy? We might not see eye to eye, and, yes, I think the lad'd be better off here where there's someone at home all day, but I'd not keep quiet about something like that. What do you take me for?'

Cicero again felt the distress beneath the indignation, but he was a policeman, not a counsellor, and there were points to get clear.

'Why wouldn't it have been easy to let her know if Oliver had turned up here?'

'Because I don't have her address!' she burst out. 'There, that surprises you, doesn't it? Four months since she left, and I still don't have an address.'

'But how do you keep in touch?'

'She rings me, usually on a Sunday. We never talk long. She rings from a call box and them pips are forever pipping. I tell her to reverse the charge but she's not a one to be obligated, our Jane.'

'Did she ring this Sunday?'

'No. Something better to do, I expect. Hold on! He's not been missing since Sunday, has he? Not since Sunday?'

The thought constricted her throat, turning her voice to a thin squeak.

'No,' said Cicero. 'So you've no way of getting in touch with her direct?'

'She told me in emergencies I can ring that friend of hers, that Maddy.' Her lips crinkled in distaste as she spoke the name.

Maddy. The name in the copy of *Songs of Innocence and Experience.*

'Who's Maddy?' he asked.

'One of her college teachers she got friendly with. Too friendly.'

'Why do you say that?'

'Family comes first in my book, mister. Besides, she must be near on my age!' said Mrs Maguire indignantly. 'If you must have friends, stick to your own age, your own kind, that's what I say. I knew this Maddy would be the cause of trouble, and wasn't I proved in the right of it?'

She nodded with the assurance of one used to being located in the right.

'Was it this Maddy you quarrelled about then?'

'It was too! Maybe only indirectly,' she qualified with reluctant honesty. 'But she was behind it all the same. Why should her telephone number be such a secret? It's public property, isn't it? It's in the book.'

'It is if you've got a surname and address,' said Cicero. 'Do you?'

'No. I never cared to ask what she might be called and I've no idea where she lives,' admitted the woman.

'And who was it you gave her number to?'

'It was this friend of Jane's, a really nice girl, well spoken, the kind of friend Jane ought to have if she must have them. She'd lost touch with Jane since college and she was so keen to see her again that I saw no harm in giving her this Maddy's number. It was shaming enough to have to admit I didn't have an address for my own daughter without pretending there was no way I could get in touch with her.'

'What was her name, this girl? And when did she call?'

'Week before last it was. And her name was Mary Harper.'

'Did Jane remember her?'

'No. But the girl was wearing a ring so it seems likely it was her married name. But whether she knew her or not, there was no reason to get in such a tantrum when I told her I'd given this

Mary the telephone number. Well, I wasn't about to be lectured in my own house by my own daughter, I tell you! So we had words and she stalked out.'

'What time was that?'

'Not long after they arrived. About half past four.'

'How did she look, your daughter?'

'Like she always does. A bit pale maybe. She doesn't eat enough, never has done. All this athletics stuff, it's not right for a girl. The men are built for it, well, some men, but it's a strain on a female, bound to be.'

'And Noll? Oliver?'

'Now he looked peaky, I thought. I said to her, what're you thinking of, putting that child through such a journey . . .'

And once more she stopped in mid-stride as the fear she was trying to control by words, by anger, by indignation, was edged aside by a darker, heavier terror.

'All these questions, what have they got to do with anything? What's really happened, mister? He's not just wandered off, has he? Well, *has he*? What's really happened, mister?'

He said, 'We don't know, Mrs Maguire, and that's the truth. But we've got to face the possibility that your grandson may have been abducted.'

It was a choice of horrors. Little boy lost, wandering around in the cold midwinter weather, or a kidnapped child in the hands of a deranged stranger. She sat there rocking to and fro, in the delusive belief that she was facing the worst. This was no time to hint at the third and most terrible possibility.

The door bell rang. He looked at the woman. She showed no sign of having heard it.

He went out into the tiny hallway and opened the front door.

Father Blake was standing there, his face pale with anger. Before Dog could speak, the priest demanded, 'What the hell are you playing at, Inspector? Coming here with your stupid lies! What sort of man are you?'

'I'm sorry. I don't understand . . .'

'No, you don't, do you? That's clear enough. It's people

you're dealing with . . . Why couldn't you come right out and say it? Don't we have a right to know what's going on? Suppose that was how Mrs Maguire got to know, for God's sake!'

His anger and anguish clearly went deep.

Dog said, 'Please, Father. What's happened? Tell me what's happened and maybe I'll be able to tell you what you want to know.'

The priest regarded him with deep mistrust, but he was back in control of himself.

'All right, Cicero,' he said. 'I'll play your game a little while. I've been sitting in my car listening to the radio, and I've just heard some policeman from Essex, Romchurch, isn't it? That's where you're from?'

'Yes,' said Dog. 'What was it you heard?'

'I heard this man, Parslow, saying the reason you're interested in Jane Maguire is because her son's missing, that you believe he's dead, and that you want to find his mother in order to charge her with murder!'

## 12

It wasn't as bad as the priest made out, but almost. Close questioned, Blake calmed down enough to admit that Parslow hadn't stated categorically that it was a murder hunt, only that the child was missing, the police were anxious to interview his mother, and the possibility of foul play could not be ruled out.

'Look,' said Dog. 'Why don't you go in and see what you can do for Mrs Maguire? She knows the boy's missing and that's been shock enough. I'll get onto my office to see if anything else has come up.'

'And you'll let me know? The truth this time?' said Father Blake harshly.

'I'll tell you everything I can,' said Dog jesuitically.

Reluctantly, the priest went through into the sitting room leaving Dog to his thoughts.

The whole thing stank of Tench. He must have decided his devious purposes would best be served by going public. And he'd get no argument from Parslow. Steady Eddie would have made the statement dressed as Santa Claus, so long as his pension rights were safe.

Dog cooled down a little. Perhaps he was being unfair to both Tench and Parslow. Perhaps something new had come up.

He picked up the phone from the hall table and dialled.

'Romchurch police, can I help you?'

'CID, Sergeant Lunn.'

When he heard the sergeant's voice, he said, 'Charley, are you alone? What's going on?'

'Maguire, you mean? There was some kind of media leak, I gather, so they wheeled out the super to make a statement. But why he decided to throw petrol on the fire beats me, specially as I'd talked to the social worker who tried to see

Maguire, and while he said a couple of odd things, there was nothing there to reinforce the murder theory.'

'Tell me,' said Dog.

'This chap confirms he rang Maguire's bell and got no reply. Then he had a word with Mrs Ashley, the old lady who'd made the complaint. He wasn't all that worried, it seems, 'cos evidently it's quite a hobby of Mrs Ashley's ringing up with allegations about domestic mayhem. And in this case he reckoned she'd really slipped over into fantasy land because there was no record of a child living in the flat anyway.'

'Maguire hadn't been in the area all that long,' said Dog.

'All the same, kids usually figure in the records very quickly. Health, education, that sort of thing. I checked with the DHSS about Child Allowance and there's no trace there either.'

Cicero said, 'Would going to a private kindergarten make a difference to the records?'

'Officially, no. I mean, children have to be accounted for and County Hall would have a record of all the Vestey Kindergarten kids. But until someone bothers to do a cross check, the fact that a pupil at the kindergarten doesn't figure elsewhere wouldn't come up.'

'Whereas if the child had been registered at a local authority nursery school, it would automatically be fed into the whole system?'

'Right. Why so interested in that aspect, Dog? It was the same when I told Parslow. That chap, Tench, from the funny buggers, was there and he didn't seem much bothered that the child abuse thing was probably a fake alarm either.'

'Oh, I'm bothered, Charley. Anything else?'

'No. Oh yes. Five minutes ago they rang up from the desk to say there was this woman asking for you and did we know when you'd be back. A Miss Edmondson. Said she worked with Maguire.'

'First name Suzie? Long blonde girl, not bad looking?'

'Don't know. Never saw her.'

'You mean you just let her go?'

71

'Of course not. I went down but by the time I got there, your Mr Tench had swallowed her up. Willy on the desk, though, did have a languid look on his face so maybe your description fitted. She's probably still in the super's room . . . hang about, I hear Mr Tench's merry laugh now . . . I'll just have a word . . .'

'No!' snapped Dog, though why the word came out he did not know. But it was too late anyway. There was nothing on the end of the line but background noise of footsteps and a door opening, voices, distant and tinny, silence, more steps, then in his ear Tench, merry and bright.

'Dog! Just been talking about you. How goes it, my son?'

'What's going on?' said Dog. 'Why have we gone public?'

'No choice, had we? Press got onto it, probably one of the mums at the kindergarten tipped them off. You've got to cooperate with the media, Dog, or they won't play ball with yours.'

'But why stress the possible murder angle?'

'Because that's what it looks like more and more. Don't knock it, my son. Once we're absolutely sure it's some batty slag topping her toddler 'cos he got on her nerves, I'll be on my way and you can get back to the five-hour siesta!'

'What did Suzie Edmondson say?' said Dog, refusing to let Tench irritate him off course.

'What? Oh, the girl from the Health Centre, you mean. You didn't mention her, did you? Saving her for yourself, were you? Don't blame you, very tasty. But she just about wrapped it up, Dog. Thought you were just enquiring about the Jacobs business till she heard the news. Then she recalled a couple of odd things Maguire had said to her this morning. Like when she got bawled out for being late, she'd told Suzie she was sick of this and was thinking of looking for a real full-time job with better money. Suzie said, what about the kid? And our little charmer shrugged and said she had a life to live too. Now I know it's hearsay and what Suzie says about Maguire's tone of voice would not be admissible, but it all adds up, my son. How've you got on with the mother?'

'Maguire came up at the weekend. Saturday. With the boy. They didn't stay. There was a row and she left.'

As he spoke his hand toyed with a spring-loaded index by the phone, its right angles exactly matching those of the highly polished table. He touched M. There was only one entry: *Maddy*, with a number after it.

'A row, you say? What about? Any idea where she went?'

'Oh, just the usual mother and daughter thing,' said Dog. 'And Mrs Maguire assumed she'd drive home.'

'But we know she didn't. Could be that's when it happened, Dog,' said Tench. 'And she spent all Sunday thinking up her fantasy. Well, it'll all come out in the wash. What time will you be back?'

'Oh, a couple of hours,' said Dog vaguely.

'See you then if I'm still around. Take care, old son.'

'I will,' said Dog, replacing the receiver. He'd no idea why he'd lied, except as a defensive response to a gut feeling that Tench was lying too. But about what? He picked up the phone again, dialled Directory Enquiries, identified himself, gave the number next to *Maddy*, and asked for a name and address. It took half a minute.

Madeleine Salter, The Warden's Flat, South Essex College of Physical Education, Basildon.

He went back to the sitting room. Father Blake was kneeling beside Mrs Maguire, holding her hands and talking urgently to her in a low voice, but there didn't seem to be any response. Dog motioned with his head and the priest followed him into the hall.

'Look,' said Dog. 'I've been on the phone to my station and it's not as bad as it sounds.'

'Will you spell it out to me, Inspector,' said the priest grimly. 'If I'm to help this poor creature, I've got to know how much reassurance I can honestly give her.'

'Fair enough,' said Dog. He gave a rapid digest of the facts, missing out any reference to Special Branch.

'So there's nothing to show that Janey had hurt the boy?' said

Blake fiercely.

Dog hesitated. Then he said quietly, 'Father, be as comforting as you can, but until we can see our way clearer, it would be wrong to promise certainties.'

The gazes locked. It was Dog who turned away first, unable to meet the pain and anger he saw in the priest's eyes.

'I'll get the local force to send someone round,' he said. 'It won't be long before the press get onto her, I imagine, and it'll take a uniform to fight those boys off. Take care of her, Father.'

He made for the door. At the telephone table he paused, wondering whether to ring the local station. Better to call personally as he passed. There would be anger there if they'd heard Parslow's statement especially as Denver already suspected he'd been holding out on him earlier. He shrugged. The anger of colleagues was nothing compared with the pain he was leaving here.

He noticed he'd moved the telephone index slightly off square. Carefully he realigned it before he left.

It was the least he could do for Mrs Maguire.

Worse, it was probably the most.

# 13

The trip south was no better than the trip north. It felt like the wee small hours when Dog hit home territory, but his dash clock told him it was only eleven.

He saw the Romchurch sign, but kept his foot hard on the accelerator. When you're on a rush, you don't eat, you don't crap, you hardly breathe. Just play. Gospel according to Endo.

Basildon. He looked at a map as he drove, located the college. Five minutes later he was parked on the verge by the main gate.

The college occupied a flat windswept site south of the A127. There was still agricultural land here but it would have taken an unreconstructed East Ender, or an estate agent, to call the location rural. The lights of housing prickled in all directions and there was a constant drone of traffic from the arterial road.

But, set in a couple of acres of playing fields, and emptied now for the Christmas vacation, these inelegant boxes of concrete and glass still managed to chill Dog's heart like a Gothic mansion.

There was a hoarding by the gate bearing a diagram of the complex. He studied it, located the warden's flat, then slipped through the gate. There was a caretaker's lodge just inside but he didn't want either the bother or the disturbance of explaining his presence so he cut away from it across the grass to minimize sound. The rain had finally stopped and the skies were clearing. Tendrils of mist from the sodden ground curled around his ankles and from time to time he stumbled in the tussocky grass. He doubted if this was doing his expensive shoes much good. Or his career.

He reached the block where the flat was located. The main double glass door was locked, but presumably the warden would have her own personal entrance. Even a college lecturer was entitled to a private life.

He moved cautiously along the flagged walkway running alongside the building. He had to make a full circuit to the other side before he found what he was looking for. There was a car park here with a solitary car parked in it, right outside a conventional single door with a bell push.

He could make out no light from behind the curtained windows. Cautiously he tried the door handle but it was locked. There seemed nothing to do but the obvious. He reached out to ring the bell. But even as he pressed it he caught the sound of light steps coming up fast behind him. He turned, but not fast enough. A fist drove into his kidneys, not hard but with painful accuracy. He flung out his left hand in a flailing blow. His wrist was seized, twisted, and as he involuntarily came round to negate the twist, his legs were swept from under him and he crashed heavily to the ground.

Suddenly he was bathed in light. The ebbing cloud had pulled back from a soaring moon. Standing above him was a tall, thin figure in a track suit with one foot raised threateningly over his neck. He fought off the temptation to grab at it. So far every one of his reactions had been expertly prompted and devastatingly countered. First break the cycle, then take control. He feinted at the foot and swung both his legs round in an effort to sweep his attacker off balance. But the track-suited figure rose easily in the air, to let the attack pass harmless beneath, then came down with both knees into Dog's exposed stomach.

Or at least would have done.

But Cicero wasn't there. Like an engine slow to start after long disuse, his body was at last reacting with the speed of trained instinct rather than the languor of rational thought. He pivoted his whole body through ninety degrees on his right elbow and as the falling figure took the sting out of its collision with the flagstones by turning its aborted attack into a forward roll, his knee came up into the base of its spine. The figure arched, screamed, then its head hit the ground and it lay there, crumpled and silent.

Dog scrambled to his feet, panting heavily. He had deluded

himself that he kept in condition but now he knew differently. Ten years was too long between fights. Or too short.

He stooped cautiously over the recumbent figure before him. In the bright moonlight, the face confirmed what the scream had made him guess. It was a woman. American army fashion, there was a name on the track suit breast.

Madeleine Salter.

'Oh shit,' he said.

He felt in the pocket of her track suit tunic and found a Yale key. It fitted the door lock. He opened the door, found a light switch and flicked it on.

The woman groaned. He watched and did nothing. If there was any spinal injury, interference on his part could just make it worse.

She raised her head, looked at him.

He said, urgently, 'Miss Salter, I'm a police officer. Look, there's been a mistake but we can sort that out later. Main thing first of all is to check you're OK. How's your back? Can you move your legs?'

For an answer, she raised them slowly in the air one at a time, then gently flexed her back and, gradually taking her weight on her arms, sat upright. She winced as she did so.

'Pain?' he said anxiously.

'Just my head.'

She touched it gingerly. He stooped and had a closer look through the short black hair.

'There's no bleeding,' he said, 'but I reckon you'll have quite a bump. Here, let me help you inside.'

Her body felt tense against his as he helped her to her feet. He couldn't blame her.

He said, 'I really am a policeman. Detective Inspector Cicero from the Romchurch force. I wanted to talk to you about your friend, Jane Maguire.'

He felt her relax slightly. He steered her inside. She pushed open the door of a book-lined sitting room and flopped into an easy chair.

77

'Can I get you anything?' he asked. 'A drink?'

She said, 'Not yet. I'll wait till I see how I am.'

She turned an assessing eye on him and said, 'How are *you* feeling?'

He had forgotten his own pains but now they came shooting back.

Massaging his kidneys gingerly, he said, 'I'll survive. Do you always come on so strong with intruders? Could be dangerous.'

'I usually cope,' she said.

'I meant for the intruder.'

This brought a faint smile. She was a good-looking woman in her forties with a determined jaw and probing blue eyes. He wondered about her relationship with Maguire. Mother substitute or something closer?

'Your average man would have been finished by the time you hit the ground,' she said. 'Someone trained you well.'

'That was a long time ago,' he said. 'Are you ready for that drink?'

'Meaning you are. In that bureau. I'll have Scotch.' As he poured two stiff measures, she said, 'You mentioned Jane . . .'

'Yes. When did you see her last?'

'Why?'

'Will it alter your answer, knowing why?'

'I wouldn't be at all surprised,' she said.

He gave her a glass. She took a long pull.

He said, 'Her child's gone missing. Mrs Maguire was in hospital. She'd fainted and banged her head. Like you. Then she vanished.'

Salter was regarding him with a face blank of emotion. How much did she know? Would a woman who'd just heard the news he'd given her react this way?

She said, 'I feel sick. Excuse me,' put her glass down and ran from the room.

He waited a moment. It could be that Maguire was here at this moment and Salter was putting her in the picture. He rose and went to the door. He heard the sound of a lavatory flushing, then the woman came out into the narrow passage wiping her face with a towel.

'Are you OK?' he said.

'Yes. The bang. And the news. I've just taken in what you're saying . . . Noll missing. Christ, that's terrible. Poor Jane, she must be out of her mind . . .'

'That's why we're so eager to get hold of her,' he said, ready to play along with this line, if line it were. 'So please . . .'

She led the way back into the sitting room.

'She was here Saturday evening,' she said.

'You mean she stayed the night?'

'No. She stayed till late, then she headed home.'

'And the boy was with her?'

'Yes. He was asleep by then, of course. He half woke up as she took him out to the car.'

'And he was well? I mean, then. And generally. He was well looked after?'

'Yes,' she said. 'What are you getting at?'

He finished his drink without taking his eyes off her.

'I think you know, Miss Salter. Could she harm him?'

She shook her head in disbelief, not denial, saying, 'You men. Always wanting simple answers. Could *you* harm your wife, Inspector?'

'I haven't got a wife.'

'Perhaps that's because you're frightened of what you might do to her. Jane loved . . . loves that child. But she lives in fear of what she might do to him.'

'Because of her upbringing, you mean?'

'You've met Mrs Maguire? Of course, that's how you got on to me. I've never met her or even spoken to her. She had my number but she never used it. But what I learned from Jane was that for her mother, physical violence was a first disciplinary sanction rather than a last resort.'

'And what was that?'

'The threat of hellfire. Northern Ireland Catholics get it drummed into them early on that there's a place for little children who do not toe the line.'

'Are you a psychologist, Miss Salter?' he asked, glancing at her book case.

'I've done a degree in educational psychology. I started with physical education but somewhere along the road I've moved on to minds. Self-protection. It'll keep me in work when I can no longer climb up the wall bars.'

'So no doubt you talked about these matters with Mag . . . with Jane, both as a teacher and a friend?'

'If you're asking whether Jane knows that the children of parents who used violence are most likely to use violence on their own kids, then yes, of course she does. If you're asking whether awareness of the danger removes it completely, no, of course it doesn't. In choice situations, the violent option may cease to exist, but in moments of stress the concept of option itself ceases to apply.'

'Hold on,' said Dog mildly. 'This isn't a post-graduate seminar. You mean she could strike her son?'

'Possibly. In the right circumstances . . . the wrong circumstances . . .'

*I shouldn't have hit him. It was all my fault.*

'Hard enough to cause real damage?'

'As opposed to unreal, i.e. psychological, damage? Now that's a policeman's question! Answer it yourself. Out there you weren't sure whether you'd hit me hard enough to break my back or just to give me a bit of a headache, were you? Damage, inside and out, is totally unforecastable, Mr Cicero. But I dare say you know that already.' She looked at him closely. 'Incidentally, don't I know your face?'

'Which half?' he said.

She said gently, 'See what I mean?'

He said abruptly, 'What was your precise relationship with Jane Maguire?'

She smiled thinly and said, 'Meaning, am I gay, like most middle-aged academic spinsters? That's my business, Inspector. But I'm happy to admit I've always loved grace and strength

80

and athletic beauty. That's what first attracted my attention to Jane. Poetry in motion ceases to be a cliché when she runs. With full-time training she might have managed world-class times, but that kind of existence wasn't right for Jane. But if they'd given points for style and artistry, she'd have won every gold medal in sight.'

'So your initial interest was . . . aesthetic?'

She laughed and said, 'Let us say educational, shall we? As I got to know her, I got to like her. She really opened out a lot during her time here.'

'And you thought she'd make a good teacher?'

His voice was casual but she picked him up instantly.

'You heard about what happened, I see. Yes, I was sure of it. Still am. God knows what went wrong up there on Ingleborough. I wrote, but she didn't reply so I only know what I read in the papers. Hey, wait a minute, that's where I've seen you before. In the papers. But that was years ago . . . one of the South Essex local rags. Army hero joins the police. From platoon commander to police constable . . . it *was* you, wasn't it?'

'Probably. So you had no contact with her after she left teaching?'

'One postcard, postmarked Boston, saying she was well and intended settling in the States. No details. No address. No follow-up. I thought that was that. Then one day about four months ago, there she was on my doorstep with child in tow.'

'What did she say?' asked Dog.

'That she'd been widowed. That she had got a flat and taken a job in Romchurch.'

Widowed. So Maguire had stuck to that version even here.

'Had she changed much, did you think?'

'Yes and no. She'd matured, certainly. She was no longer just a girl. And she was watchful, reserved, even after the initial awkwardness was over.'

'And did you resent this reserve? Resent the child even? Just a little?'

She said, 'You're a sharp old war hero, aren't you? Yes, a little, in both respects. At first. But not for long.'

'Did it surprise you when she asked if you'd mind if she gave your telephone number to her mother?'

'No. She said it was just for emergencies. She didn't want the expense of putting a phone in her flat when she wasn't sure how long she'd be staying in it.'

Also a phone listing made you easy to trace. Why was Maguire so keen to cover her tracks? Because she feared the Americans might try to pursue her with their arrest warrants?

'Do you know someone called Mary Harper?' he asked.

'That's what Jane asked, or rather if anyone with that name had been in touch.'

'And had they?'

'No. But I'd not been around much last week. And there were several Marys it could have been, assuming it was a married name.'

'Close friends of Jane?'

She shrugged, winced.

'They might have thought so. Few years away from college, taste of the restrictions of married life, it's surprising how nostalgic some girls can get for those days of freedom. And even the most casual acquaintance can start figuring as a spirit of delight in that golden landscape. Have you never looked back yourself, Inspector, and thought, God, if only I'd known how happy I was then?'

'Was Jane convinced?'

'No. She got very agitated. When I asked her why it mattered so much she tried to pretend it didn't. I got irritated. I like to help my friends but it's two-way traffic and I don't care to be used. I'd had the sense of something bugging her ever since she returned, but I thought, in time she'll tell me. Now time was up.'

She spoke defiantly, even defensively. Dog said gravely, 'Was that all?'

She said, 'That really is a detective's nose you've got there! All right, it was me too. I wasn't in the mood for offering tea and sympathy. I shouldn't have been there at all. I'd planned a weekend away with a friend, only everything had gone wrong, we had a bust-up and I came back after only one night. So Jane picked the wrong moment to irritate me.'

'What happened?'

'One thing led to another. We exchanged mutual insults, hers about whether someone with my tastes in sex was fit to look after students, mine about whether someone with her track record in teaching was fit to have children. It was nasty, it was loud. It woke Noll up and he started crying. It ended with her picking him up and walking out . . .'

So, three times in a single day Maguire had taken it on the lam – from the social worker, from her mother, from her friend. She must have been really strung out.

Madeleine Salter was still speaking, in a low, almost inaudible voice. 'If anything happened because she didn't stay the night here, I'd never forgive . . .'

Dog cut in. 'If cause and effect were as simple as that, the dole queues would be full of bookies. Save your guilt and your grief till we find out what has happened, Miss Salter. I assume Jane hasn't tried to contact you tonight?'

'I don't know. I only got in half an hour ago. I felt so miserable all day yesterday that I decided this morning I couldn't face another day like that. So I jumped in my car and drove down to Devon to see my friend, the one I'd had the bust-up with. I was ready to grovel, only grovelling's scored for a duet, and there was somebody else there . . . I just got back half an hour ago. It was a nightmare drive, lots of flooding, and I felt I just had to stretch my legs after all that time in the car. Then I saw you . . .'

'I remember,' said Dog. 'You were pretty quick on the draw.'

'Women alone can't afford to shout *Who goes there?* And the caretaker had reported seeing someone prowling around the previous week. Look, Inspector, what can I do? Even if I didn't feel as guilty as I do, I'd want to help all I can. I love Jane, and her kid too, and you can take that any which way you like.'

Their gazes locked, both steady, unblinking. He thought, she can't have been listening to her car radio or she'd be even more upset than she is.

He said, 'You can let me know straightaway if Jane contacts you, or if anyone contacts you about Jane . . .'

As if it had been waiting for the cue, the telephone rang.

Madeleine reached for it automatically, then withdrew her hand sharply as the possible implications struck her. She looked at Dog, who said, 'Answer it,' and moved close to her so he could listen.

She picked up the receiver and said, 'Hello?'

'Miss Salter?'

'Yes.'

'Miss Salter, my name's Blake, Father Blake. I'm a friend of Mrs Maguire, Jane Maguire's mother, and she's been trying to phone you to ask . . .'

Dog took the receiver from the woman's hand.

'Father Blake,' he said. 'Inspector Cicero.'

'You're there, are you, Inspector? I should have guessed. Is there any news? Mrs Maguire's distracted, as you can imagine, and there's not been any reply from Miss Salter's number, and she doesn't have any other way of getting in touch . . .'

'No,' said Dog. 'I'm sorry. No news. Jane hasn't been in touch here.'

'Are you quite sure, Inspector? I mean, them being such good friends, maybe the lady wouldn't be as open with you as she should.'

'I do know my job, Father,' said Dog.

'Yes. I'm sorry. But I know mine too. Listen, my visit to the Priory is over, but I've got to visit a couple of text-book warehouses in London before I head back to Dublin. Mrs Maguire's asked if I'd take the trip out to Romchurch to see you while I'm down there.'

'I don't see any point . . .'

'She wants to come herself, Inspector,' said Blake grimly. 'The only way I could stop her was to promise.'

'I wouldn't want you to break a promise,' grunted Dog

ungraciously. 'A priest, Father Blake. Friend of Mrs Maguire's,' he said as he put the phone down. 'I met him up there. Now he's coming to see me.'

'Thinks he's Father Brown, does he? Sorry. Don't mean to offend the faith. You're one yourself, aren't you? Catholic, I mean.'

'Why do you say that? The name? There are Italian protestants.'

'Not just the name. Something in the way you spoke to the Father.'

'It's a virus that stays in the blood,' he said. 'Did Jane ever talk much about Ireland?'

'Of course. She grew up there till she was seven or eight. We all like to talk about when we were kids.'

'Why did they leave?'

'Her father was killed. There was an incident, some shooting. He got caught in the crossfire. After that her mother decided she'd had enough. She went to Northampton because that's where her brother was.'

'The priest?'

'Yes. Brother and Father. A troublesome combination for a bossy sister.' Maddy managed a faint smile. 'Jane says they were never ten minutes in each other's company without bickering. He was a teacher at some big Catholic boarding school in the area. When Jane was fifteen, he took ill and when they diagnosed cancer, his Order sent him back to Ireland to die. Mrs Maguire thought of going with him but the end came very quick, so she and Jane stayed put.'

'How did they live?'

'There was a small pension, and Mrs Maguire worked as a seamstress. Also there was the compensation money.'

'Compensation?'

'For the shooting. It was a Brit bullet that killed Jane's father.'

Dog could detect no note of accusation in the statement but it felt like one. He rose, frowning, and went to the door. He stood there a moment looking round the room.

'You've a lot of friends,' he said.

'What? Oh, the cards. Everyone likes to be teacher's pet,' she said, self-mockingly.

'Including Jane Maguire?'

'Could be. But not everyone runs like a red deer in full flight. You'll find her, won't you, Inspector?'

It was almost casually put, but he felt the passionate need for reassurance behind the question.

He thought, she's in full flight now. I wonder if she still looks like a red deer.

'We'll find her, Miss Salter,' he said. 'Wherever she is, whatever she's doing, we'll find her.'

# 14

Jane Maguire lay on her back, felt the rough hands squeezing her nipples, felt the hot hard flesh forcing its way into her unwelcoming dryness, felt the desperate mounting rhythm of his thighs.

It didn't last long. He was young and impetuous and came quickly. He rolled off her, panting heavily, his narrow chest palpitating like a frightened bird's. It disgusted her that someone so young should be so unfit. This was the only emotion she let herself feel.

He reached down to pull his jeans up, not for decency but to take a pack of cigarettes from the pocket.

'And what were you thinking of, Janey, my love?' he asked between puffs. 'I hope you weren't lying back and thinking of England. A good Irish girl should get a lot more excited when she thinks of England.'

'I was thinking of Noll,' she said in a dead voice.

He turned towards her and blew smoke across her face. She didn't turn away. His power over her was absolute. There was nothing he couldn't make her do, and, knowing that, she knew it was futile to waste energy in resistance or debate. There was a strength in her body and her mind which was best left hidden until it could once again be profitably tapped.

'You'll need to do more than think,' he said. 'Thinking's not going to bring him back.'

She said, 'All I want is . . .'

'Yes?'

'You know what I want.'

Pretending to misunderstand her, he put his hand on her breast and said, 'Now you'll have to wait a wee while for that, at least till I finish my fag.'

The door opened, a voice said, 'I thought you might like . . .' and a woman came in holding a cup of tea. Her voice choked in disbelief as she took in the scene before her.

Then: 'What the hell is *this*?' she shouted.

The man rolled sideways off the bed, the woman flung the cup at him, missing by a yard, but splattering hot tea over his shoulder.

'Jesus, you stupid cow!' he screamed. 'What the hell . . .'

But his words thinned out to another scream as she sank her fingers in his stubbly blond hair and dragged him towards the door. His jeans slipped back down over his knees, forcing him to half hop, half hobble, and any resistance he might have contemplated was dissipated in the effort of keeping his balance.

She thrust him out of the door. Jane heard a crash as he finally tripped to the floor outside, but she showed no more interest than she had when the woman arrived. She sprawled on the bed as he had left her, her face a blank, not even moving to cover herself up.

The woman stood by the door looking down at her.

'And you,' she said contemptuously. 'Lying there with his slime seeping out of you. What kind of creature are you, for God's sake?'

Jane lay quite still for another ten minutes or more after the door had slammed. She hadn't flinched when drops of hot tea had spattered her body, so words were not going to move her. There was a strength in not feeling, in not allowing herself to feel, that only those who had experienced it could understand.

Finally she rose. There was a hand basin in the corner with a mirror over it. She studied herself in the glass. What kind of creature? It was a good question but not one she was willing to answer. Not yet.

She turned on the taps. Carefully, methodically, she began to wash her body from top to toe.

In the room next door, the woman who'd thrown the tea heard the taps running. After a while she rose and went out across a hallway into a bright modern kitchen. Here she made another pot of tea, poured a cup and took it into the bedroom again.

The naked woman by the wash basin turned to look at her.

'I'm sorry,' she said. 'He made you, didn't he?'

Jane Maguire didn't reply, but the other woman nodded as if she had.

'There's your tea,' she said, putting the cup on a bedside table.

Back in the living room, she turned the television on low and flicked around between news programmes.

After about half an hour she rose and went through into the hallway again. In her hand was a Charter Arms Police Bulldog revolver.

After a few moments the handle of the outer door turned silently and the door began to open. She stepped forward, gun raised.

The man standing there regarded her and the weapon without surprise.

'You could try having my slippers warming in front of the fire for a change,' he said.

'There'd be land mines in them if I did,' she answered.

His still, narrow face flickered into a smile and he stepped forward and took her in his arms. For a second they embraced fiercely, then broke apart.

'Did you find out what's happening?' she asked, as they went through into the sitting room.

'Yes. I spoke to our boy. It's like we thought. Tench playing clever.'

'I don't follow.'

'For the time being we're playing the same game. But he likes to be the one forcing the pace. *I* call the papers, *he* starts hinting at murder.'

She considered a moment, then said, 'But how will that help him?'

'A dead child interferes with rational thought. That's how he sees it. And he can tie up the points of entry far better than us. That suits me too. Our boy will keep us posted.'

'It's nearly Christmas.'

'Meaning he could be here already? Tench knows that too, knows it'll be me he comes looking for.'

She thought again, then looked alarmed again.

'That only makes sense if Tench knows where we are.'

'Oh, he does. Round-the-clock surveillance. It must be costing the tax payer a fortune.'

'Did they see you come in?' she demanded.

'I doubt it. And if they did, what odds? You don't shoot a tethered goat. Also, the good thing about tethered goats is they all look alike in the dark.'

'You're being very enigmatic, Jonty,' she said.

'Isn't that how I keep my youthful good looks? What I'm saying is I want you to move out in the morning. Somewhere they can't keep such a close eye. Where's Billy the Kid?'

'Sulking in his bedroom. We had words. I caught him screwing Maguire.'

'Did you now? Rape, you mean?'

'I don't think he used physical force, but he certainly didn't use charm. Jonty, he's trouble, that one. Didn't I always say so?'

'Why else do you think the old men in Dublin wished him on us? Either I bring him to heel, in which case they've got themselves a top gun, or he brings me down, in which case they've got rid of an insubordinate bastard.'

He sat in thought for a moment, then he said, 'At least it shows we've got her the way we want her.'

'For Christ's sake!' she exclaimed. 'Is that all it means to you?'

He looked at her quizzically and said, 'I hope you're not going to go feminist on me, Bridie. Or worse still, sentimental. You've seen her, heard her. She's the enemy. A slag.'

His voice was soft and light, but she responded as if to a threat.

'Yes, of course, Jonty. All I meant was, you can't let Flynn get away with it. It's a question of authority.'

'You leave that to me. Get him in here, will you? Give us a couple of minutes then bring Maguire in.'

She went out. A moment later the blond-haired youth came in, his face sulky with defiance.

'There you are, Billy. Come over here, will you?'

Billy Flynn moved slowly to stand in front of the seated figure who smiled up at him benevolently.

'Billy, you've done me a bit of a favour, and that's good. I like people who do me favours.'

'What fav . . .' The words exploded into a scream of agony as Thrale's left hand shot forward, seized his testicles beneath the tight denim jeans and twisted mercilessly.

'But I don't like people who do me favours without asking first. You can use that thing to piss with, Billy, since that's a call of nature. But use it, or any part of you, to do something I haven't told you to do, and I'll pull it off, whether it's your prick or your head. Do I make myself clear, Billy?'

'Yes!' the youth gasped.

Thrale relaxed his hold and Flynn staggered back into a chair where he sat doubled up, his face pale as his hair.

The door opened and Jane Maguire came in, with the other woman close behind. Jane didn't even glance at Flynn but fixed her gaze unblinkingly on Jonty Thrale. He nodded approvingly. He liked people who understood priorities.

'Mrs Maguire,' he said gently, 'I think you've been telling me the truth.'

'What else would I tell you?' she said lifelessly.

'Just so. And I don't doubt you feel the better for it. Confession cleanses the soul. It can even set you free. And that's what I'm going to do for you, Mrs Maguire.'

'What?' the woman Bridie ejaculated. Even the youth registered alarm through his pain. Only Jane Maguire did not react with any sign of surprise or hope, and it was on her that Thrale's eyes were fixed.

'Good,' he said softly. 'I see we understand each other, Mrs Maguire. It's no use confessing, then going back to sinning. You've got a lot more confessing to do before you and I are through. A lot more before your soul will be clean enough to be set free along with your body. So sit down quietly and pay attention while I spell out your act of contrition.'

# 15

Dog Cicero rolled a cigarette and asked himself what he was doing here.

It was after midnight. He still had not reported in to the station. He was in possession of what might be important information on a serious case. And he was standing outside the house where Suzie Edmondson lived.

Why the hell had she wanted to see him?

To put the bubble in for Maguire, Tench had said. And it was true she'd shown no special liking for her colleague. *Bit stuck up. Keeps herself to herself.* But there'd been no sense of active dislike nor had the girl herself come across as malicious.

Even less had she come across as the civic conscience type who'd feel duty bound to pour her thimbleful of water on a drowning woman.

He went up to the door of the house, which was in the middle of a tall Victorian terrace long since declined to bedsit level. A man went up the steps before him, opened the door with a key and turned to look suspiciously at Dog as he prevented him from closing it.

'Suzie Edmondson,' said Dog.

This switched off suspicion, switched on a knowing grin.

'Oh, Suzie. Yeah. Second floor, straight ahead.'

The stairwell was lit by a single distant bulb. Paint was peeling off the walls and the carpeting was threadbare, but at least it all smelt quite clean.

There was a line of light beneath the door of Edmondson's room. He tapped the woodwork gently.

'Who's that?'

'Inspector Cicero. We talked earlier. About Jane Maguire.'

The door opened on a chain. An eye regarded him. Then the

door was opened fully.

'You wanted to see me,' he said.

'Yeah. I saw your boss. I thought it was all settled.'

'It was me you wanted to see.'

'Only because you were the one who came asking. I don't know a lot of cops, thank God.'

'Can I come in?'

She stood aside. He went into the room. It was sparsely furnished with a sofa bed against one wall. The only item not looking to have seen better days was a huge television set.

The woman was wearing slacks and a blouse. The blouse was half unbuttoned, as if she'd been getting ready for bed. She refastened the buttons as he looked.

'My boss?' he said. 'You mean Mr Tench.'

'That's the one. He is your boss, isn't he?'

'My superior,' said Dog carefully. 'But he works in another section and he'd gone home by the time I got back. So if we could just go over it again.'

'Oh, all right.' She sat on the bed and lit a cigarette. Dog sat gingerly on what looked like a bean-bag with ambitions.

She said, 'I heard about Jane on the news, about her kiddie and all, and it gave me a turn. And I got to thinking, that was probably what you were round at the Centre about, not the other, but the other would make things look worse, and that wasn't fair. I mean, when I heard she'd got the heave, I thought, no skin off my nose, she's not what you'd call a mate, and losing a lousy job like that's no big deal, is it? You've got to watch out for yourself these days, haven't you?'

Dog smiled wearily and said, 'Yes, you have. Then you heard the news . . ?'

'Yeah. And that made it different. I mean, OK, if she's killed her kid, she deserves what she gets, I suppose, though God knows it can't be any fun being by yourself and trying to cope . . . well, I don't know if I could manage it, I tell you.'

'So you decided to tell the truth?'

'Truth? Who knows that? All I'm doing is guessing what

really happened. Didn't matter before, but now I reckon she's got enough hassle without that. Look, your boss, that other one, he said it was going to be all right, no comeback, everything under the carpet, OK? That still stands, does it?'

He nodded. It was a reassurance at least as reliable as any Tench was likely to have given. Tench who didn't give a toss who he lied to, including his own colleagues. His mind had already leapt to the truth of Suzie Edmondson's evidence, but he wanted to hear it from her lips.

'Go on, Suzie,' he urged.

'The thing is, I sometimes do a bit for the odd customer, not them all, and only when I get the message that they wouldn't say no to a helping hand, know what I mean?'

'I get the picture,' said Dog. 'And Councillor Jacobs was on your help list?'

'That's right. Twice a week, regular as clockwork. Only today I wasn't around, I had to go to the dentist's, so Jane got landed with him instead, and the silly old sod probably thought a change is as good as a rest, and expected Jane to get on with it. She must have told him to get knotted and walked out. And he suddenly got all worried about his reputation, so thought he'd better get his retaliation in first, in case Jane started stirring things up.'

'Did the Grangers know what was going on?'

She shrugged. 'Don't know. Her, probably not. Him, well, maybe he had a notion, but he wasn't going to do anything to upset Jacobs, was he? I mean, he has to be council-licensed, doesn't he? And I've heard tell that it was Jacobs who fixed it for Granger to get the old youth club dirt cheap when it was sold off by the council.'

So. Jacobs, the fixer. Everyone owing him, including the police. But not Tench.

'And Mr Tench said . . ?'

'He said I was quite right to come in to talk to someone, but it didn't have any bearing on the investigation, in fact it just complicated matters, so all things being considered, it was probably best to say no more about it. He promised me that as far as Jane went, it wouldn't figure at all, and he saw no reason why Councillor Jacobs needed to know I'd been talking to the police.'

He caught Tench's avuncularly reassuring cadences in the girl's words. He'd sent her away with the pleasant glow that comes from doing the right thing and finding it's not going to cost you after all.

As he rose to leave the girl said, 'Do you really think she did it, killed him, I mean? That's what it sounded like on the radio.'

'And what did it sound like when you talked to Mr Tench?'

'Don't know. He's an odd one, isn't he? Reminds me a bit of Councillor Jacobs. Very friendly, but I wouldn't like to get on his wrong side.'

She wasn't stupid, this girl. And she'd known she was taking a real if relatively small risk in letting the cat out of the bag about Jacobs.

He said warmly, 'Thanks a lot, Suzie. You've been a great help.'

It wasn't till he was back in his car that he realized he'd evaded her question. Did he think Maguire had killed her child? Put another way, did the fact that she hadn't propositioned Jacobs make it less likely? Or put another still, was someone like Suzie, who freely admitted to maximizing her income by jerking off middle-aged men, more or less likely to harm a child?

The answer was so clearly 'no' that he felt a pang of self-revulsion at the way he had let his judgement of Maguire as a mother be clouded by his opinion of her sexual mores.

On the other hand plenty of contra-evidence remained – her family background, her record, her own words, the judgement of her friend, the absence of support for her story of this morning's sequence of events, the boy friend she denied having but who had called for her at the Health Centre.

Also – and while he was facing up to things he might as well confront this – the fact that she had red hair, spoke with the lilt of soft flowing waters, and had been the mistress of a man who fed money into the ravening maw of the IRA.

He headed back to the station. It was quiet as the grave. Monday was usually the best night of the week. Fewer people went out on Mondays, meaning there was less drunkenness in the pubs, less opportunity for break-ins at empty houses, less traffic to get involved in accidents.

He found a note from Tench on his desk.

Dear Dog, where've you been? I'm pretty sure it's a murder enquiry with nothing in it for the Branch. No doubt Mr Parslow will brief you. But if you do get a sniff of anything that might interest me, give me a bell on Extension 477 at the Yard, and in any case, next time you're up West, let me know and we'll have a jar and a jaw about the good old days. Watch how you go! Toby.

Nice letter. The letter of a man who wasn't going to let divisions of rank stand in the way of old friendship. The letter of a man happy to relinquish his special interest in a case and let the local lads get on with it.

Like hell!

Dog screwed up the note and tossed it into the waste basket.

One thing was certain. When Toby Tench extended the hand of friendship, a wise man reached to cover both his crutch and his wallet.

97

# 16

Next morning the story hit the papers. A revolution, an explosion, and a Royals-spending-Christmas-apart scandal kept it off the front pages, and the 'qualities' put it on hold, simply stating the facts. The tabloids would probably claim the same if they ever got sued, only they concentrated on the missing mother rather than the missing child and it didn't need a medium to get the message.

At eight-fifty, Dog Cicero was standing in Charnwood Grove. He watched as a succession of elegant cars drew up, and matching mums escorted gleaming children into the Vestey Kindergarten.

By five past nine the street was empty. He stood for another ten minutes. A couple of cars turned into the far end. He stepped out into their path, forcing them to stop.

The first driver said he hadn't come this way the previous morning. The second said he had, but it had been at nine-thirty, pissing down, and he hadn't noticed any women or a child or a rusty mini.

At twenty past nine a woman with a dog walked by on the opposite side. Yes, she walked this way at the same time every morning. And yes, despite the dreadful rain she hadn't missed the previous day. But she had had her head buried beneath an umbrella, and though she thought there might have been someone talking on the pavement opposite, she couldn't swear to it.

Dog got her name and address and then went into the school.

Mrs Vestey was not overly pleased to see him. Dog put up with her chilliness for a while, then offered to return at a more convenient time, like say three P.M. with a couple of police cars and half a dozen uniformed officers to take witness statements from parents. After that things improved.

'But there's nothing more I can tell you,' she said. 'And I thought from the papers . . .'

'You thought we were following the line that Mrs Maguire herself might be responsible for Noll's disappearance,' he said bluntly. 'In which case your involvement would be minimal. I can see how that might relieve you.'

'Inspector, I don't like your . . .'

'But what *that* would mean,' he cut across her, 'is that everything that happened here was a set-up to misdirect our enquiries. And that would include the phone call you got saying Noll was ill. How certain are you it was Mrs Maguire's voice?'

She thought, then said, 'Certain enough not to have had any doubts when she identified herself, if you see what I mean. It had the timbre and the intonation, that slight Irish brogue, of Mrs Maguire's voice. And I assure you that since yesterday, I've gone over it a hundred times in my mind and I still can't think of anything odd about it.'

'OK,' said Dog. 'Let's go back to last Friday. Mrs Maguire says she met this Miss Gosling . . .'

'There's no such woman,' said Mrs Vestey firmly. 'That I can be sure of.'

'No such new member of staff,' said Dog. 'But was there anyone here that afternoon who wasn't normally present?'

'Of course not! Do you think we let strangers roam around at will?' she said indignantly.

'No, but you must have visitors,' he said reasonably. 'LEA officials, suppliers, and so on.'

'Of course. But all we had on Friday afternoon were two mothers who are considering putting their children in our care.'

'Strangers to you, then?'

'Only by sight. I assure you we vet prospective parents far more closely than they vet us.'

The vetting seemed to be mostly concerned with credit ratings once the customer made up her mind, but there were some preliminary precautions, such as getting a telephone number to check back to after the initial appointment had been made, and matching the number with the address given.

'There are some weird people in the world,' said Mrs Vestey, with expert authority. 'And where children are concerned, you can't be too careful.'

'What about Mrs Maguire?' said Dog. 'She had no telephone. And I doubt if she had a credit rating.'

It turned out that cash payment of a term's fees in advance obviated these difficulties. But in the case of Mrs Tobin and Mrs Osterley, Friday's visitors, the addresses and numbers had been checked out and Mrs Vestey was not too happy at handing them over to Cicero.

'They seemed most impressed,' she recalled. 'A heavy-handed approach from the police could quite undo that good impression.'

Dog smiled and made no promises. He needed to squeeze Maguire's story absolutely dry before he committed himself to its even more dreadful alternative. And if she'd met someone on Friday afternoon who pretended to be a new member of staff, it had to be one of these two.

The fact that both women had spent most of the afternoon with Oliver Maguire's starter group gave a faint glimmer of credibility to Maguire's claim. Nor was her description of the alleged Miss Gosling made completely impossible by Vestey's account of the two mothers.

He said goodbye. He could feel Mrs Vestey's relief. Being a policeman meant never having to say sorry for leaving.

Fifteen minutes later he was entering Rhadnor House, the block of elegant apartments where Mrs Tobin lived. He pressed the bell of Number Thirty-four, felt himself observed through the spyhole, then the door was opened on a chain.

'Yes?' said a woman in a cut-glass accent.

'Mrs Tobin? I'm Detective Inspector Cicero.' He showed her his warrant. 'Could I have a quick word?'

The door closed for the chain to be removed and then the woman invited him into the hallway. She was medium-sized, nondescript, with a harassed expression not caused entirely by his visit. Through an open door off the hall he could see into a kitchen where a workman's legs were visible stretching from under the sink, and through another door he glimpsed a little girl in candy-striped dungarees chewing a huge chocolate bar as she tried to climb into an open suitcase on a bed.

'Polly, don't do that,' commanded Mrs Tobin. 'You'll get chocolate everywhere!' Then, deciding that some things are best left hidden, she closed both doors and said, 'I'm sorry. Look, we're off to Barbados tonight for Christmas, and my husband's left me to do all the packing, and the waste disposal unit's started playing up so I've had to call a plumber . . .'

'So you hope I won't take up too much of your time,' completed Dog. 'I don't think I will.'

He was right. She had nothing to tell him. She'd visited the kindergarten to check it out for her daughter, and couldn't recall anything special except that she hadn't taken to Mrs Vestey very much and wouldn't be using the school unless her other options didn't come up to scratch.

Dog thanked her and left, smiling to himself at the thought that Mrs Vestey would have no doubt as to where to lay the blame.

The second woman, Mrs Osterley, was harder to find as she lived on a new executive estate where it was clearly considered *de trop* to exhibit house numbers, but it took even less time to eliminate her from the Gosling hunt as she was six feet tall with prominent horsey teeth and twin boys clearly ambitious to fill the gap left by the Krays.

All in all it left Maguire's story not just lame, but legless.

Back at the station he met Sergeant Lunn on the stairs with WPC Scott behind him.

'Morning, Charley. Anything new?'

'Yeah. She bought some clothes at Mowbrays in the precinct. It was Scott's idea to check.'

Guilt too can be inspirational, thought Dog.

'Good thinking, Scott,' he said.

She flushed with pleasure and said, 'Thank you, sir. I won't be happy till we get her back.'

'Could be some time. If she's buying clothes, she's really on the run.'

Her face fell. She thinks it's all personal, thought Dog. Perhaps she's right.

He said, 'Have you got the new description out?'

'Just on my way to the computer,' said Lunn, holding up a sheet of paper. 'By the way, the super was asking for you earlier. He sounded hot and bothered.'

'Probably the greenhouse effect,' said Dog.

He went right up to the superintendent's office. The door opened as he approached and Parslow ushered Councillor Jacobs out.

'Ah, here he is now,' said Parslow. 'Dog, Councillor Jacobs came in to make a formal statement and he was asking me what progress we'd made in catching this woman.'

'It's very good of the Councillor to take an interest,' said Dog.

'I'm always interested in justice,' intoned Jacobs. 'A slag like this who could harm her own child, she needs to be found quick and put away, or by God there are plenty of decent people out there who'll be only too glad to do it for you!'

'Sort of lynch mob, you mean?' said Dog pleasantly.

'No, I do not. But there's something called natural justice which comes into play when civic justice drags its heels. I don't approve, Inspector Cicero, but I damn well understand. Good day to you, Superintendent.'

He walked away. Parslow said, 'Not a chap to get on the wrong side of, Dog. Come inside.'

'In a minute,' said Dog. 'I'd just like to set the record straight with the Councillor.'

He ran lightly down the stairs and caught up with Jacobs on the half landing.

'Quick word,' he said.

'It'll need to be. I'm a busy man.'

The self-important tone, the sneering lips, were suddenly too much. Dog's hand seized a bunch of shirt and he thrust the man back hard against the wall, his eyes popping in mingled amazement, indignation, and fear.

'What the hell . . .'

'You listen to me, dickhead,' snarled Dog. 'We know all about you and your dirty deals and what you get up to at the Health Centre. Your lot would get chucked out at the next local election if the voters knew what we know. But you're useful to us so we let you stay. But that doesn't mean I'll stand by and watch you drop other people in the shit to cover your own shabby name. Have you got that?'

Jacobs's face was now grey.

'This is outrageous,' he croaked.

'Yes, isn't it? Now, on your sledge, Santa!'

He went back up the stairs to Parslow.

'OK?' said the super.

'Fine,' said Dog.

'Good. Excellent fellow, the Councillor. Salt of the earth. Few more like him on every council and our job'd be a lot easier.'

'You wanted to see me, sir.'

'That's right, Dog. Fill me in. How'd you get on last night?'

Briefly, Dog described his encounters with Mrs Maguire and Madeleine Salter, then his visit to Charnwood Grove. Suzie Edmondson he didn't mention. He'd learnt by experience not to tell Parslow things he wouldn't want to know.

'So she quarrels with her mother, then she quarrels with her friend, and no one saw the boy after she left Salter's flat on Saturday night. Where did she go? Obviously to this boy friend or minder, whatever he is. Somewhere, either en route or after she got there, it happens. The child is struck, injured, dies. Which of them hit him, I don't know. It's usually the man. And it'd certainly be the man who says, dump him where he won't be found, then spends the rest of the weekend coaching Maguire in her cover-up story. Did the hospital check her for drugs, by the way?'

'I don't think so. Why?'

'She'd need something to keep her going,' said Parslow, almost sympathetically. 'Only thing that doesn't really fit is offering Councillor Jacobs this hand-job right out of the blue. You'd have thought she'd have wanted to keep everything on a nice routine even keel that day.'

Dog wondered if Parslow would reckon the removal of this small obstacle to accepting Maguire's guilt was worth having to know the truth about Jacobs. He doubted it. Also he saw no reason for helping the superintendent believe what he clearly wanted to believe. Though why he should be quite so keen to believe it, Dog could only guess.

'I gave a press conference last night,' said Parslow.

'So I gather.'

'I had to field a lot of questions about the scope of our enquiry and I couldn't leave out the possibility that Maguire herself had injured the child. I'd weighed all the possibilities and had a long talk with Toby Tench, and that did seem the most probable scenario.'

So that's it, thought Dog. And when you heard the radio reports last night and saw the tabloid coverage this morning, you began to realize what a nana you'd look if the child turned out to be kidnapped after all! No wonder you're chuffed that I've come up with nothing.

'Mr Tench went along with you, did he, sir?'

'Oh yes. He was most supportive, most helpful. It's marvellous how quickly the Branch can whip the media up. So your recommendation, Dog, is that we concentrate all our resources on finding Maguire and looking for the child's body?'

Dog regarded him almost admiringly. How casually he continued hedging his bets. The wise old super, delegating authority and accepting the advice of the officer in charge of the case!

He said maliciously, 'There is another scenario, sir. How about if Maguire just drove back to her flat on Saturday night. Got there so late, no one saw her. Found all the parking spots at the front of the building filled so had to park round the corner. Spent all day Sunday in the flat. And then went off to school with the boy on Monday morning like she said. Fits the known facts pretty well.'

'But the blood on the back seat?' objected Parslow, alarmed.

'Kid had a nose bleed on the way home. Wasn't very well on Sunday which was why she kept him inside.'

He'd got Parslow really worried. Suddenly his amusement turned to self-disgust. He didn't believe a word of what he was saying, and by saying it, he was doing just what both Parslow and Tench were guilty of – reducing Maguire and her child to counters in a personal game.

He opened his mouth to put things right, but before he could speak, the phone rang. Parslow picked it up and listened. On his face Dog saw alarm turn slowly to jubilation.

'I'm on my way,' he said, replacing the receiver. 'Well, there we are! Just goes to show the old man's nous can still beat the young man's nose, even if he is called Dog. Is that where you got the name, by the way? Never thought to ask before.'

'No, it's because I crap on people's carpets,' said Dog irritably, as he was urged through the door. 'May I ask where we're going, sir?'

'Of course you may,' said Parslow gleefully. 'We're going downstairs to have a chat with an acquaintance of yours – a Miss Jane Maguire who's just walked into the station and announced she wants to confess to killing her son!'

# 17

Jane Maguire had the look of a woman who had been to hell and knew there was no way back. Once you'd been in that place, you took it with you everywhere.

Lunn had already issued the caution, but Parslow, who liked belt and braces, insisted on repeating it.

WPC Scott was in attendance once more. The smile of relief she flashed at Dog Cicero contrasted so strongly with the tragic haggardness of Maguire's looks that he quenched it with a frown. Inside, though, he knew he preferred Maguire looking like this. Despair aged her, folded her in on herself, diluted her power to remind.

'You wish to make a statement, Mrs Maguire?' said Parslow.

'*Miss* Maguire,' she said in a low tone. 'Yes, I want to tell you what happened.'

'Good. Now what you say will be noted down, then typed out for you to read and emend if necessary before you sign it. You understand?'

'Yes.'

'Then go ahead.'

She sighed deeply. Parslow had done all the talking so far, but it was on Dog that she fixed her eyes as she began.

'I made it all up,' she said wretchedly. 'All that about being late and the new teacher . . . it was all lies so that you wouldn't know . . .'

She slurred to a tearful halt. Dog said gently, 'From the beginning. From the time you left Maddy Salter's flat.'

She expressed no surprise that he knew about Salter.

'I just drove away. I didn't know where I was going. Anywhere. Noll was strapped in on the back seat. He had started crying, not so much crying but whingeing, on and on, he wouldn't shut up, and I reached back to touch him, not to hit him, but somehow it turned into a blow, and he let out a terrible cry and when I looked back, I could see blood all over his face. I froze. I couldn't take my eyes away, and when I did, I realized the car was heading off the road into the verge, and I slammed the brakes on and went into a skid, spinning right round and the back end of the car hit a tree. Then everything was still, so very very still . . .'

'Where was this?' interjected Parslow.

'What? I don't know. Out in the country somewhere. A narrow road. Everything round about so black. That blackness you get in the country. So very very black and so still . . . it was like being dead . . .'

'Were you hurt?' said Dog.

'Me? No. I was strapped in. But when I looked back . . . Noll must have half struggled out of his straps . . . and when the car spun, he must have been thrown against the side, against the window . . . I got him out and laid him down . . . he wasn't breathing . . . I did all the things you ought to do . . . but it was no good . . . he was gone, he's gone, I've lost him, he's gone . . .'

Tears streamed down her cheeks and she bowed her head so that long tendrils of her bright hair covered her face in fuchsia-like glory.

'And then, Miss Maguire, Jane, what did you do with him then?' asked Parslow urgently.

Dog glared at him angrily. This was bad interrogation procedure from every angle, but Parslow had the scent of flesh in his nostrils.

'Do? Nothing. I told you, there was nothing I could do.'

'I mean, with the body, Jane. What did you do with the body?'

'The body?' said Maguire, as if somehow she had not made a connection between this term and her dead child.

'How long did you stay by the car, Jane?' said Dog quietly.

'I don't know. Minutes, hours, I don't know.'

'But finally you got back into the car?'

107

'Yes, that's right.'

'And you'd put Noll back inside too?'

'Yes.'

'And where did you go then?'

'I just drove.'

'Didn't you think of taking him to a hospital?'

'Yes, of course. But when I looked again, he was quite cold.'

Her voice was now drained of emotion, as if the narrative had moved on to a different level.

'So you stopped again?'

She hesitated, then said, 'Yes.'

'Did you speak to anyone? Did you go to see anyone?'

Another hesitation.

'No,' she said.

'And what did you do with Noll?' said Dog gently. 'Where is he now?'

'I told you. He's dead.'

'Yes, but we need to find him so that he can be properly buried,' he insisted. 'You're a Catholic, aren't you, Jane? You know how important it is for the proper rites and ceremonies to take place. You wouldn't want to think of him lying somewhere unhallowed without a stone to mark his passing, would you?'

She raised her eyes to meet his.

'Do you believe in God?' she asked softly.

'Yes,' he lied, frowning.

'Then you really are a fool,' she said, almost jubilantly. 'I put him in the river.'

'The river? What river?' he demanded.

'I don't know. The Thames, I expect. Yes, it was the Thames.'

'Where? Where exactly?' demanded Parslow.

'I don't know. I didn't mark the spot!' she cried. 'I drove around. I remember being somewhere near Tilbury. What does it matter? He's dead. I've told you he's dead. Isn't that enough?'

'We need to find him so we can establish how he died,' insisted Parslow. 'It could make a lot of difference to you. If, like you say, it was the result of your accident, then that's very different from, say, if when you hit him . . . and what you intended . . .'

Parslow was floundering, trying to hint a deal when clearly what she might be charged with didn't loom large among this woman's current priorities.

'I hit him. He's dead. I put him in the river. Write that down on your paper and I'll sign it. Nothing more, I don't want to say anything more.'

Parslow regarded her with unconcealed frustration. Dog said, 'OK, we'll get it typed up.'

He went to the door, ushered Lunn out, then stood and stared at the superintendent till, reluctantly, he too stood up and exited.

'We'll need more detail, Dog,' he said fretfully as they walked down the corridor together. 'Especially about where she dumped the kid. Damn. I hate it when they dry up after only half a story.'

'Let's get this lot signed before she changes her mind,' said Dog. 'Half a story's better than no story at all.'

'Yes, of course, you're right. I must give Tench a ring. He said he'd like to be kept in touch with developments.'

And you want to keep on the right side of everyone, thought Dog scornfully.

He turned on his heel and headed back to the interview room.

'Your statement's being typed up, Miss Maguire,' he said. 'Just one thing I'd like you to confirm, just so that we can keep our records straight. You left the Health Centre early yesterday. Mr Granger, your employer, says this was because you were dismissed. Is that right?'

'Yes,' she said dully.

'And he says the reason you were dismissed was a complaint laid against you by a client. Is that true?'

'Yes.'

'And was the complaint accurate? Did you in fact offer to masturbate Councillor Jacobs for a payment of twenty-five pounds?'

She looked at him for the first time since his return, shrugged and said, 'Yes.'

'You confirm you made this offer? For twenty-five pounds?'

'Yes, yes, yes! Now will you leave me alone? For God's sake, leave me alone!'

Suddenly there was life and colour in her face and the Irishness of her voice came bursting through its overlay of Midland and mid-Atlantic English.

Memories surged up in Dog's mind. Sad memories. Bitter memories.

He turned and left. Behind him was a woman he wanted nothing to do with, whose every word and feature could rouse emotions he thought he had quelled. Nothing would please him more, he thought, than to be able to take her story at face value, book her for child killing and leave her to the lawyers.

But now for the first time since he met her he was sure of one thing – that whatever else Jane Maguire might be guilty of, she had not killed her son.

# Part Two

# 1

Noll Maguire sat on the edge of the bed and looked at the woman who had stolen him.

She was of medium height, medium build, with a round pleasant face and short, light brown hair. Her voice was soft and musical, and if she kept quiet, you hardly noticed she was there at all.

Noll liked her very much and not just because her handbag seemed to hold an endless supply of sweets. He knew a secret about her. She could be anyone in the world! When she told him stories, that gentle voice could rage like an ogre's, roar like a lion's, or trill like a lark's; that placid face could twist into villainy, slacken to idiocy, go pop-eyed with fear. She could dance like a dervish, march like a soldier, or hop like a one-legged pirate with a parrot on his shoulder. She knew all the best riddles and jokes and games. He thought he probably liked her better than anyone else in the world. Except of course for one.

'Auntie Bridie,' he said. 'Will Mummy be away very long?'

'Not very long,' she answered. 'Now if you'll do me the very great favour of putting those little pig's trotters into your shoes, we'll be on our way.'

'They're not pig's trotters,' he protested.

'Surely they are,' she said. 'What else would a little piglet have at the end of his legs?'

'Then if they're trotters, I don't need to wear shoes, 'cos pigs don't wear shoes,' he argued.

'And have you never heard the tale of the pig who wore Wellington boots?' she asked in amazement. 'I'll tell it to you as we drive along in the car.'

'Where are we going?' he asked. 'Are we going to see Mummy?'

'No, my pet. Like she promised, we'll be seeing her at Christmas, never you fret. Today we're going to a new house in the country. Could be we'll find some real piglets there. Billy, are you not done?'

Billy Flynn appeared in the doorway carrying a canvas tool bag.

'What's your rush?' he said. 'You get the kid ready and leave man's work to the men.'

'Don't try that macho crap with me, Billy,' she said wearily. 'After your half-witted performance yesterday, you're on probation with this team. I thought that would have penetrated even your thick skull.'

He flushed angrily and said, 'It showed how tight we could pull the strings, didn't it? That's why she's roaming loose. Jonty said I did him a favour.'

'So he almost pulled your pecker off to show his appreciation,' she said contemptuously. 'Anyway, it was yesterday afternoon I was talking about. Last night was just the shit on the blanket.'

'How the hell was I to know she'd be leaving early? No one said . . .'

'How the hell did they ever think you were good for anything beyond burning buses and throwing rocks?' she asked. 'Hands aren't enough out here, Billy. You've got to use your head too. You've got to plan for everything, even the things you've forgotten to plan for.'

'Which is your way of saying even the famous double act can cock up?' he mocked. 'It was you who let this address out of the bag, wasn't it? And didn't Jonty say the pigs wouldn't bother us here?'

She frowned and said, 'Even the pigs have dickheads like you who don't do what they're told.'

'Pigs?' Noll caught at the word. 'Are we going to see the pigs now, Auntie Bridie?'

'Sure we are. Billy, get these cases down to the car. I'll see you down there.'

He touched his forelock in mock deference, ruffled Noll's hair and said, 'Pigs, is it? Next pig comes here, it'll be fried bacon for supper.' Out of his tool bag he pulled an Uzi 9mm pistol which he flourished melodramatically, crying, 'Bang! Bang! Bang! Bang!'

Noll's eyes grew round with envy and he said, 'Is that for me, Billy? Is that my Christmas present?'

'Will you listen to the boy?' said Flynn, delighted at the disapproval registering on the woman's face. 'Well, maybe Auntie Bridie and me'll drop Santa a line and see if we can get you one, then you could blow all your little English friends away, would you like that?'

Laughing, he went through the door.

'Will you really get me a gun, Auntie Bridie?' asked the boy hopefully.

'We'll have to see what your mammy says, won't we?' said the woman. 'Now get your coat on. It's cold out there.'

She went through into the kitchen to check it out. Everything was neat and tidy and gleamingly clean. The only discordant note – literally – was the drip-drip-drip of a tap into the stainless steel sink.

They'd blame Jonty for the loss of this safe-house, even though it was down to Billy's cock-up. And as for Billy, if his little farewell present worked, it would be marked up to him as a triumph. Life wasn't fair, never would be, especially for women. Look at her and Maguire, both where they were, what they were, because of the men they'd chosen to orbit around.

Chosen! Now there was a word.

Noll had entered the kitchen unnoticed as she stood in thought.

'Tap dripping,' he said. 'Mummy says I should turn taps off.'

He set off across the tiled floor. She caught him in a couple of strides and swung him high.

'And your mammy's right,' she said, 'only we don't have the time. Not if we're going to see those little piggies in the country. Let's have a song, shall we? When you're going on a journey, doesn't matter whether it's somewhere good or somewhere bad, you should always set out singing. Now do you recall that song I taught you?'

'Yes! *Green grow the rushes oh!*' he shouted.

'That's it! All together now. *I'll give you one oh!*'

And with the boy laughing and singing over her shoulder, she turned and went out of the door.

# 2

Dog Cicero shuffled a pack of cards and dealt himself four aces, shuffled again and dealt four kings, shuffled a third time and dealt three queens and a six. He grimaced and took a long pull from a mug of coffee liberally laced with the Strega he kept in his desk. Just when you thought you had things under control, something always went wrong.

'Is this a private game or can anyone buy in?'

Charley Lunn was standing in the doorway holding a sheet of paper delicately between the thumb and forefinger of his left hand as if it were either very fragile or very dirty.

'I only play cards with strangers,' said Dog.

'And yourself.'

'That's what I said. What's new, Charley?'

'She's signed her statement and been charged,' said the sergeant.

'Who?'

'Maguire, of course.'

'Nothing to do with me,' said Dog. 'I'm off the case.'

He had told Parslow he didn't believe the woman's confession. The superintendent had looked as sick as a dog when told of Jacobs's guilt, but to do him justice, he had listened closely and patiently before saying, 'You mean, because you reckon her small admission is false, the big one has to be false too?'

'It's more than that,' said Dog.

'It doesn't sound more. I don't know the truth of that Health Centre business, Dog, but let's accept that Johnny Jacobs likes having his bishop bashed by a pretty girl now and then. Can't blame him. Have you seen his old lady? And let's accept that Maguire's innocent of offering her services. So why does she admit to it? Because it doesn't seem important by comparison with killing her kid, that's why! Because she's so full of guilt she's ready to admit to anything we care to put to her! That's my logic, Dog, and it sounds a damn sight more logical than yours!'

He'd argued, got nowhere, felt, not altogether comfortably, that perhaps he didn't want to get anywhere, and when Parslow wondered whether he might feel better off the case, he'd taken a childish satisfaction in agreeing and dumping the file on the chief super's desk. Not that he imagined it would stay there very long.

Lunn proved him right.

'Yes, I know. I've spent the last hour going through the file, haven't I? Mr Parslow says with my promotion board coming up, a bit of responsibility will do me good. Under his even-handed supervision, of course.'

Dog smiled. They both knew about Parslow's even-handed supervision. He took the credit while you took the blame.

'You need some help, Charley?'

'You said you checked out Maguire's story about this Gosling woman, but I can't see anything . . .'

'Sorry,' said Dog, digging through a tray and producing reports on his abortive interviews with Mrs Tobin and Mrs Osterley. 'Though now you've got a confession, you hardly need these.'

'Always keep a tidy file,' said Lunn, echoing one of Parslow's maxims. 'Anyway, I thought you didn't rate Maguire's confession?'

'I don't. But if she's willing to make a false confession of killing her kid, what's she really guilty of, eh?' It was a feeble attempt to assuage his own guilt at letting himself be so easily edged off the case. Charley Lunn raised his eyebrows and Dog went on irritatedly, 'Her confession might well be a lie, but her original story certainly is. There's the boy friend she says doesn't exist, who we know does. And there's Gosling, who we know doesn't. No, whatever's going on is very dirty and I'm glad I'm out of it. But keep me posted, Charley, especially if

118

you feel anything's been laid on you that doesn't feel right.'

This was more than just a conscience-salver. He genuinely liked the brash young sergeant who came as close to being a friend as anyone he'd met during his decade in the Force.

'Thanks, Dog. And, taking instant advantage, what do you make of this?'

He placed the sheet of paper he was carrying on the desk. Dog glanced through it once very quickly, then again more slowly and with growing incredulity.

'Bail? She's being given bail? Has she had her brief in?'

'No brief. No request. Bail on her own security.'

'But why? Up before the beak, remanded for psycho report, that's the form even with a clever brief shouting the odds. What's Steady Eddie playing at?'

'I don't know. What I do know is he had a long phone conversation after you left him. So my snout on the exchange tells me.'

'And does your snout say who with?'

But Dog knew the answer before Lunn said, 'Your old oppo with the funny fellows.'

Tench. So keen yesterday to have her accused of murder. So keen today to let her run free. What kind of game was being played here?

Lunn said, 'What's it mean, Dog? It don't feel right. Is there anything we should do?'

Dog regarded his eager face affectionately and shook his head.

'*We* should do nothing. This is crusty old bachelor country. Man with a promotion board coming up and family responsibilities should keep his nose clean.'

Lunn had married young and had a boy and a girl aged four and six. Dog had been to his house and met his wife, a sharp-eyed, sharp-minded young woman who had smiled and made herself pleasant. But he'd overheard a snatch of conversation as he returned too silently from the bathroom. '. . . But be careful, Charley. Cold bastards like that can get you into trouble without even trying . . .'

He didn't want to prove her right.

He handed back the sheet and with it his own reports.

'Now bugger off and get that file nice and tidy for Mr Parslow.'

When Lunn had gone, he picked up the cards, shuffled, and dealt five. Slowly he turned them over. Royal flush in spades.

He swept the cards into a drawer and reached for his topcoat.

He'd been sitting in his car for the time it took to smoke three of his skinny cigarettes when Maguire came out of the station. She stood on the pavement, sniffing the air like a rabbit suspicious of an open meadow. Then she made up her mind and in two strides changed from frightened coney to red deer. Red deer. Madeleine Salter's image, Madeleine who loved her, who felt responsible for what had happened, who felt herself judged that she hadn't been turned to in Maguire's time of despair.

So who had she turned to? And what had happened to make her confess to the unthinkable?

Suddenly his recent certainties felt solid as a sandcastle. His intention had been to follow, but he no longer had the patience. In any case, God knows who else was following her! There was probably a procession as long as the Lord Mayor's Show.

He started the engine and kerb-crawled till she started to cross a side street. Then he swung sharply in front of her, flung open the passenger door, leaned across and snarled, 'In!'

She froze, shock on her face, flight in her mind. He reached out, grabbed her hand and pulled. As she fell into the car he pressed the accelerator and began to move away, giving her no choice but to scramble in.

'You crazy bastard,' she exploded.

'Pull that door shut,' he ordered.

'What the hell do you think you're doing?' she demanded. 'What do you want?'

He said, 'I'm sorry. You're needed. They've found . . .'

He let his voice tail away.

'What?' she screamed. 'Noll, you mean? Is he . . . hurt? Oh

Christ! He's not dead? Tell me he's not dead?'

'No, Miss Maguire,' he said softly. 'It's you who are telling me that.'

For a second she looked at him uncomprehendingly. Then she said in a low, intense voice, 'Oh, you bastard. You unfeeling bastard! Let me out of here.'

She would have got out even with the car moving at speed if he hadn't grabbed her arm again.

'For Christ's sake, how will it help anyone if you kill yourself?' he cried. 'How will it help Noll?'

That locked her muscles, but mind and spirit were still in a turmoil which showed clearly on her face.

He turned down a service road behind the shopping precinct and ran the car between a pantechnicon and a loading bay.

'We should have a few minutes before they find us,' he said. 'Let's use them well.'

'Before who finds us?'

'Does it matter? Tench. The people who made you come to the station this morning. They'll all be watching. Look, you're everyone's puppet. Is that what you want?'

He had meant to be reasonable. Instead the question exploded out of some underlying emotion he didn't understand. But his agitation had the effect of caulking hers.

'There's only one thing I want,' she said. 'What about you, Inspector? Which of my strings is it you want to pull?'

He said, 'You've got to trust me. There's no time for explanations.'

'Make time.'

He frowned and said, 'It might take ten years. And I'd probably end up talking myself out of it.'

'Out of what?'

'Out of trying to help you, you stupid bitch!' That confusion of emotion again! This was no way to play cards. On the other hand it was probably his unfakeable rawness which was keeping her listening. If you're sick on the table, watch who wants to keep playing. The bastard must really need that pot. He smiled.

She said, 'It's so funny, calling me a stupid bitch?'

'I was thinking of something my Uncle Endo said. Sorry. And I'm sorry for yelling at you. Listen, Jane, I want to help, that's all that matters.'

'And I want to know why I should believe you.'

'Because I know you didn't harm your child any more than you offered to jerk Jacobs off.'

'And knowing that makes me worth helping? Funny it doesn't work with all your colleagues!'

She was right, Tench certainly knew as much.

He said, 'OK. I don't give a toss about you, Maguire. It's your boy I want to help. It's Noll I care about.'

That was the Open Sesame. He could see her wanting to believe, perhaps needing to believe. But there were obstacles to trust beyond belief. Time to hit hard.

He said, 'Your son's under threat, isn't he? Who's holding him? Who's threatening him? Is it the one with blond hair? The one called Billy?'

His bluff of knowledge was counterproductive.

New distrust flared in her eyes. She said, 'How do you know all this, you bastard? What are you . . .?'

'I don't know anything,' he said swiftly. 'I just want to help Noll. This Billy, is he your boy friend or what?'

Now incredulity edged out distrust.

'Boy friend? Jesus! You are crazy . . .'

'Is he the one threatening Noll?' he demanded harshly. Find the weakness, keep hitting it.

'No. I mean, yes. Oh yes, he makes threats.' Her face twisted in disgust and hatred and for a moment he thought she was going to spit. Then she said quite calmly, 'He raped me.'

'*What?*'

'He told me he would cut off Noll's ear. I believed him. So I let him . . . fuck me!'

Now she did spit the word out. He said helplessly, 'I'm sorry.'

'For what? You think I should have taken the ear? I'm not

telling you this for sympathy, Inspector. I just want you to be clear there's nothing I won't do to keep my son from harm.'

She spoke with an unnatural calm. He said gently, 'But there's someone else, is there? It's not this Billy you fear the most?'

She put her hands to her face and spoke through her fingers, as though trying to hold in words that were forcing their way out.

'Oh yes . . . another man . . . a terrible man . . . Thrale his name is . . . Jonty she called him . . .'

She shuddered as she spoke the name and deep down in Dog something shuddered in response, like the first stirring of a dormouse after long hibernation.

But he had no time for himself, far from enough for this tragic woman. He should be trying to win her confidence, to coax the truth from her. Instead he had to press hard, to force as much as he could through the fine mesh of fear and evasion.

'What did he say to you? Was it him who made you come to us with this cock and bull story? Is that it?'

She took her hands from her mouth and cried in anguish, 'Why should I trust you?'

'Who else have you got to trust?' he demanded savagely. 'A man so terrible you can hardly bear to think about him?'

He saw that he hadn't said anything new. She was agonizingly aware of how frail a thread she was hanging her hopes on. And now she was looking at him desperately, begging him to convince her that he could offer something stronger.

Then suddenly they were out of time. In the mirror Dog saw a car nose round the end of the pantechnicon, then quickly reverse out of sight. He started the engine and realized too late that the way ahead was now blocked by another lorry which had backed right up against the loading bay.

He dug his fingers into his breast pocket and pulled out a card. 'That's my home number and address,' he said, urgently thrusting it into her hand. 'Go there. Or ring. Now get out of here quick.'

She didn't ask questions. He admired her for that. She got out of the car. A man came round the back of the pantechnicon. Dog

123

got out too. He said to her, 'Through there!', pointing to the bay doors which had opened to let a trolley-load of boxes out. From the shop behind drifted the distant strains of 'The Holly and The Ivy'. It came to him then that every carol note, every thread of tinsel, every plastic holly leaf, must score her soul.

She looked at him once. Not in thanks, not in promise, but as if in search of a sign. He had nothing to show her.

'Go!' he urged.

And she went. *Oh the rising of the sun, and the running of the deer* . . .

The newcomer broke into a trot too. Dog watched his approach, then stepped in his way. The man, heavy, thickset, and already panting, tried to shoulder him aside. Dog swayed gently, let the shoulder slide across his chest, locked his knee against the man's inner thigh and next moment sent him sprawling to the ground.

Jane Maguire had paused at the doorway and was looking back. A car rolled into sight round the pantechnicon. A door opened and Tommy Stott, the lovely Special Branch sergeant, jumped out. Suddenly the fallen man half rose and grappled with Dog's legs. A gentle pressure of fingers against his neck had him subsiding again. Then Dog turned and smiled a welcome at Stott, who was moving forward menacingly.

'Morning, sergeant. No need to risk damaging that pretty jacket of yours. I think I've got things under control.'

'What?' said Stott, pausing uncertainly.

'This would-be mugger. Broad daylight too! Look, you're welcome to the collar if you think it might help your career.'

For a moment he thought the sergeant was going to burst out of his Gaultier jacket and launch himself at him. Then the car's rear window wound down and Toby Tench's amiable face peered out.

'All right, Tommy,' he said. 'Pick that useless wanker up, and if he moans about being stiff, offer him a few years back on the beat to walk it off. Dog, would you like to step in out of the cold?'

Dog looked towards the loading bay. It was closed and there was no sign of Jane Maguire.

'My pleasure, Toby,' said Dog Cicero.

# 3

The car door closed behind him with a clunk like a bank vault; in the front the driver was talking rapidly into his radio.

'. . . Captain Hook to all units, Tinkerbell is in Hartley's furnishing store on the Central Mall. Rear is covered. Cover all customer exits. Repeat, Tinkerbell is . . .'

Tench pressed a button which brought a glass barrier purring down, cutting off the driver's voice.

'Dog, how are you, my son?' he said. 'Didn't expect to see you again quite so quick.'

'That's how it goes,' said Dog. 'You don't meet for years then you can't stop bumping into each other.'

'That's where I think you're wrong, Dog. I think we *can* stop bumping into each other. With a bit of goodwill on both sides. And Tommy too. You've bumped into him once. I thought for a moment you were going to bump into him again out there. Not advisable, my son. Tommy's worse than me for bumping into.'

'You reckon? You'd think a good-looking boy like that would try to keep out of the way,' mocked Dog.

'Yes, he is a handsome lad, isn't he?' agreed Tench, unperturbed. 'I always liked the nice-looking ones in my gang, eh, Dog? Like what you were. Don't think you'd qualify now though, would you?'

'Thanks for that at least, Toby,' said Dog. 'Is that why you asked me into your lovely car, to talk about old times?'

'No! I've had enough reminders of my age today without digging up the past. For instance, I reckon I'm going deaf. I could have sworn I heard old Eddie Parslow tell me you were off the Maguire case.'

'That's right,' said Dog. 'So I am.'

126

'Really? In that case, how come you're still sniffing around her like she was a bitch on heat, Dog?'

'Is that how it looked? I'm sorry. I saw her walking along and like any well brought up boy would, I offered her a lift. She said thank you kindly and asked to be brought here. Then she said thank you kindly again and walked away. Then your lad came running up. I thought he was a mugger. Sorry about that. I hope he'll be OK. Incidentally, why are you still interested in Maguire? Yesterday you seemed determined she was a killer. Well, now she's admitted it. So what's your problem, Toby?'

Tench sighed deeply.

'My problem? Normally I ain't got no problem, leastways no more than any other Branch cop working under the Prevention of Terrorism Act to try to keep this little realm of ours safe for Her Majesty's Subjects to live in. But you look like you might be about to turn yourself into my problem, Dog. So let's try to get you solved before you get out of hand, shall we? No more questions 'cos I know the answers. You reckon she didn't kill her kid and you're wondering what would make a woman confess to something like that and you can't see any better way to find out than blundering around after her. Right?'

'I thought you weren't asking any more questions,' said Dog.

'You really want to play it hard, don't you?' said Tench. 'OK, get this. Me, I don't know if her kid's alive or dead, and it doesn't bother me that much. What does bother me is whether his father's alive or dead. Yeah, that's it. Oliver Beck, your friendly Noraid man. Now our mole Paddy – we call all our Irish moles Paddy, it saves on the headstones – tells us that it wasn't just the IRS who were bothered by Beck's creative accounting, it was the IRA. Seems there's hard men from South Africa to Libya asking for payments that never came. And there's lots of Micks catching cold on lonely beaches at midnight watching out for arms shipments that are never going to come. And it all adds up to somewhere around three million. Pounds sterling, I mean. Not dollars. Where's it gone, everyone's asking. Three possibilities. One, it's salted away and no one but the dead man knows where.

Two, it's salted away and Maguire knows where, and is just marking time till she feels it's safe to pick it up. Three, Beck's not dead at all. He just faked it to get out from under before the IRA's hard men found out what he'd been up to and sent in their own special brand of debt collector.'

'And Maguire?'

'She'll join him when the time seems ripe.'

Dog frowned and said, 'But wasn't there a body . . ?'

'Which she identified. That's right, Dog. If Beck is still alive, then someone else got killed, and she knew all about it. Oh yes, just because you think you've proved she doesn't jerk off old men for pocket money, don't imagine she's the Virgin bloody Mary! At the very least she knew how he made his living and it didn't bother her. She's a thief and that doesn't bother her. And she could be party to murder, and I doubt if that'd bother her either. Another nice girl you've got yourself mixed up with, Dog.'

'I'm not mixed up with her.'

'Sorry. Mixed up *by*, I should have said. Dog, let me tell you, I punched up what happened to you over there. It's all in the files, everything that's happened since sixty-nine, and you're part of it. A little part, but with lots of detail, more than you imagine possible, I dare say. There's even a photo of the girl. And I looked at her and I could see how Maguire might get to you . . .'

'What the hell are you talking about? There's no resemblance . . .'

He stopped as Tench laughed at the giveaway denial.

He tried to open the car door but it was locked.

'Not in the features, no,' said Tench judiciously. 'But the eyes, Dog. And the hair. But above all, Dog, it's in you that the resemblance is most marked. The same doubts, the same ambivalence. The same wanting and not wanting . . . I told you the record was detailed, Dog. Pity you can't see it. Might put you out of your misery . . . if you want to get out of it, that is.'

'All I want to get out of is this car,' said Dog softly. 'Do I have to break a window?'

'You'd need a pneumatic drill, old son!' laughed Tench. 'But I can see you're in a hurry, so there you go.'

He pressed a button and the door handle moved. Dog thrust the door open and got out.

'Just remember one thing, Dog,' said Tench cheerfully through the window. 'This slag's ours. She can lead us to a lot of nasty people. It's a boggy enough path without sinking my feet into your neuroses every two minutes. So be a good little old soldier, Dog, and simply fade away. We'll take care of everything, I promise.'

'Including the child? You'll take care of the child?'

'Don't get sentimental, Dog. Of course we'll take care of the child, though I don't know why. With his background, when he grows up he'll be a natural for putting bombs under cars, wouldn't you say? You worry about yourself, son. Take a few days off. You're looking a bit peaky to me.'

He pressed the button which wound down the barrier so he could speak to the driver. As he did so, the car radio crackled. The driver picked up the mike and said, 'Captain Hook. Receiving. Over.'

'Wendy One. No sign of Tinkerbell in Hartley's store. I say again, no sign of Tinkerbell . . .'

Tench seized the mike from the driver and snarled into it, 'You load of wankers! Don't hang about repeating yourself. Get out there and find her. Captain Hook, out!'

He tossed the mike back into the driver's lap.

Dog grinned at him through the window.

'Having trouble, Cap'n?' he mocked. 'If you can't catch Tinkerbell, how do you expect to lay your hands on Jonty Thrale?'

Tench's face smoothed into a puzzled blank.

'Who?' he said. 'Where'd you pick up a name like that?'

It was an unconvincing performance, but it was his own reaction rather than Tench's which disturbed Dog. He'd tossed in the name just to stir things up, but even as he spoke it, he was aware of that deeper resonance, something more personal, more buried, which he hadn't had time to examine when Maguire had mentioned the man with such fear.

'Must have been something you said,' he lied. But it didn't feel altogether a lie . . .

'Never heard of him,' said Tench. 'Dog, my son. There's an old Irish proverb. Half a face is better than no head. Take care.'

The window purred up, the car accelerated away.

Dog watched it go, debating his next move. Would the woman contact him at his flat? Doubtful. In any case he couldn't sit around waiting. Inside him, in that tangle of wreckage he'd thought he was walking away from for ten years, something was stirring. Brought to life by Tench's mocking reference to his file? Or by a name he'd never heard before but which tolled like a passing bell? Or by a red-haired girl with a voice full of music?

He made for his car. It was time to call in a favour owed for many years, perhaps time to do himself a favour he had owed for almost as long.

He got in the car, drove back through town till he hit Eastern Avenue and then turned west towards London.

# 4

The ringing of the door bell startled Madeleine Salter into waking. For a moment she did not know where she was, only that she was not in her bed where she expected to be. Then she sat upright and the unfamiliar ceiling gave way to the familiar walls and pictures and furnishings of her living room.

She had slept badly, risen early and made herself a pot of tea which stood by a half-filled cup on the table by her sofa. Sleep had come unasked as so often it does when you stop chasing it, and it had swallowed her deep for many hours.

The bell rang again. Suddenly she was certain it was Jane. Pulling her thin silk robe around her, she ran to the door, undid the chain and flung it wide.

A man stood there, swathed in a long dark overcoat, buttoned up to the neck against the chill wind. She slammed the door shut, refastened the chain, then opened it a crack through which she said, 'Yes?'

He hadn't moved but stood there still, smiling slightly.

'Miss Salter, is it?' he said. 'You're wise to take care.'

'Who are you? What do you want?' she asked.

'It's about your friend, Jane Maguire,' he said. 'Can I come in?'

'Who are you?' she repeated. 'Police? I'll need to see some identification.'

'Of course,' he said. 'Like I say, you're very wise. Let me introduce myself.'

And he began to unbutton his coat.

It was two hours later that Jane Maguire arrived at the college.

In Hartley's furnishing store, she had paused briefly to wrap a headscarf round her giveaway hair. As she approached the main exit, she saw a woman trying to negotiate it with a pushchair and a crammed shopping bag.

'Let me give you a hand,' said Jane, taking the bag and holding open the door so the chair could get through.

'Thanks a lot,' said the woman on the pavement outside. 'It must have been a man who designed that place.'

'It's the same everywhere,' said Jane. 'Mine can walk now, thank heaven.'

It came out automatically as part of her cover as she walked down the mall chatting animatedly, two friends out shopping together. But as she spoke, the brightness of tone hit her like a betrayal and when the other woman said, 'How many have you got?' it was all she could do not to choke as she answered, 'Only the one. A little boy.'

'Are you all right?' asked the woman, concerned.

'Yes, fine, just a bit of a cold. Bye.'

She hurried across the mall, dodging between the crowds of Christmas shoppers. Everything seemed to be closing in on her, the canned carols, the glittering decorations, the festive windows, and everywhere the young children. Every woman she saw seemed to have one by the hand, or in her arms, or on her back, or in a pram. She saw a sign saying TOILETS, hurried in, shut herself in a cubicle like a coffin, and let the tears flow. It was, she told herself, the right place to be. Her tears were a waste product, a necessary relief of pressure. From time to time they would build up till they had to find release. But in between times, she would be cool, calm and collected as a woman must be whose every decision is life or death. Her son's life or death.

In her mind she went over Thrale's instructions again. She'd hung on to his every word, terrified she might miss something and give him an excuse for hurting Noll. And she'd carried out his orders to the letter. But they had stopped with the confession. There'd been nothing after that, no contingency plan for what she should do if they let her out on bail.

Suppose they had seen her get in the car with Cicero, what

would they make of that? Surely they'd guess that she had no choice, surely they wouldn't blame her? Wouldn't blame Noll . . ?

She was still clutching the card the detective had given her. She ripped it in half as though it were evidence against her. But as she made to drop it into the pan she hesitated. What game was he playing? She'd looked back and seen him floor the fat man who was trying to follow her. That could be evidence of his good faith. Or maybe just part of an elaborate charade.

No, Cicero was definitely a last resort. But when your options were as limited as hers, it was wise to keep them all open.

She put the pieces of card in her pocket and tried to work out her next move. She needed somewhere to go. Her own flat was out. There would certainly be watchers there. Worse, Noll would be there, in everything she saw.

Her mother's then? She longed to go, was appalled at the prospect; longed for the welcome and comfort that ought to be there, felt sick at the prospect of reproof and priests and prayer.

Or there was Maddy's. Again. She'd gone there yesterday (was it only yesterday?) in search of refuge and found instead . . . But that was nothing to do with Maddy. Perhaps she would be there now. At the very least she ought to make sure she was all right. But no bus this time, no long walk. She came out of the toilet, washed her face, repaired her make-up, then set out briskly towards the taxi rank at the entrance to the shopping precinct.

Her years with Oliver had stopped her feeling guilty about riding in taxis, but something of the old feeling returned as she watched the meter ticking up a day's pay. The driver looked at her curiously as he dropped her by the gate.

'This it, darling?' he asked, casting a distrusting urban eye over the desolate and deserted-looking site.

'This is it,' said Jane, paying him.

He drove away and she set out down the driveway towards the residential block. There was no sign of life anywhere. If there were watchers, they were a long way off and well concealed. But she did not feel herself observed and she was beginning to trust her instincts.

Rounding the end of the block she saw with relief that Maddy's car was there. But when she rang the door bell, she got no reply. She dug into her purse and found the key she hadn't had to use on her last visit. Memories of that came flooding back and when she unlocked the door she pushed it open and took a quick step backwards. But there was no one waiting to greet her this time.

Cautiously she entered.

'Maddy?' she called. 'Are you there? It's Jane.'

There was no reply, but the flat didn't feel empty. Or perhaps it was simply that her subconscious had already spotted what her eyes now began to take in – the raincoat hanging behind the door, the scattering of letters on the mat, the purse and key ring on the mantelpiece.

She moved slowly, reluctantly, towards the bedroom.

The door was ajar. She pushed it wide. And felt a great surge of relief.

Maddy was lying in bed, looking towards her.

'Maddy,' she said, moving forward. 'Are you ill? I just came straight in because . . .'

Her voice tailed away though she would have liked to keep on speaking, just for the comfort of the sound. The eyes were still staring at her but they were unblinking with a steadfastness beyond simple control. The skin of her face was translucent as the membrane of an egg with the creases and lines of middle age all smoothed away. But she did not look young. Only dead.

A scream of grief, of terror, of something more unbearable than both, welled up from the pit of Jane's being. She tried to stop it in her throat with her fist in her mouth, biting on the knuckles. But it forced its way through and filled the tiny room with an almost visible pulse of sound.

Slowly it faded, slowly the ripples of echo smoothed out like the skin on the dead woman's face, till the room became again a solid cube of silence with the two figures fixed in it, the living as still as the dead.

# 5

Dog Cicero knew there was no point in bullshitting David Westmain.

When you'd pulled a man out of a burning personnel carrier eleven years ago and made no attempt to contact him for the last ten, he would have to be a fool not to hear alarm bells jangling when you walked into his office.

Westmain was no fool. He'd been a captain in Intelligence the night he'd decided to take a personal look at a border operation he'd helped set up. Now he was a full colonel, though he didn't look in the least military in his grey business suit.

'Dog,' he said, rising and reaching out his hand. 'I haven't seen you since . . . ages.'

The last time they'd met had been in hospital, but it had been Westmain who was visiting. He'd looked down at the recumbent figure, forced himself to meet the one eye visible through a cocoon of dressings, and murmured something idiotic about the marvellous things the quacks were doing these days, hadn't they got an old crock like himself back on his feet in a couple of months?

Shortly after, they'd flown Cicero back to England. Westmain had written a couple of times, got no reply, and accepted the rebuff with the guilty shrug with which most men accept the chance to step aside from anticipated awkwardness. But it's a long step that's forever.

'I'm a policeman,' said Dog.

'Yes, I did hear something. The lure of uniform, eh? Will you have a coffee? Or something stronger?'

'I want some help,' said Dog. 'Some information.'

'Is this official, Dog?'

'Depends. Jonty Thrale. Does that mean anything official to you?'

Westmain pursed his lips, shook his head.

'Sorry. Rings no bells.'

Truth? Lie? It didn't matter.

He nodded at the keyboard and screen on Westmain's desk.

'No bells, eh? Suppose you try Big Ben there, see if he rings?'

'Dog, even if we've got something, you know I can't just . . .'

'Why don't you check first, then decide if they'll send you to the Tower for passing it on?'

It was the gospel according to Endo. The weaker your hand, the tighter you took control.

Westmain turned the screen so that it didn't offer his visitor even an oblique view, and his fingers ran lightly over the keys. Dog watched, unblinking. The hands, not the face. In poker, faces tell nothing because they can be made to tell anything.

'Yes, we've got something. But I'm sorry, Dog, it's got a classification way above anything I dare pass on without top-level authorization.'

His voice was at the same time pleading and adamant.

Dog said, 'OK. What about me? Am I in that thing?'

'You? You mean . . . yes, I suppose you would be.'

'Could you try?'

The fingers moved again.

'Yes, you're there, Dog. The whole thing.'

'How's the rating?'

'Lowish after all this time.'

'Low enough for you to leave it up there while you get me that coffee you offered?'

Whenever you can, offer an option. Show them the big rock, and they'll chew on the pebble like it's new-baked bread.

Westmain hesitated. Dog said, 'I need to see it. It's in my system, David. Working its way through, but it needs an impetus.'

'Sort of an enema, you mean?' Westmain joked. Dog didn't smile. Awareness of his bad taste could be the last straw of guilt the Intelligence officer needed.

'How do you like your coffee, Dog?' said Westmain resignedly.

'Espresso. Take your time. Espresso means pressed out, not quick.'

He took the vacated chair and started reading the lines of green light.

*Cicero, Julian. Lieutenant Royal Essex Light Infantry . . .*

It went on and on. Christ, they knew details of his life he'd forgotten! He skipped till he caught his father's name.

*Giuliano Cicero, Italian national, son of Antonio Cicero secretary of Genoan branch of Italian Socialist Party who died in prison 1934 . . . emigrated UK 1935 naturalized 1938 served in Far East with Royal Essex L.I. 1940–45, corporal at discharge, joined British Labour Party 1946 . . .*

The bastards were into everything! But there was no time for this, not now. His hands hovered over the keyboard then dipped like a pianist's and his fingers moved lightly, echoing the motions of Westmain's earlier.

All the psychological skill in the world wouldn't help you win at poker unless you could remember the cards. Uncle Endo had delighted him with tricks of memory as much as prestidigitation, till one day he had amazed his uncle by first equalling, then surpassing his feats. A couple of dozen letters and numbers pressed in sequence on a keyboard was child's play.

*Thrale, Oscar Johnson, ka Jonty Thrale b Shrewsbury England 5.7.58. Mother, Jennifer Teresa nee Mahoney. Father, Antony Johnson Thrale solicitor d heart attack 1969. Thrale ret Dublin to mother's house 1970 . . .*

There was a footstep outside the door. He looked up, alarmed. The steps moved on. But this was too slow. He pressed the print-out key. It was one of the superfast silent printers, thank God. He glanced at the last line. *Known associate: Heighway, Bridgid.* His fingers flickered again. The printer performed its silent magic. He tore off the print-out, folded it, tucked it beneath his shirt under his belt, punched up *Cicero, Julian* and once more keyed the printer.

Enema or irritant, there was no point in not knowing anything

Toby Tench knew.

Westmain returned a few moments later with two cups of coffee.

'Done?' he said.

'Yes.'

'Good. Would you clear it?'

He studied the keyboard carefully, one finger poised.

'Is it this one?' he said.

Westmain smiled slightly.

'I'll do it. Tell me, Dog. Why were you asking about Thrale?'

His voice was lightly curious, but Dog knew he'd been checking on current security operations involving Thrale. Like Uncle Endo said, at Fourth Street in Hold 'Em, the best bluff could be the truth.

'The Branch have been on my patch. Overlapping cases. I heard one of them mention Thrale. I know Tench, their chief man, from way back. We don't get on. I thought I might put one over on him by twisting your arm. Also he made some crack about my file. I reckoned if my enemies could read it for entertainment, I was entitled to my share of the fun.'

'Fair enough,' said Westmain. He was six to four convinced. If you were to make the grade in Intelligence, those were the best odds you ever allowed.

Dog downed his scalding coffee.

'I've got to go,' he said. 'I've got an appointment.'

'It's been nice to see you again, Dog. Let's make it social next time.'

Interpretation: OK, perhaps I still owe you, but professionally, the bank is closed.

Dog nodded and offered his hand.

'Watch how you go,' said Westmain. 'By the way, all these years, one thing I never knew, how come they called you Dog?'

'You know the Army. I was very good at obedience tests.'

Later he sat in his flat which ten years of occupancy hadn't personalized beyond the laundry mark on his sheets. In front of him were the print-outs. He tried to start on Jonty Thrale and

Bridgid Heighway but it was no good. A man's ghosts are stronger than living flesh. So he started reading about himself, and soon it ceased to be a reading and became a renewal.

He was sitting in his car in the shadowy car park of that Belfast pub. Beside him Maeve Mooney was putting the key in the ignition. She looked at him anxiously, eyes huge in that luminously pale face all shadowed by an exuberance of rich red hair.

'You OK?'

'Fine,' he muttered.

She switched on the engine. The starter had been playing up but tonight it caught first time. You want an ace for three hands, you'll get it when your straight needs a deuce.

'You're sure? You're not going to be sick?'

'Only for the rest of my life.'

Even in his drunkenness he recognized that the melodramatic phrase marked a point where self-reproach was becoming self-indulgence and he looked at her and tried to smile apologetically.

Her lips twisted in wry acknowledgement, then she found reverse gear and let in the clutch to back out.

The explosion drove right up from beneath the front offside wheel. It was channelled right at the driver's seat and it blew her apart. Literally. Him it flung sideways out of the car, breaking bones in his legs, arms and rib cage and laying waste the right side of his face.

There was nothing heroic about what followed, no desperate efforts by a wounded hero to rescue the woman he loved. He lay there, his head in a frozen puddle, his clothing scorched by the blazing car, and screamed till someone started to drag him clear. Then he fainted.

He struggled free from that terrible memory and read on. He saw himself in hospital and there was the memory of comfort here, not from the medical staff, though the Army had seen he got the best of care to heal his body, but from the man they'd sent to heal his mind, the only person whose visits he ever looked forward to. 'Bear with me now,' that soft voice had insisted. 'You may not feel the benefit for months, for years even, but what we're doing will help, believe me.'

He'd wanted to believe, in the end had come to believe. That soft, undemanding voice was the only good memory of that time, one of the few good memories of any time since.

But now as he read on, he felt himself squeezed and torn apart as the explosion had torn at his body. For here in the print-out it was clear beyond any doubt that the psychiatrist's equal if not prime concern had been to get at the truth for Army Intelligence. He and the debriefing captain had been working as a team! Hard man, soft man, the commonplace of interrogation technique.

The captain had flung questions at him like blows.

'Did you ever suspect that Maeve Mooney was working for the IRA? Hadn't you been warned that her family had strong Sinn Fein sympathies? Didn't your CO suggest that your association with this woman was inappropriate? Did she ever question you about your work? Did you at any time discuss operations with her? Hadn't you met her that night to talk about the incident earlier that day?'

*Incident!* How easy to shrink the monstrous with jargon.

Incident . . .

On patrol – everything quiet – routine, almost over, his mind drifting ahead to his date that night – out of nowhere a flurry of shots and suddenly it was combat – a figure bent low scurrying across the street – the challenge and the shot almost simultaneous – echoes fading, silence flooding in like a choking gas, and combat reduced to a fourteen-year-old boy bleeding to death in a gutter.

Yes, of course he'd have talked about the incident to Maeve. Where else could he take his guilt?

But what the captain alleged . . . 'You were drunk, vulnerable, ready for squeezing dry. She offered to take you home, said you wouldn't want to go back to your quarters in this state. Oh yes, you'd have told her everything she wanted to know, and if you hadn't, there'd have been a couple of the boyos in the next room ready to start pulling your plonker less gently. Believe it or not, Cicero, you were lucky. Because you shot that kid, some more of the boyos decided to fix you quick. Leaving your car in that pub car park must have seemed a heaven-sent opportunity. But they got their wires crossed. Mooney saw her chance too and decided to make her move. That's all that saved you, Lieutenant. A typical Mick cock-up . . .'

'No! No! No!' he'd screamed. And his screams of denial were still echoing when the other had come with his soft voice, his sympathetic ear, his promise of healing.

*'In my opinion Lieutenant Cicero was ignorant of Mooney's probable terrorist connections and did not knowingly offer her any classified information. But it is at least possible that, but for the car bomb, there would have been a breach of security by this officer and it is therefore not recommended that he continue in the service.'*

Not because of his scarred body, not because of his agonies of mind, but because he might have been going to be a security risk. For years he had felt sure that resigning his commission had been his own indisputable decision, the only course possible for a man of feeling and honour. But now he saw that it had presented itself as the easiest course for the Army, and he of the soft voice had spared no pains to direct him to it.

His decision to join the police had baffled people, baffled himself. How could a man who'd walked away in disgust from one form of uniformed law enforcement so quickly embrace another?

But he hadn't walked away. It was not in his nature to walk away. Uncle Endo had seen this when he had fallen seriously ill during one of the old man's visits from the States. 'This kid will make it,' he'd said confidently when his parents' fear had been turning to despair. 'He doesn't know how to give in, believe me!' And he'd recovered against all the odds.

No, he wouldn't have walked away. He'd have stayed and done things his way. But all the Army could see was a flaw, a potential embarrassment. So he of the soft voice, the man he'd trusted as healer and friend, had opened the door and gently ushered him through.

'Bastard!'

He spat the word out like an explosive sneeze, and like a sneeze it cleared his head.

The print-out shouldn't make him angry, it should make him glad! It made more sense out of the last ten years than all his soul searching had managed. It could help him bring his life back into focus.

But it still left him not knowing, never able to know, what Maeve had had in mind when she had helped him into his car.

Now here he was again faced with the ambiguities of a woman, the ambiguities of Ireland. This time he needed no urging to walk away. Everything in his being cried out against re-entering this dangerous maze.

Everything except the knowledge that there was an innocent child out there in the hands of people who had never let innocence come between them and their cause, being sought by a policeman who would rather collar the perpetrators than recover their victim.

Noll Maguire was the same age as Dog Cicero had been when he lay dying in the eyes of everyone except old Endo. The fears of parents are too easily turned into a communicating despair. A boy needs someone else reading the cards for him.

He turned to the print-outs on Jonty Thrale and Bridgid Heighway again.

Thrale had started a course in law at Dublin University, joined Sinn Fein in his second year, abandoned his course shortly afterwards, travelled extensively in Europe and America, and returned to Ireland in 1979. It was believed he had fallen out with his immediate political masters who were keen for him to complete his studies and serve the cause with the respectable face of professional expertise. But Thrale had opted for direct action. He had no convictions but the list of suspected complicities ran through several lines over more than ten years, building from simple bombings and hit-and-run killings to big mainland ops.

It was couched in the distancing abbreviations of the intelligence gatherer's trade, and with Dog's eyes drawn to the later headline-making stuff, he almost missed it.

Then it burned out of the page at him.

*10.1.80. sit Bluebell Inn cp Bel. c bm ft off whl trig. 1 civ d 1 sec w rec*

One civilian dead. One member of the security forces wounded, but recovered.

Recovered! As one part of his mind tasted the bitter irony of the word, another part was racing back into the past, the near past, the distant but ever-present past; Jane Maguire's mention of Thrale, Tench's unconvincing denial, his own sense of significant echo but so far away, so deep buried . . . then he was there . . . the crowded bar, the need for another drink, the barman setting a Guinness and chaser before him, 'with compliments', but not just anyone's compliments. He had said, 'With Mr Thrale's compliments.'

And once again he saw across the smoke-filled room the narrow face shaded under the old tweed hat, the raised glass, the sardonic smile.

Strangely, he had never felt individual hatred till this moment, never thought of the blast as the work of an individual man, but of a monstrous machine. Perhaps it had been necessary for his survival that his mind should generalize the vileness which had wrecked his life. How could anything so cosmic be put down to one man?

But God, who loves a revenge tragedy above all things, had finally tired of this dilatoriness which made Hamlet look like Indiana Jones, and He had shoved Thrale onto stage with a thunder roll of winks and nudges.

Great players don't think of money lost, only money loaned. They know they'll get even.

God and Uncle Endo both.

Time to get back to the cards.

He turned to the Bridgid Heighway print-out. Born in Cork in 1957, she had come to Dublin in 1973 and worked as a waitress for two years before getting taken on as an ASM at the Abbey Theatre. It was believed her acquaintance with Thrale began during this period. There had been walk-on parts, small speaking roles, understudy work, and during the period Thrale was on his travels, her career had looked as if it might be about to take off. Shortly after his return she had been given her first leading role in a new play. Two months later, the day before opening, she vanished. By the time she returned, the play had gone on with an understudy and folded. She offered no explanation, but there had been a botched border ambush the day she took off, shots had been exchanged and the Army were sure they'd hit one of the attackers. Word was that it had been Thrale, and that Heighway had rushed off to be with him. Whatever the truth, she was thrown out of the Abbey for it, worked intermittently with other companies, resting as much as she worked, till gradually she dropped out of the acting scene altogether. Meanwhile Thrale was evolving from gunman to undercover operative and frequently using a woman as his principal aide. Heighway had no convictions either. There were plenty of pictures from her Abbey days, but as she looked completely different in each of them, they weren't much help.

One thing was certain. If Heighway had been involved in half the ops Thrale was suspected of masterminding, then she was just as dangerous as he was.

Another woman willing to kill, maim, extort, abduct, all for the sake of a cause. Or for the sake of a man.

And for the sake of her child, what might a woman be willing to do?

He stared unhappily at the print-outs. There was nothing but grief for him here. Past grief certainly, and future grief too if he came back to life only to recreate the sorrows of the past.

With luck it might all pass by. There was nothing he could do, there were no more leads to follow. This too could be buried. Tench would mistake impotence for obedience. He could let a few more months slide by, quietly fold, leave the table, go and sit in the sun somewhere. Show Uncle Endo he'd been wrong about him all these years.

The door bell rang, a long desperate peal.

He knew who it was without recourse to the peephole. He flung open the door and stared at her silently, his face showing neither the welcome nor the resentment he felt. She stared back at him, her eyes huge in a face so pale, her hair seemed to burn around it like fire in the snow.

She said, 'There was nowhere else . . .'

Then she swayed forward and he caught her in his arms.

# 6

It was when he was five and convalescing from his near-fatal illness that Dog Cicero really started learning cards. Endo sat by his bed hour after hour, dealing cards onto the counterpane and talking nonstop. And because he talked about poker as if it were the most important thing in the world, that's how it came across to the young listener.

Once when Dog had had a run of luck, Endo said, 'Looks like you got your poor old uncle by the short hairs this time, boy.' He spoke so piteously that Dog had pushed half of his matchstick winnings across the sheet towards him but, instead of the thanks he expected, Endo had looked at him grimly and said, 'Nice thought, Dog, but let it stay a thought. Kindness and cards don't sit easy together. What a man does with his winnings is his own affair. But they ain't winnings till the game's over. While you're still playing, you see someone in trouble, that's the time to hit hard!'

Jane Maguire was in trouble. Dog felt the pressure on him to persuade her that her friend's death was not her fault. He kept quiet, fed her whisky and water, listened to her low musical voice playing its fugue of guilt and grief, and finally crashed in discordantly: 'Who killed her doesn't matter. So she's dead and you're sorry. She'll still be dead and you'll not be so sorry next week, next month, next year. Why she was killed, *that* matters. Did she know anything?'

He'd cut through the shock, at least temporarily. She looked at him with loathing but she answered, 'No, nothing, I'd told her nothing, that's why we quarrelled. I would have told her everything when I went back last night, but he was there . . .'

'Billy, the one who raped you?'

He was beginning to make sense of it now. They'd wanted to

147

find what she knew about Beck, about the money. They'd tracked her down through her mother, through Maddy. And they'd decided the way to do things quietly and get her fullest cooperation was to get hold of the boy first. Which they'd done, though he wasn't yet quite sure how. Part two of the plan was for Billy to pick her up as she left the Health Centre on her way to the Vestey Kindergarten. Only she'd got the sack and left early. By the time he realized something was wrong, she'd reached the school and their quiet operation had gone public. Back to the drawing board. Maguire had given them a second chance by walking out of the hospital. She'd either been spotted, or they'd guessed she would head for the college. And Billy had been waiting once more.

'Where did he take you?' he demanded.

'I don't know. I got in a car. He gave me a pair of dark glasses and said if I took them off, he'd poke one of Noll's eyes out. I believed him. The glasses were absolutely black and fitted tight like goggles so I couldn't see a thing. I don't know how far we drove, then we went into a building, up some stairs. Then someone pulled the glasses off. There were two more of them . . .'

'You saw them plain?'

'I saw the woman. They called her Bridie. She looked different but I'm sure she was the same woman who took Noll . . .'

'Miss Gosling, you mean?' he said. 'The one you met that morning? The one you'd seen in the school the previous Friday?'

He wanted her to deny it, to produce some other explanation.

'Yes, that's right,' she said.

There was no hesitation in her voice, no sign she was lying. Worse, there was no reason for her to be lying. But in that case . . . His mind was racing through a maze to a centre he didn't really want to discover. He forced himself back to what she was saying.

' . . . The other one, Thrale, I never got a really good look

148

at. Sort of a thin face, not someone you'd pay much attention to, except for his eyes . . . I think I saw him in town earlier, watching me when I was on my way to the bus station.'

*. . . a narrow face, a faint smile, a raised glass . . .*

'What happened then?' he asked.

'The woman took me into a bedroom to see Noll. I was so happy I could have kissed her. She warned me not to say anything to upset him. I was to call her Auntie Bridie and to say I wanted Noll to stay with her a few days while I went to see Santa Claus about his Christmas present. She sounded kind, I wanted to believe she was kind. But the man Thrale said, "You can make it easy for him or hard for him. It doesn't matter to us," and his voice was like ice. Then Bridie took me in. He was in bed, very sleepy, I think they must have given him something. He was so pleased to see me but he didn't seem unhappy . . . he talked about Auntie Bridie and how funny she was and I told him that I had to go away to see Santa Claus to get this bike he'd been wanting and his eyes lit up and then he was so tired he fell asleep . . .'

He was losing her to grief again.

He said, 'What happened then? Come on, Jane. Stop being so bloody self-centred! Stop thinking just of yourself. Think about your son!'

The so obviously unjust accusation hit her like cold water.

She cried, 'What the hell do you think . . .' but he cut across with 'What did they want from you, Jane? They wanted to know about Beck, was that it? About the money? Is he alive, Jane? Come on, tell me. *Is he alive?*'

She took a long pull at her whisky and water, then she said dully, 'Of course he's bloody well alive.'

There it was at last. It had been inevitable, there was no other explanation. But he realized he hadn't really wanted to hear it. For there was a body in Beck's grave, and this woman had identified it, and that made her an accessory to a lot more than the theft of Noraid funds . . .

He said, 'Tell me about it.'

Something of his disappointment, perhaps his distaste, must

149

have come through for she began to talk rapidly, self-justifyingly.

'I didn't know about Oliver, not until . . . All right, I'm not such a fool I didn't guess he was the kind of businessman who shaved corners, so I wasn't too surprised when he came along and told me he was in trouble with the IRS. The Inland Revenue Service. He said he'd been juggling his taxes for years and now they were catching up with him. He said they could strip him clean, and probably put him away for five to ten as well. He said everyone was at it, he'd just been unlucky. I believed him. Why not? It's in the papers all the time, and you never think it's all that bad, cheating on taxes, do you?'

She spoke defiantly, not challenging his possible disapproval so much as her own sense of poor judgement.

'So he decided to fake his own death,' he prompted.

'That's right. He said he couldn't take being locked up, especially not when he knew me and Noll would be left destitute. So he came up with this plan, and I went along. He was Noll's father. And I loved him. What was I supposed to do? There didn't seem to be basically anything wrong with it, a few lies, nothing that a couple of "Hail Marys" wouldn't put right even if I hadn't stopped going for all that junk!'

The thought of the body she'd identified hit Dog again, but it still wasn't the time to turn over that stone.

He said, 'When did you find out the truth?'

'The whole truth you mean? He wasn't lying, you see, just being a bit selective. The IRS came first. I was ready for them. I wasn't ready when his wife showed though. She was supposed to be living abroad. It turned out she was shacked up with a lawyer in New York and she'd come ready to fight me through the courts to get her hands on Oliver's estate. That cheered me up a lot. I just introduced her to the IRS men and told her to get on with it. But then the FBI showed up too and began asking all kinds of incomprehensible questions, till finally I caught on.'

'You'd no idea he worked for Noraid?' said Dog incredulously.

'None! Hard to believe? Listen, we'd talked about Ireland when we first met, naturally. He wanted to know all about my background and I knew he had Irish blood in him. But it must have come across quite clear what I thought of the bastards who kill and maim innocent people, whatever cause they claim they're fighting for. My dad died in the middle of it. So British soldiers, Irish bombers, they're all the same to me. Scum.'

She spoke with burning passion. Dog's hand touched the side of his face. He said, 'So what did you feel when you found out the truth?'

'Sick. Sick because of what he was. Sick because he hadn't felt able to confide in me. Sick because I saw my life, and Noll's life, in tatters.'

'So what did you do?'

'I got more and more desperate. I felt I was being watched all the time. I don't think they suspected Oliver wasn't really dead but they certainly suspected I knew where a lot of money was stashed.'

'Why didn't you just tell them what had happened?' he asked.

She looked at him scornfully.

'You don't just betray someone you've loved,' she said. 'Not even when you fear they've betrayed you.'

He nodded and said, 'So you did what?'

'I ran. I ran home to mother.'

'Using what for money?'

'Oliver had dumped a suitcase full of mixed bills in a locker at the bus station,' she said.

'You didn't object to using this money, knowing where it came from?'

'Yes, it crossed my mind to object, but I needed to get away. And I needed money to keep me going till I could take care of us both by working. If I'd been by myself, who knows what I'd have done? But there was Noll. And when we came down here, I had to have a decent home for him, and I needed to get him into a nursery school so I could work, and I went private because I didn't want to answer a lot of questions and leave a trail . . . So yes, I've used the money, but not for myself. For your child you don't ask the same questions, that's all.'

It was a moving declaration.

He said, 'Well, that sounds reasonably honest of you. Would it surprise you to know there are theft warrants out for you in Massachusetts?'

It obviously would. At least she contrived to look dumbfounded.

He said, 'When you vanished, everything of any value in your husband's house vanished with you.'

Suddenly she smiled, a glimmer of sun on a frost-bound field, showing him what she could be like if summer ever returned.

'Babs,' she said. 'His wife. We didn't get on, but when I told her she could stop worrying about me as I was heading for home, she helped all she could. No wonder! The house was full of lovely things but the IRS had them all inventoried and valued. Me taking off gave Babs the chance to fill her boots, with a ready-made culprit laid on!'

It was plausible. It was also unimportant.

He said, 'There must have been plans for you to get together again?'

'Of course. I was to wait six months then head back to England.'

'So you've carried out phase one,' he accused.

'No!' she said fiercely. 'I didn't wait six months. I ran. And I came back here because it was the only place I had to run to. And I've been trying to cover my tracks ever since.'

'Who from? FBI? IRS? IRA?'

'All those, obviously. But above all, from Oliver,' she said.

'Of course. I was forgetting your moral indignation. So you were to come back to England. What next?'

'Nothing. I don't know. He would get in touch.'

'How? Via a medium? Come on, you can do better!' he said, disbelieving.

'That's the way he was,' she cried. 'He kept things to himself.

152

And he said, the less I knew, the easier I'd find it to carry things off.'

'OK. So he's the macho type. But you must have thought about it.'

'I suppose so. I guess I just assumed he'd make contact through my mother. He had her address.'

'And that was the first place you headed in this great flight from evil,' he mocked.

'Where the hell else should I go?' she demanded angrily. 'It was my home, for God's sake. I needed a base. But I didn't stay, not long. Six months, he said. I was out of the States in three, out of my mother's house in another. I came down here to hide. I didn't even give my mother my new address.'

'But you gave her Maddy's telephone number.'

'Yes. I gave her . . .' Her voice choked as she thought of her dead friend. Dog watched stonily as she took a series of deep sobbing breaths. Her voice was steady again as she resumed. 'I had to let Mam have some way of getting in touch. I owed her that. I made her promise not to tell anyone else. When I found out she'd given the number to this Mary Harper I'd never heard of, I panicked. I was sure it must have something to do with Oliver. I went down to Maddy's that night to find out if anything had happened, but things went wrong between us. It was my fault . . . I'd taken advantage . . .'

Her voice faltered again. Dog said impatiently, 'Yes, I know. What happened after you left?'

'I drove back to the flat. It was very late. No one saw me. And I stayed in all Sunday . . .'

'Where did you park?'

'Round the corner in the next street. I couldn't get in my usual spot. On Monday I thought, this is stupid. I can't stay indoors forever. And Noll was getting fractious. So I set off for school as normal. And the rest is like I told you. When I realized Noll had gone, I thought I'd go mad. But when I woke up in hospital, I started thinking logically, at least I thought I did, and I worked out it must be Oliver who'd got him . . . I suppose I wanted to believe it was Oliver, that way at least he'd be safe . . . I didn't know what to do, I didn't know how best to answer your questions, so when the chance came, I took off from hospital, and that's it. You know the rest.'

He didn't, of course. There were gaps big enough for a man to fall through.

'They asked you about Oliver and the money. What did you tell them?'

'The truth.' She looked at him in surprise. 'What else would I tell them with Noll asleep in the next room?'

'And they believed you? About not having any way of contacting Beck?'

'Of course they believed me. I let that bastard rape me, didn't I?'

'And then Thrale told you to go and confess to killing Noll? Didn't you ask why? Didn't the others say anything?'

'Me, I was past asking questions. The woman wondered if it was a good idea to let me loose. Thrale said something like, the more distance there was between me and Noll, the less likely I was to act stupid. Also it would give someone called . . . Trent I think it was . . . something to worry about.'

'Trent? Could it have been Tench?'

'Maybe. I can't remember. That fat slob Trent, I thought he said.'

That did it. But what the hell did Thrale know about Tench's involvement? The rest was easy to figure. Thrale had been quickly convinced that Jane had told him all she knew. He'd leaked the story to the press to get publicity to attract Beck's attention. Tench had responded by upping the ante and hinting via Parslow that the child might be dead. Thrale had then contemptuously dropped Maguire back in his lap with a confession, which move Tench had countered by turning her loose on bail.

Bait, that's all she was, tossed around between two predators, each with a disturbingly accurate picture of what the other was up to . . .

Dog's mind was getting dizzy. Sometimes a man can get so snarled up working out possibilities, he loses sight of the cards on show.

And there was one problem still unresolved.

He said, 'This place they took you to, what was it like? Furniture, lay-out, decor, anything.'

Her face screwed up with effort. She wanted to believe his questions were significant. She said, 'It's hard, I didn't pay much attention . . . It was pretty smart, I think . . . newish . . . but neutral. Mushroom emulsion, brown upholstery, that sort of thing . . .'

'Noll, then. What was Noll wearing?'

'Pink pyjamas,' she said promptly. 'And I noticed some striped dungarees draped over a chair. I remember thinking they were a bit girlish then telling myself not to be so stupid, that buying Noll clothes meant they didn't intend harming him . . .'

She was begging him to approve her judgement, but the rising panic in his mind washed away kindness.

'You said Noll kicked you when you were talking to this Gosling woman,' he snarled. 'What happened to your torn tights?'

'I dumped them in a litter bin,' she said, baffled. 'Bought a new pair at a corner shop. But why . . ?'

'No reason. Look, pour yourself another whisky. I won't be a sec. There's a call I need to make.'

He went into the bedroom and dialled the station. Asking to be put through to Charley Lunn, he found himself talking to a DC called Mawson.

'The sarge isn't here, guv. You just missed him,' said the man.

'Shit. Look, you'll do, Mawson. I want you to contact the Registrar, the Health Authority, the Child Benefits office, anywhere else you can think of, for any record they've got of a girl called Tobin, Polly Tobin, that's probably Mary or Pauline on the birth certificate, aged four or five, address Flat Thirty-four, Rhadnor House.'

He'd been aware of would-be interrupting noises from Mawson

as he spoke but had ridden right over them. Now the constable said, 'Yes, guv. But listen, I've been in the sarge's room for the last half hour and he's been doing that already, checking round just them places from what I heard. And I heard him mention Tobin. Do you still want . . .'

Dog cut in. 'Did he say where he was going?'

'No, guv.'

'Did he say *anything*?' The extrovert Charley Lunn was unlikely to make a quiet exit.

'Yes, guv. One of his jokes, though I didn't really get it. He said, "You know, Pete, there's a lot more than home-cooking that crusty old bachelors miss." Then he laughed and went off. About those calls, guv . . .'

'Forget it,' snapped Dog, putting down the phone.

'What's up?' said Jane Maguire anxiously.

She was standing in the bedroom doorway.

He said, 'Scared I was turning you in again?'

She said, 'I need to know what you're doing till I can understand why you're doing it.'

'Fair enough. OK, what I'm doing now is leaving you here. I've got to go out.' He let his mind run quickly over his call. How much had she heard? 'I've got to see my sergeant. He may have some information. Probably not, but worth checking.'

She regarded him suspiciously, but she must have missed his mention of the child or she surely could not have held her peace.

'You'll wait till you hear from me?'

'Yes.' The word carried no conviction but there was no time for persuasion.

'Right,' he said. 'I'll be as quick as I can. Make yourself at home.'

He pulled on his coat and left without further words from either side.

It wasn't till he was sitting in his car that he recalled he'd left the computer print-outs on his dining table.

*Shit!* He hesitated, but only a moment.

Live with your mistakes, said Uncle Endo. Tidying up usually just fucks up your next play.

He turned the ignition key and forced his way aggressively into the heavy afternoon traffic.

# 7

Click!

Charley Lunn in mid-stride.

Click.

Charley Lunn pausing at the entrance to Rhadnor House, scuffed briefcase in hand, like an absurdly young Chancellor on the steps of Number Eleven.

Click.

Charley Lunn disappearing inside.

The man in the blue Sierra put the camera down and reached for his radio mike.

'You there, sarge? There's a geezer just gone in. Looks familiar. I think he's a DS from Romchurch nick. Instruct, please.'

'Wait.'

The man yawned. Poured himself a cup of coffee from a flask, drank, grimaced, lit a cigarette.

'OK. Wander over there, check out what's his game, but don't make contact.'

'Right.'

He got out of the car and strolled towards the flats. Five minutes later he was back.

'He's knocking on doors, letting on he's selling encyclopaedias.'

'Jesus. Clever idea like that, they'll make him Head of CID in a fortnight. Wait.'

Time for another fag.

'OK. Let him be. He's not official. He can't do any harm and when he gets back to his nick, that prat Parslow will really chew his bollocks off. Out.'

\* \* \*

Charley Lunn would have made a good salesman. In the interest of verisimilitude he had worked his way steadily towards his goal along the top floor and had twice had to accept cups of coffee and interest in his alleged product or blow his cover. The second coffee maker, a parti-coloured blonde, hinted she was more interested in barter than purchase and Lunn only avoided a down payment by promising to return when he'd canvassed the whole building.

'Well, you've finished on this floor,' she said sulkily. 'Next flat's empty, and the one at the end, they've gone out.'

This was the Tobins'. He said, 'Oh yes. Any kids? So I'll know if it's worthwhile coming back.'

'Oh, it'll be worth your while,' she said.

'I meant, for a sale.'

'A little girl, I think. I only saw her this morning as they were going out. They've not been there more than a week.'

Lunn managed to take his leave, was watched to the stair head, then doubled back when the door closed. At least it made his mind up for him. There was no point in hanging around debating legalities. He took a quick look at the lock, delved into his briefcase, selected a bunch of adjustable keys and after a little trial and error, found a combination that turned.

Slowly he pushed back the door. The flat lay before him, empty, innocent.

He went inside.

When Dog Cicero arrived there was no time for the man in the Sierra to get a snap.

'Sarge! That Romchurch DI, the one with the frozen face, who was here this morning. He's back! Drove up like a bat out of hell and has gone in at the run. Instruct.'

'Wait.'

He waited, sensing trouble.

'OK. Enough's enough. Get them both out quietly as you can. Jesus! What a pair of plonkers! Out.'

He got out of the car and stretched. Life would be so much

159

easier if it was just the boyos you had to deal with. He began to walk slowly across the road.

There was a lift but Dog ignored it. There was too much adrenalin burning through his veins to tolerate that sense of boxed-in nowhere. He went up the four flights of stairs without slackening speed. As he hit the top floor, he shouted, 'Charley!' He couldn't have said where this imperative to speed came from, but he obeyed it absolutely, like a man who knows against all reason that the next card will fill his inside straight.

The Tobins' door was ajar. He burst through it and skidded to a halt on the polished tiles of the narrow hallway. Relief drained the strength from his muscles as Charley Lunn's head appeared round the half-open kitchen door, his mobile features rounded like an Allegory of Surprise.

'Dog. What the hell are you doing here?'

'Looking for you,' gasped Dog, leaning back against the wall. 'What the hell are *you* doing here?'

'Me? Easy! I got to thinking, crusty old bachelors can't tell boys from girls, not without the help of big tits and a squeaky voice. So I started checking out the Tobin kid and came up with zilch. I reckon little Miss Maguire could have been telling the truth, Dog. This place is empty. I mean really empty, not just gone away on holiday empty.'

'OK, Charley,' said Dog. 'Now just come out of there and we'll hand the flat over to Forensic and ourselves over to Mr Parslow.'

'Oh God. Will we get a lecture?'

'At the least. Come on!'

'OK. Just a moment.'

He turned, moved out of sight. Dog heard him say, 'What's the difference between a drippy super and a dripping tap? You can turn off a dripping tap.'

It took a split second to sink in.

Then Dog Cicero screamed, 'Charley, don't touch . . .'

The blast came funnelling across the kitchen, tearing the door

160

off its hinges and smashing it against Dog, who slid slowly to the floor. Behind it came a huge tongue of flame spitting shards of glass and metal and wood and stone. Half conscious and not yet feeling pain, he struggled to move the door . . . beside him the car burnt, the woman in the driving seat was a Guy Fawkes doll, the only sound above the crackle of flames was his own voice screaming . . . then hands were under his shoulders and, cursing and grunting, the man from the blue Sierra dragged him out of the reach of the fire into the smoke-filled corridor.

# Part Three

# 1

Jonty Thrale dreamt he was questioning Oliver Beck and woke with a throbbing erection.

Only Bridie Heighway understood the physical bonus his work for the Cause brought him. It would have been good to find her on the narrow hotel bed by his side but she had other work to do. Relief was only a brief friction away, but though the anti-orgasmic beatings doled out by the watchful Fathers at his boarding school had often been counterproductive, the associative guilt was deep grained in his soul.

He went into the bathroom and turned on the shower. Prayer and cold water was all that a growing boy needed for salvation. But a man needed to add works to faith and, as he took back control of his body, his mind focused on the current operation.

The old men across the water might be saying that things were falling apart, but that was why they were sitting on their arses in O'Connell Street, unable to raise much more than their voices. They it was who'd insisted he took Billy Flynn on board. From time to time they elected some dickhead wild boy flavour of the month because he reminded them of their own imagined youth. Well, Billy Flynn's balls-ups were well documented. He'd been told to follow the woman to work and sit outside the Health Centre till she came out again. Instead he'd wandered off God knows where, come back at her normal leaving time and found the bird had flown. So there they were in the public domain from the start and instead of being able to sit quietly and wait for an unsuspecting Oliver Beck to drop into their laps, suddenly they had to contend with that tricky bastard, Tench, and his storm troopers. Not forgetting Cicero. Not that he was any danger, but when God made you a gift of a bit of unfinished business, you didn't throw it back in his face!

But first things first. Oliver Beck and three million dollars was the prize. Miss out on that, and those wanked-out warlords in Dublin wouldn't be interested in blaming Billy Flynn. He'd made too many of them look foolish over the past few years. There'd be a lot of private rejoicing behind the official regret if Jonty Thrale failed.

He smiled to himself. He didn't intend to fail.

He came out of the shower, dried himself, got dressed. Finished, he studied himself in the mirror, checking focal points. It was Bridie who'd taught him that technique. It wasn't possible to be totally unmemorable, so you had to make sure you gave potential witnesses something positive to fix on. Henry Ward, commercial, from Ipswich, had a gold filling in an upper left incisor and a small mole under his chin. He wore a chain store suit, a club tie, and a slightly peeling 'gold' watch. This last was pure stage dressing. Jonty Thrale had never needed a watch. He had an inner clock which let him go to sleep when he wanted, woke him when he needed, and permitted him to ignore most normal temporal cycles of activity. For instance this afternoon, after thirty-six hours without rest, he had allowed himself two hours' sleep, and now the peeling watch confirmed the accuracy of his inner alarm.

He picked up a scuffed plastic briefcase, and went out.

The girl on reception took his key and flashed him a smile as meaningless as the token tinsel which fringed the desk.

He glinted his gold tooth back at her and went out into the night.

There was a feel of snow in the air. The bookies would be shortening their odds on a white Christmas. Not that he would be tempted. He wasn't a gambling man, despised those who were. Not for him the artificial thrill of betting on the turn of a card, the stride of a horse. Not while he still had the will, sinews and heart to play that first and only game which others palely imitated – the grand old game of death.

Only Bridie had ever heard him talk like this. The others thought of him as a cold fish, a man whose deadliness came from the ice water in his veins. They didn't know how his blood sang and his heart exulted as the bombs he planted exploded, the bullets he fired struck home, the enemies who thought they had him in their grasp fell back in confusion and disarray.

There was a telephone box ahead. A man entered it, tried the phone, banged it down in disgust and came out.

'Knackered,' he said to Thrale. 'Like everything in this fucking country.'

Thrale watched him out of sight then went into the box, removed the tiny pin with which he had short-circuited the cable earlier, and dialled.

He got a reply almost instantaneously.

'It's me,' he said. 'How are things?'

'Chaotic. Maguire's loose again. We checked out the college where her mate lives and found her dead. Tench has put it down to you.'

There was a question in his voice.

Thrale said, 'The transfer to Warwickshire, that went OK?'

'Fine. There's a twenty-four-hour team on them. Look, Tench is still holding off but if he decides to go with what he's got, I can't guarantee . . .'

'Leave me to worry about that. No sign of our main man yet?'

'No. We've got the ports and airports plugged tight and round-the-clock on the old girl in Northampton. Anything stirs, I'll let you know.'

'You'd better,' said Thrale coldly. 'Anything else?'

'An explosion at Rhadnor House. One of the Romchurch plods bought it.'

'Cicero?'

'No. A sergeant. Cicero was there, injured but he'll survive. He'll maybe wish he hadn't when Tench gets through with him.'

'Where is he now?'

'At the hospital. Tench has gone to see him.'

'Right. I'll keep in touch.'

He put the phone down and went on his way. A police siren sounded in the distance, approaching fast, but he neither turned

167

his head nor altered his pace as it swept past. He was the model of the good citizen who knows the forces of law are on his side. As indeed they were. The idea made him smile. Tench thought he was using Jonty Thrale's bait to capture Beck while the truth was, *he* was using Tench's eyes to spot the bastard first. And if he couldn't get hold of him alive, he would at least make sure Tench got hold of him dead. Though that would be a pity. He was looking forward to asking Beck a few questions. He was a slippery bastard but he wasn't going to slip out of this one.

And Cicero. Unimportant. No danger. But another slippery bastard, or, just as bad, a lucky one.

He'd survived twice.

Though he was not a gambling man, Jonty Thrale resolved as he walked the bright Christmas streets that for Dog Cicero, third time was going to be unlucky.

# 2

'You're a very lucky boy, my son. A very lucky boy.'

Dog continued fastening his shirt across his bruised chest. It was a painful process but he didn't wince. He deserved the pain.

'Charley Lunn's dead,' he said in a low voice.

'Yeah. Well he would be, wouldn't he, standing where he was. But not you. Two IRA bombs and still here! Should've called you Cat, not Dog. That door! Like a riot shield after a bad day in the Bogside. Oh yes. God must be saving you for some special purpose, my son!'

Now Dog swung round to face Tench.

'Like pulling your face off maybe,' he grated. 'That was your man who got me out, wasn't it?'

'That's right. No gratuities necessary. Just a simple thanks and a bunch of roses on mother's day . . .'

'You were watching the place! You saw Charley Lunn go in and you did nothing about it!'

'What did you want us to do, Dog? Arrest him?'

'You must have known the place was empty. You know those bastards don't leave their bolt holes unprotected . . .'

'Right, Dog,' interrupted Tench. 'But we didn't know that you've got your lads trained as burglars when they ain't got no warrant.'

'Lunn wasn't acting on my instructions,' interjected Dog.

'No? Not directly maybe, but you want to ask yourself why he'd do a thing like that. Not to impress Mr Parslow because we all know what Steady Eddie feels about making waves. So who was he hoping to get his Brownie points from? Which brings us to another question, Dog. What the hell are you playing at? You're off this case. You've been taken off it and you've been warned off it. So how come you and your oppo are still plodding through it with your size elevens?'

169

'Because we're policemen, not secret bloody policemen!' snarled Dog. 'Now if you don't mind, I'd like to get out of this place.'

They'd had to force him into the ambulance. All he could think of was Charley. The pain, the physical pain, hadn't started till they confirmed Lunn was dead. Then he felt as if his own body had been ripped apart in the blast. And when they told him nothing was broken, that he'd got away with severe bruising and contusion, there was no relief, just an even greater agony of guilt.

He pushed by Tench and strode down the hospital corridor. Only yesterday he'd been here trying to sort out the truth from the lies in Jane Maguire's story. Sort out the truth! What kind of task was that for a man who couldn't even pin down the truth about himself?

Except for one thing – he dragged those he loved into disaster. That was indisputably true.

As he crossed the reception area, the glass-plated door ahead swung open and Charley Lunn's wife came in. She was deathly pale, those bright searching eyes sunk deep in shadows. He halted, sought for words, but didn't need them as she swept by without a pause or a glance.

'That his old lady? Poor cow,' said Tench at his side. 'Don't worry. I'll see he gets the full hero bit even though he acted like a right prat.'

Dog nearly hit him then. Tench saw it in his eyes but he didn't flinch, nor did the amiable Pickwickian smile fade from his round and rubicund face.

'Take a swing if you like, my son,' he urged. 'Go on. Why don't you?'

He'd like me to hit him, thought Dog. Then he could really get me out of his hair.

Knowing he'd be playing into Tench's hands didn't lessen the temptation. His fist stayed balled, but he was saved by an intervention which came as close to the divine as a man could expect in Romchurch.

'Inspector! Inspector Cicero! Are you all right?'

Hurrying towards him, flushed with haste and concern, was the black-clothed figure of Father Blake.

'I called at your station and they said there'd been an accident,' panted the priest. 'I didn't know what to expect.'

'I'm fine,' said Dog. 'Look, Father, I can't talk just now . . .'

'Don't let me interrupt the Holy Office,' said Tench. 'Didn't know you'd got your own personal chaplain, Dog. Why don't you present me?'

Briefly Dog introduced the two men. Tench's heavy lips puckered disapprovingly when he heard of Blake's connection with the Maguires.

'If you don't mind me saying, Father, I reckon you should stick to comforting the afflicted and leave police matters to the laity. Dog, when you've made your confession, perhaps we could have a word in my car?'

He strode away. Blake said softly, 'That is not a godly man.'

'You're right there, Father,' said Dog. 'Look, like I told you on the phone, there's nothing you can do here . . .'

'But I think there is,' insisted Blake. 'When I called at your station and mentioned Jane Maguire, the desk constable said she had been let out on bail. What does this mean, Inspector? Have you been lying to me? Was she already in custody when we spoke together last night?'

Dog groaned gently.

'No,' he said. 'She came into the station early this morning.'

'Voluntarily, you mean? What did she say? What has she been charged with? What has happened to the child?'

The questions came at Dog with a force and anger he had to admit were justified. With Maguire's mother agonizing over the fate of her daughter and grandchild up in Northampton, it must look like an act of gross callousness for the police not to have got in touch.

He said, 'Father, I'm sorry. But the reason no one's contacted Mrs Maguire is that we still don't know what's happened to Noll, except that his mother came in this morning to confess to killing him.'

The priest shook his head in pained bewilderment.

'I don't understand . . . they said she'd been given bail . . .'

'Yes, she has. It's difficult to explain . . . look, can you hang on a moment? I've got to speak to Mr Tench.'

He had seen one of Tench's underlings come into the hospital vestibule and gesture imperiously towards him. Normally, he might have returned the gesture with interest, but now he was glad of an excuse to take time out from the angry priest.

He found Tench waiting in the back of his car.

'For Christ's sake, close that door, Dog. I've just worked up a nice warm fug. Finished with your tame priest, have you?'

'He's not mine. He's just genuinely concerned about Maguire and her child,' snapped Dog. 'And I don't blame him.'

'Ooh, temper!' reproved Tench. 'We're all concerned, Dog. So let's get things cleared up between us, shall we? Cards on the table, none of your fancy gambling games, nothing in the hole. Do you still play? Remember those games in the bicycle shed? You took all our sweetie money, you bastard! No one would play with you in the end!'

'Cards on the table,' snapped Dog impatiently.

'All right, you first. Come on, Dog. What have you been up to that I ought to know?'

Dog flexed his fingers. Cards on the table, was it? Never show a man more than he's entitled to see, said Uncle Endo, not unless you're softening him up for next deal.

He said, 'I looked up an old mate in Intelligence, tried to twist his arm to tell me something about Jonty Thrale.'

'Who?'

'Come off it, Toby. Cards on the table, we said.'

Tench smiled and nodded. He said, 'This mate of yours let you look at Thrale's file? I don't believe it, not unless you had him by the balls.'

'He accessed my file and when he left me to look at it, I accessed Thrale.'

'Naughty. How'd you know your mate's entry code?'

'I watched the way his fingers moved.'

172

Tench chortled admiringly. 'Those old memory tricks. They'll get you into bother one of these fine days, my son. So tell me, now you've seen Thrale's file, what is it you know, or imagine you know?'

'I think Thrale is after the money Oliver Beck embezzled from Noraid. I think it was his sidekick, Bridie Heighway, who lifted the boy to put pressure on Maguire.'

'And she knows where the money is?' said Tench tentatively.

'Don't bullshit me,' said Dog. 'You know she doesn't. They'd never have let her go if she'd known that.'

'So they've had hold of her, have they?' said Tench. 'And they let her go because she knows nothing?'

'They let her go because she told them Oliver Beck is still alive,' said Dog quietly. 'Thrale wants the headlines to bring him out of his hidey hole. She confesses to murder, we lock her up, and that turns her into tethered bait. When Beck appears, Thrale probably reckons he can move twice as fast as you lot. And if the worst comes to the worst, a bullet certainly can.'

Tench whistled admiringly.

'You're not daft, are you, Dog? You'd almost think you'd been having a good chinwag with Thrale himself. Or at least with Maguire.'

He regarded the inspector shrewdly.

Dog said, 'If you tell me where she is, I'd like nothing better. You did catch up with her again, I take it?'

'Not yet. Not that it matters,' said Tench indifferently. 'She leaves a wide trail. First off, she went to see that old college chum, the butch lecturer. We found the poor cow dead in bed, smothered with a pillow, Maguire's prints all over the place. Lover's tiff, maybe. She's one to steer clear of, Dog, believe me. Sooner her old man catches up with her, the better for everyone. We'll be waiting. And even if he gets to her before we do, no matter. We've got a fool-proof long-stop.'

He watched Dog work out the implication.

'You were onto Rhadnor House *before* they left, weren't you? Leaving your man on watch was just a precaution. Which means

173

you've followed them . . . Why the hell haven't you picked them up and got hold of the boy?'

He guessed the answer even as he put the question, but Tench didn't mind spelling it out.

'Priorities, old son,' he said. 'We pick them up, what've we got? A few more Micks for the tax payer to feed. They're not the type to give us anything. They'll sit inside, painting their cells with shit, till either someone busts them out, or there's a deal done. No, I've got bigger game than even Mr Jonty bloody Thrale. Yes, you're right. Oliver Beck. You see, with Oliver I get, first of all, the money; second, the propaganda coup when it gets out in the States where all their money's been going; and third and most important of all, I get a man who knows all the ins and outs of the Irish–American connection, who can supply top names on both sides of the water, who can detail commercial channels to all the terrorist supplier countries, and I get him by the balls! All I've got to do is tell him he either talks or he gets dropped off in the Falls Road on a Saturday night with his name tattooed across his face. So you can see I've got to take the long view! For a while at least, me and Thrale are playing the same game. He'll use the boy to smoke Beck out, then I'll move in and pick him up, and probably the others with him.'

He finished and regarded Dog complacently as if expecting congratulation.

There was a long silence.

'Cat got your tongue, Dog?' enquired Tench finally.

'No,' said Dog in a very low voice. 'I was just trying to be sure I heard properly. You've let Charley Lunn get blown up, and you've let a child stay in the hands of his abductors, and you've let his mother remain in a state of mortal terror, all for a propaganda coup?'

'And the rest, Dog,' said Tench, aggrieved. 'Don't forget the rest.'

'Fuck the rest! And fuck you too, Tench. I should have known from way back that beneath that revolting exterior there was something really evil waiting to get out.'

He opened the car door and began to climb out. Tench grabbed at his arm.

'Dog, wait. At least be honest and admit what's really getting your knickers in a twist. It's not this Irish tart and her precious bastard, is it? It's that other one, the one Thrale blew up. You read the file, Dog. Don't tell me you missed that! But you didn't mention it, Dog. And for why? Because it's eating your guts so badly you don't dare to let it show. It's Thrale you want! All right, you shall have him. Soon as we've got him banged up, I promise you half an hour alone with him, no questions asked, OK? But till then steer clear, my son, or else. I'm not having my operation fucked up by a jumped-up wop with half a face!'

Dog had dragged himself free and was walking away towards Father Blake, but Tench continued to yell at him through the open door.

'You stay out of it, Dog, you and that poxy priest both. This has fuck all to do with revenge or religion, this is politics, and you'd better remember that!'

Curious heads were turning, attracted by the noise, but Dog Cicero did not turn as he walked through the frost-edged December gloom to where the broodingly still figure of the priest waited beneath the huge red cross painted on the lintel of the hospital door.

# 3

'This is the first time I've made my confession over a cup of tea,' said Dog Cicero.

'Over anything at all for a long time, I suspect,' said Father Blake dryly. 'And you don't sound all that contrite to me.'

'It's not absolution I'm after, just confidentiality,' said Dog. 'I don't want you blundering around causing more confusion than we've got already.'

'You've got it, I promise,' said Blake impatiently. 'So far I've heard that Janey Maguire has been let out on bail after confessing to killing her son, and that you believe her child is alive and well anyway! In God's name, Inspector, I need to know what's going on!'

They were in Dog's office. The station was in a state of shock from the news of Lunn's death, and the sight of Dog turning up, with hair singed, face cut, clothes crumpled and bloody, accompanied by a priest, had cast even more darkness. He'd volunteered no information, merely demanding a pot of tea which he'd reinforced from his Strega bottle.

Quickly he filled the priest in. His motives were both humanitarian and practical, but also he felt a need if not to confess, at least to confide, and he detected a strength and resourcefulness in Blake which, added to the certainty of his silence, made him an ideal confidant.

Also, with Charley Lunn gone, Dog realized with a devastating sense of loss and loneliness that there was no one else he could talk to.

The door burst open as he finished and Parslow came in. He was grey-faced.

'Dog, they said you were here . . . this is terrible . . . Charley Lunn . . .'

Dog looked at him keenly, seeking hints that the man was viewing Lunn's death in terms of its effect on his own standing. He found none and felt guilty. Parslow had been a good copper longer than he'd been a complacent time-server.

'Yes, sir. Terrible,' he said. 'The Branch let him go in there. They should have warned him.'

He spoke with a bitterness aimed at Tench, then saw too late that Parslow had taken the reproof to himself.

'I'm sorry, Dog. They warned me off, but it's my patch . . . I should have . . .'

'It's OK, Eddie,' said Dog. 'Not your fault. There was nothing you could do, nothing any of us could do.'

He didn't believe it, but it wasn't Parslow's shoulders he wanted to drop his own share of guilt on.

The superintendent left. Dog doubted if he'd even registered Blake's presence.

The priest said, 'That's your top man, is it?'

'Yes,' said Dog challengingly.

Blake shrugged and said, 'He looks like he needs help.'

'Light a candle,' growled Dog, suddenly wondering if he'd made a mistake in taking this man into his confidence. Never sit down with a priest or a Chinaman, Endo had warned. They both got an edge.

As if sensing this revulsion against his spiritual function, Blake suddenly became very down-to-earth.

'So you think the boy is alive? But the main watch will be on his mother because she's the bait for this man, Beck, when and if he gets word of what's allegedly happened?'

'Oh, he'll get word,' said Dog.

'It may take time,' said the priest. 'If he's hiding out in South America, say.'

'I'd say Europe myself,' said Dog. 'Spain, perhaps. He spent a lot of time over this side of the water on his Noraid business, so he'd have plenty of opportunity to set up a bolt hole. Also he told Jane to make back to the UK after six months so presumably he wanted her here so he could make contact.'

177

'But she doesn't want to see him, you say?'

'Not since she found out where his money was coming from. But he'll go after her for sure. Where else can he go? I almost feel sorry for the poor bastard, thinking his son might be dead, then finding he's walked into a trap, either the Branch's or the IRA's. I'm not sure which would be worse!'

Blake regarded him ironically.

'I would have expected a man in your position to have more faith in British justice, Inspector,' he said. 'So, the way I see it, what we've got to concentrate on is the boy.'

Dog rolled one of his cigarettes and said, '*We?* I'm not in the market for a partner, Father.'

'Aren't you?' said Blake softly. 'I got rather a different impression. But this isn't about you or me, Inspector. It's about a child in danger. And from what you say, you reckon his well-being is not a priority of this man Tench's.'

'No, but I assume the Branch are keeping an eye on Heighway and the child,' said Dog. 'And once they get hold of Beck, they'll move in.'

He saw no reason to communicate the full depth of his unease about Tench's attitudes and plans, but Blake was well ahead of him.

'Look,' he said grimly. 'We both know who we're talking about here. If Heighway and her chums get cornered they'll use the boy as a hostage, and do you think your friend, Tench, is going to let a child's life stand in his way? And if they did get clear, they won't be wanting to slow themselves down with a four-year-old boy.'

'You think they'd kill him?' said Dog, distressed to hear his own fears echoed by this man of peace.

'He's got eyes, ears, a memory, a tongue,' said Blake grimly. 'This is Ireland we're talking about, remember? Now I don't know about your job, Inspector, but mine's got a moral imperative. I can either go back to Mrs Maguire and tell her that her grandson's alive but for God knows how long, or I can do something about keeping him alive.'

'Fine words, Father,' said Dog, with the mockery of impotence. 'But that's the speciality of your trade, isn't it? Remind me to look you up when it's a moral imperative I'm after, not some practical help.'

The priest did not react to the sarcasm but regarded Dog with a quiet smile. Then he said, 'How come they call you Dog?'

There were half a dozen flip answers at his disposal, but he didn't feel like being flip. Why lie to a priest anyway?

He said wearily, 'I was very ill when I was a kid. My Uncle Endo was the only one who didn't give up on me. When I got better, he said, "So what did I tell you? No way this kid'd give up. This kid's Endo Cicero's nephew and he ain't got no dog in him." And after that I was called Dog, like calling a big man Tiny. It's a gambling expression, for *underdog*, they use it in odds, like eight to five dog means . . .'

But he saw no explanation was needed.

'Cicero? Endo Cicero? Not the Endo Cicero who took the World Series poker title back in the seventies?'

'My God,' said Dog. 'You're never a gambling man, Father?'

The priest grinned and said, 'It's our only permitted vice, my son. Within reason. I'm a matchstick millionaire, and I've got a bishop who, if he'd backed every classic winner he's picked in the past twenty years, could have saved the Vatican bank all that embarrassment!'

Dog didn't return his grin. A priest was only a priest, but in a tight corner you could put your trust in a gambling man.

'OK,' he said. 'Where do we go from here?'

Blake immediately became serious.

'I don't know,' he said. 'But I surely know someone who does.'

For a disappointing moment, Dog thought he was being invited to pray. But Blake was looking far from pious.

'Tench,' he said. 'Your friend Tench knows where they are, doesn't he?'

'Yes, sure, but you don't imagine he's going to tell us, do you?'

'Not if you ask him, he's not. But there's bound to be an

operational plan, I'd say. And that'll all be mapped out in a computer program, won't it? And from what you've been telling me, Dog, you're no slouch at getting into other people's programs.'

Dog nodded slowly. He'd been right. You can rely on a gambling man to spot the angles you should have seen yourself.

'Hold on here,' he said rising. 'Have another cup of tea.'

'No thanks, but I'll have another drop of that Italian milk, if I may.'

Leaving the priest with the bottle of Strega, Dog headed down to the basement room that housed the station computer terminal.

WPC Scott was watching a print-out of car registration details.

'Anything I can do for you, sir?' she asked, with that false brightness the English adopt when uncertain whether to offer comfort or discreetly ignore a bereavement.

'No, I'll manage,' he said. Her list came to an end and she made for the door where she hesitated and said, 'I was so sorry . . .'

'Yes, I know.' He smiled at her and she left. He felt touched that the girl had put him at the centre of loss rather than indulging in an expression of personal grief. His affection for Charley Lunn must have shone through chinks in the barriers he thought he'd erected.

He turned to the computer. There was no way it was going to tell him what he wanted to know legally. He would have to use David Westmain's access code again and hope to hell that Tench hadn't got round to advising of the need to change it.

His fingers ran lightly over the keys.

It worked. He was in. Special Branch operations lay open before him. All he had to do was ask. But what was the question? Trial and error would probably get him there eventually, but not without attracting attention. He closed his eyes, shut off the conscious level of his mind, and let his fingers choose whether to bet or fold.

They ran across the keys, inviting the computer to access Operation Tinkerbell.

He opened his eyes. There it was. Old conditioning kept all emotion off even the mobile half of his face, but beneath the blank surface a deep sigh of relief imploded.

He keyed up personnel disposition. It was clearly a big operation. Tench was pulling out all stops. Possibly he'd put his reputation on the line which would make him all the more dangerous. Dog's eyes sought the groups of six which indicated round-the-clock surveillance teams. There were two of them, each with a grid reference, one with a car number, but before he could probe for more details the door opened behind him.

He turned. Two men were standing there. One of them was Tommy Stott, his classic features a mask which didn't quite conceal his anticipated pleasure.

'Sergeant Stott,' said Dog pleasantly. 'What can I do for you?'

'Sir,' said Stott stiffly. 'I am investigating a possible breach of the Official Secrets Act through unauthorized use of the Central Police Computer to obtain classified information. You are not obliged to say anything unless you wish to do so . . .'

'Are you saying you're arresting me?' asked Dog, his tone politely puzzled.

'No, sir. Just inviting you to accompany me to a senior investigating officer who wishes to put to you certain questions about your possible involvement in this crime.'

Tench. He hadn't rushed off to alter or cancel Westmain's access code. He had left it as a bait to lure Cicero into an indisputable illegality. Whether he'd go as far as a charge was another matter. But Dog knew the thousand and one delaying devices which could keep a man incommunicado for a couple of days or more, with at the end of it a suspension from duty pending further enquiries.

The man accompanying Stott was taking photographs of Cicero beside the still active screen. Dog took one last look then played a little arpeggio on the keyboard and the screen went blank.

'You got enough, Fred?' said Stott.

'Plenty.'

'Right, sir. If you wouldn't mind . . .'

He stood aside and motioned Dog to the door. He really was a thing of beauty, perfectly balanced, both hands free, with the look of a man who, while he doesn't expect trouble, would be more than happy to accommodate it.

Dog paused alongside him and said, 'This is absurd. I demand to see Mr Parslow at once. Someone's going to suffer for this.'

His indignation washed over Stott like a Tuscan storm over the Boy David, leaving him untouched, unmoved. Then the computer let out an ear-piercing howl as his last entry triggered its illegal access alarm system. The beautiful head turned, and Dog drove his knee into the sergeant's balls. Now the lovely mouth opened wide to let out a second howl in concord with the computer's.

Dog stepped through the door, took out his key, turned the deadlock, and ran up the stairs to the ground floor. Here he met WPC Scott.

'Are you finished, sir?' she asked.

'Almost. I've just got a little program running. Do me a favour, Scott. Pop up to my room and tell Father Blake I've had to go out and could he call back in a couple of hours?'

He made for the exit to the car park. His own car was still presumably in the street outside Rhadnor House. Blake had driven him here from the hospital and it was to his old Popular that Dog now headed. The priest practised the trust he preached and the door was open. Dog climbed in the back and lay down on the floor.

It seemed an age before Blake turned up though it was probably less than two minutes. Coming from the hospital Dog hadn't noticed what a lousy driver the priest was, but now he flinched as gears crashed and the car lurched out onto the road. He was wondering how to reveal his presence without causing a crash when Blake said casually, 'You can sit up now,

Inspector, and tell me what in the name of heaven's going on.'

'You spotted me,' said Dog, rising cautiously.

'Is there a prize?'

'Just my thanks for not making a fuss.'

'That's an option I've not abandoned,' said Blake dryly. 'Now perhaps you'll explain how a man in my line of business comes to be smuggling a man in yours out of a police station.'

'I'm on the run,' said Dog bluntly. 'I got caught lifting classified computer information. In fact, I reckon Toby Tench laid a little trap for me to give him an excuse to put me out of commission for a while.'

'That means he must be worried about you,' said Blake. 'I like the sound of that. And did you manage to find out anything before the trap was sprung?'

Dog didn't reply at once. Listening to Blake's suggestions was one thing. Letting the priest get deeply involved in the action was quite another. Yet he needed transport and he needed it fast.

But Blake, like a good gambling man, was reading his mind.

'If you're thinking of hijacking my car, forget it,' he said softly. 'What's mine is yours, but you get me with it. And look at it this way before you start arguing. OK, this old car won't get spotted in a hurry, but you're not the most unnoticeable man in the world. Whereas who'd look twice at me, especially without my collar?'

He pulled it off as he spoke and dropped it into the glove compartment. Dog glimpsed a copy of the *Ordnance Survey Atlas*. He leaned forward and pulled it out.

'Father, you're wasted in education,' he said. 'You should be in missionary work. All right, but when I say genuflect, you get down on your knees pretty damn quick. Now pull into that pub car park. I need to be steady while I'm doing this.'

Blake obeyed. Dog closed his eyes to conjure up the two grid references he'd seen next to the surveillance teams, then tracked them down in the atlas. He found them both on the same page. One was on the edge of Northampton and he didn't need a larger-scale map to tell him it would be Mrs Maguire's house. The other, some twenty miles to the west, was more problematical.

'Well?' said Blake impatiently.

'According to what I saw, Tench has ordered a twenty-four-hour surveillance on a piece of open countryside in Warwickshire.'

'You couldn't have copied it down wrong?'

'If I'd copied it down, perhaps. But as I didn't, no way. I have a car number too, though why they should have parked their car in a field . . .'

'Perhaps they're camping?'

'At this time of year? Not likely. They'd stick out like a sore thumb for a start.'

'There's only one way to find out,' said Blake, starting the engine.

He was right. No point in hanging around here where he was more likely to be spotted than anywhere else. Tench probably had his boys out looking already . . .

'Shit!' he said. They'd go straight to his flat. And Jane Maguire was still there unless she'd got impatient and run.

'Hang on,' he said. 'I need to make a call.'

He got out and went into the pub. There was a public phone just inside the door. He dialled his number. It rang endlessly. Then at last it was picked up. He could hear breathing. He said, 'It's me.'

Silence. Then her voice. 'Where have you been?' Low, taut, accusing.

'Having the time of my life,' he said savagely. 'Listen, you've got to get out of there. You'll have visitors soon.'

'Where shall I go? Have you found anything out?'

Her voice was desperate. She needed something to cling on to. And he needed to keep in contact with her.

He said, 'Look, I don't know. Perhaps. Just get out. Head up to Northampton. There's a motel on the ring road not a million miles from your mother's. The Clareview. Do you know it? Opposite a new superstore.'

'Yes.'

'Head there. I'll try to be there tonight but leave a message anyway. OK?'

She didn't answer. He could feel the waves of doubt and distrust coming down the line but there was not time to try to stem them.

'Go now,' he ordered. 'At once.'

And rang off.

Back in the car, he sat silently in the passenger seat while Blake jerked out into the traffic.

'Something up?' asked the priest.

He almost told him but changed his mind. Jane Maguire had no time for priests. She had been betrayed enough without this further small betrayal of talking about her with Father Blake.

'Only your driving,' he said.

'They used to call me Jehu at the seminary,' laughed Blake. 'You remember? Second Kings, he was the one who drove furiously.'

Dog found himself smiling.

Battered, bruised, on the run from his own colleagues, driving north with a crazy priest to an empty spot on the map in search of a kidnapped child, he had no right to feel anything but the depression of insanity.

But suddenly he felt almost lighthearted.

And that was something he hadn't felt in more years than he cared to recall.

# 4

Toby Tench shook his head sadly and said, 'You're a great disappointment to me, Tommy. I always thought you had nuts of reinforced concrete and here you turn out mortal flesh like the rest of us.'

The sergeant shifted gingerly in his chair and said sullenly, 'It was that bloody machine starting to scream. I took my eyes off him.'

'Yes. Always was a clever sod, that Dog, credit where it's due,' said Tench. 'Now, more important than your knackers, how much of the Tinkerbell file did he see?'

'Not much,' said Stott. 'And he didn't have time to take no notes or get a print-out.'

'Makes no matter, my son,' said Tench. 'Not with Cicero. I've seen that sod look at a page of Shakespeare, close the book, then recite the lot. It wasn't fair. Me, I always had to do things the hard way at school. Cheat.'

He laughed, became serious and went on, 'So let's assume he remembers what he saw. Where will that get him?'

'I don't give a toss as long as it gets him in arm's length of me,' growled Stott.

'Don't make it personal,' advised Tench gravely. 'Priorities. First and foremost, to get our hands on Oliver Beck. Then to take out Thrale and his team. After that you can start thinking about kicking Cicero's head in. At the moment all I want to know about him is where he is so I can be sure he's not sticking his nose in. So let's assume that he's done his memory trick on the bit of the file he accessed. What was that?'

'Surveillance disposition,' said Stott.

'And what could that tell him he didn't know already? Salter's flat, Maguire's house. And Warwickshire. That's the one.

That'll set his nose twitching. Tommy, you'd better get yourself and a couple of extra bodies up there just to make sure old frozen face don't throw no spanner in the works.'

'It'll be a pleasure, guv,' said Stott, rising.

'No it won't, my son,' said Tench softly. 'Not yet. Not till we've got our result. And then the pleasure will all be mine. Now sod off and try to keep the family jewels under lock and key this time! I ain't got no use for geldings, you should know that by now.'

After the sergeant had gone, Tench sat for a while studying the file on his desk. He had a great deal riding on this operation. While disaster might not break him, it would certainly fix him where he was until an uncomfortably early retirement. He'd pushed his way to his present moderate eminence by a mixture of hard work, brown-nosing, and ruthless opportunism. But he'd pushed too hard and taken too little care of those he had pushed by. Not every face that gets trodden on remains in the mire, and even in the Lodge which was the centre of his social life he was regarded with a distrust which not all the fraternal vows in the world could overcome.

What can't be won by worth may still be claimed by right of conquest and from the moment a rumour had surfaced of the IRA's belief that Oliver Beck was not dead, Tench had seen a unique opportunity. His efforts to persuade his superiors to put Jane Maguire under permanent surveillance after her return to England had met with failure but at least he had put his marker on the case. And when the flag he'd put on police computer queries about Maguire had popped up, he'd been ready. Intelligence had already suggested that Jonty Thrale was on the mainland planning an operation. Tench had linked Thrale, Beck and the missing child in a bold hypothesis which his superiors had recognized as providing a blueprint for either an anti-terrorist coup or Tench's own downfall. Either way, they won.

He had moved quickly. While Cicero was still trying to unravel the truth of the woman's story, Tench had accepted it as gospel. He had made no attempt to interview the two women who had visited the kindergarten as prospective clients but had put a watch on both addresses. Any doubt that Rhadnor House was the one vanished when Billy Flynn was seen escorting a dark-glassed Jane Maguire into the building. Tench could have moved in then, recovered the child, picked up Flynn and Heighway, and perhaps Thrale too. But he held back. His masters said nothing. For them, as for him, Beck was the big noise. Get hold of him, and he knew that the men who moulded careers wouldn't give a toss what happened to Noll Maguire and his mother.

This was the world according to Toby Tench. At the moment he felt pretty much in control of it. He had Maguire covered, had the boy and two of Thrale's team covered, had old Mrs Maguire's house covered. Cicero he guessed was heading for Warwickshire where he'd soon be picked up. Thrale was roaming loose, but he had Thrale on a string, and could jerk him hither and thither at will.

At least that was the grandiloquent way he put it when self-doubt crept in. But he'd been too long in the game not to know a string has two ends and can be pulled from either of them. Also this was a very private string. He'd never seen any reason for letting his superiors or his rivals dip their bread in his gravy. But there came a point where secrecy became illegality; worse, unprofessionality. He'd long passed that point and knew now that the string to Jonty Thrale was a tightrope he could easily fall off.

Except if he grasped the magic jewel which enabled a man to fly.

Success!

He picked at his teeth with a bent paper clip and let his mind drift from the rocks below to the cloudless blue sky above.

He knew exactly what he needed to soar over the rainbow.

Beck in his hands. Thrale in his grave.

Nothing – not a kidnapped child, not a distraught mother, not a meddling priest, and certainly not a childhood friend – was going to get in his way now.

# 5

Father Blake's driving got better as they sped up the M1, and after a while Dog drifted off into a fitful sleep.

He awoke to find Blake's elbow digging into his side.

'Next exit,' said the priest. 'Then I'll need navigation.'

The sign showed Northampton a few miles to the east. As he massaged the fatigue out of his face, Dog thought of Mrs Maguire. A cold woman, he'd felt, but what kind of coldness? He knew from experience about the frost that comes after sorrow, binding together what else must fall apart. But if this in its turn is thawed by a stronger, hotter grief, what happens then?

It struck him he didn't know if he was thinking about Mrs Maguire or himself.

'Are you with us yet?' demanded the priest.

'West,' grunted Dog. 'Head west.'

Along the motorway the air had been like a wintry breath, hazing the headlights. But as they headed west along the narrower A road, the haze thickened as tendrils from the surrounding fields began to link fingers ahead of them, and when they turned into a winding unclassified road, it was like moving into the gas tunnel Dog recalled from his army training days. Blake almost missed a sharp bend, hit the brake, made it, and swore in a most unpriestly fashion.

'I see why you wear the collar,' said Dog. 'It's a symbolic gag.'

'I thought everyone knew that,' said Blake. 'Damn this weather.'

'We may be glad of it later. Easy now. We can't be too far away. Ah, that must be it. Don't stop! Tench's men could be watching for any vehicle showing a special interest.'

What he had spotted was a large sign off to the left and reading CLAYPOLE QUARRY: COUNTY COUNCIL TRAVELLERS' SITE.

'What's that?' demanded Blake.

'I'd have thought you'd know,' said Dog. 'Lots of your flock in there, Father. Local councils can't just keep moving gypsies and travellers on any more. The law says they've got to provide permanent sites with facilities laid on. The art is picking some spot so out of the way or so completely derelict that none of your ordinary fixed voters will complain. A disused quarry must have seemed just about perfect, to the council I mean. And to Jonty Thrale too.'

'I thought that gypsies were very clannish,' objected Blake.

'Real gypsies, maybe. But I reckon what we'll find in there is everything from sixties hippies in beat-up transits through teepee people to your scrap metal dealers in sixty-foot trailers. One thing they'll all have in common, though, is a deep and abiding distrust of the law. Pull in here and let's have a look at the map.'

Blake pulled in by a gate leading into a field. Dog spread the map out on his knees and studied it carefully. After a while Blake said impatiently, 'What's the problem?'

'No problem. Just a matter of tactics.'

'Let's see.' The priest leaned over and peered at the map. 'OK, so we don't want to go down the main approach. But what's wrong with this farm track here? It takes us close round this north side and there seems to be another track winding down here.'

Dog said patiently, 'True. That's the first thing I saw, so it's also the first thing Tench's team saw. If I were in charge I'd put a car here to cover the approach track and a man up here with night glasses and a radio. The relief team are probably resting up in one of these two farmhouses with some story about druggies or car thieves among the travellers. Farmers hate them and are ready to believe anything about them.'

'Sorry,' said Blake. 'I'm teaching my grandmother, aren't I? What do you suggest?'

'I can't see any alternative to slogging cross-country,' said Dog. 'You don't happen to be carrying two pairs of walking boots and a couple of anoraks, do you?'

'Hold on,' said Blake. 'We're getting company.'

There was a growing radiance in the mist ahead. Soon it was joined by the noise of an engine even more erratic than the Popular's, and finally an ancient camping van came lurching out of the white swirl. Once it had been gaily decorated in rainbow whorls, but now rust was erupting through the flaking paint, and the effect was like smudged make-up on a very old tart.

The van stopped alongside them, a window wound down in spasms, and a man with a flowing salt-and-pepper beard and a friendly smile leaned out and said, 'Peace, brothers'.

'Hi,' said Blake, out of his window.

'You folk in trouble?' enquired the man.

To Dog's surprise, Blake said, 'Afraid so. The engine's just packed in and we were wondering where the nearest phone might be. You're not heading anywhere near one, are you?'

'Well, we're making for the campsite at Claypole Quarry just a ways down the road here. You're welcome to a lift.'

'Is there a phone there then?'

'No, but some of the gyps with the big trailers have car phones now and they might let you ring a garage if you flash some folding money. Only I shouldn't let them know where your car's situated, else by the time the breakdown people get here, you'll likely be short of a couple of wheels. Hop in the back. Frodo, open the door.'

'Perhaps you should teach your grandmother after all,' murmured Dog as they got out of the car.

The van door was opened by a sullen-faced youth in his late teens, presumably Frodo. A girl of about ten was lying on a bunk. In the passenger seat was a thin-faced woman of indeterminate age with a small child asleep across her lap and a very young baby in her arms.

'Have you been to this site before?' asked Dog.

'Just once,' yelled the driver over the grind of the engine. 'Don't much care for organized sites, and in any case, the gyps usually get there first and make sure what they call the hips aren't welcome. But the people got established here in numbers early on so the gyps have just had to put up with it. And with Christmas coming on, we thought it would be nice to head somewhere with a few facilities and a bit of company.'

They reached the direction sign and turned off the road. The combination of grimy glass and swirling mist made it impossible to see anything out of the side windows. Presumably it was as difficult to see in from outside, but Dog kept well back just in case.

The track descended quite steeply then levelled out, and now over the driver's shoulder he could see lights, the vinegary glow of electric bulbs through trailer windows and the dancing red of camp fires burning holes in the mist. Even this brief glimpse showed the described apartheid, with gleaming trailers and a couple of traditional caravans at one end of the site and a more battered and eclectic collection of hippie vehicles at the other.

The quarry had been dug out of the face of a hillside leaving a broad arena, backed by fifty-foot cliffs to the north with open ground sloping away to the south. Under the cliffs ran a row of sentry box toilets with standpipes between them, presumably in compliance with some official version of 'permanence'. On the blasted rock above the toilets someone had aerosoled some words. Dog made out a couple of them through the swirling mist and his schoolboy memory supplied the rest.

*Look on my works, ye mighty, and despair.*

There was an ironist at work here. Perhaps irony was all you had left if, as he guessed of their driver, you had started down the love, peace and flower power trail in the sixties and found a quarter-century on that it petered out on this derelict margin of society.

The van came to a halt, reversed, halted again, and the driver said, 'Here we are, folks.'

Frodo opened the rear doors and jumped out. They were backed close up against another van, providing useful cover. Dog did not doubt that powerful night glasses would be trained on the new arrivals and while Blake might pass as just another traveller, he himself was too readily identifiable.

Blake said, 'What now?'

'First thing is to spot the car number.' He recited it to Blake who repeated it, nodded, and said, 'Then?'

'Then you do nothing,' said Dog grimly. 'If they're here, they'll be armed and they'll be ready to fight.'

'Look, I'm not afraid . . .'

'I am. Not just for you. For all these other people. For myself. For the boy.'

'Are you coming out, brothers?' enquired their host, who had walked round to the back of the van. 'We'll be joining our friends in a brew and you'll be very welcome.'

'That's kind of you,' said Dog.

He turned up the collar of his coat and climbed out. He was relieved to see just how dense the mist was. The walls of the quarry seemed to hold it in and he doubted if even good night glasses could make out much of what was going on down here. Nevertheless he kept close to the driver, endeavouring to keep him always on the open side.

Already his eyes were taking in vehicle numbers. What happened if he spotted the one he was looking for he didn't know. His warning to Blake to keep out of it masked a complete blank. His forward thinking hadn't got any further than finding a vantage point from which to spot the boy and his captors. Now Blake's quick thinking had got them right into the thick of things, but he doubted if the priest could think quickly enough to get them out if Bridgid Heighway and her young sidekick came at them with Armalites blazing.

He realized he'd made up his mind that Thrale wasn't here. No way that he would be sitting on his arse in this dump when all the traps for Oliver Beck were set elsewhere. He was pleased with his logic. It cut down the odds. Also it meant his mind could concentrate on rescuing the boy without any distractions of revenge. And it would be a distraction, he admitted, touching the stiff side of his face and watching the flames leap around a blackened kettle on the camp fire. It would certainly be a distraction.

Someone thrust a tin mug into his hand. He could feel the heat of the scalding tea through the metal but he did not flinch.

'I'm Gandy,' said the bearded driver, by way of introduction.

'Like the Mahatma?' enquired Dog.

'A happy coincidence,' grinned the man. 'No. Short for Gandalf. I got rechristened twenty-odd years back. Hell, that was some ceremony! Total immersion of *everything!*'

'I bet. I'm Dog.'

Blake was sitting on a rock by the fire, deep in conversation with a group, very much at his ease. So far Dog had to admit he'd been an asset, but how would his godly principles react if and when the blood began to flow?

'Dog, you say? I like it. But why . . ?'

'It's God backwards. Do those toilets work?'

'Who knows? But the night is dark and the countryside wide and empty.'

'Never believe it, Gandy,' said Dog. 'Excuse me. Nature calls.'

He set off towards the line of boxes, weaving in and out of the scatter of vehicles. Their variety was great. Caravans, campers, canvas-topped pick-ups, transits, beat-up estates, and an ancient bus still carrying a destination board which read Woodstock.

But nothing with the number he sought for. Could they have changed it? Then Tench's men would have recorded the change and it would have been entered on the computer.

He had reached the line of toilets. His pretended need was now real and he went into the first. It was relatively clean and worked perfectly well. He washed his hands under the standpipe, dried them on his handkerchief, wondered if this behaviour might be aberrant enough to draw attention, then grew angry at himself at the thought. These people so far had shown him nothing but courtesy. What right did he have to patronize them?

But when he returned to the camp fire, all attitudinal analysis washed from his mind.

Father Blake had vanished.

He looked around and could see him nowhere. Gandy was in the van holding a feeding bottle to the baby's lips.

'What's happened to my mate?' demanded Dog.

'Gone over to the gyps to try for a phone, I expect,' said Gandy cheerfully. 'He should have waited for you. You need someone to watch your back when you're talking to a gang of Irish tinkers.'

*Irish tinkers*. That was the phrase that did it. He'd been looking in the wrong place. If Thrale's team was going to lose itself in a group of travellers, it wouldn't be these freaky drop-outs he'd choose but that other more rigid and strongly capitalist society with its strong Irish links and fierce tribal loyalty.

'Isn't she gorgeous?' said Gandy, holding up the baby. 'She's my seventh, you know. That's meant to mean something, special powers, that kind of stuff. You like to hold her, Dog?'

'Later maybe,' said Dog. 'I think I'd better check on my friend.'

Trying to avoid the appearance of hurrying he made his way across the divide between the two encampments.

He spotted the car number almost immediately. It belonged to a Ford Granada parked alongside a blue and gold caravan, slightly travel-stained but otherwise in good condition. The side door was open and there was a sound of upraised voices from within.

Dog rushed forward. The watchers would have been alerted by now so there was no more need for discretion. He went in crouched low. If there were guns waiting, speed and surprise were his only defence, and pretty feeble at that. But as his eyes took in the scene he saw he needn't have worried. Muscular Christianity was in control.

Father Blake was holding a young man against the wall in a judo lock which forced his arm where no arm was supposed to go. A terrified-looking woman crouched in an armchair clutching a young girl who was the only one present not registering any extreme of emotion. Dog recognized none of them. Certainly the woman and the child were not those he'd seen at Rhadnor House, though at a distance they might have passed for them.

At a distance . . . His mind had already read the script before Blake looked towards him and shouted angrily, 'It's not Noll! But this bastard's going to tell me where he is!'

'I don't know! For God's sake, it's the truth. I don't know!'

Dog believed him. But whether it was the truth or not, there was no time for further questioning. There were several men crowding at the steps leading up to the doorway.

'What the hell's going on here?' demanded a burly man with a broad Galway accent. 'Sean, boy, are you all right?'

'Blake, we've got to get out of here,' said Dog urgently. 'Tench's men will be on their way.'

The priest turned and looked at him, weighed what he'd heard, then nodded.

'Let's go,' he said.

He released the young man who slid to the floor. The threatening group at the door saw the look on Blake's face and melted away like snow off a boiler. Dog leapt after them with the priest close on his heels. Across to the left he could see headlights sawing madly at the mist as a car came bucketing down the track into the quarry.

'Where to?' demanded Blake.

'*Now* you want instructions!' groaned Dog. 'Round here.'

He ran behind the next trailer. Blake thought he intended to head for the cliffs but Dog grabbed him and pulled him to the ground.

'Under here!' he hissed, rolling beneath the trailer.

'They'll find us in no time! We can climb out of here, get back to the car.'

'It'd take at least half an hour, probably more. By that time they'll be sitting there waiting for us. What the hell did you think you were doing in there?'

'I'm sorry. I lost my rag when I realized it wasn't Noll.'

'Isn't wrath still a sin? Just stay calm, will you? Say a prayer, and move when I tell you.'

The car was in the arena now. It came bouncing over the frost-rutted ground, skidded to a halt in front of the blue and gold caravan, both front doors flew open, two men rolled out and came up carrying guns. One was Tommy Stott. He scurried forward to crouch on one knee against the side of the caravan holding his weapon in two hands aimed at the door. The second man dived past him to the other side of the door and adopted a similar pose.

'They've been watching "Miami Vice",' said Dog. 'Come on. Nice and easy.'

He got to his feet. Most of the inhabitants of the other trailers had emerged, but their attention was riveted on the live cop show unfolding before their eyes. There was a short hiatus while the two armed men seemed to have a silent debate as to which was going to have the possibly fatal honour of going in first. Then Stott jumped forward and threw himself through the door while his mate followed behind, to crouch at the foot of the steps aiming into the caravan.

'Let's go,' said Dog.

He walked easily forward towards the car which stood there with its doors wide open, its engine still running.

The second cop followed Stott into the caravan and the spectators were emboldened to press forward in their eagerness to miss nothing.

'This time I'll drive,' said Dog.

He got into the driver's seat, pulled the door quietly shut.

Someone saw them and shouted. Tommy Stott came out of the caravan, hampered by the crowd, his mouth open wide in a yell of fury, his gun held high. Dog let in the clutch and stood on the accelerator. Behind them was a confusion of noise, perhaps even a shot but he couldn't swear to it. The mist was confusing and he momentarily lost the entry track. When he spotted it, they were almost past. He swung the wheel over, they ran up a shallow embankment, and for a moment he feared the car was going to flip over.

Then they were on the track, bouncing upwards out of the quarry.

197

There was a voice squeaking at them out of the car radio. Dog plucked the microphone from the dash and yelled into it, 'Major incident, Claypole Quarry! Request armed assistance, ambulance, fire brigade, May Day, May Day, May . . .'

He pulled the mike loose and threw it out of the window.

'What the hell was that in aid of?' demanded Blake.

'It's better than the kind of discreet help the Branch will be trying to whistle up,' said Dog.

A few moments later they saw Blake's car ahead.

'Hold on,' said Dog.

He aimed at a thin section of hedge and ran the police car through it.

'Jesus,' said Blake as he cracked his head against the roof.

'I told you to hold on,' said Dog. 'This'll do.'

He left the car hidden from the road behind a clump of trees. They ran to the Popular. Once more Dog got into the driver's seat. It started first time and he sent it hurtling along the narrow country road at a speed far too high for the conditions.

Blake flinched away from his window as the branches of a hedge whipped against it.

'I'm sure you have a plan,' he said. 'Does death figure large in it?'

'No. That's in God's plan,' said Dog. 'Mine's much more short term. To get us out of here. I can drop you off to make your own peace with the authorities if you prefer.'

The priest sighed and pulled his seat belt tighter.

'I'll think about it. Look, I'm sorry I went off half cocked back there but I thought . . .'

'You thought you'd found the boy. Me too. But this Thrale's too clever for that. He knew the flat had been spotted but instead of running for it, he arranges a switch so that Tench will still imagine he's got him under surveillance.'

As he spoke it occurred to Dog again that Thrale must have been very confident that Tench's immediate strategy was limited to surveillance . . .

'So where is the boy now?'

'God knows. That's your department, Father.'

'I'll keep asking,' said Blake. 'Those sirens are getting nearer.'

'We're getting nearer to them,' said Dog. 'That's the main road ahead.'

They came up to the junction. A sign post told them they were fifteen miles from Northampton. Dog swung the wheel in that direction. A few moments later they met the first of a line of police cars and ambulances. As they flashed by, he felt a pang of guilt at turning them out on a false alarm on a night like this.

'What now?' said Blake wearily. The priesthood was fine for long-term optimism, thought Dog cynically, but CID got you more used to short-term disappointments. Then he reminded himself how much purer this man's motives were than his own and felt guilty.

He said, 'If Beck makes it back to England, Mrs Maguire's his only point of contact. That's where Tench and Thrale will be waiting for him. The way things stand, Northampton's the only place to be.'

'You reckon so?' said the priest. 'Then so be it. I'm in your hands.'

'I'd stick with the Holy Trinity if I were you, Father,' said Dog Cicero.

# 6

They didn't speak at all on the way to Northampton. Dog peered through the windscreen into a mist-shrouded road which seemed a fit emblem of his own future. He found himself examining his recent actions and their motives with that cynicism which is the last boundary before despair. He'd thrown up a career which he'd been ready to junk anyway. He'd set off on a mad quest to rescue a missing child because he'd needed to fill the blank space which lay between him and a featureless horizon. He'd lost the trail with no real hope of picking it up again, and all he was doing now was thrashing around blindly, trying to pretend there was still an immediate objective between him and that emptiness. Not even fantasies of revenge had any power to push back this pressing fog of despair. He imagined having Thrale at his mercy. What would he do? Kill him slowly? Kill him quick? Hand him over to the authorities for judgement?

Nothing stirred the blood in his veins. He was like a tortoise who has emerged from hibernation only to find it is still winter.

'Isn't there a bloody heater in this car?' he demanded, suddenly needing to break the silence.

Father Blake, who had been plunged into a reverie which seemed as deep and black as his own, said shortly, 'Yes. It's on.'

A mile passed, then Blake said, 'Look, I've been thinking, I need to contact my people and let them know where I am. All this has happened in such a rush that I've not had time to put anyone in the picture and they'll be getting worried about me. So can we stop somewhere with a phone and maybe get a bite to eat and some hot coffee in us while we take a close look at what to do next?'

'I see my turn in charge hasn't lasted long,' grunted Dog.

In fact it suited him very well. He wanted to check at the

Clareview Motel to see if Jane Maguire had left any message. There was an outside chance she might even be there in person. If so, she'd have to face Blake, whatever she felt about priests. Anyway, this one had surely worked his passage.

He postponed the problem, drifted southwards on the ring road till he hit the roundabout where the motel was situated, and pulled in, saying, 'This should do'.

Blake climbed out and looked with distaste from the scattered blocks of the motel to the solid bulk of the superstore across the carriageway. He said, 'What happened to the green and pleasant land?'

'All you've got to do is scratch the surface,' said Dog. 'With a bulldozer. It's down there somewhere.'

They went into the reception area.

Blake said, 'I'll make my call. See you in the diner. Order me something, will you? Better make it fish and chips. I've lost track and for all I know it could be Friday.'

He went towards the line of telephone cubicles.

Dog waited till the priest was out of sight then moved swiftly to the desk.

'Any message for Cicero?' he asked.

There was none.

'Do you have a Ms Maguire registered?'

The clerk checked, shook her head.

Unsurprised, but disappointed, Dog headed for the cafeteria. He ordered haddock and chips twice and a pot of coffee from a cheerful waitress in a gingham dress. The coffee came instantly but he was still waiting for the food when Blake joined him. He started to fill another cup but the priest stopped him.

'No time,' he said. 'Look, I'm sorry, but they're not pleased with me. I stood a couple of people up, taking off like I did, and there's a lot of ruffled feathers to smooth. I really think I should head on to the school and sit down with a phone for an hour or so to put things right. I doubt if there's anything more we can do tonight, is there?'

'No,' said Dog.

'Then I'll probably stay over at the school. I could beg a bed for you too if you like. The boys have gone now and there's whole dormfuls of the things!'

Dog shook his head.

'I'm not that tired,' he said.

'You're probably wise,' laughed Blake. 'Can I at least drop you somewhere?'

'No. I'll have something to eat then call a taxi if I decide to move on. Thanks for all your help, Father.'

The priest reached out his hand. Awkwardly Dog stood up and shook it. Blake laughed and said, 'You're a good man, Dog Cicero, don't let anyone tell you different. But what I wanted was the car keys.'

'Of course. Sorry.'

He handed them over and sat down. The priest made the sign of the cross over him, his lips moving in a silent blessing, then he turned and left.

Dog felt deserted and desolate. For a man who prided himself on his self-sufficiency it had been surprisingly comforting to have Blake by his side. Now with the priest gone, and Charley Lunn dead, and not the faintest shadow of a lead in sight, he felt totally alone.

He drank more coffee, rolled a cigarette, lit it, drew in the acrid smoke, closed his eyes.

And when he opened them, she was there, looking down at him, her expression uncertain and wary, as if the slightest sound would send her flying for cover.

He sought for something to say, rejected everything that came to mind. Then the waitress arrived with two platefuls of fish and chips which she set on the table with a smile.

Dog Cicero returned her smile and let it spill over to include Jane Maguire.

'I bet you're starving,' he said. 'Why don't you join me and eat?'

# 7

They were both surprised to discover how hungry they were and nothing was said till their plates were empty. Dog ordered more coffee. After it came and the waitress had gone, he said, 'Have you just arrived?'

'No. I got here about an hour ago. I took a room.'

'Not in your own name. I asked.'

'I called myself Smith,' she said. He smiled and she said, 'I couldn't think of anything else.'

'I thought you must have decided not to come,' he said.

'I didn't know whether I was going to or not. I told myself I was driving north to go to my mother's. I knew her house would be watched, but I didn't care. There was nowhere else to go, and anyway I knew I had to talk to her. We've never seen eye to eye, and I don't doubt we'll be quarrelling again soon after we meet, but she loved . . . loves Noll too, and it's not right to leave her not knowing what's going on.'

'So what made you divert here?'

They were talking politely, only cautiously edging near the doubts and suspicions and accusations which lay between them.

She said, 'I heard on the car radio about an explosion . . . it said an officer from Romchurch police had been killed, another injured. It said they thought there was an IRA connection . . .'

Suddenly she seemed to take in his appearance for the first time, the bruises and scratches on his face and hands.

'It was you, wasn't it? That's where you went when you left me? I need to know what happened, I've got to know what it means.'

Her voice began to lilt upwards.

He said, 'Can we go up to your room?'

'What for?' she demanded suspiciously.

'So you can shout at me without an audience, that's all.'

He only meant he didn't want to attract attention from other tables, but her reaction was disproportionately fearful.

She said in a low voice, 'Oh God, you don't think . . . if *he* sees me talking to you, God knows what . . .'

No need to ask who *he* was.

He said reassuringly, 'I'm sure we're OK here, but just to be on the safe side. What's your number?'

'Two one two.'

'OK. I'll catch you.'

She rose and left. He paid the waitress then followed.

The door of 212 was ajar. He went in. It was a decent-sized room with two single beds but only one chair on which she was sitting, very stiff, like a nervous interviewee. He sat on the end of the bed.

He said, 'OK. Here's what happened.'

He told her the story plainly, factually, without attempting to explain or interpret his own or anyone else's motives. She listened intensely, her eyes never leaving his face. He finished by saying, 'As far as Noll is concerned, nothing has changed. They've still got him, but he's just as safe as he was before.'

It was a feeble and ambiguous reassurance, but as much as he dared offer.

She said incredulously, 'So Special Branch knew where he was?'

'They thought they knew,' Dog corrected. 'There'd been a switch either en route for the quarry, or more likely as soon as they arrived there.'

'But they knew before that? They knew they were in that flat? And they did nothing?'

Her voice was on the rise again and he knew he'd been wise to talk up here.

'I'm afraid so.'

The explosion didn't come, not yet.

'But why?' she said helplessly. 'Why? How could they sit there knowing a little boy was . . .'

He tried to sidestep the truth because it would seem

monstrous beyond belief, because he could not bring himself to say that to Toby Tench, the kudos of catching Beck rated immeasurably higher than her son's safety, her son's life even.

Instead he said, 'They'd be waiting their moment, waiting for a chance to move in with minimum risk to Noll.'

'Liar!' she said with instant scepticism. 'If that was true, you wouldn't have done what you did, you and that meddling priest!'

He said, 'Father Blake was just doing the same as me, trying to save Noll.'

'Is that so? You, you were there! You actually saw him in that flat and you did nothing, spotted nothing. She talked you out of it! What sort of policeman are you for God's sake?'

Her scorn was almost tangible. He felt himself beaten down by it.

He said defensively, 'I didn't believe you, that's the truth of it. What had you done to make me believe you? I was expecting to find nothing to support your story . . .'

'So it's my fault, is that it? Not yours, not the great Inspector Cicero's!'

'No!' he snarled. He was wearier than he'd realized and he felt his own self-control close to snapping. He breathed deep and took a grip. 'No, it's my fault. I should have worked it out, I should have been sharper. I'm sorry.'

'Sorry?' she screamed, rising. 'Is that all you can say? What's the use of that when if you'd done your job, Noll could have been safe at home now?'

'If I'd done my job, Charley Lunn could have been safe at home too,' he said bitterly. Suddenly the flow of compassion was cut off. He wanted to remind this woman there was pain in the world beyond hers.

'You stupid, insensitive bitch! Your son's still alive and well and may yet come home safe and sound,' he snarled. 'You think you hurt! There's a woman and two kids in Romchurch who could tell you what pain really is. He was my friend. He was, God help me, my only friend. So stop pouring guilt and blame on me. Believe me, lady, it's superfluous to requirements!'

The passion of his outburst drove her back onto her chair. They sat facing each other with gazes locked, two pale, weary, frightened people seeking strength in anger.

Finally he rubbed his hand down the frozen side of his face and said quietly, 'What's done is done. You've got to take what help you can get. From me, from Father Blake, from anyone. Even from Toby Tench. OK, he puts capturing Beck before rescuing your son, but that doesn't mean he won't get Noll out if he can.'

'And you?' she said with equal quietness. 'What do you put first? When I was waiting in your flat, I found some computer print-outs. I had plenty of time to read them, waiting for you to come back. You must hate Thrale.'

'Must I? I suppose so. I haven't had time to think about it,' he said. 'But I didn't leave Noll in that flat because I wanted to wait till Thrale was in the net too, if that's what you're thinking.'

'No!' She shook her head, tried a smile, and said, 'I may be a hysterical, obsessive woman, and Jesus! I've got cause to be! But my mind still works. I know you didn't. I just wanted to know, if it came to the point, which would come first – killing the man who ruined your life? Or rescuing the child of a woman you don't much care for?'

'What gives you that idea?' he asked.

'I may be a stupid, insensitive bitch, but I can still taste vinegar,' she said. 'Do I remind you of her, the one who died, is that it? Trouble with an Irish accent? Trusted like the fox?'

She was far from stupid, very far from insensitive. He pretended to misunderstand, saying, 'She had red hair too, yes.'

'Did she? So it's outside as well as inside that bothers you?'

'Only as much as me being a Brit soldier bothers you. What was it you said? "Bombers and soldiers alike, they're all scum!" Something like that.'

'You stopped being a soldier,' she said.

'You stopped being an IRA woman,' he said.

He stood up, felt himself stagger slightly.

'Jane,' he said. 'There's nothing more to be done tonight. I reckon we're both out of insults. So can we finish this talk in the morning? I'm done in.'

'What'll you do?' she asked.

'Go downstairs and book myself a bed.'

'You don't look like you'll make it,' she said. 'Why bother when there's a spare one here?'

She spoke in a matter-of-fact tone with no overlay of sexual invitation.

He echoed her tone. 'You're sure you wouldn't mind?'

'As long as you don't snore. Or smoke.'

'Snoring I can't guarantee. Smoking I can.'

It seemed to make perfect sense. He went into the bathroom, stripped down to his underpants, washed, looked at his face in the mirror and for a brief moment saw in his eyes that this was perhaps not the wisest thing he'd ever done. But he'd waved goodbye to wisdom much earlier that day and he was too tired to renew acquaintance now.

He went back into the bedroom, slipped into the nearer bed, said 'Goodnight' without looking at her, and fell asleep as he closed his eyes.

Jane looked down at him as he slept. Why had she suggested he stayed? She made no attempt to persuade herself it was a logical or even commonsense decision. A woman who believes that inviting a strange man to sleep in her room is logical needs her head examined. So, was she attracted to him? He twisted in the bed, pushing down the duvet, and she saw again the old burn marks on his chest which she'd noticed as he came out of the bathroom. Scarred without and scarred within. Perhaps that was the attraction, the visible flaws to set against Oliver Beck's deceiving flawlessness. Or perhaps it was simply the attraction of availability, of proximity. That deep sensuality which Oliver Beck had awoken hadn't left her with his pretended death. In the months since, she had often lain in bed and yearned for love but had never come close to giving way to the yearning. She had steered clear of men and had foreseen no difficulty in continuing this nun-like regime into the most distant future. What had happened last night with the revolting Billy she did not count at all. Her mind had closed time over it like a skin. It might fester and throb beneath and break out in remembered pain at some later date, but for now it hadn't happened. All she knew at this moment was that her body had not known the comfort and the pleasure of a man since the eve of Oliver's death.

So if Cicero woke in the night and came across to her bed, what would she do? Time enough to decide when it happened, she told herself. She undressed and climbed into bed, put off the light and fell asleep almost as quickly as the man.

She awoke. Four hours had passed, the luminous face of her watch told her. There was no movement from the other bed but she sensed he was awake too. She lay tense and waiting, till she thought, 'What the hell century do I think I'm living in?', rolled out of bed, crossed the couple of feet between them and slipped in under his duvet.

He was ready for her, almost too ready. She felt his effort of will as he held back to synchronize his passion with her needs and it wasn't till she dug her nails into his shoulder and cried 'Yes!' in his ear that she felt his lean and wiry body relinquish its control and thrust uninhibitedly into hers. She felt her mind, her spirit, her flesh dissolving into a nebula of pure ecstasy burning across the blackness of outer space. For the first time since Noll's disappearance she was completely beyond the reach of pain. And even when the blackness began to flow back, gobbling up her light till she was reduced to one single burnt-out planet again, there was comfort to be found in wrapping herself round this man and feeling his sunlike warmth.

She said, 'Tell me what happened in Ireland?'

'You read it.'

'No, you tell me.'

So he told her.

She said, 'So you don't know if . . .'

'If Maeve was working for them and died by accident?' he

interrupted fiercely. 'Of course I know. I loved her.'

'Then it's better not to know,' she said almost inaudibly. 'Tell me about your father. He sounds an interesting man.'

'He was. He came to England in the thirties to get away from the *fascisti*. They wanted to intern him when the war started but he actually talked them out of it and joined up instead. After the war he stayed in England. He thought that this was where the future shape of Europe would be decided. He thought there'd be a socialist democratic state here for evermore. By the time he realized how wrong he'd been, he'd got married and established the family business, a café and fish and chip shop in Romchurch. My mother was a local girl. Her family didn't much care for her marrying an Italian so she told them all to go to hell. She died seven years ago. Car accident. After that Papa just collapsed. Cancer. He was eaten away by it, as if the cells had just been biding their time till his grasp on life weakened. He died in Romchurch Hospital, where I first saw you. I smuggled him in Strega and tobacco. He wasn't supposed to, of course, but he said, what the hell was he supposed to do with the few extra minutes he might save by giving them up?'

'No brothers? Sisters? How about your mother's family?'

'They never made up the quarrel after she married Papa. Funny. In that at least, they turned out more Italian than the Italians.'

'And on your father's side? Didn't you once mention an uncle?'

She felt him chuckle in the dark.

'Endo. Yes. Papa's elder brother. He left Italy at the same time but not for the same reasons. He just wanted a different kind of life. He headed for America, did all kinds of things. But mainly he settled for gambling. He used to visit, not often, every two, three years maybe. I first remember him when I was very ill, age four or five. That's when he started teaching me to play cards. Papa didn't approve, but Endo was the elder brother and that carried weight in Italian families. And also Endo loved us all, and that carried even more weight. Last time I saw him was at Papa's funeral. He said, "Next time you'll have to come to see me, Dog.

I'm getting old and besides, your friends, the fuzz, ain't keen on letting me in for anything but funerals, and there ain't nobody left to die.'' I said there was me and he laughed and said, "No, you'll live for ever, Dog. Didn't I always say so?" Then he went to catch his plane.'

'Why did he say the police weren't keen?'

'I didn't enquire too closely, but he's got his own hotel and casino in Vegas and I don't doubt he's had to run with some pretty heavy people in his time.'

It was good to lie here in the sealing dark, her head against his chest, the warmth of his body against hers, its scent in her nostrils, its taste on her tongue. It was good to be sharing his memories just as she had shared his senses.

He felt it too for now he said lazily, no hint of anything more than a lover's curiosity, 'Your turn. You're an only child too, right?'

'Yes. But not spoilt like you. Ouch.'

He pulled her hair with his teeth.

'The truth,' he said sternly.

'All right, Daddy did spoil me. But he needed to. My mother made up for it, with interest.'

*Slap! The hand across the leg . . .*

'So. A typical little daddy's girl,' he mocked.

'Till there was no daddy.'

'I'm sorry. I didn't mean to . . .' His arms tightened round her.

'It's OK. Really.'

'Everyone says you were a great athlete. I talked to someone called Denver, his daughter knew you, seemed to think you were England's answer to Superwoman.'

'Denver? Sally Denver! I haven't seen her for years. We used to . . . well, we were best friends for a long time.'

'*Best*,' he echoed. 'Funny how temporary an absolute can be. So you ran . . ?'

'Hurdled, long jumped, even threw things when the fancy took me.'

He felt her muscles flex and relax as though they were remembering too.

He said, 'Which is why you opted for a PE course.'

He hadn't intended for this to become even a gentle probing, let alone anything like an interrogation. But though by no means as strong, as urgent as once they had been, his doubts and uncertainties, like her darkness, had returned.

She said, 'Yes. We don't all make the right choices. Look at you, going for a soldier.'

He said, 'That choice was unmade for me. Yours too, I gather.'

'Yes. I changed direction.'

She was stiff in his arms now.

'What happened?' he said casually.

*Mist on Ingleborough* . . .

She said flatly, 'You know what happened.'

'You knew what happened to me in Ireland, but you wanted to hear me tell it,' he reminded her.

'It was misty. These two had dropped back to have a smoke. I told them not to lose contact with the rest of the party. They were cheeky. One of them said . . . well, it doesn't matter. But she took another drag at her cigarette. And I tried to knock it out of her mouth. That was all. But she must have swayed forward . . . I hit her . . . and she ran. It was misty, there's a lot of old shafts up there . . . she was badly injured and she said . . . and the other girl said . . . I never meant to hit her!'

'Yes, yes,' he said soothingly. 'And you were exonerated, weren't you?'

'You mean I got away with it? That's what everyone said . . . I got away with it. That finished me for teaching. I ended up on the liner and that's where I met . . .'

Suddenly the blackness was racing back and his questions were rearing up strong and irresistible. They moved apart, only a few inches in the narrow bed, but it felt like a ravine.

She said, 'Is there anything else you want to ask, Inspector?'

He wanted to reach out and pull her close again and spin around them once more that warm, dark and timeless cocoon.

But, check to the dealer as much as you like, the moment comes when you've got to make your play.

He said, 'When Beck faked his drowning, there was a body. You identified it as Beck's. Where did that body come from?'

There was a long silence, then she sighed deeply. He felt her breath warm on his face, like a breeze in the desert.

'From the sea,' she said in the lifeless voice of a child reciting a rote-learned lesson. 'It came from the sea.'

'Just like that? Gift wrapped?' he said.

'Just like that,' she agreed. 'The evening before Oliver was going to disappear. He was down at the boathouse checking the yacht. Then he came running up to the house calling for me. I went out. He said a man had been washed up on the beach. I went to look. He'd been in the sea long enough to get roughed up but I could see he was a man of Oliver's build and colouring. I said that we'd better call the coastguard or the police or someone, but Oliver said no, he didn't want to focus attention on himself so close to his own disappearance. He said it would look very odd if, the day after finding a drowned man, he went out alone in lousy weather and got wrecked. I said, what then? And he said at first we should just dump the body back in the water. Then he got this idea. Why not take it out with him the next day, put some identification on it, rings, watch, that sort of thing, and if it washed up again after they'd found the wreckage of the boat, it would confirm his death.'

'And you went along with this?'

'It wasn't difficult,' she said dully. 'What is it they said about that Frenchman who walked three miles after his head had been chopped off? It's the first step that counts.'

He knew what she meant. He wanted with all his being to believe her. There were other questions demanding to be asked but he forced them back down and reached out and laid his hands on her unresponsive body.

'What's this?' she said. 'Interrogation broken off for refreshments?'

'I'm sorry,' he said helplessly. 'I didn't mean to . . .

Sometimes we have to act as if . . .'

'As if we don't belong to ourselves? Oh yes,' she said. 'I know that.'

Her tone was still harsh and mocking, but she rolled close to him once more, only this time when he made to lay her on her back, she resisted and forced him supine, and, straddling him, brought them both to a climax which did not so much blot out the darkness and doubt as intensify them, like a distant storm's lightnings making lurid a hot tropical night.

Afterwards he fell into an uneasy sleep and when he woke she had returned to the other bed. He lay with his eyes open, but their focus was inward and he hardly noticed as a feeble wintry dawn struggled to dilute his darkness to a paler shade of grey.

# 8

A few miles away, Billy Flynn too was staring into the darkness of a strange bedroom.

He had no idea where he was, only the certainty he was not where he ought to be. As his eyes tried to form shapes from the lumpy greyness and his furred tongue sought dampness in his dried-up mouth, his mind teetered uncertainly back to the previous night.

He had been restless from the moment they arrived. He was a man who needed the buzz of action. The switch had given him a bit of a charge but it had gone almost too smoothly. Down into the quarry, straight out of the car into a truck with its engine revving, and while a man, woman and child dressed like them transferred cases from the Granada to a caravan, they were bucketing up the track past the Branch car at the top while its occupants were probably still reporting their safe arrival.

Thrale might get up his nose with his Mr Wonderful act but, credit where it was due, he was a great orchestrator. Only he hadn't orchestrated this lumpy bed in this frowsty room, and, as Billy knew to his cost, he didn't care for unrehearsed variations on his careful themes.

He reached out his hand. He was alone, but by the warm hollow at his side, he hadn't been alone for long.

It was coming back to him now. Playing with the kid in the small garden of the cottage they'd been dropped at, hearing on the radio that his little dripping tap trick had burnt a pig . . . that had cheered him up a lot, but it had also made him feel more restless. He fancied a few bevvies, a bit of company, a celebration. It wouldn't have been so bad if there'd been any booze in the cottage, or if My Lady bloody Heighway had shown any sign of being willing to pass the time profitably. He'd

taken a shower and wandered out naked to give her a chance to
size up the goods. She'd taken a long cool look and said, 'OK,
Billy, I've seen it. Next time I see it, I'll chop it off.'

He'd almost hit her then and forced her head down between his
legs . . . even the thought excited him, but the remembrance of
Jonty Thrale played across his mind like a cold jet and he'd got
dressed and sat in a sulking silence till approaching ten o'clock,
she'd closed her book and stood up, saying, 'I'm off to bed, Billy.
I'd advise you to do the same. Jonty should turn up tomorrow and
he'll look to find us wide awake and ready to go. Goodnight.'

It was the kindly voice that did it, like a schoolmarm talking
to a child. Seething with resentment, he followed her upstairs
and banged his door. His window was open. He went to shut out
the cold night air but found himself hesitating with his hand on
the latch. Right outside, its branches touching the sill, was an old
wych-elm. Almost without conscious thought, he slid out of the
window, grasped a branch and swung himself through the
whippy boughs to the ground.

They had no car and in any case he wouldn't have dared risk
starting one. But in a tumbledown garden shed, he and the boy
had found an ancient sit-up-and-beg bike whose wheels still
managed to turn. He carried it on his shoulder up the long rutted
track which ran through a stretch of unkempt woodland to a
narrow country road. Here he mounted the cycle and began to
pedal. He had no lights but the earlier mist had risen and the road
flowed like a river before him, all silvered by a frosty moon.

They'd skirted a substantial village as they were driven here
from the quarry, the kind where the old centre was being
swallowed up by new estates. There should be real pubs here, not
just ancient ale houses where you banged your head on wormy
beams and got clocked by a load of nosy yokels.

He was right. He heard it before he saw it, a brand new road
house called the Snooty Fox, with loud music beating out of
misted windows across a GTi-crammed car park.

He hesitated on the threshold. A pair of cold eyes seemed to
be fixed on him and a soft level voice to speak in his ear. Then

a group of late arrivals swept him forward and drove him through the crush up to the bar.

He drank hard and fast, partly because of the late hour, partly to make sure Jonty Thrale didn't gain admittance to his mind again. At some point he got talking to Yvonne. She was a type his louche expertise thought it recognized. Mid-forties dressed like mid-twenties. Not yet paying for it but not wanting to be paid for it either. And best of all, with a place of her own. No parents or husband to make the evening end with a contortionist's act in the back of a car or a cold-arsed knee-trembler up against a tree.

A room. A bed. That's where he was now. His eyes strained against the dark, but his mind welcomed it. Waking up to daylight would have been disaster, but there was probably still time to get back to the cottage without the slag Heighway knowing he'd been out.

And now the gloom was giving up its secrets to his adjusting sight. A wardrobe, a dressing table, an open door, its space lined with a very faint difference of light . . . He sniffed the air. Tobacco smoke. Someone was smoking a cigarette in there.

Silently he slipped from the bed and approached the doorway. Through it he could make out the gleam of a washstand. It was a bathroom. He stepped inside, his hand brushed a light pull, he caught it and jerked.

Sitting on the lavatory bowl, cigarette in mouth, was a naked woman. She looked startled by his sudden appearance. But it wasn't just the shock of the light that brought alarm to her eyes. In her hand was a leather wallet, its contents spread neatly on the bath ledge at her side.

She said, 'It's all right, lovey, I wasn't taking anything, just curious, you know, a good-looking boy like you, a girl wants to keep in touch . . .'

'Girl!' he said viciously. 'I've got a granny who looks younger than you, you stinking slag.'

'Is that right?' she said, rising. 'Then I'm surprised you couldn't get it up last night, 'cos you Micks spend most of your

216

time fucking your grannies, don't you? There, take your bloody wallet and sod off!'

She flung it at him. He let it bounce off his chest, then moved towards her.

'Come on,' she said in renewed fear. 'No rough stuff, eh? Not with your granny.'

He hit her with all his strength and felt something break in her jaw. She shrieked and began to fall back into the bath. He caught her on the side of her head with his other fist. The back of her head cracked against the tiled wall. Her shriek died to a long bubbling groan, but he kept on hitting her till there was no sound at all.

Then he stood there and looked down at her in a growing horror which derived partly from the deed itself but mostly from the fearful prospect of Jonty Thrale's reaction if he found out.

He turned on the tap in the wash basin and let the water run over his bloodstained hands. Then he went back into the bedroom and pulled on his clothes which lay strewn over the floor. Once more he had to go into the bathroom to gather up his wallet and stuff the contents back into it. But he kept his eyes averted from the woman in the bath who had still not moved and was making no noise.

He opened a window and looked out. He was in a ground floor maisonette and was able to drop out of the window onto a concrete pathway. The moon was still up and by its corpse-light he could see that the block of maisonettes lay on the fringe of a new estate. Over the road were the foundations of more buildings and beyond them, trees.

He set off towards them at a run.

It was more by luck than any judgement that he found himself on the road that he'd cycled along earlier. As he jogged along he glanced at his watch. It was later than he thought, after six A.M. The midwinter darkness had deceived him, and though the sun was not yet up, the east was a paler shade of grey and there was already traffic on the road. Each approaching headlight sent him into the hedgerow until at last, scratched and exhausted, he

217

reached the lane to the cottage. Another set of headlights was approaching. He dropped into the ditch till they should pass, but to his horror he realized the car was slowing down.

He couldn't have been spotted, he tried to assure himself. But the car was down to a crawl now, and his mind was already trying to cope with the greater problem of what to do about the driver. The cottage was too close for mere evasion to be enough. Now, the man might be merely curious, but when news of the attack on Yvonne became public, the memory of a dishevelled figure hiding on the roadside would rise strong in his mind, and the first place the police would look at was the nearest habitation.

But what was the alternative to letting the man drive off? Another assault, leaving a body to dispose of? And a car, he'd have to get rid of the car . . .

Oh shit, shit, shit, shit! Billy groaned inwardly. It didn't seem possible that things could get any worse.

Then they did.

The car wasn't stopping, it was turning into the lane!

'Oh shit!' he cried aloud.

Driven on sidelights only, the car was bumping gently towards the cottage. For a moment Billy thought of leaving Bridie Heighway to look after herself. It wasn't heroics that made him go on, simply the realization that, as he was, he had nowhere else to go.

He followed the car down the track, keeping well back out of sight. By the time he came in sight of the cottage, the car had stopped, and the driver was opening the little gate into the garden.

Even from behind in silhouette, Billy recognized the figure and had a millisec of relief that at least it wasn't the pigs. Then the front door opened and Bridie Heighway came flying out into Jonty Thrale's arms and it occurred to the watching youth that if he didn't get back into his room before they finished kissing, he might wish that it *had* been the police.

He began to move sideways into the wood, planning to work

his way round the back. But the cow Heighway must have been snogging with her eyes open for she broke away from Thrale, speaking urgently, and he came spinning round with a SIG-Sauer P226 conjured out of nowhere into his left hand.

'Right, let's have you out of there. Right now!'

Slowly Billy stepped forward. There was no point in running, not with Thrale at the other end of fifteen nine-millimetre Parabellum rounds. But his mind was racing madly in search of that safety he knew his legs could never find.

'Well, well, well. If it isn't Superboy,' said Thrale softly. 'Now there's a thing. And what have you been up to, Billy, to get yourself in such a state?'

Billy Flynn tried to speak, found how hard it is to get out words which might be your last, hawked, spat, and said, 'Christ, is it only you? I heard a car, thought I'd better take a look, so I climbed out of my window. There's a tree, but a branch broke and I fell.'

For a long moment Thrale regarded him in silence. Then he smiled and the gun vanished as swiftly as it had emerged.

'So you've found at last that you really can't fly, Billy! Never mind. Full marks for being so alert. We'll make a fieldman of you yet. Now let's all go inside and have a cup of tea. There's work to be done, or will be soon.'

'Work?' said Bridie Heighway. 'Does that mean you've made contact with Beck?'

Thrale smiled again. He was in a high good humour, thought Billy. It had probably saved his life.

'Better than that,' said Thrale. 'Beck's snapped. He's in the country and he's made contact with the Listeners. And he's missed me so much, he's invited me along to a little reunion!'

# 9

They breakfasted together in silence till their hands touched as they reached simultaneously for the coffee pot. Dog's fingers curled round hers.

'Look,' he said. 'I know it's not the time, and probably for you last night happened because . . . well, because of everything. But I wanted to say, for me it was . . . more. End of speech.'

She said, 'Maybe for me too. I don't know . . . I mean . . .'

She looked at him and wondered what she did mean. Her heart, her body, might be making decisions that could be binding, but they were being stored in a bottom drawer till her mind had leisure to examine them. Last night had been . . . last night. A necessary interlude, a longed-for respite. But *here* and *now* are creditors who always claim their due.

She tried again and said, 'I can't think of anything but Noll. And Oliver . . .'

'What do you think of Oliver?'

'Where is he? Has he heard yet? What does he think? What will he do?'

'And what do you feel about him when you think about him?'

She shook her head impatiently.

'How should I be able to answer that? I ran from him, from part of what he is. But only part . . . And you might argue that it was illogical to run from a man for helping something you hate when it turns out what he was really doing was robbing it blind!'

He shook his head and said softly, but forcefully, 'No, I wouldn't argue that.'

She pulled her hand free. He lifted the coffee pot, poured more coffee.

'You'll go to your mother's now?' he said.

'Yes. I think so. Unless you've got any idea . . ?'

She looked at him desperately and when he shook his head, tears started in her eyes and she said, 'It's hopeless, isn't it?'

'Yes,' he said gravely. 'I'm afraid it is.'

Then as her face registered her dismay at not getting even some token disagreement, he smiled and said, 'But like Uncle Endo used to say, there's guys sleeping in the subway for not knowing the difference between no hope and no chance. There's always a chance till the last bet's laid, Jane, and we'll find it.'

Somehow this flimsiest of straws was more comforting than a whole rhetoric of reassurance.

'Will you give me a lift into town?' he asked. 'My heavenly driver with his chariot of fire has deserted me. Can't say I'm sorry. He relied a bit too much on divine intervention.'

'Sure. I'll just get my things from the room.'

'And I'll settle the bill. No,' he added when she demurred, 'I'm sure they've spotted there were two of us in there and will probably take great pleasure in pointing it out.'

In the event the cashier who was sitting tapping out figures to the rhythm of some music from her Walkman clearly couldn't have cared if the Ball of Kirriemuir had been held in the room. She removed her headset as she printed out the account. The radio was tuned to the local station and as Dog waited he heard the music fade and the announcer start to speak.

'An update on our earlier item about the discovery of the body of Mrs Yvonne Ellings in her maisonette at Little Staughton after neighbours reported a disturbance early this morning. The police would like to interview a man in his early twenties, with spiky blond hair and wearing jeans and a mottled brown leather bomber jacket who was seen leaving the Snooty Fox public house at Little Staughton with Mrs Ellings late last evening. If you think you can help the police with this or any other information please ring the following number . . .'

'Ready?' said Jane Maguire behind him.

He turned. Either she hadn't heard the item or the echo of her description of the youth who had fixed her car, the youth who had raped her, hadn't registered. Why should it? Blond hair, jeans, bomber jacket . . . it could be any one of a million kids.

To a man too broke to make the next ante, it could be all he was going to get.

As she drove towards the town centre she said, 'How will we keep in touch?'

He said, 'I'll ring your mother's with a message for Father Blake. I'll say it's the school calling and ask him to be there at a certain time. I'll be waiting at the Clareview an hour before that time, OK? But take care. You'll be followed. You can drop me here.'

She pulled in and he climbed out of the car. He sought for some parting words of cautious comfort and could find none.

Then he thought, to hell! He'd chucked everything else to the wind, why hang on to caution?

'Don't worry,' he said, leaning down. 'We'll get him back, whatever it takes. I promise.'

He didn't wait for a reaction or a reply but straightened up and walked swiftly away.

Two minutes later he was pushing open the door of the Central Police Station. His logic was simple. He doubted if Tench would have put out a general alert on him. A story like that would soon have leaked and Tench would want the media interest to centre on the vanished child, not on a detective inspector on the run. Walking into the station was the quickest way of testing this theory.

More important, it was the only way he could hope to check out his single flimsy lead.

For all his logic, he felt a great surge of relief to find that, though Denver's welcome was chilly, it was not the greeting of a man about to make an arrest.

'Oh, it's you, Cicero. Still acting as a messenger boy for your funny friends, are you?'

He guessed at the cause of the irritation. It wasn't hard.

'No,' he replied forcefully. 'Not now, and I wasn't last time

222

either. I'm trying to do my job and I don't much care to have those bastards creeping out of the woodwork telling me what I can and can't do . . . I'm sorry, sir. I shouldn't be talking like this . . .'

Denver had visibly relaxed.

'Don't worry,' he said. 'I know just what you mean. We've had them on our backs too. Worst was the last, smarmy fat sod smiling all the time, like a spiv selling dodgy cars. I came close to putting my boot up his arse, I tell you!'

So Tench himself had turned up. This must be the place to be.

Dog said, 'If you ever need a witness that you were only raising your foot to tie your lace, look no further, sir.'

Denver barked a laugh and the relaxation was complete. He ordered up some coffee and asked Dog what he could do for him.

'Well, it's really a courtesy visit,' said Dog. 'This Maguire case has to all intents and purposes been taken out of my hands. I've been instructed to liaise between my chief and the Branch and to assist where I can. Well, I've offered my assistance and more or less got told to run off and play with myself. So I thought the best thing I could do was come along here and talk to some real cops again.'

'And pick our brains, you mean?' said Denver.

'Well, that too,' grinned Dog. 'I can't deny it would give me great pleasure to turn up something those sods had missed.'

The coffee came, strong and hot. Denver sipped his, grimaced, and said, 'Sorry, Cicero. Wish I could help, but we've been pretty well sidelined on this too. I don't even know what the hell it's all about, apart from the missing kid. Or is he dead, do we know that yet?'

Dog shrugged.

'The father's an American. There's an FBI interest, that's all I know,' he said vaguely. 'No doubt it'll be tossed back to us when things fall apart. Meanwhile I'm just going to be hanging around twiddling my thumbs, so if you've got anything an idle detective can do, just say the word. You're being kept pretty busy by what I hear on the radio.'

'You're right there,' said Denver. 'Lots of fun and games last night. Major alert to start with, not on our patch but we went on stand-by. Some riot out on one of these gyppo sites. Turned out a false alarm in the end. There was a lot of smoothing over went on and it smelt a bit of the Branch to me. Nothing to do with this Maguire thing, was it?'

'Not that I know of,' said Dog.

Denver looked at him sharply then went on, 'Then there's been a murder out at Little Staughton. Not so little now and growing fast, that's the trouble.'

'Lot of men tied up on door to door, eh?'

'Door to door, yes. There's a lot of doors out there now with all these new estates. But it's the buggers who are putting the doors in and the bricks down and digging the new roads that are taking up the time.'

'Sorry?'

'The building workers, the navvies. Area's full of them. Hostels, digs, caravans, and with half of them on the lump, their bosses don't bother keeping records.'

'I heard on the radio you were looking for some youngster,' said Dog. 'But the description was pretty vague. What makes you think he might be one of these building workers?'

'There was something else we didn't give to the radio. No use letting the world know everything you know, is there? Not that it's much, just that the landlord reckons the man we're after was drinking Guinness and spoke with a bit of a brogue, and these building sites are full of Micks, so that's our lead if you can call it that.'

And my lead too, thought Dog, feeling a little surge of excitement. It would probably turn out to be simple and sordid, some Irish brickie picking up a tart and things getting out of control. On the other hand . . .

He said, 'Sexual, was it?'

'She'd had it, but willingly, the M.O. reckons. The injuries came later. She was well known for bringing strange men home. Not a pro but always on the look out for a drink, a laugh, a bit of company, know what I mean? Almost sure to go sour in the end, but it's a hell of a price for being lonely, wouldn't you say?'

A hell of a price for being Catholic, Protestant, rich, poor, black, white; for simply being there. The price of admission and the price of exit all in one.

'A hell of a price,' agreed Dog Cicero.

# Part Four

# 1

Three people watched Jane Maguire arrive at her mother's house.

Two of them were Tench's men, one outside and one in.

The third was Oliver Beck.

He'd spotted the outer watcher without difficulty. He'd had years of practice spotting all sorts and conditions of security men. Technique becomes habit, and habit is the great betrayer of human beings. After a while even attempts at variety form a pattern.

Being aware of this, he had schooled himself over the years to leave layer after layer of variants, each one sufficiently detailed to make the keen seeker after knowledge think, this is the true pattern of Oliver Beck! But when the last one was peeled back they would find . . . nothing.

Jane Maguire had changed all that. First she'd been a simple pick-up, a ship-board affair. Then he'd fooled himself into thinking that by setting her up in his house on Cape Cod he was merely laying another diverting trail for the hounds that followed.

That was another way men betrayed themselves, by not examining their own motives with the same cold clarity they turned on others. We're the Immortals, he'd told her, we're the Gods. But even the Gods can get it wrong. You'd only got to look at Ireland to see that.

But when his son was born, self-deceit went out of the window. The simple and complete disappearance he had been toying with for years was no longer possible. That he himself could vanish beyond all trace he did not doubt. Hadn't invisibility been his metier? But a woman and a small child could not be so easily spirited away.

Alone, he would have been happy to be alive and defy the hounds to find him. Now, he had to be dead and hope they would stop looking.

He needed Jane's cooperation but he hadn't told her everything. His reasons were mixed; all good in themselves, but not perhaps the ideal mixture. First he hadn't been sure of her reaction. To go on the lam from the Revenue Service was one thing. But to let her know the true source of his wealth and the kind of people who might be looking for him was something else. Besides, she'd got enough acting to do, identifying 'his' body and faking grief. The genuineness of her reaction to the news of his Noraid connections would be a real protection to her. So his divine logic went.

How it would affect her feelings for him he didn't know, but flight was a possibility not overlooked in his scenario. In the end there was only one place for most people to run to, and that was home.

And there she was now, walking up the little path alongside the starched and laundered garden, to ring at the shining front door.

But the rest of his plan was in tatters. Jonty Thrale had seen to that. Jonty Thrale who, when the cards had all been dealt and all the delicate groundwork of bluff and double bluff gently laid, had reached across the table with a cut-throat razor and flicked over the hole cards.

The door opened. She paused and looked around, as if sensing the other watchers. He put his hand to his face though there was no way she could see him. Then she disappeared inside.

For a moment he allowed himself the indulgence of examining his feelings for her. Their strength still surprised him. Women had always been a short-term investment with him ever since the disastrous mistake of marriage. But Jane was different, perhaps because she never asked for anything. In fact she never behaved as if she believed she had any real right to happiness. Maybe this had helped when he broached his plan for disappearance. Maybe she had taken it all so calmly because she'd never really regarded those years of happiness as permanent. And because she made so few demands on him, he had come as close to loving her as he had ever loved a woman. But not as he loved his son. Life without Jane was conceivable; he might always remember her but not always with pain. But life without Noll would be a maiming, an emptiness, an absence, which nothing could ever fill.

So, if it came to choices, Noll first, Jane second. He didn't feel guilty at thus articulating priorities. He had no doubt that Jane had already done the same.

He walked slowly back to his car.

Soon it would be time to meet Jonty Thrale.

In the house Jane Maguire sat opposite her mother and felt ashamed. Here was the woman she had longed to love but only feared, striven to please but always failed. Whatever she had done in her life, she had always been aware of this judging presence. And always she had fled for comfort to that other presence, the gentle, laughing, soothing wraith of her dead father.

Now, sitting before this hunched and somehow shrunken figure who had put on twenty years since last they met, Jane realized what she had never admitted before: that all her life she had blamed her mother for her father's death. Because she had never articulated the accusation, there was no detail, just a conviction that it was this rigid, icy woman who had driven her man to the warm consolation of the pub which had left him too befuddled to dive for cover when the firing started.

Even now Jane could not entirely explode this notion, but it had ceased to be simple black and white. How could anything be black and white ever again now that she realized that all the barriers which she had felt her mother set up against true closeness with her daughter were nothing compared to this one great invisible unsuspected barrier she had built up around herself?

They had exchanged few words. When she came into the room, her mother had looked up and said, 'Any news?' And Jane had said, 'None.' And the brief flicker of animation had left the older woman's face.

She reached forward and took the unresisting hands in hers. They felt skeletal and cold.

'It's going to be all right,' she urged. 'Really it is. Noll's alive. He's going to stay alive. We'll get him back. I know we will.'

The eyes met hers, in them an intensity of longing to be convinced which almost made her drop her gaze, but she kept it steady as her mind desperately sought for some authenticating gesture.

She said, 'And when he comes home, we'd better have his room ready. You sit here and rest, Mam, I'll see to it.'

She pulled her hands free and stood up.

As she reached the door she hesitated, thinking wretchedly that her pathetic effort at stimulation wasn't going to work.

'Shall I use the blue sheets?' she said.

And at last her mother spoke, in a voice as frail as her looks.

'Sorry?' said Jane. 'I didn't catch that.'

'I said, you can't use blue sheets with that wallpaper,' said Mrs Maguire. 'You never had any sense of colour, did you now? Green's what you want. The green sheets with the pink flower on the pillowcases.'

'Yes, of course. Where would they be kept?'

'Do you not know anything?' The voice was almost back at normal strength. 'I'd better see to it myself. If you want something done properly, do it yourself, that's what they always say.'

She got to her feet. There was something over-deliberate in her movement just as there was something slightly stagey in her speech, as though to mark her awareness that this was a charade. No, Jane corrected herself. Not charade, but ritual, like those religious ceremonies performed as acts of faith even though the faith they witness is close to annihilation.

Jane stood aside to let her pass. It is love of my son that has brought her to this, she thought, and, for the first time in more years than she could recall, felt a gush of pure affection for her mother.

'Don't just stand there,' ordered Mrs Maguire. 'Make us a pot of tea. That useless item through there shows it a single tea bag and that's it.'

The 'useless item' was the Special Branch officer who'd let Jane in. She could hear him talking into his radio in the next room. Presumably her arrival was now fully recorded. As she put the kettle on the gas stove, he came into the kitchen.

'Good to see you've got the old lady up and moving,' he said. 'I was starting to get a bit worried.'

'Not worried enough to have a nurse in? Or get her into hospital?' she flashed.

'Hang about. She's had the doctor looking at her and he wanted her to have a nurse, but she told him to push off,' he protested.

So she'd still had enough strength left to refuse to let herself be ordered about. This, with the noise of her feet above as she moved about making Noll's bed, brought fresh reassurance. Jane felt almost lighthearted as she made the tea. Perhaps everything really was going to be OK. Perhaps even as she stood here watching for the kettle to boil, Dog Cicero was hot on the trail of the gang who'd taken Noll.

Dog Cicero. Why should she place such reliance on him?

Forget last night. Forget bodies meeting and mingling. Forget promises half made. The answer was simple. There was no one else.

If Noll was going to be returned to her safe and sound – and she had to believe that or else collapse into a state which would make her mother's condition seem like rude health – then she had to place her faith in Dog Cicero. To use his own idiom, he was the only game in town.

The kettle was boiling. She poured the steaming water into the tea pot and wondered what he was doing now.

# 2

'Not another one,' said the landlord of the Snooty Fox. 'I've got work to do as well!'

Dog put away his warrant card.

'Sorry,' he said pleasantly. 'Just need to recheck a couple of details. This youth who left with Mrs Ellings, did he seem to know anyone else in the bar?'

'How should I know? We were packed to the ceiling last night. I only noticed him at all 'cos I came up from the cellar as they were going out into the car park.'

'But you remember him ordering Guinness?'

'I think it was the same geezer, yes, but I wouldn't swear to it.'

What the hell am I doing here? thought Dog. Answer: backing a hunch. Only fools and Texans back hunches, Uncle Endo had said. But there's a lot of rich Texans, so if a hunch is all you've got, back it.

'This Mrs Ellings, you know her well?'

'Only as a punter. She was in a lot.'

'Liked a drink, did she?'

'Drink and a bit of company. But like I told your mates earlier, she wasn't on the game. I don't allow any of that in my boozer.'

'Very moral of you,' observed Dog. 'Did she always go for the young stuff?'

'Not particularly. And she didn't always take 'em home.'

'She took this one home. How would she do that, by the way? You said they were going out into the car park. Did she have a car?'

'Yeah. Banged-up old Maxi. Some of the lads had to give it a push start a couple of times.'

'I see. It was this door they left by?'

Dog went out into the car park, followed by the landlord. He looked around. It was empty. Litter blew aimlessly around at the whim of a cold gusting wind which was plastering sheets of newspaper against a wire-net fence.

'Was the car park empty when you locked up last night?' asked Dog.

'Yeah. Not a dicky bird. Except that.'

'What?'

The landlord seemed to be pointing at a recess in which stood three large wheelie-bins.

'That heap of junk.'

Against the wall behind the bins, looking like a collapsed marathon runner, leaned an ancient bicycle. Dog went to it and took hold of the handlebars. The metal was rusty, the tyres half deflated and the seat a threat to manhood, but when he tried the pedals, the rear wheel turned with only a mildly protesting squeal.

'You didn't think it odd for someone to come on a bike and just abandon it?'

'What?' The man laughed. 'Oh, I'm with you. But you don't think anyone actually rode that thing here, do you? Just look at the state of it. No lights, no brakes either I bet, and it must weigh a ton. No, it's just been dumped. Happens all the time. People bring sackfuls of rubbish in their boots, dump them against the fence, have a pint or two, then drive off and leave their crap for me to clear up next morning. We're a disgusting lot when you look close at us.'

'You're probably right,' said Dog. 'But I'll take it just in case.'

'Please yourself.'

'Is there another pub in the village? Somewhere a little . . . older?'

He looked neutrally at the hectic red brick and leaded-light-effect windows of the Snooty Fox.

'There's the Compasses in the High Street if it's spit and sawdust you're after. Down the hill, turn left.'

'That'll do me nicely,' said Dog Cicero. 'Thanks for your time.'

235

He wheeled the old bike out of the car park. Glancing back to make sure the landlord had gone inside, he threw his leg over the cross bar, gingerly sank onto the seat and began to pedal.

He soon discovered the landlord was right in every particular. The descent into the old centre of the village confirmed that the brakes didn't work and once the perilous velocity had been absorbed by the slight uphill slope of the High Street, the man's estimate that it weighed a ton didn't seem exaggerated.

The Compasses was as far removed from the Snooty Fox as the bike from a GTi. He ducked his head under a low lintel and wheeled the machine into a narrow stone-flagged passage which led into a broad, shadowy room. There was no bar, only a single huge table which must surely have been built inside these walls for there was no way it could have been introduced along that narrow passage or through either of the two small windows. At the table sat three old men on three old chairs with which they looked to have a common ancestry. In front of them were three half-filled pint glasses.

Dog leaned the cycle up against the wall, nodded at the drinkers and sat down. Nothing was said. After a while footsteps were heard along the corridor and a fat man in shirtsleeves filled the entrance.

'Yes?' he said.

'I'll have a pint of best,' said Dog. 'Perhaps you gentlemen would care to join me?'

The glasses were raised and emptied in a unison which would have won points for a team of synchronized swimmers. The landlord swept them up in one huge hand and vanished, appearing a minute or so later with a loaded tray.

'Good health,' said Dog.

'Good health,' said the trio.

Silence returned. Dog knew about silences and recognized the curiosity behind this one. But he knew also that any sign of a respondent curiosity on his part could raise impenetrable barriers. He emptied his glass, rose and said, 'I'll be off. Cheers.'

As he reached the entrance to the passageway one of the trio said, 'Hey'.

'Yes?'

'Aren't you forgetting something?'

Three heads nodded towards the bike.

'Not mine,' said Dog. 'It was lying on the ground outside. I brought it in, in case it got stolen or damaged. Thought it must belong to one of you.'

They examined the heap of rusting metal which this foreigner had been at such pains to preserve.

'Not ours,' they pronounced.

'I'm sorry,' said Dog. 'Well, as you don't know whose it is, I'd better put it back.'

He took hold of the handlebars and made to wheel the machine out. At the last moment the provocation of imputed ignorance worked.

'That's old Edgar Blackett's bike,' said one of them and the others nodded accord.

'Oh. Then perhaps I'd better return it to him,' said Dog.

They laughed as at a Wildean shaft.

'It'll be a downhill ride for sure,' said their spokesman. 'Old Edgar's been dead these three years.'

'That's a real mystery then,' said Dog. 'I'd better leave it with the village bobby. He'll be able to sort it out.'

The threat of losing their status as local experts finally got him what he wanted.

'Shouldn't bother with him today. He'll be up to his eyes with this murder out on the new estate. Off-comers. Nothing but trouble.'

'Oh yes. So who *can* help me get the bike back where it came from?'

'Must have come from Edgar's cottage, I reckon. Grazey Lane Cottage off the Framley road. Went to his daughter but she don't use it much, living down in London with her fancy man, so she lets it off.'

'And it's let now, is it? Funny time of year for a holiday.'

237

'Don't know about that, mister,' said the spokesman defensively. 'Some folk likes a country Christmas. Log fires and all. Mind you, they'll end up well kippered, the way old Edgar's chimney always smoked!'

Dog left on the wave of laughter, wheeling the bike out with him. At the village post office he purchased the OS 1:25000 sheet for the area and found Grazey Lane Cottage marked. As its name suggested, it was situated at the bottom of a green track off an unclassified road.

He reminded himself this was all still speculation. But when the antes have eaten up your pile, you've got to go with whatever you've got.

There was a phone box outside the post office. He hesitated by it. Did he really have anything to tell Jane Maguire? Not yet, but if he did get a line on the boy, it could be useful to have her close at hand. Young Noll was clearly very much at home with Bridie Heighway. He would come running at his mother's call, but was more likely to turn to his captor if a stiff-faced stranger did the calling. But suppose he'd got it all wrong and Grazey Lane Cottage proved a dead end? Even then, he argued, it might be that Jane herself had picked up something useful and was even now fretting that their agreed line of communication was one way only.

It was only after he had entered the box and dialled that Dog admitted another, and perhaps the most powerful, reason. He wanted to see her again.

'Hello.'

It was her voice. Hearing it confirmed his need.

'Is that Mrs Maguire?' he asked in a gruff brogue.

'No. This is her daughter. Who's speaking?'

'This is Father Kylie from the school. Is Father Blake there, please?'

'No, I'm afraid he's not.'

'Now that's a nuisance. Look, if he turns up could you ask him to get in touch? But he'll need to contact me before two o'clock as I won't be in after that. Many thanks.'

He put the phone down. Would it fool the listeners? Possibly. Would Jane be able to slip the watchers? She'd managed it twice already so there was a fair chance. Except of course that Tench's men would be on their mettle to make sure third time wasn't lucky.

He mounted the bike and began to cycle out of the village.

# 3

Two hours earlier Jonty Thrale had been in the same phone box.

At ten o'clock precisely he had dialled. The phone at the other end had been picked up immediately.

'What's new?' he said.

'Maguire's at her mother's.'

'Any sign she's made contact with Beck?'

'Not unless she's a better actress than Bridie Heighway. My guess is Beck's still sunning himself on some tropical beach. Maybe he hasn't even seen an English paper yet.'

'You could be right. Fill me in on the rumpus at the quarry.'

'Tench is raging about that. He'd like to make out he knew all the time and he was just playing along to fool you, but you really had him going. Me too. That was a good trick, the switch. You got 'em somewhere safe now, I hope?'

'Safe enough. But I'd rather you lot were still watching the quarry. What sparked it off?'

'That frozen-faced cop from Romchurch. Christ knows what he's playing at, but I shouldn't like to be in his shoes when Tench catches him. He'd accessed the computer and must have spotted the surveillance team.'

'And you let him run loose?'

'He slipped us. We reckon that priest, Blake, helped him.'

'And where are they now?'

'God knows, but we'll get 'em. Listen, about my retainer. Christmas coming up and all, how about a big drink on the house? It's a risky game I'm playing . . .'

'Me too. I'll see what I can do.'

Thrale put the phone down. It was good that Special Branch still thought Beck was out of the country. If that's what they did think. Tench was a tricky bastard, capable of conning his closest

240

colleagues. Certainly he was capable of spotting a leak from his own team and instead of plugging it, feeding the leaker disinformation.

Or using him to set his contacts up.

He stepped out of the box. There were two policemen standing by his car.

His hand slipped into the broad pocket of his car coat, but only for a second. If this *was* a set-up, then the two uniformed constables were a mere diversion. There'd be hard-eyed men with high-powered weapons lurking close, ready to blow him away at the slightest sign of menacing movement. But since Gibraltar, they no longer had quite the same freedom of interpretation, so with people on the street and his hands in clear view, he should be safe.

He walked towards the car.

'This your vehicle, sir?' asked the older constable courteously.

'That's right. It's OK parking here, isn't it?' he said, making a play of looking for yellow lines.

'Yes sir, that's fine. Were you around the village last night? Or early this morning?'

His mind raced. If this was Tench's game, there was no way out, not for the moment anyway. So play along.

'No,' he said. 'I've just driven up from London today. I only stopped to phone my office.'

They checked his licence off-handedly. It told them he was David Coe with an address in Ealing. If they ran it through the computer, all the details would check, and the car would come out as part of a fleet belonging to one of the country's largest DIY manufacturing and retailing companies.

'Something happened, has it?' he enquired, as he put his licence back in his wallet.

'Just an enquiry, sir,' said the older man, but the younger, with a vain effort at insouciance, added, 'Murder case. Some tearaway beat up an old lady.'

'I'd not say forty-eight was old,' corrected the other man, with a grin at Thrale. 'We're just interested if anyone in the village last night saw anything or anyone.'

'I'm sorry I can't help you. Any leads?' asked Thrale, getting into the car.

'There's a chap we're looking for who might be able to help us,' said the older policeman. 'His description's been on the radio. Young, medium build, blond hair, short and spiky. Jeans and a brown bomber jacket. Could be anyone, I know. But if you spot someone like that trying to thumb a lift, sir, I shouldn't pick him up. Drive to the next phone and give us a bell. Cheers now.'

Thrale drove carefully away. Could be anyone, the man said. Yes, it could. But he was recalling Billy Flynn's unexpected appearance outside the cottage. Out of his window and down a tree when he thought he'd heard an intruder. And he'd actually complimented the youth on his alertness! Something else came to him now. He'd told them about Oliver Beck making contact with one of the Listeners. There was a whole network of these throughout the UK, people whose sole function was to take messages they didn't understand and pass them on to people they'd never seen. Interpreted, the message had read *Beck for Thrale. Woodall Service. First phone. Twelve noon.* He'd expected Billy to come at him with some gungho notion of providing cover and taking Beck out as soon as they spotted him. But the youth had said nothing, not even when Bridie had asked, 'Will you be wanting cover, Jonty?'

'I think not,' he'd said, willing to explain his reasons to her, though Billy would have got a simple, terse *no.* 'I think this will be the old telephone runaround till he makes sure I'm by myself. There'll be no trouble this time. All he wants is to find out the starting price. He'll probably make an offer. I'll tell him that's fine. If he wants to pay on the instalment plan, that's how he'll get the boy. In instalments. In fact maybe I should take a finger on account so he'll know we're serious.'

Bridie had regarded him thoughtfully, then said, 'He's surely known you long enough to know you're a very serious person, Jonty.'

And Thrale had laughed. Bridie Heighway was the only person who ever made him laugh.

'You're right. And knowing me, he'll know the starting price, and the finishing price too.'

'So why does he want to see you?'

'To make arrangements. He'll insist on confirming the boy's alive. And because he's a real tricky bastard, he'll hope when that happens that he can find a way to get him away from us.'

'You think the money means that much to him?'

'I think he knows that whatever the starting price, my finishing price includes his bones,' Jonty Thrale had said.

And during all of this, Billy Flynn had said nothing, had offered none of his usual stupid suggestions, had not even uttered that faint incredulous snicker which was the nearest he dared come to saying out loud that he thought they were a pair of outdated old farts.

Thrale knew he should have taken more notice, made enquiry – made very serious enquiry if need be – as to the state of Billy's mind. But he'd been tired after the drive, conscious of the need for rest before he set out for his rendezvous with Beck, conscious too of the closeness of Bridie, of the warm, exciting and excited smell of her flesh beneath her old woollen dressing gown.

He hadn't slept long but he'd slept deep. Bridie did that. She pursued every last pulse of pleasure along his veins, breathed on every last ember of desire in his flesh, till finally there was nothing left, just dead meat with his mind a blank screen from which all disturbing images had fled. He'd always been able to make do with very little sleep, but a couple of hours of this kind of unconsciousness saw him rise rejuvenated.

They'd breakfasted alone. Billy was out in the little garden, kicking a ball around with the boy while the transistor blared pop music from the top of a frozen water butt.

'He'll disturb the beasts,' he'd said.

'The beasts are all safe inside this time of year,' Bridie had laughed. 'And what would the local peasants expect from the mad townies but a lot of that kind of row?'

It had occurred to him how pleasant this was, sitting over their coffee together, chatting idly like any other couple in any other house. And then he had reacted against the soft sentimentality of the thought and stood up abruptly, saying, 'I'd best be going. I've a call to make.' But the feeling hadn't left him and it had been strong enough to mask again any curiosity as to Billy's cooperative behaviour, Billy's tuning of the radio to a non-news programme.

Now he knew. His first instinct was to head back to the cottage, pack up, put Billy – willing or not – into the boot, drive away. But that would mean another safe-house. Easy to arrange, but not without the old men in Dublin knowing. And they'd know already that his 'quiet' operation was making far too much noise. And when, as he certainly would, Oliver Beck contacted one of the Listeners again, they'd know Thrale had failed to keep his appointment with the man this was all about.

It wasn't the old men's anger he feared, it was their joy. A Thrale operation falling apart. And though he might blame Billy and make him pay the price, the old men would know where to lay their blame.

He turned onto the motorway approach road. Billy wasn't going to show his face, that was for sure. The police were looking for some building site worker who had probably had it away on his toes. They might do house to house in the village and all its new development, but they probably wouldn't bother with a cottage three miles out in the sticks.

He was, he acknowledged with that cold clarity of vision which had always kept his head and his hand steady in the most terrifying of situations, into excuses rather than reasons. Reasons decided what course of action you should follow. Excuses might sound just the same but they came after the decision.

He was heading north partly to protect his reputation, but mostly because he had the scent of Oliver Beck in his nostrils, and it had one thing in common with the scent of Bridie's body on heat – it was not to be denied.

He drove steadily northward, five to ten miles per hour under the limit, and reached the Woodall service area of the M1 in South Yorkshire at ten to twelve. The main restaurant complex was on the other side of the motorway. He crossed the bridge and descended into the foyer where the phones were. The one he was supposed to stand by was occupied, but after a couple of minutes the woman using it moved away. He examined her closely, decided it would be a pointless risk for Beck to have put someone in there to hold the phone for him, and moved in himself. Pretending he was making a call, he held the cradle depressed and waited for his instructions.

Twelve noon came and passed. After five minutes he began to feel uneasy. After ten, he reviewed the situation coldly.

Two possibilities. One was that Beck had been prevented from making contact. It wasn't worth speculating about possible reasons. The other was that Beck had deliberately not made contact. Here speculation ran rife, but one possibility headed the pack.

Suppose he was here because Oliver Beck wanted him to be as far away from Grazey Lane Cottage as he could get him?

His mind turned it round and round. From one angle it looked absurd. There was no way that Beck could have uncovered the boy's hiding place. No way. Then his heart twitched like a small fish that feels the bent pin in its palate. Beck's message had been for him personally. *Beck to Thrale*. How had he known? A not unlikely guess? Or a leak in the system? Or a direct sighting?

And if either of the last two . . . Suddenly he was looking at things from quite another angle and it no longer looked absurd.

Suppose he was here because Beck was planning a rescue attempt and wanted to get the man he most feared well out of the way?

He stared in cold, helpless fury at the phone. It was no use to him. Grazey Lane Cottage didn't have one. There were others he could ring of course. He could have reinforcements round there in half an hour. But not without the risk of drawing attention from curious locals already alerted by the murder hunt. And not without the certainty of the old men in Dublin drooling over another crack in the Thrale crystal.

No. His fears might be groundless. Or, if not, there was still Bridie, who had proved herself the match of many a man. And young Billy might be a Grade A idiot, but when it came to action, he had a proven track record.

In any case, he himself could be back there almost in the time it would take to raise assistance and get it in position. Whatever the reason, the bastard wasn't going to ring now.

He banged the phone back hard on the rest and set off at a trot up the stairs to the bridge.

Oliver Beck watched him go. Standing by his car with a small pair of field glasses he tracked Thrale's progress across the bridge, then he got into his car and started the engine. There was no need to hurry. Thrale had a three-mile drive north before he could turn and head back south. Carefully Beck slipped into the traffic. He drove steadily, using only the two inner lanes. After twenty minutes, he spotted Thrale in his mirror coming up fast in the outside lane. He let him get by, then he stamped on the accelerator and, smiling complacently at his own cleverness, let himself be hauled along to his kidnapped son.

# 4

Dog Cicero squatted on a mossy log under the trailing branches of a willow tree and waited.

He was forty yards from Grazey Lane Cottage. Between him and the building was a wedge of coppice badly in need of trimming, but at one point the lattice of twigs and branches left a small diamond of clear space through which he could see the front door. Thirty minutes earlier as he approached from the road he had heard a child's voice. Silence might have tempted him closer, but after hearing that unrepeated noise, he had not been able to take any risks. So here he sat, oblivious to the cold seeping slowly into his bones, unmoving, unblinking, waiting for one confirmatory glimpse.

He was not going to tell Jane Maguire that he *thought* he knew where her son was or that he *might* have heard his voice. He wanted to give her certainty.

His left leg suddenly raged into pain from cold and cramp. Still he did not move. If you can't keep still then move all the time, Endo had advised. But stillness is best. Then anything you do, picking up your cards, pushing out your chips, *anything*, gets them worried shitless.

But why suffer when there was no *them*?

There's always a *them*, said Endo.

The door opened.

A woman came out and stood on the threshold. It could be the woman he had met as Mrs Tobin but he wasn't one hundred per cent sure. That woman had been middle-class English with the poise, the facial set, the physical carriage, of her type.

This one had an air of animal wariness which still remained even as she relaxed and held her face up to the wintry sun and took in deep draughts of the wintry air.

247

Then she smiled, said something, stood aside, and through the door came a blond-haired youth, stooping low to avoid banging the head of the child who clung to his back.

Even now there was no positive identification, but it would be a coincidence beyond . . . then as the youth straightened up, the child threw back his head and laughed, and Dog forgot all about coincidences. This was Jane Maguire's son. He had seen and heard her laugh only once but this came unbearably close to a second time.

They moved out of sight now. He massaged his cramped leg and began to retreat through the copse to the road. His mind was already racing through methods of getting the boy out safely. But one image remained constant through the mental turmoil.

It was the look he imagined in Jane Maguire's face when he told her he'd found her son.

'Tinkerbell's on the move,' said Sergeant Stott, turning from the radio.

'Good,' said Tench. 'Seems you were right and two meant one. Who's tagging her?'

'Young Gill.'

'Tell him to keep her in sight. I've known them bugs fall off before now.'

Stott obeyed. They were sitting in what from the outside looked like a small removal van. Inside, it was a mobile surveillance HQ. It was cramped but Tench preferred it to taking over a room at the local station. He liked to keep the plods at arm's length unless he wanted to punch their silly heads. There were too many flapping ears beneath those pointy hats.

'Think it was Beck who made that call?' said the sergeant.

'No. Whoever it was, she'd met him recently to make the arrangement, and if it had been Beck, I doubt if she'd have put herself back near us.'

One of the three phones rang. A young woman picked it up, spoke softly into it, listened, then passed it to Tench.

'Captain Hook,' he said.

He listened, smiled, tossed the receiver back to the girl.

'Tommy, on your feet. Cynthia, my sweet, get onto young Gill and tell him I'll be coordinating from my car. When I give the word, I want him to close up and let her know she's being followed. She'll try to lose him. I want her to succeed.'

As they made their way to Tench's car, Stott said, 'You onto something, guv?'

'Could be. That call. I had Fred Harper checking out hotel registers in the area. Tinkerbell had to stay somewhere last night and I thought it might be interesting to find out if she'd made any calls, or taken any. Long shot and tedious, but Harper needs his nose held to the grindstone from time to time. Well, this time it hit bone and struck sparks. The Clareview Motel. No Maguire on their books, but there was a Miss J. Smith, and you know whose plastic paid the bill? My friend and your friend, DI Dog Cicero, suspended!'

They got into the car. Stott started it up while Tench made radio contact with Gill.

'Captain Hook to Wendy One, await my instructions,' he said. 'All right, Tommy, straight ahead, turn left when you hit the junction and I'll see if I can get this box of tricks working.'

He started fiddling with the knobs on the electronic bug decoder but all he got was a lot of static. Then the radio crackled and Gill's voice said urgently, 'Wendy One to Captain Hook, I've lost Tinkerbell. I say again, I've lost Tinkerbell.'

'I said, wait till I give the word,' Tench yelled into his microphone.

'She can't have heard you, guv,' said Gill. 'She went up on the pavement, cut up a lorry, jumped a light. She must've turned off and got a couple of blocks between us because I'm not getting a dicky on the detector.'

'You'll get more than a dicky when I see you,' retorted Tench. 'Out.'

He started poring over a street map.

'He's a cheeky young sod, that Gill,' said Stott.

'Remind me to kick his arse. Turn right, Tommy, then straight over the roundabout.'

'You reckon she's going back to this motel to meet Cicero?'

'We'll make a cop out of you yet, my son,' said Tench. 'Aha! There. Listen.'

A faint pulse began to sound, growing stronger.

'Seems you were right, guv,' said Stott. 'It'll give me great pleasure to get my hands on the bugger's collar!'

'Yeah? Well, it's a pleasure you'll have to defer. I want Dog running loose a bit longer.'

'Eh?'

'He's not rendezvousing with Tinkerbell to enquire after the state of her health,' said Tench patiently.

'You reckon he's onto something? Don't seem likely, guv,' said Stott doubtfully.

'You reckon? Listen, my son, that bastard without any help or encouragement has managed to stick his finger deeper into this pie than our whole team put together. It wouldn't surprise me in the least if old Dog had managed to dig up something interesting. So you behave yourself till I turn you loose, right?'

As they talked the signal had grown stronger.

'She's behind us,' said Tench. 'And there's the Clareview up ahead.'

'Shall I go into the car park?'

'No. If Dog's waiting for her, he'll be keeping a watchful eye. Turn in here and make like a customer.'

They turned into the car park of the superstore opposite the Clareview and took up a position which gave them a clear view of the motel.

The beep got louder.

Behind them Dog Cicero came out of the superstore entrance with a large carrier bag. It was the car number he spotted, not the occupants. The Branch had its own range of numbers. If a traffic cop checked one out via the police computer, he would be warned to stay clear. At some time in the past Dog had had occasion to glance down the complete list. Now they were all imprinted on his memory. He sat down on a low wall and opened his bag. His heart sank as he regarded the odd collection of items it held. He hadn't purchased according to a plan but had moved swiftly through the store, impulse buying. The nearest he had managed to real weaponry was a gardener's pruning knife and a child's water pistol which bore a distant resemblance to a Beretta Model 20. His final purchase had been a pair of tennis shoes. He removed his brown slip-ons which were fine for driving and the office, but not for action man. The tennis shoes fitted snugly and gave him a sense of buoyancy and athleticism. From the bag he now took a small aerosol can of black paint which the label assured him was a perfect match for small scratch repairs on most Ford models. The Branch vehicle was a Vauxhall and it was blue, but in the circumstances it didn't seem to matter.

A dirty white Metro came into sight, flashing to turn into the motel car park. He caught the glow of the driver's red hair and felt his heart lift up. Then he was moving swiftly forward.

The Branch watchers had spotted the Metro too and their engine was running. He walked casually past, turned, met Toby Tench's unbelieving gaze, then obliterated it with a haze of black cellulose paint across the windscreen.

Now he was nimbling across the carriageway, dodging between braking cars, leaving an audio-trail of blaring horns and swearing drivers. Jane was negotiating gingerly into a parking space when he pulled open the door and slid in beside her.

'Keep going,' he ordered.

She was startled but she obeyed without question, sending the Metro screaming across the car park and out of the far exit. After a couple of hundred yards they had to stop at lights behind a builder's pick-up. Dog opened the door, got out, went round the back of the car and stooped out of sight. The lights changed. He reappeared, and lobbed something into a pile of sand on the truck ahead as it edged forward and turned right.

'We go left,' said Dog, getting back in. 'No need to rush now.'

He smiled at her and she made herself smile back at him. It was not the faith of trust but the faith of necessity, he recognized that. But it was faith and for the moment it would do very nicely.

It was twenty minutes before Tommy Stott, peering waterily through the hole he'd smashed in the windscreen, came up behind the pick-up. The detector was beeping madly on Tench's knee. He switched it off.

'Oh, what a clever little Dog it is,' he said softly. 'Full of tricks. I wonder if he knows how to roll over and die for his country.'

'Do I stop him, guv?' asked Stott, nodding at the pick-up.

'Certainly. Can't have government property roaming loose across the country. You sort it out, my son, while I whistle up the local plods to get us a change of transport before we freeze to death. Then it's back to the magic box.'

He patted the detector.

Stott began flashing his headlights as he overtook the truck.

'You mean there's another bug?' he said.

'In her handbag. She'll be sending out more signals than a bitch on heat. All we've got to do is get in range, and then I've a feeling the whole bloody shooting match is ours.'

He put his hand on the sergeant's knee and squeezed reassuringly. But beneath the calm smiling face he felt such a rage of hate that had he been offered at that moment a choice between having Oliver Beck at his mercy or Dog Cicero, he would hardly have known which pleasure to opt for.

# 5

They sat in the car on the grass verge at the brow of a narrow country road. To a passer-by they must have looked like a pair of quarrelling lovers.

'No!' said Dog Cicero. 'No way.'

'He's my son,' cried Jane.

'Mother love may move mountains but it doesn't stop bullets,' said Dog. 'These people are armed and dangerous.'

'Then let's get some help that's armed and dangerous too.'

He sighed and said, 'I thought of that, naturally. If I call Denver, one of two things happen. Either, the area Task Force takes over and we could end up with a nice little siege with Noll as the main bargaining counter. Or, Tench gets in on the act. What he will want to do is nothing. He'll just be delighted to be back to where he was before, knowing Noll's location and sitting it out in the hope that Beck will hove into view.'

'So why did you contact me then? It must be because you daren't contact anyone else. So let me help you!'

'I contacted you because I need someone at my back with a car, not someone at my side with a black belt or whatever it is you've got. Two bodies trying to get near Noll will make twice as much noise as one.'

She glared at him, unconvinced, and he went on swiftly: 'Also I called you because you've a right to know, a right to choose, as long as you understand that the options don't include you getting in the front line. So what's it to be? I try it alone with you as back-up? Or I ring Denver and try to get him to set things up without reference to Tench?'

She hid her face in her hands. When she revealed it again, all anger had vanished.

'I'm sorry,' she said. 'You've done far more for me than I've any right to expect and all I can do is complain. My choice, you say? I choose you. So where do we start?'

'Right here,' he said.

He delved into his carrier bag, came up with a child's telescope, got out of the car and started to scan the countryside below. From here he could see the woodland through which he'd approached Grazey Lane Cottage earlier that day. The magnification wasn't great but enough to convince him nothing was moving down there. He snapped the telescope shut and went round to the driver's door.

'Move over,' he said.

'What's up? Don't trust lady drivers all of a sudden?'

'Just move,' he said harshly. But when he was behind the wheel he gave her his twisted smile and said, 'Sorry. I'm on edge.'

'I know all about edges,' she said.

He started the engine, moved forward till they picked up momentum, then slipped into neutral and coasted quietly down the slope.

Suddenly to Jane's horror he twisted the wheel sharply and ran the car at an apparently solid wall of undergrowth. Briars clawed the windscreen and scraped at the paintwork, then they were through and into a small clearing among close-pressing trees.

'Holy Mary!' she gasped. 'No wonder you wanted to drive.'

But he was out of the door and moving forward before the words were spoken.

In the cottage doorway Bridie Heighway said, 'What was that?'

'What?' said Billy, pausing in the game of football he was playing with Noll.

'Did you hear something?'

'Nothing. What did you . . .'

'Hush.'

They listened.

'I thought there was a car. A long way off. Then a crackling

. . . like brushwood.'

'I'll take a look,' said Billy.

He went inside and came out almost immediately, carrying an automatic.

'For Christ's sake, Billy!' said the woman, glancing at the boy who was looking at the gun with wide envious eyes.

'Are we going to play cowboys?' said Noll.

'Something like that,' said Billy Flynn.

'You come inside with me, Noll.'

'No. I want to play.'

'We'll play inside. And I'll see if I can find any more of that chocolate.'

'And you'll tell me a story?'

'Yes, I will. Billy, for God's sake, put that thing away till you need it.'

The youth slipped the weapon inside his jacket and moved forward into the woods.

Dog heard him coming before he saw him. Billy Flynn was a town rat. The streets were his jungle. Down alleys and entries he might flit unobserved, but out here he signalled his progress with every step.

Now Dog saw him. Saw and understood the hand hidden beneath the jacket. In his own hand the pruning knife was ready. He stood motionless behind the bole of a sycamore and willed the youth to come to him. To take him out here would cut the odds by half, always assuming that Thrale had not joined them. There'd been no car in sight on his last visit, and he couldn't see one now, but that wasn't the only reason he had for guessing that Heighway and Flynn were on their own. No. If Jonty had been in the cottage, he was sure that Billy Flynn wouldn't be wandering loose in the woods like the last of the Mohicans.

Another ten paces would bring him within striking distance. He didn't underestimate the problem Bridie Heighway would present. She was probably a more formidable opponent than Flynn. But with the youth's weapon in his hand and the element of surprise on his side, he felt confident he could cope.

Flynn stopped. If there was anything out here, he couldn't see it. And if it could see him, then out here was no place to be. Billy Flynn was arrogant, self-absorbed, but he wasn't stupid. He tried to focus those urban sensors which had so often saved him from walking into trouble in the Belfast shadows, but here all he felt was a general jumpiness which had more to do with nerves than threats. The sooner he was out of all this, the better.

He turned and went back to the cottage.

'Anything?' said Bridie.

'Not a thing,' he said, with aggressive scorn. 'Just you hearing things, that's all. Bad time of the month for you, is it?'

'Every time's been a bad time since they wished you on us, Billy,' she replied.

'Ha ha. Where's the boy?'

'Upstairs. In case of trouble.'

'That's great! If we ever do get trouble and it's not just your hysterical imaginings, it's down here in front of us we want the kid,' he snarled. 'He's our best protection!'

Suddenly, without quite knowing how it happened, he found himself back up against the wall with Bridie's face close to his and the cold barrel of his own gun pressing against his belly down the front of his jeans.

'*My* way, Billy,' she said, her breath warm on his face. 'And when Jonty's here, *his* way. But, and this is the last time of telling, we never do things *your* way. Understand? Or shall I squeeze this trigger and see if you keep your brains down there with the rest of your valuables?'

'For Christ's sake, are you mad or what?' he cried, not daring to push her away.

'I must be mad not to shoot,' she said, stepping back, leaving the gun tucked into his trousers. 'Now you watch the front, I'll watch the back.'

'For how long, for God's sake?'

'Till I decide there's nothing out there,' she said.

Dog watched Flynn return to the cottage then moved carefully back through the copse to the car. Jane Maguire hadn't moved.

'Sorry about that,' he said. 'I needed the car off the road to make sure we weren't spotted by anyone coming to the cottage. And I had to make sure we hadn't been heard.'

'You don't leave much margin for error,' said Jane, looking at the close-crowding trees. 'Had anyone heard us?'

'They'd heard something,' he said. 'The blond boy came out. Not close enough for me to make contact unfortunately.'

She looked at the knife in his hand and said, 'Would you have . . ?'

'If necessary,' he said. 'Wouldn't you?'

'Noll's my son,' she said simply. 'He's my reason for going on living. I'd do anything. But you . . .'

'I've elected him my reason for living too,' he said. 'It's a commodity I was growing short of. OK. I want you to sit here in the car watching and listening. Put it into reverse. Keep your foot on the clutch. First sound of any activity from the cottage, you turn the engine on. Three possibilities, progressively harder. One: I come running out of the wood with Noll. We get in the car. You don't talk or do anything, but get out of here backwards like a bat out of hell. Two: I come running by myself. Just the same. Go! No questions. Last, and hardest. You hear a noise. It could be anything. A shout. A gun. Glass breaking. Anything. You count up to a hundred, slowly. Then you take off by yourself. Or if you see anyone else but me coming, you stop counting and go. This is the most important. If I don't get Noll, it's no use coming after me. You've got to go for help. Do I make myself clear?'

'Yes.'

He regarded her doubtfully.

'Do anything else,' he said slowly, 'and you've probably killed all three of us. Me, yourself, and Noll. Trust me.'

'You men!' she burst out. 'You and your plans. Trust me, I know best! Is that all you can ever offer?'

He closed his eyes and his hand went to the frozen side of his face. When he looked at her again, his eyes were cold.

'I think maybe we're mistaking each other for two other people,' he said. 'Do what you think best.'

He reached into the back seat, picked up his plastic carrier bag.

Then he was gone.

She almost called after him, realized in time how stupid that would be, and slumped forward over the wheel. Then she sat upright, let in the clutch, found reverse gear, took hold of the ignition key, and stared fixedly ahead as though by will alone she would penetrate the woodland and draw her son safe home.

# 6

There was cover to within twenty yards of the cottage but after that, every approach was overlooked by at least one window.

Four sides. Two watchers. His mind assessed the odds. On the surface they looked evens, but they weren't. There's guys standing in line for soup 'cos they couldn't figger odds. So Endo Cicero.

Four sides. But he could only pick one. Two watchers. Meaning any one side could either be watched by Billy, or watched by Bridie, or not watched at all. So the odds on the side he chose being unwatched weren't even. They were two to one against.

Other factors. Four windows and a door at the front. Three windows and a door at the back. Two windows, one ground, one first floor at one side. One window, first floor at the other. A waste pipe emerging below window level and a small overflow pipe alongside indicated a toilet.

Defend your weaknesses. In this case, doors and ground floor windows.

Conclusion. The most unassailable side was the least likely to be watched. Odds? When you decide to go, fuck odds. So Dog Cicero.

He stood upright and walked steadily forward towards the side of the cottage with the single window.

Nothing happened. Which only meant that Billy wasn't at this side. He'd have shot him, no sweat. But Bridie might hold her fire, not out of female softness but because she'd be looking for a quieter solution in case he wasn't alone. Or in case he was, for that matter. Good odds, when you won either way.

Pressed against the rough stone wall, he waited. Nothing. He tested the down pipe. It seemed firmly anchored.

Hooking the plastic bag over his arm he began to climb.

Now he was totally vulnerable. He felt a sudden surge of exhilaration. There's only one thing to match winning the final pot and that's losing it, said Endo. You gotta watch that, Dog. Man can get hooked.

At times in the Army, he'd got close to the habit. Not since. When you didn't value your life, there was no kick in risking it. Now the kick was back.

But this wasn't the time for self-analysis. He was close to the window. Cautiously he peered in. As guessed, it was a loo. The window was far too small for him to get through, even if he'd been able to open it without detection. One-handed, he opened the bag. Sometimes impulse buying was better than all the shopping lists in the world. He reached in and took out an aerosol can of vaporized lubricant. It had a thin plastic tube attached to it for squirting the lubricant into awkward spots like key holes. He fixed one end to the nozzle and fed the other into the overflow pipe. Then he pressed the trigger till the aerosol was empty. He did the same with a second and third canister, reserving enough to impregnate a length of lint bandage thoroughly. One end of this he twisted into a wad which he then put into the pipe. Using a knitting needle as a ramrod he pushed it as far up as it would go. Then with a pair of pliers he crimped the pipe as tightly as he could without entirely cutting off the source of air.

Satisfied, he dropped lightly to the ground. The bandage dangled above his head. He took out a book of matches, flicked one into flame on his thumb nail, and touched it to the end of the bandage.

Flame ran up it and vanished into the overflow. There was a moment's pause, one of those year-long moments like that in which the eye sees but the mind refuses to register whether your last card is the right number and the right suit.

Then it came. Not an earth-shaking explosion but a gentle *whoof!* Hardly enough to shake the lavatory window. But in the cottage, with ears and eyes strained to detect an enemy, it would sound like a stun grenade.

He moved round the corner to the rear of the cottage. Front doors had Yale locks, but people who lived in the country didn't risk locking themselves out at the back.

He was right. The rear door opened to his touch and he stepped into a tiny old-fashioned kitchen with a blue-veined pot sink and brown stone jars on the shelves. In his left hand he held the water pistol, in his right the pruning knife. He realized he was counting slowly under his breath . . . fifteen, sixteen, seventeen . . . Jane Maguire would be counting too. At least he hoped to God she was counting! Had he given himself enough time? Plenty! If he wasn't out of the house and running back to the car in the space of one hundred slow seconds, he would be . . . his mind pushed the thought away, not out of fear but because it was too fascinating . . . twenty, twenty-one, twenty-two . . . he was through the kitchen door into a narrow passage alongside a steep flight of bare wooden stairs high kicking from a gloomy hallway with an elephant-foot umbrella stand to an even gloomier landing from which drifted smoke and the smell of burning and the sound of a child crying.

If Jane heard that, she would stop counting and start coming.

A woman's voice cried, 'Billy, for Christ's sake! Check downstairs!' and Dog stepped sideways, pressing close against the warped panels of the boarded stairway. Footsteps sounded, descending fast, leaping two or three stairs at a time. He reached up through the rickety rail, and grasped a flying ankle.

The result was spectacular. Billy went into a limb-flailing dive which ended when he crashed into the front door. His body spasmed for a second then went still.

'Billy!' screamed Bridie Heighway from the top of the stairs.

For a moment she was exposed, uncertain if Billy had fallen or been attacked. If he'd had a gun, Dog would have come round the foot of the stairs, blazing away. Now he could only hope she came down to look at Billy and gave him the chance for the same trick.

But she'd been Jonty Thrale's partner too long for such a risk. Her footsteps moved away. A door opened. Cautiously Dog moved forward. The only thing moving on the landing was smoke. His improvised bomb must have started a fire. He bent over Billy's body. The youth groaned. Dog dragged him onto his back, desperately looking for the automatic he'd seen in Flynn's hand in the woods. There was no sign of it either on his person or in the shadowy hallway.

He looked wryly at the water pistol. Perhaps it was the best weapon in an age when even money was plastic. He began to move up the stairs.

He'd only taken two paces when the swirling smoke on the landing parted and Bridie Heighway stood there. In her arms was the boy.

She screwed up her eyes to make him out.

'It's you,' she said, puzzled. She'd been looking for combat jackets, blackened faces, machine guns, not a tennis-shoed inspector with a small pistol. But it was held very steadily.

'It's me,' he said. 'You're not thinking of walking out behind the boy, are you?'

'And why not?'

'Because you know if he's in your arms they'll shoot your legs off and if he's on the ground, they'll shoot your head off.'

'Is that a fact? Well, it's nice to know I've still got options.'

He almost smiled. Then he said urgently, 'Think of the boy, Bridie. He's clinging to you because he's scared. Noll, will you come with me? Noll, shall I take you home?'

The boy looked towards him with huge, frightened eyes, then he tightened his grip on the woman's neck, buried his face in her shoulder and said in a muffled, tearful voice, 'Don't want to go . . . want to stay with you, Auntie Bridie . . .' then started coughing as the smoke caught his lungs.

'He trusts you,' said Dog. 'Do you really want him harmed? I don't just mean physically. Imagine your brains all over him . . . that could do damage that'd remain for the rest of his life.'

'Not to mention mine,' said the woman, patting the boy's

back. 'There, now, I'll not be leaving you, my little piglet. We'll be walking out of here together and the nice gentleman's not going to get in the way, is he?'

Dog felt a surge of despair. She was too close to lose now.

He said urgently, 'Bridie, listen. Put the boy down, and you can walk away from this safe and free. I'm alone, but it won't be long till this place is swarming. Fifteen minutes max, plenty of time for a woman of your talents to disappear. What do you say?'

She looked at him disbelievingly. He slipped the water pistol into his pocket, glad of an excuse to get it out of sight before she spotted what it really was.

'I mean it, Bridie,' he said. 'The boy's all I want.'

Perhaps it was his despair which persuaded her. He saw decision in her eyes. Then she started to set the boy down.

It wasn't easy. The only place the scared child wanted to be was in his 'auntie's' arms. She prised his fingers apart, murmuring reassurance. Dog watched with growing irritation. If Jane had moved quick, perhaps run into some of the police round Little Staughton . . . Bridie Heighway counted odds too, and the sound of a fast-approaching siren might throw her into reverse.

If he'd found Billy Flynn's gun, the wise thing would have been to shoot her now as she lowered the boy to the floor.

Would he have done it? Could he have done it?

'Hurry it up,' he urged.

She straightened up. 'Why am I trusting you?' she wondered.

'Because I've got an honest face?'

The words came out more savagely than he intended.

'Oh yes. That was Jonty, wasn't it? That makes it even odder. Is it the girl, then? You've still got a soft spot for red-haired colleens, is that it? If that's the case, then you're on the wrong side, Mr Cicero. You should be with us, trying to put that traitorous bastard Beck out of the way.'

Too late it dawned on him that she wasn't just idly passing the time of day with this provocative talk. It was for a purpose that she'd so totally engaged his attention.

His first thought was Billy. He half turned, drawing back his foot to kick the youth back into submission. But he was still far from fully conscious.

Then Bridie screamed, 'Jonty! He's armed!'

And now he turned fully, his hand dragging the plastic water pistol from his pocket.

A man was standing in the hallway beneath him. He wore a crumpled blue business suit and a homburg, and on his thin, unremarkable face was the melancholy expression of an insurance salesman about to remind you of your family responsibilities.

But it was a gun in his hand, not a policy.

'It's all right, Bridie,' he said. 'I don't think Mr Cicero's going to squirt us to death.'

There was another figure behind him. Tall, red-haired, wild-eyed.

She said, 'I'm sorry, Dog. I *was* going to go . . . then he came . . . I had to tell him, else he said he'd hurt Noll . . . Where is he?'

Dog glanced up the stairs. Bridie Heighway had swept the boy out of sight. To protect him? Or merely clearing the decks in case of action?

Jane followed the direction of his gaze and tried to push past Thrale but he swung his free arm savagely across her breast and snarled, 'Wait! If you please, Mr Cicero, will you drop that thing? It may be only a water pistol, yet I find it strangely distracting.'

Dog looked down at the piece of moulded plastic in his hand and shrugged ruefully.

'I knew I should have got the cap gun,' he said. And squirted a jet of household ammonia into Jonty Thrale's face.

The man's control was tremendous. The burning liquid hit him full in the right eye. He cried out once, turning his head away. The automatic he held wavered a fraction, then steadied. He squeezed the trigger. If Dog had stayed upright he must have been hit. But he had launched himself forward over Billy Flynn and hit Thrale's knees in a flying tackle.

He heard the gun's explosion, heard the unmistakable sound of a bullet excavating flesh, heard a shriek of pain, and did not know if it was his flesh, his cry, his pain. There was no time to find out. As Thrale was driven backwards, he was twisting to his left to keep his gun arm free. Dog thought, a man with a bullet in his body ought to be able to think at least as fast as a man with ammonia in his eye. The gun came crashing down on the back of his skull and waves of agony delivered the message that whoever got hit before, it wasn't him. He'd got hold of Thrale's gun arm now. He grappled it to his chest like a passionate lover, dropped his head to the taut and twisting hand and sank his teeth into the thumb's hard ball. Now it was Thrale's turn to cry out. And his cry brought Bridie Heighway running out of the bedroom where she'd deposited the boy and unearthed the old army revolver which she held unwavering in both hands. But there was nothing for her to shoot at for Jane Maguire came leaping over the struggling bodies in the hallway and blocked her passage down the stairs.

'Noll!' she cried. 'Where are you? What have you done with him, you bitch? What have you done?'

'Stand aside!' ordered Bridie, in a harsh, unfemale voice. 'Or I shoot.'

'Oh, I should, if I were you, I should!' said Jane, beyond reach of threat or reason. And she began to ascend.

The revolver held steady on her breast. Bridie Heighway had no thought for anything but Thrale struggling in the hallway below. Her finger tightened on the trigger.

Then a voice behind her said, 'Mummy'.

Distracted, Heighway turned her head – only for a second, but it was enough.

The supple, high-tuned muscles of Jane Maguire's long legs exploded her up the remaining stairs beneath the extended arms. She drove her fist into Heighway's solar plexus and as the woman doubled over, Jane rose to her full height, got her shoulder into Heighway's rib cage and heaved her backwards like a sack of coals.

Her triumph was Dog's disaster. His assault on Thrale's gun hand was close to success. Flesh had parted and he could taste blood. He bit harder, certain now the man must release his automatic very soon. Then a heel crashed into the back of his neck with a force that made him gasp with shock. Thrale wrenched his arm free, raised his bloody hand high and brought the butt of his gun down on Dog's head again and again. He tried to maintain his grip on Thrale's body but the blows were dissipating his strength like morning mist and he had no power to resist as the Irishman hurled him backwards.

The blow to his neck had been inadvertent. Bridie Heighway had come rolling down the stairs in a series of uncontrolled somersaults and her foot could as easily have hit Thrale as Dog. She lay stunned but she hadn't let go of her weapon. Now she raised her head, glanced back, saw that Thrale was now in total command of the lower battle, and turned her attention to the enemy above.

Jane Maguire was kneeling beside her son. The little boy was terrified by the noise and violence and the smoke, but he had no doubt where he wanted to be. He flung his arms round her neck in a grip which came close to strangling her, but she had no thought of complaint as she folded him in her arms and sank her face into his tangle of rich brown hair. Then she let her gaze drift down the stairs to see Bridie Heighway looking up at her, her face twisted with hate. Jane smiled. The world was full of terrors. But this moment's joy was, for this moment, more powerful than all these terrors put together.

Dog had passed beyond terror almost to acceptance. He lay back, all strength gone, and watched his death approach. Once before he had escaped this man. But death is not escapable. All death needs is patience. The best a man can hope for is to die in comfort, and he felt surprisingly comfortable. His right arm was resting on the elephant-foot umbrella stand and his head was reclining against something nice and soft. What was it? he wondered. He turned his head slightly and found himself looking into a wide, staring, unseeing eye.

Billy Flynn. That was where that first flesh-crunching bullet had gone. Poor Billy. So evil, yes. But so young.

There was something else about Billy he couldn't quite remember . . . a mystery . . .

But now the time was close for an end to all remembering . . . all mysteries . . .

Jonty Thrale had brought his automatic forward till the muzzle touched Dog's cheek on the frozen side of his face.

'It was me who did this, did you know?' said Thrale.

Dog regarded him with indifference. Man who gloats ain't thinking of the next pot, said Uncle Endo. Only this time there wasn't going to be a next pot. Like Billy Flynn, he was all played out. Billy Flynn . . . he remembered the mystery now. What had happened to his gun? Down the stairs . . . body flying through the air . . . gun flying through the air . . . then disappearing into the air! It wasn't possible . . . there had to be an answer . . . he was sure he could tease it out if only he had time . . .

But time was up. The gun had moved across to his good cheek.

'I always hated leaving a job half done,' said Jonty Thrale.

'Was she one of yours?' said Dog hoarsely.

He didn't want to know. He'd realized some time earlier how little it mattered. But he suddenly wanted that extra time. Resignation and acceptance might be a comfortable way to go, but not for a man taught to play cards by Endo Cicero, one time Poker Champion of the World, who'd lifted an ailing child in his arms and said proudly, 'This boy's going to make it. This boy's my nephew and he ain't got no dog in him.'

'Oh yes,' said Thrale, with slow delight. 'She was definitely one of ours.'

'You're probably a liar,' said Dog. 'But thanks for taking the time.'

And he put his hand into the elephant's foot, grasped Billy Flynn's gun, and shot Jonty Thrale twice in the stomach.

Bridie Heighway had brought her gun up to fix on Jane once more. Neither it nor her gaze wavered, but still she did not squeeze the trigger. She had learned many strange and terrible

267

things since some trick of her genes had intertwined her life so utterly with Jonty Thrale's. But she was not yet sure if she had learned how to shoot a woman she was sure she hated who had her arms around a child she was sure she loved.

Then the sound of the shots behind her temporarily postponed the problem.

She turned in time to see Thrale falling backwards, his face twisted with shock and pain.

'Stay still, Bridie,' said Dog. 'Drop the gun.'

Naturally she paid no heed but kept turning.

He would have shot her, he had no doubt of that. But he needed to get the gun out of the elephant's foot before he could manage that and his hand was tangled up with God knew what rubbish.

It was Jane who saved him again. The smoke on the landing was dense and choking now. The fire in the bathroom had burnt its way up into the attic and there was an explosion as it burst its way through the roof tiles and sent a tongue of flame licking into the cold night mist. Not even the threat of the gun could have kept her up there any longer. Clutching Noll tight in one arm she came down the stairs, and with her free hand chopped Heighway viciously at the base of her neck. The Irish woman sighed like a sated lover and collapsed with the slow grace of a stage swoon.

Dog looked up at Jane and tried a smile of love, of trust, of gratitude. But she wasn't looking at him. Her eyes were on the front door which was swinging slowly open till it came to a halt against the recumbent figure of Thrale, lying on his back with his hands clasped across his bleeding belly.

Cold mist drifted in to mingle with the swirling smoke. And now the vapour coagulated, took shape and substance, and became a man.

Dog looked at him in disbelief, then coughed a painful laugh.

'Where the hell have you sprung from?' he demanded. 'A priest is just what we need round here!'

But the bearded figure of Father Blake had no eyes for him.

His gaze was fixed on Jane Maguire.

Now she moved slowly forward, stepping over Dog without even looking down at him.

He heard her say, 'Oliver?', then she repeated it, certainly. 'Oliver!'

He wanted to believe she was talking about her son, but he knew she wasn't. She was face to face with the priest now and his arms went round her and round Noll, and the three of them held still for a long agonizing moment in a triangle of total exclusion.

Then the fire raging above sucked up this draught of new energy pouring through the front door and came exploding through the ceiling of one of the downstairs rooms, and for the first time, Dog saw as well as heard the flames.

'Quick, get out!' cried Blake/Beck. 'My car's up the lane. I'll take care of things in here. Hurry!'

Jane Maguire hesitated, looking at Dog. He wanted her to go. He wanted her to stay. He wanted above all to know how much she knew, how deeply he was betrayed.

Then Noll's terror at the flames burst out in a long cry of 'Mummy!' and she turned and vanished through the door.

Beck stooped over Jonty Thrale. Interesting rescue priorities he has, thought Dog, struggling to rise and finding the pistol whipping he had received had damaged the link between his brain and his muscles.

Then he realized Beck's priorities had nothing to do with rescue.

He straightened up with Thrale's automatic in his hand. Deliberately, he put it to the Irishman's head and squeezed till the magazine was empty.

Blood, bone and brains fountained out and, as if excited by this rival destruction, the fire came roaring through the kitchen ceiling and sent its red tongues licking into the entrance hall.

Dog was on his feet, moving towards Beck. Or perhaps he was moving towards the door. Whatever, Beck took it for menace, and lashed him back with a blow to the head from the empty gun. He fell across Bridie Heighway, saw Beck step forward as if to finish the job, saw him hesitate as a sound of distant bells drifted through the door, saw him turn and run.

Once more Dog rose. Something very serious was happening in his head. Whole areas of his body seemed totally disconnected from his mind. His right arm and right leg swayed in and out of control as if not yet decided whether to commit themselves wholly to the mutiny. All he wanted was to get away from this heat, to see the sky again. But as he began to crawl towards the door, something stirred and moaned beneath the pressure of his weight. It was Heighway, still unconscious from the power of Jane's blow.

He shrieked at his limbs with the voice of his old RSM, and muscles that a moment ago had hardly got the strength to move his own body to safety now began dragging the woman's, inch by painful inch. The heat was tremendous. Only the solid stone walls and the flagged floor saved him, giving the fire nothing to get a purchase on. The bells were louder now, but whoever was coming on their peal would be too late. His mind was computing odds. Without Heighway, he could probably get evens; with her, he'd be lucky to get eight to five dog. But they were his kind of odds. Hadn't Uncle Endo said so? No use giving underdog odds against a kid who ain't got no dog in him. They just don't mean a thing!

The door was close now. He knew now he was going to do it again. But how much longer could he go on hobbling, crawling, slithering away from death?

How much longer did he want to go on?

That was a question to be set aside for later . . . like the other question, the one about Jane Maguire . . . Now he just wanted to lie and look up at the grey uncaring sky. It had started to snow. The bells sounded louder and louder. Soon it would be Christmas, the children's time . . .

He closed his eyes, but his mind stayed full of snow and bells. He shook his head violently, crying out at the pain, but he kept on shaking it till snow and bells ceased together.

# Part Five

Part Five

Parslow said, 'How could you do this to me, Dog? I took care of you, spoke up for you. There were plenty who didn't like you, you must have known that. Man with your background . . . and you didn't try to be liked, did you? But I went out on a limb for you, and this is how it ends . . .'

Dog Cicero looked at him curiously. Did he really believe all this? Then he turned his curiosity inwards, and wondered if perhaps there was not something believable there after all.

He tried to lift his head and winced at the pain which still whispered in slow swirling currents beneath the oil slick of drugs.

'Eddie, I'm sorry . . . Is there any news?'

'There's going to be an enquiry, naturally. You'll be dismissed from the Force, there's no doubt of that. And there'll probably be criminal charges. The papers are onto it and there've been questions in the House and the Branch want to throw the book at you . . .'

Dog shook his head gently. A busted flush is like a busted skull. Shake it any which way you like, you ain't going to get nothing but grief. Endo. Or was it Endo? He sometimes suspected he'd got into a habit of authenticating his own half-baked apophthegms by ascribing them to his uncle.

He said, 'I meant, news of . . . Beck.'

He couldn't bring himself to mention her name.

The fire brigade and the police had found him unconscious outside the charnel house of Grazey Lane Cottage. They hadn't come there because of any startling piece of detective work but because a neighbouring farmer had spotted the smoke and dialled 999.

It wasn't till Dog recovered consciousness an hour later that a true picture of events could be put together. By that time Oliver Beck and his family had vanished completely. With air- and seaports jammed for the Christmas exodus, they had probably slipped out of the country with no bother.

'News of Beck? What do you expect? A postcard?' snapped Parslow. 'All our fault, of course. The whole fiasco. All the blame dumped on us, except what's spilled over onto Northants.'

'Blame?' said Dog. 'All right, yes . . . but surely with Thrale and Flynn dead, Heighway in custody, not to mention a murder case cleared up, there has to be some credit . . .'

'Oh yes. There's credit,' said Parslow bitterly. 'And can't you guess who's got it? Your chum Tench and his wild bunch, that's who. You've a lot to answer for, Dog. A hell of a lot!'

There was a limit to the crap even a man staked out on a dunghill could take.

As Parslow made for the door, Dog said faintly, 'Eddie'.

'Yes?'

'In case I don't see you again. Happy New Year.'


New Year came and went. Dog didn't celebrate. He would have discharged himself from hospital if the neurologist hadn't warned him sternly that he wasn't yet out of danger from his severe head wounds. The threat of death wouldn't have stayed Dog. The threat of vegetabilization did. So he rested quiet in his bed, a model patient, shuffling and dealing a pack of cards, charting his recovery in the dexterity of his fingers and the accuracy of his memory.

Tench came to see him, flushed and jovial like the Spirit of Christmas Present, bearing a bunch of red roses and a basket of green grapes.

'Still playing with yourself, my son?' he said amiably. 'You look well. Have you out of here in no time!'

'And out of the Force too, I hear, Toby,' said Dog.

'You wouldn't want to stay, would you?' said Tench.

'I like to make my own decisions,' said Dog, dealing five cards.

Tench turned them up. A royal.

'So I see,' he said. 'Well, maybe we can do something there.'

Dog eyed him coldly. This was a different tune from the one that Parslow had said the Branch was singing. He slipped the cards back into the pack, shuffled, cut, dealt again. Tench turned them up again. It was the same hand.

'Clever,' said Tench. 'That Oliver Beck's clever too. Only he plays cards with people. Makes them disappear. You've got to admire him, Dog.'

'Why?'

'Just think about it. He must've been planning the big drop-out for yonks. I mean, even the thick Micks are going to notice they're three million light in the end. But suddenly he finds he's got himself a family to disappear too. Does he panic? No. He's got his own little hidey hole all set up by now, but he doesn't want to risk taking Janey and the kid directly there. No way he can fake all three deaths, and a trio on the move leaves too big a trail. So he uses her to authenticate his own demise, leaves her completely in the dark about his destination just in case anyone gets to her, and sets up this other cover so he'll be able to get access to her whenever he thinks the time is ripe.'

'The Blake scam, you mean?'

'That's it.' Tench shook his head admiringly. 'Over three years ago it started. He must have pumped Janey for details of her family, and every time he made one of his little trips across the pond, he'd divert to see Mrs Maguire and chat about her brother, the priest. There is a Father Blake who does the job he claimed, a big, bearded fellow, so his cover went really deep. And when our lot and the Micks started sniffing around Janey's connections after the drowning, who was going to pay any attention to a priest who'd been a friend of the family for years? Brilliant!'

The cards were flying in Dog's fingers, expanding and contracting like a squeeze box.

He said, 'Did she know?'

He'd asked a similar question of Thrale. Then it hadn't mattered any more. Now . . .

'Know he was IRA, you mean? Or that he was coming for her at Christmas? Who can tell, Dog? Who can tell?' said Tench, almost sympathetically. 'All we can assume is he was planning to contact her and the boy during their Christmas visit to Northampton. Only, when he met you at the old lady's that day, suddenly it was a new ball game. He was up shit creek and he stuck to you, Dog, 'cos you were the nearest thing he could find to a paddle. Good instinct as it turned out, even if you did lead him into that farce at the quarry. He struck out on his own after that, somehow psyched Thrale into leading him to the cottage. Clever, that. Any sod who can psych Jonty Thrale gets my vote for cunning bastard of the month. But he only comes out equal first with you, Dog. My God, I wish I could have got you on my team! But maybe it's not too late, eh?'

Here it comes, thought Dog.

'What do you want, Toby?' he said.

'What do you mean, old son?'

'There's no such thing as a free bunch of grapes,' said Dog.

'These grapes are seedless, my boy,' said Tench. 'Slide down a treat, and nothing left to show you've had 'em, know what I mean?'

'Tell me.'

Tench pulled his chair closer to the bedside.

'No fooling you, is there, Dog? All right, here's the pitch. You'd think my guvnor would be well pleased with me for smashing the Thrale cell, wouldn't you? But he's a hard man to satisfy and all he can say is corpses can't talk, not even Irish corpses.'

'You've got Bridie Heighway,' said Dog.

'Yeah. But what have we got her for? Kidnapping? There's no evidence with that red-headed tart long gone. We've got her tied in with most of Thrale's ops, but it's all circumstantial, and as Thrale's not going to come up for trial now, we can't even look for a spin-off result, can we? Time was when I'd have typed out a full confession, stuck a Sterling up her fanny and invited her to sign. But an admission's not good enough any more, not without AV support and a deposition from the Virgin Mary. And I doubt if Bridie would have signed anyway. She's a hard nut, that one. But Beck now . . .'

'What about Beck?'

'Well, he's travelling heavy now, isn't he? Woman and a kid pin you down in all kinds of ways. If we can find out where he is, he's ours.'

'Time it takes for extradition, he'd be drawing his pension, even supposing he's somewhere that's got a treaty with us.'

'Extradition? Who gives a fuck about extradition? Christ, if we bring this guy to trial, best we can hope for is a five stretch on what we've got on him. No. What we want is not him inside, but what's inside him. In his noddle. Supergrass of the century, he'd be. And he's there for the squeezing once we can track him down.'

Dog said, 'You mean, we tell him we'll leak his whereabouts to the IRA unless he cooperates, is that it?'

'Bang on. Offer he can't refuse, wouldn't you say?' said Tench, with jovial complacency. 'And this is where you might be able to help us, Dog. You spent a lot of time with him, OK, I know he was Blake then, but maybe he said something which, looking back and knowing what you do now, might give us a pointer. I know you, my son. Every last syllable he spoke will be fixed in your bonce. And the girl too. You got pretty close to her, didn't you? Anything she might have let slip. Just give us it all verbatim, my boy, and we'll go over it with a fine tooth comb. Though maybe we won't need to. Maybe you've got a scent already, Dog! You're the talk of the Branch, I tell no lie, the way you sussed things out all on your tod. We'd be glad to have you aboard, all of us!'

He paused. Dog had closed his eyes. Only the cards in his hands still moved.

Then he said, 'Down and dirty, Toby. If I help, if I *can* help, I get to stay a cop, no criminal charges, no disciplinary hearing even?'

'You help me out on this one, Dog, and I think I can even guarantee a promotion in a few months once the dust has settled,' said Tench. 'Do we have a deal? What have you got?'

Dog smiled and dealt a hand.

'Let's see what you've got first of all, Toby.'

Slowly he turned up the cards. Two, three, five, seven, eight, every suit.

'Well, what have we here? All rags, Toby. A real bag of shit. And you're trying to bluff me off the pot with that! Forget it. You have to be desperate even to think of trying this game, old son!'

Tench sat very still for a while, and all his jollity drained from him.

Finally he stood up.

'You're a fool,' he said. 'I've always wondered how anyone so fucking clever can be so fucking stupid. You're finished, Dog. You must know that. Out of the Force, that's for certain. And if I've got anything to do with it, it won't end there. You've broken the law, my son. You've aided and abetted criminals to evade justice, you've obstructed police enquiries, you've illegally accessed and misused confidential security files, you've assaulted one of my officers . . . Oh, I reckon we can close the door on you for a couple of years at least, old son.'

He turned to leave.

Dog said, 'As long as I don't have to share a cell with Tommy Stott.'

Tench froze.

'Not that they won't be falling over themselves at the Scrubs to be bunking down with a good-looking boy like Tommy,' said Dog.

'What the hell are you talking about?' snarled Tench, spinning round.

'They had a pipe into your section,' said Dog. 'Stands to reason. Thrale knew things. Has to be Tommy Stott. I'll give you chapter and verse if you like, but there's a simpler test. If you want to know the time, ask a policeman, and if he looks

278

at a Cartier watch, you can be sure he's bent.'

'You're living in the past,' said Tench, recovering. 'Anyone can get a five thou Swiss watch for a pony these days, long as you don't mind it being made in Hong Kong.'

'It's real. Real as his Gaultier labels. I can tell,' said Dog. Then he frowned. 'So can you, Toby. Let's have another look at this flop before I bet.'

He thought a moment then smiled.

'You knew!' he said. 'Of course. That explains a lot. Tommy was only feeding Thrale what you wanted fed to him. He was doubling, in other words.'

'Well done, Dog. You've got there,' applauded Tench. 'I admit everything. It was a set-up to fool the Micks. So where's that leave you, old son? With egg on your face, as per usual.'

His mockery didn't quite ring true.

Dog smiled and said, 'Now I've got it. OK, it *was* a set-up, but I reckon it was a private arrangement, not one with your bosses' official seal of approval.'

'Now why should I want to do anything crazy like that?'

'First, it put you and you alone on the inside lane, not having to share any info with the rest of the Branch. Second, it probably meant you didn't have to be too choosy what info you passed to the Irish. In fact, knowing you, Toby, I wouldn't be surprised if you'd deliberately nobbled some of your oppos' operations if they looked like getting too much credit for them. And thirdly, which explains Tommy's timepiece, not going through official channels means you and your boy friend get to keep the IRA sweet money!'

He could see that each of his inferences hit home.

But Tench was an old pro, well versed in riding the storm, covering up till his chance to counter came.

'Good try, Dog,' he said. 'Pity your credit's so low just now. The more you badmouth me, the deeper the shit's going to pile up over you. Do yourself a favour. Keep your head down and your mouth shut and maybe you'll get off with a suspended sentence, OK?'

'Now that's big of you, Toby,' said Dog. 'Only I wasn't really thinking of trying to convince the authorities, was I? Like you say, who's going to listen to me, unless I've got absolute evidence?'

'I'm glad you've still got some sense left . . .' began Tench, but Dog interrupted.

'No. It was a *real* question, Toby, not rhetorical. Who's going to listen? I'll tell you. A lot of big ears in Dublin and in Belfast, that's who. They'll put your Tommy on the same list as Oliver Beck, men who've fooled them out of hard cash. And we know how they like to deal with people like that, don't we?'

'What are you trying to say, Dog?' said Tench softly.

'I just want to be sure you're joking about these criminal charges,' said Dog. 'So what's it to be, Toby? Me walking free, or Tommy Stott not walking at all? Take your time. I'm curious to see if there really is another person in this world you care about.'

There was. The pain in Tench's eyes told him that, though probably most of it came from having to acknowledge such a weakness. But one thing you had to give the man, he didn't mess around when the cards were down.

'All right,' he said. 'You've got it. No charges, no trial. But you're out of the Force, no way will I fix that.'

Dog shrugged and nodded. There was no pain. He said, 'I was going anyway.'

'Yeah. If I were you, I'd keep going, Dog. As far as you can get.'

'Oh, I shall,' said Dog Cicero. 'I shall.'

# 2

The old man was thin to the point of emaciation. The tee shirt
he wore hung so loosely on his narrow rib cage that its inscription
THE CHAMP was almost unreadable in the folds. But his eyes still
shone bright in the wrinkled olive face and his step as he came
across the room was steady, though slow.

'Dog? Is this really you? At last you've come to see me after
all this time! Come here, let me be sure you're real.'

He folded Dog in his arms, ran his hands over his back and
shoulders, pushed him away and put one hand up to his frozen
face, touched it lightly with his fingertips.

'Hey, they did good work. At your father's funeral, it still
looked like old Scarface had just climbed out of the grave, but
now . . . OK, maybe it don't move so good, but that's no
disadvantage when you're trying to finesse a pot with a pair of
deuces.'

'Uncle Endo, it's great to see you,' said Dog Cicero, with
warm affection. 'And you're looking very fit.'

'Fit? You think that, maybe you should think about a guide dog.
Vincent, no need to stand there looking menacing. This is him,
my nephew, Giuliano, known as Dog. I gave him the name and
you know why?'

'Because he's got no dog in him,' said the man called Vincent.
He it was who had escorted Dog from the hotel lobby to the
penthouse suite after a long telephone consultation. He wore a
soberly expensive suit and horn-rimmed bifocals and could have
been a banker, except that bankers, in Britain anyway, rarely had
perfect tans, an athlete's muscle tone, and a Benelli B76 tucked
under their left armpit.

He smiled now as he took Dog's hand and shook it.

'Welcome to Vegas, Dog. We've heard a lot about you from

Endo over the years. Glad you finally made it here.'

There was a hint of reproach. As if he was saying that an old man shouldn't be kept waiting so long for a visit from his favourite nephew.

Endo heard it too and clearly didn't like it. He was a man who would make his own reproaches.

'OK, Vincent,' he said. 'We'll catch you, later, huh? Dog and me have got a lot of talking to do.'

'Sure. Nice to meet you, Dog.'

He left. Endo said, 'Take no notice of Vincent. He gets a bit over-protective, like I'm in my dotage or something.'

'He's obviously wrong there,' smiled Dog. 'But he's right. I should have come earlier.'

'But you didn't, worrying like you musta done about the company I keep. No need to look embarrassed! All the boasting I've done about my marvellous nephew over the years, you don't think I ever let on you'd become a cop!'

The two men laughed together, then Dog said, 'No need to worry any more, Uncle Endo. I quit.'

'Yeah? Well, me too. This is a legitimate concern except maybe for a bit of laundering in the casino. What are we standing here for? Come and sit down.'

He led the way through into a long, cool room with a mosaic floor, a high frescoed ceiling, and windows with old-fashioned wooden shutters. The walls were hung with *settecento* paintings which to Dog's untutored eye looked genuine, as did the classical busts and assorted statuary displayed on plinths about the room.

'You like it?' said Endo, observing him keenly.

'It's fantastic,' said Dog.

'Fantastic? Yeah, that's the word,' said Endo. 'A real fantasy. I always told myself ever since I came to this country, if I got rich I would go back home and buy myself one of those fancy villas, a palazzo even. But when push came to shove, I didn't want it. I went back on a visit, and it was OK, but I knew it wasn't for me. Too far from any real action, know what I mean?

Then I thought, what the hell, in Vegas they got everything, Caesar's Palace, Circus-Circus, Aladdin's, the Sahara, you name it, we've got it. So why shouldn't I indulge myself with my own custom-built palazzo? Sit down. Let me fix you a drink. What'll it be?'

'A glass of Barolo would be perfect, if you have one,' said Dog gravely.

The old man chortled.

'Still them good eyes, Dog! Still taking everything in, looking for the best angles! If I've got one!'

He went to a distant corner where, half hidden by a huge porcelain lamp, stood an open bottle of Barolo.

Returning with two brimming glasses, he said, 'And now let's talk.'

Talk they did, for more than an hour, mainly of the old days; of Dog's childhood which the old man, despite the distance separating them for most of their lives, seemed to recollect better than Dog; of Endo's early adventures in the New World, and above all of cards; of famous pots, of towering triumphs and deep-plunging disasters, of players – the great, the eccentric, the rash, the cautious, the successful, the broken – and at some point a deck of cards appeared on the table between them and they started playing their own version of seven card stud called Cheat 'Em, in which anything went, and the only rule was you didn't get caught. The old man's fingers weren't what they used to be, and Dog let several blatant substitutions pass till finally he said, 'OK, I've got you this time'.

'You think so,' said the old man. 'So what have I got and why shouldn't I have it?'

Dog studied Endo's show cards. A pair of red fives, deuce of clubs, ace of spades. His own show was king of spades, six of clubs, and two aces, clubs and diamonds.

'You're guessing you'll have to beat a house,' he said. 'Could be aces up, so you'll need a four which means you've got yourself the other two fives in the hole, only I stacked the five of clubs two hands back along with the king of diamonds, king of spades, ten of hearts, eight of hearts, six of hearts, four of diamonds and trey of diamonds.'

'So you're calling me. You want to put money?'

'As much as you like,' said Dog.

Slowly the old man turned up his hole cards. They were rags, not a five in sight.

'You crafty sod,' exploded Dog. 'You let me see you fiddling the cards so I'd have to call you.'

Endo laughed with real pleasure.

'Fingers ain't what they were, Dog, but like I always told you, nothing's so bad you can't make use of it, if you look at it right. Now why don't you tell me what brings you here?'

As always the old man had got it right. Through the talk and the cards they had got past the awkwardness of long separation and rediscovered in each other those ties of family, of thought, of affection which bound them so close together.

Dog said, 'Remember when you saw me in hospital after *this*.' He touched his cheek.

'I remember.'

'You said then, did I want you to find the man who did it? I said what would be the use of that? It wasn't a man, it was a madness, and all I wanted was to get as far from it as I could.'

'I remember.'

'But if I'd said, yes, find him, you could have done?'

'Maybe,' said Endo, his keen brown eyes never leaving Dog's face. 'I'd have certainly tried. Not me personally, you understand. I ain't equipped to be no avenging angel. But I got friends, influence.'

'That's what I reckoned. Well, I want to find a man now.'

'Hold on, Dog,' said Endo urgently. 'I ought to tell you, I put out feelers among my people then, never mind what you said, I was so mad on my own account. Only the word came back, they were sympathetic with me in my grief, but there was no way they could justify starting a vendetta with the Shamrocks over a guy who wasn't one of their own and wasn't even dead! I could see their viewpoint. Things won't have changed. And

284

that trail's ten years old . . .'

'Uncle Endo,' interrupted Dog. 'It's not that man. I found him myself. Or rather he found me. Yes, he's dead. But it wasn't a vendetta killing. Just a necessity. No, this is another man. And I want to find him for another reason.'

'So tell,' said Endo.

As briefly and as unemotionally as he could, Dog told the story. Endo listened without interrupting and when Dog had finished, he poured another two glasses of wine.

Then he said, 'This woman had a choice and she went with him?'

Dog said, 'Her son had been kidnapped. There were three IRA killers in the cottage. She knew there were plenty more where they came from. What kind of choice was that?'

'It still doesn't mean she's not where she wants to be.'

'All I want is the chance to ask her myself,' said Dog.

Endo considered, then nodded twice.

'OK. OK.'

'You really think you can find him?' said Dog, suddenly reacting into scepticism now his uncle had agreed.

'Not him maybe. People are hard to find,' said Endo. 'How much do you say he looted from the Shamrocks?'

'Three million, I heard.'

'Dollars?'

'Pounds.'

Endo whistled. 'That's some pot. That's much easier to find. The days of gumshoes and hound dogs are over. Now it's all done in bank computer rooms. They'll find him. But it'll cost, Dog. This ain't no favour anyone's doing me for free.'

Dog shrugged.

'You find him, *he* can pay. He's got the money.'

Endo laughed so much he almost spilt his wine.

'Dog, you're a chip off this old block! Wait here.'

He left the room and Dog leaned his head back in the deep armchair and closed his eyes. He felt a deep sense of relief. Without Endo's help, he was lost. Nothing that Blake/Beck had said had given him any clue as to where the man was hiding, and he had found himself totally barren of intuitions. Tench had been bidding for a dead hand.

He opened his eyes and for the first time really took in the ceiling paintings. They filled four panels and were a classical depiction of the four seasons, except that each panel was also a playing card, with spring a diamond, summer a heart, autumn a club, and winter a spade.

'You like it? My own design,' said Endo. 'Life's a gamble, that's the message, and the only loser is the guy who won't play. Dog, I can set the wheel spinning, but this thing will take some time. Can't have you sitting around wasting your life, so I thought, what's best to do with the boy?'

'And what did you come up with?' asked Dog.

Endo went to the window and pressed a button which slowly unfolded the wooden shutter to give a view over the garish Vegas skyline to the shimmering desert.

'You could play cards,' he said.

'What? Here? In your casino?' said Dog.

'Hell, no! That's for the tourists. Besides, I don't want you robbing me in my own backyard. No, I was thinking, there's a real high-rolling game goes on downtown, what we call Glitter Gulch. I used to sit in there pretty often, but lately I've been losing my edge, not much, but enough not to be on top, and when that's where you've been, that's what you're used to. You, though, Dog, you remind me of me twenty years ago when I was still the Man.'

'Uncle Endo!' protested Dog. 'I haven't played competitive poker in years, and never then for real money. This game, you'd need what? A couple of grand to buy in? I don't have that sort of money.'

'A hundred grand. And yes, you do. Here, this gets you two hundred k's worth of credit.'

He fluttered a piece of paper onto the table in front of Dog.

'I can't take this, Uncle,' protested Dog. 'I don't have the nerve to play for this kind of money.'

'Man who's got the nerve to come here asking help to find his fancy woman's got the nerve for anything,' observed Endo, smiling to take the edge off his comment.

'But what if I lose it all?'

'In that case,' said Endo, 'like you said before, that rich friend of yours can pay, can't he?'

Dog shook his head, then began to laugh. There was nothing else to do.

He tucked the paper into his pocket, picked up the deck from the table, shuffled, made a deliberate mess of it and scattered cards all over the floor.

'OK,' he said to Endo. 'You win. Let's play cards.'

# 3

'Life is either comedy or tragedy or soap,' said Oliver Beck.

'And what's ours turned out to be?' asked Jane Maguire.

'I won't know till I've seen the end.'

'You mean this isn't it? I thought we'd ridden off into the sunset and opted for happiness ever after.'

She made a gesture which took in the long white villa before which they were sitting, the pool terrace below where Noll played with his Brazilian nursemaid, the steep gardens which cascaded in a gaudy torrent down to a granite balustrade, beyond and far beneath which sighed the long blue swell of the sea.

Ignoring her irony, Beck said, 'You're right. You'll not find anything more like Paradise this side of Eden.'

'You think so? OK. So we've climbed back into the Garden. Question is, can we stick the apple back on the tree?'

Now he frowned. She thought, he's lost most of his Peter Pan quality. Perhaps masquerading as a middle-aged priest dowsed the magic. In repose, he now looked his age, in anger a decade more. But his smile still had a rejuvenating charm, and catching her close study of his face, he conjured up a smile and reached out to squeeze her hand.

'Give it time, honey,' he said. 'That's what we agreed.'

'It's been six months.'

'Six months,' he laughed. 'That's a pig's fart in a Mick's memory, you of all people should know that. They're still working off quarrels that started centuries ago. I mean, give it a year at least, maybe two. Main thing is, Noll's happy.'

It was the one button he could always press, the one analgesic he could always pop into her mouth. She knew he was doing it, but was helpless to stop him. She followed his gaze now to where the little boy was chattering away to Maria. Already his speech was laced with Portuguese words. When Jane had bridled at the notion of a 'nanny', Oliver had coldly asserted he wanted someone with Noll one hundred per cent of the time. Jane couldn't be expected to provide that degree of cover, and even if she did, it wouldn't help Noll if he got smothered by too much maternal attention. As for the Portuguese thing, where was the harm in Noll growing up bilingual? The girl, Maria, had been properly trained in child management and she came from an educated background. What Noll picked up from her would be all for his benefit.

'If we stay here,' Jane had said.

'Where were you thinking of going?' he'd replied.

That had been shortly after they arrived and her words had been weightless, a feeble counterblow to his heavy reasoning. She was then still bobbing mentally and emotionally in the turbulent afterwash of those dreadful December days back in England, and she had no idea yet what she truly felt about life in this place with this man.

He had been all patience and consideration, she had to give him that. She had her own room. He came to her one night soon after their arrival and she accepted him because of what they had been to each other, and still were, and also because her body wanted him. Physically it had been as mind-blowingly explosive as ever, but afterwards, when the dust began to settle, she found the same granite doubts and reservations still standing there.

He had said nothing then. The next night he came again. This time the thoughts were not pushed back so far, but for him the experience must have been indistinguishable from their old ecstasies, for later he said in the voice of a man who expects no opposition, 'Tomorrow we'll move you into my room'.

'No,' she said, without hesitation. 'I want a room of my own.'

Then, because she didn't want to leave it to him to choose whether this was the time or the place for confrontation, she got out of bed and put on the light and, wrapping her robe around her long beautiful torso still reverberating from the pleasure of his caresses, she said, 'In case there's still any doubt, Oliver, I wasn't following your plan. I ran away, and if you'd simply made contact with me in England, I'd have told you to go to hell.'

'Yes. I'd worked that out,' he said.

'So you know I'm here because I needed a safe place for Noll and there was nowhere else to go.'

'I hope that's an over-simplification, but I understand what you're saying,' he replied calmly. 'You think I deceived you.'

'I *know* it!' she said fiercely. 'You left me ignorant. Exposed.'

'I left you innocent and safe,' he snapped back. 'At least so I thought. I wanted you to believe it was all about money I owed, not money I had, so anyone close-questioning you would pretty soon realize you were in the clear. And I left pointers to a Swiss account that no one was going to prise open in a hurry. They'd all reckon the three mill was safely stowed in there, and Swiss bankers have a religious objection to giving up money which, in the absence of any legitimate claimant, they've come to regard as their own!'

'So what went wrong?' she asked.

'God knows,' he said. 'For some reason, Dublin didn't buy the drowning story. I knew they'd be suspicious but I really thought I'd got it tamper proof. Look, I'm not doing any accusing, but maybe something you said . . .'

'So it's going to be my fault after all,' she exclaimed. 'Noll being kidnapped and terrorized and nearly killed . . .'

'I didn't say that!' he said harshly. 'But it can't have been easy doing that acting job. You're no Bridie Heighway!'

'No, I'm not,' she said. 'But I was convincing. Oh yes, I was surely convincing! They had to sedate me after I identified your body, did you know that? And I genuinely needed it, that's how convincing I was!'

'Janey, hon, I'm sorry,' he said, starting to get out of bed.

'No! Don't come near me,' she protested. 'Let me tell you why I needed sedating. It wasn't the state of that poor man's corpse, though Christ knows, that was bad enough. It was when they mentioned his dental records. I nearly fainted then. We hadn't thought of that, I told myself. The game's up! Then they went on to say that they'd checked your record and the drowned man's teeth matched. That's when I really flaked out.'

'But why? I told you I'd fixed everything,' said Beck.

'You told me that this poor guy died by accident and you'd got the idea of substitution only when his body washed up on our beach. A lucky break that he was your height and build, you said. But there was no way you could have faked his dental record and substituted it for your own in the time you had, Oliver. No way!'

He nodded as if approving her logic.

'So you decided I was probably a murderer. Then later you found out I'd been working for the IRA. And you ran. Is that it?'

'Do you blame me?' she said dully.

'No,' he said. 'What puzzles me is, feeling like that, why didn't you tell the cops the whole story?'

'Because you're Noll's father,' she said slowly. 'Because that entitled you to a chance to defend yourself.'

'Which you were going to give me by never setting eyes on me again? That's what you wanted, isn't it? Hardly logical, Janey.'

'Logic's for computers,' she said. 'I'm a human being, a mother with a child to bring up, a daughter with a father killed in a crossfire between the people whose money you stole and the people who wanted to stop them getting that money and any like it. Show me the space to fit logic into that lot.'

Now he got out of bed, but not to approach her. Instead he made for the door.

'You've changed,' he said speculatively, pausing on the threshold. 'You've changed a lot, Janey. Remember that when you pass your verdict on me. It's too soon now to talk this thing out. I deny nothing, admit nothing. But when you think of condemning me, remember the change in yourself.'

He smiled then, so that his face matched his young, fit body. Then he left.

He hadn't been back to her room since. They had slipped into a routine which had most of the appearance and some of the reality of domesticity. Sometimes politeness merged into affection, occasionally comfort almost became content. And in their shared love of Noll they found common cause which would have made a much harder existence bearable.

Together they watched their son now. He saw their interest, called, 'Watch me!' and turning, flung himself fearlessly into the deep end. He vanished completely, and for a moment Jane's skies went dark also. Then his head burst back into the sunlight and he waved triumphantly. Now Maria rose with unhurried grace and moved to the edge of the pool. She did not need to shout, 'Watch me!' Her body did it for her, its unblemished olive brown rippling sensuously beneath the token restraints of the three scraps of white bikini. Her voracious appetite for all things sweet was already causing her waistline to thicken, Jane assured herself. Another ten years would see her plump as a pigeon. But now she dived into the water with scarcely a cormorant's splash and came up alongside Noll who greeted her with a joyous laugh.

'Time for my swim, I think,' said Oliver, rising.

She watched as he ran down the steps to the pool terrace and plunged in. He surfaced between Noll and Maria, splashing them both and sparking off some three-cornered horseplay. As Maria tried to duck him, Jane wondered how often before those slim brown arms had twined round his muscular shoulders. She had no firm evidence, had sought none. But when she found herself lying awake at night feeling the temptation to go to his room, she knew how strongly he too must feel the same urges. Yet when they were together during the day he showed very little sign of frustration. That, plus a change in Maria's attitude, a shift from the status of employee to something more equal . . . she broke the chain of thought. It led to jealousy, and jealousy implied assertion of rights, and that implied commitment.

She was still far from ready to contemplate renewing that. She looked at him and saw a dead man on a slab, she saw Jonty Thrale and the other filth he had tracked into their lives. But, being honest, she knew she saw them less clearly than once she had done . . .

Meanwhile, she would bear her frustrations and, if he couldn't bear his, he was welcome to seek relief in that lithe brown body.

'Senhora.'

It was Antonio, the gardener. At least that was his official designation, but his role was to guard as much as to garden.

'Car coming,' he said. 'Taxi.'

Jane stood up.

'Thanks, Antonio,' she said. She looked down at the pool. The water fight was still going on. She pulled on a light wrap to protect herself both from the sun and Antonio's assessing gaze, which was almost as disturbing as open lust, and walked round the terrace to the side of the villa. From here you could look all the way down the long track which led to the road spiralling into the mountains from the town below.

The taxi was moving fast, hotly pursued by a cloud of dust. A telescope was fitted onto the terrace wall and she stooped to peer through it. The driver's face leapt up towards her, anonymous behind the inevitable sun spectacles, and she could make out only a shadowy figure in the rear seat. The vehicle reached the gate. The driver got out, rattled the iron bars, got back in and spoke over his shoulder.

'Who is it?' asked Oliver behind her.

'I don't know. A taxi. Were you expecting anyone?'

'No one I want to see,' he said grimly.

The taxi door opened. A man got out, walked to the gates and stood there, very still, looking up towards them as if he could see them as clearly with his naked gaze as they could him through the telescope.

Strangely she felt as little surprise as if she had issued a formal invitation and her guest had turned up dead on time.

'It's Dog Cicero,' she said, without emotion.

He pushed her aside and looked for himself.

Then he straightened up and looked at her.

'What are you going to do?' she asked.

293

'Do?' he said, turning to the mechanism which opened the gate. 'A man doesn't come such a hell of a distance without a very good reason. We'd better let him in.'

# 4

They drank tea on the terrace. It was poured from a silver tea pot into bone china cups. There were toasted teacakes and petits fours. It was Oliver Beck's attempt at a scornful mockery of things English but it fell sadly flat. Dog Cicero examined the teacakes with the polite curiosity of an Italian prelate shown a pagan sacrifice and shook his head. Jane echoed the gesture more freely so that her flowing hair rippled redly in the sunlight like the tresses of the Celtic princess whose toilette in the evening and in the morning caused the sunset and the dawn.

Beck himself, his damp hair slicked back in thirties style and wearing a Noel Coward robe over his swim trunks, looked the most Anglo-Saxon thing there. Finally he too tired of this charade of a polite English welcome and drawled, 'OK, so you've tracked me down, Inspector Dog. That's quite a nose you've got.'

Dog produced his tobacco and papers, looked enquiringly at Jane, read her blankness as permission and rolled a narrow cigarette.

'Forget the "inspector",' he said. 'I'm no longer a policeman.'

'You've left the Force?' said Beck.

'We left each other,' said Dog.

He lit his cigarette and through the smoke watched their reactions. Beck, he assessed, was nimbling feverishly round all the angles while Jane had fixed on one. He avoided meeting her gaze. It was too early to seek positive reaction.

'If you're not a cop, then what the hell are you doing here?' asked Beck.

Dog shrugged.

'What would I be doing here if I were a cop?' he asked.

For a second Beck looked angry, then he laughed.

'That's a good question,' he said. 'Special Branch, the FBI, the Garda, none of them's got any standing here. But mine was a good question too. What do you want, Dog?'

'That's a large question, if not necessarily good. May I answer it frankly?'

'I'm all ears.'

Dog Cicero hesitated as if Beck had said something worth close consideration, then said, 'I would like to speak with Jane. There are things I need to say to her, things I'd delayed saying till after Noll was found. But, as you may recall, when that happened, I didn't get the opportunity.'

Beck sipped his cold tea.

'OK,' he said. 'There she sits. The floor's yours.'

'I should prefer alone,' said Dog apologetically.

'I bet!' Beck considered a moment then said, 'OK. You've got it.'

He rose and looked down to the pool where Maria and Noll were still playing. They saw him watching and waved. He waved back then went through the sliding patio door into the villa.

'So here we are,' said Dog.

'Say what you've got to say!' These were the first words Jane had spoken since his arrival. She had been sitting trying to guess what he was playing at. Knight errantry was out of fashion. Not that he looked like a knight errant. But what else was she to think of a man who, uninvited, had put her needs before his career and now followed her halfway across the world?

'How's Noll?' he asked. 'How's he settled down after . . . everything?'

She'd noticed this ability he had to go off in an unexpected direction, usually as now in a manner which forced you to follow.

'He's fine,' she said shortly.

'No after effects?'

'I don't think so. I've watched him very carefully. We talk about it as if it was all a game. It means having to listen to him burbling on about his fabulous Auntie Bridie, but that's a small price to pay for having him happy.'

'And you? Are you happy?'

'What the hell kind of question's that?' she blazed. 'And what gives you the right to ask it?'

He didn't reply and his silence forced her to answer herself.

'I'm sorry,' she said. 'You deserve better than rudeness after what you've done for us. But what do you really want? Some kind of explanation of why I came here? It seems a long way to come for an explanation if that's really why you've come.'

'It'll do for starters,' he said. 'You seemed pretty certain things were over between you and Beck . . .'

'What did you expect me to do?' she demanded. 'All right, if I'd got Noll back and there'd been no sign of Oliver, I'd have got my head down somewhere, changed my name, asked for police protection, done anything to keep him safe. But it didn't happen like that. Oliver *was* there. Tench was probably on his way and I can guess what protection from that bastard would mean. Flynn was dead, Thrale looked like he was dying, and Irish memories feed on dead flesh. Above all else, Oliver was ready to take Noll with or without me, he made that quite clear. So tell me, Inspector, sorry, *Mister* Cicero, what choice did I have?'

He took a deep breath. It would be easy to offer sympathetic agreement. But whatever came out of this encounter, for good or for bad, there had to be no ambiguity.

He said carefully, 'The absence of choice is a circumstance more rare than most people suppose.'

She looked at him incredulously, feeling anger tightening her throat. Worse than a knight errant, this was a missionary priest!

She said, 'Is that one of Uncle Endo's little saws for winning at cards?'

'He puts it more graphically. Choice and breath run out together, something like that.'

She leaned across the table and looked directly into his eyes.

'OK. So tell me about my choices.'

He didn't flinch from her gaze.

'Specifically, you could have held on to Noll and said no. I doubt if Beck would have shot you. More generally, it was a choice between this . . .' he gestured around . . . 'which is reasonably safe, extremely comfortable, and very dishonest, and other kinds of existence which would be none of these things.'

She shook her head in disbelief.

'You really have come all this way to preach at me!' she said.

He rolled another cigarette. One suck. One exhalation. It was gone. It occurred to her that this was the pleasure of a man who scorned to assume more than the briefest fragment of futurity.

'No,' he said. 'I let myself be diverted. But I didn't want to risk deception merely for the sake of sticking to the point.'

'Deception?' She frowned. 'How could you deceive me? And even if you did, why should it matter?'

He said, 'I'm going to invite you to come away with me. In the unlikely event you agree, it would surely matter if I'd obtained that agreement by a deception, wouldn't you say?'

Her eyes rounded in amazement. Every time he opened his mouth, he came up with some new occasion of anger or surprise. It occurred to her that she was being bounced from one reaction to another without ever getting the chance to settle into a studied and developed response. With this man, you should never forget Uncle Endo!

She said, 'By "with you" . . ?'

'It's an offer of help, it's an offer of love. Acceptance of one is not conditional on acceptance of the other.'

'Love,' she said softly. 'Because we made it together? I needed . . . someone; you needed . . . God knows what. But love . . !'

'Yes, love.' He had the absorbed look of a man who has been running on instinct but has at last reached the point where he can sit quietly and sort out his own motives. 'From the start. Well, almost from the start. I thought it was complicated and confused, but it wasn't. It was simple. That's why I behaved as I did. That's why I had to track you down across the world.'

'But it's crazy! Things don't happen that way outside of soap operas, not without hope, encouragement, a future . . .'

'Oh, but they do. It's happened twice to me. Perhaps that says something about me you'd rather not know. No one should get mixed up with a man who's always drawing to an inside straight. Last time it happened, it left her dead, me not much better. This time, God willing, it won't come to that. But the worst thing of all last time was, it left me not knowing. Never able to know. I told Thrale he was lying. In that situation, he would lie. Equally, in my situation, I would want to believe he was lying. This time whatever else happens, I need to be sure I've got things straight, that I've heard the truth, no matter what it might be. No hole cards. I've paid to see.'

'You want to know whether I'm in love with you?' she asked.

'Don't be silly,' he laughed. 'We've got to clear away need-to-know before we get on to want-to-know. What I need to know is the truth, or rather a series of truths. You had no suspicion Beck was a Noraid bagman till he "died"? You really believed the substitute corpse had drowned accidentally? You came back to England to hide from him, not meet him? You had no knowledge of his Father Blake disguise till that day in the cottage? You thought he was hanging back to rescue me?'

'Yes; yes; yes!' she blazed. 'I guessed about the body later but at the time . . . And what do you mean, *thought* he was going to rescue you? He did. You and that *woman*. It was in the papers. You were pulled clear of the fire . . .'

'Yes, yes,' he said impatiently. 'We survived. One more need-to-know. Do you still love him?'

She said, 'No.' And wondered how she would answer his next question. Wrong. She knew how she would answer it, but she wondered how she would want to answer it.

When he spoke, so sure was she of what he was going to say that she had to ask him to repeat what he actually did say.

'I went to see your mother before I left England.'

'My mother? How is she?'

'Fine. No. Not really fine. But better now than she was. It

really knocked her about, worrying what had happened to Noll and you, then not knowing where you were. I told her you were all right. I said I was sure she would hear from you eventually.'

'I wrote. Oliver said we couldn't risk posting it here but that he'd get someone to post it from the States or somewhere else.'

Dog said, 'That would take time. I'm sure she'll get it eventually. She's thinking of selling up and moving back to Ireland.'

Jane said, 'But why? I thought she'd never go back, that's what she always said.'

Dog said, 'I think she feels she moved to get away from the troubles, but what happened last December made her think there was no getting away from them, so she might as well be near them rather than waiting for them to catch up with her.'

Jane put her hand to her face.

'I never brought her much joy, did I,' she said. 'We were always so different.'

'Alike in one thing,' he corrected. 'You're both strong. And you both learn. She'll make it, I'm sure. And most of the changes in her will be for the good. She never uttered one word of blame for you, I thought you'd like to know that. She cried when she spoke of Noll. The only thing she really let herself go on about was Beck. I'm afraid that pretending he was a priest was in her eyes a long way beyond the unforgivable. Whatever other good reasons he has for not going back to Britain, your mother doubles them!'

He managed to make her smile. And seeing the smile, he asked the next question.

'Do you want to come away with me?'

It was not the form she had expected. Will you come away with me? was easily answered. But this . . .

Still they were playing the truth game, so she said, 'Some of me does. A lot. Maybe most.'

He nodded as if she'd confirmed some basic intuition. Then he reached over the table with his left hand and took her right. She didn't pull away. So hand in hand they sat in silence for thirty seconds or more.

'Now isn't this a touching scene,' said Oliver Beck.

He had changed into slacks and a tee shirt and he no longer looked Anglo-Saxon. He sat down and glowered at Dog and said, 'You've got a hell of nerve, coming here and sweet-talking my wife.'

Dog met his gaze for a moment then dropped his eyes to the tea tray, picked up the silver dish with the teacakes on it, turned it over so that its contents fell onto the tiled floor, and looked at the small cube of plastic stuck underneath.

'I should have believed you when you said you were all ears,' he remarked.

'You've been listening to us?' exclaimed Jane. 'Why did you do that?'

'He wanted to know if my intentions were dishonourable,' said Dog. 'More important, he hoped I would let slip how I got here.'

'Now why should that bother me?' asked Beck.

'Because if you thought I'd got here purely under my own steam you'd get your minder in there to take me on a little walk to the bottom of the garden, then toss me over the terrace.'

He glanced through the open door of the villa where, almost invisible in the shady interior, the man Antonio stood with a machine pistol in his hands.

Jane said, 'Oliver, for God's sake!'

'Don't worry,' said Dog. 'Oliver knows it's royal flush odds against me picking up his trail on my tod. No, I got help, Beck. Family help. I asked my Uncle Endo. And he asked his friends. You owe them a million, by the way. Dollars, not pounds, so it won't hurt all that much.'

'You what?' exclaimed Beck. 'I owe . . . you've got to be joking!'

'There were expenses,' said Dog apologetically. 'Friendship only goes so far. I said you'd pick up the tab. It's up to you whether you pay or not. That's for finding you, by the way. If I don't get home safely, the price goes up. I think they reckoned everything you've got would just about cover it.'

301

Beck said softly, 'And to think that just a couple of minutes ago you were shooting Jane the heavy moral line. You've got strange friends for a preacher.'

'In my time I've met some very strange preachers,' said Dog. 'Way I look at it is, what's the best use for all that Noraid cash? Buying bombs to blow up civilians? Not good. Buying you all life's little luxuries? Better, but not much. Buying me a chance to offer Jane and Noll another chance? Well, there's no competition, is there? It would be cheap at twice the price!'

'A chance to do what?' enquired Beck.

'To talk to visitors without a gun-toting heavy in the background, for a start.'

Beck made an impatient gesture and Antonio slipped out of sight.

'Now let's hear it,' he said.

Dog leaned forward and spoke with sudden urgency. But it was Jane, not Beck, he was addressing.

'This isn't a life,' he said. 'It's a siege. With him, this is it forever. You know what he is. He's a thief, a cheat, a killer. You've admitted you want to come away with me. So do it!'

Jane tensed her muscles to stop them from shaking. She had felt like this before races. All the training, all the preparation seemed to count for nothing; body limp, mind unfocussed; the running track a desert road; the finishing tape the unattainable line of the horizon.

She said, 'He's still Noll's father.'

'Yes. And he'll be Noll's mentor and exemplar if he grows up here,' said Dog grimly.

'At least he'll be safe here!' she cried.

'Safe? I found you, didn't I? At least away from here the danger stops at kidnapping. But when they find Beck, they'll come with guns blazing!'

'Very colourful,' said Beck dryly. 'But perhaps, Mr Cicero, you ought to tell us something of your financial background and prospects before Jane makes up her mind. Or do you anticipate subsidizing your new life with a little of my tainted wealth?'

He was back to his English parody, this time the paterfamilias interviewing a suitor for his daughter's hand.

Dog smiled thinly, knowing he had cards that Beck had not yet guessed at.

'I'll get by,' he said. 'Uncle Endo bankrolled me into a big Vegas game while his friends went looking for you. It lasted a fortnight. I'm glad you were so hard to find, Beck. After a week I was well down. But then I started getting into the swing of things and by the end of the second week I'd won myself a barrowload of chips. Jane, what do you say?'

She looked at him in such a distress of uncertainty that he had to look away. Suddenly his voice became harsh and loud, his expression aggressive and challenging. 'OK,' he snarled. 'Let's check to the dealer. Beck, what do *you* say?'

This was the way he'd played the last big pot in that smoke-filled room in Glitter Gulch. For thirteen days he had kept his face and mind a blank, his voice a monotone, unchanged from when he was losing heavily to when the chips started to flow his way. Now unexpectedly, shockingly, he had been all naked aggression. He had caught Endo's eye in the shaded rank of spectators beyond the sharp cone of light stamped down on the table, and he had seen surprise and doubt there. He had bounced them all out except for the other big winner, a lean, drawling sixty-year-old from Texas who looked like an extra in a John Wayne movie. He read the change of tactic as a giant bluff and he smiled almost sympathetically as he pushed forward the huge pile of chips needed to cover Dog's bet. Forty years of making a living at the tables showed in that smile when Dog turned up the card which filled his running flush. It didn't flicker or diminish, though it turned a little rueful as the Texan said over his shoulder, 'Knew I should never have taken those two dollars off you at blackjack in sixty-four, Endo'.

Now here he was again, forcing the play he wanted. All Beck had to do was say, 'Jane, don't go,' and he guessed the game was over. But the man was smiling like the Texan and behind those eyes too a computerful of calculation was clicking.

'What do I say?' said Beck. 'I say, Jane, you're an independent adult. Go, if that's what you want. I won't try to stop you. Only I can't let Noll go till I'm sure he's going to be safe. Now don't look like that. Isn't it reasonable? Dog, don't you feel it's only reasonable? You two get yourselves settled somewhere if that's what you want, then get back to me here and we'll settle on some mutually beneficial arrangement about Noll.'

Dog let out a long slow sigh of relief. The man was greedy. He thought he saw a chance of getting everything he wanted with minimum hassle. But best of all, or worst if you looked at it from Jane's point of view, he had just revealed that despite their years together, he didn't know her, didn't understand the tempered steel which formed the core of her being. No hope ain't the same as no chance, Endo had said. But in this case it was the same. There was no hope, no chance, of Jane Maguire leaving the villa without her son, and a man who truly loved her would have known that.

Jane said, 'You bastard. You stupid bastard! Do you think I'd just up and leave . . . how could you even dream . . ?'

It was time to cut in and play his winning card. Or perhaps his losing card. Bearers of bad news are rarely rewarded with their heart's desire.

He said, 'He didn't dream. He just hoped. It'd make things a lot easier, wouldn't it, Beck?'

'What the hell does that mean?' demanded Beck, and Jane looked the same question. It was her look that Dog answered.

'For a million dollars, Endo's friends did the thing thoroughly. They needed to be sure they weren't offending anyone really important before they pinpointed Beck. Well, they weren't. He'd bought a few minor officials, that was all, and they were anybody's for a handful of cruzados. But he needs protection, not against Thrale and his ilk – only self-help, big guns and eternal vigilance can protect him there – but against official hassle. If the Americans and my lot find where he is, they're going to start serving extradition papers like a short-order cook serves breakfasts. Now there's one certain protection against getting extradited from this country. If you're married to a native Brazilian and have a child by her, it doesn't matter who waves what papers, they won't send Daddy away.'

Jane said, 'So what are you saying? That Oliver . . ? But that's absurd . . .'

Dog's gaze slipped from hers and slowly turned till he was looking down at the pool. Jane's followed. Noll looked to be asleep now in the huge chair but it wasn't Noll they were looking at. Flat on her back, legs splayed in an unconsciously abandoned pose, lay the gleaming figure of Maria.

The thickening figure of Maria . . ?

'You're saying he's got her pregnant? Oliver . . ?'

She didn't need to complete the question. Beck smiled at her a boyishly rueful smile and said, 'You called the shots, honey, when you held out for your own bed.'

'My fault, you mean? My fault *again*? To hell with that! One thing's for sure. You can't marry her. Or have you forgotten Babs back in New York?'

Beck shrugged, looked at Dog and said mockingly, 'Low man brings it in.'

Jane looked blank. Dog said, 'It means, to get players really committed at stud, it's the one with the lowest hand who has to lead the betting.'

'And your hand's really low, ain't it, *Dog*?'

He thinks I can't win, thought Dog. He knows what I want and he thinks there's no play to get me it. He knows all I can do is pour pain on Jane. And the bastard doesn't care.

He said, 'It's Reno rules all the way with you, isn't it? That was where you got your quickie divorce five years ago, only you didn't shout it around. An estranged wife often came in useful. But you showed the papers quickly enough last week, didn't you?'

'Last week?' echoed Jane.

'When he married Maria,' said Dog flatly. 'For the past seven days you've been a guest in the house of Mr and Mrs Oliver Beck.'

There was no struggle for belief. Everything Jane recalled of the change in Maria's attitude, plus the change in her appearance, fell into place. And if any doubt had remained, Oliver Beck's face would have dissolved it.

He said, 'Well, there we have it, folks. Bet you really enjoyed that, Dog. Jane, I'm truly sorry it didn't work out. I could see how things were going to be between us, and once I knew Maria was in the club, I had to take the chance to protect my back. Don't worry. I'll see you right . . .'

'No you won't,' said Jane. 'Noll and I don't want anything from you . . .'

'You speak for yourself, hon,' he said easily. 'But as for Noll, he's going to get the best.'

She turned to Dog then, looking for help. He could see she was ready to offer him anything for a way out of this dilemma, but he knew he had nothing to offer.

Beck spelled it out.

'No use looking at Dog, hon. Dog's all chained up in his kennel! He can tell the Feds and the Branch, but they can't touch me now. Or he can drop word to Dublin, but he knows that'll mean a Semtex tea party round the pool one day with everyone getting a piece of the cake, so he's not going to do that, not with Noll here, and here Noll stays!'

He was right. It was the end of the game, even though he still had a hole card. Endo had said, 'You want this guy taken out, say the word. They'll throw it in for the million.' But it was not a card he knew how to play. Jane was still regarding him with hope born of, and almost indistinguishable from, desperation. He had nothing to give her, nothing to say. He looked away from her, looked behind her into the open door of the villa into the shade as dark as his future. His eyes bored into the darkness in search of some symbol of hope, but all they found was the figure of Antonio. He had after all only retreated into the depths of the room where he still remained, gun in hand, ready to advance again as soon as his master snapped his fingers.

And now he must have realized Dog had spotted him for he was advancing anyway. And now he was at the doorway unblinking in the sunlight which limned his face and form. But it wasn't Antonio. It was his own death Dog saw standing there and it had the features of Bridie Heighway.

# 5

She said, 'Stay still. No use looking over my shoulder, Beck. Your handy man's not coming. Don't you recognize his gun?'

She motioned Beck into a tighter group with the two seated figures. Now the Beretta 93R's twenty-round magazine would be quite enough to cut them all down in a single burst.

Beck said, 'It's Bridie, isn't it? We met a couple of times in Belfast way back. And how are things with you, Bridie? You look a tiny bit peaky to me.'

She looked like a ghost. Pale beyond remedy of even the Brazilian sun, flesh honed almost to the bone, she was herself at last, undisguised with only a single role to play.

She had been rehearsing it for months as she sat in a series of cells and interview rooms. There had been no trouble not answering the endless stream of questions. Most of them she didn't even hear as her mind roamed forward to a time beyond this when the man who had murdered Jonty Thrale and the man who had led him to his death would be in her grasp.

She set no period on her revenge but, if forced to an estimate, would probably have guessed at a couple of years minimum, and possibly a lot longer if the Brits managed to manufacture the serious evidence she knew was lacking. It didn't matter. When life ceases to have meaning, time is no longer of the essence.

'Did you break out, Bridie? Or did Tench turn you loose?'

It was the killer who spoke, the frozen-faced soldier who had murdered her love.

She almost shot him then but a desire to prolong the moment, perhaps an awareness of the utter emptiness that lay beyond it, stayed her finger on the trigger.

'Yes, that would be it,' Dog Cicero went on. 'Tench let you

go. He must have decided he could get a better result that way than putting you behind bars for a two or three stretch.'

He didn't sound afraid, and that was bad. She wanted him to be afraid. Her last memory of Jonty was of a man sobbing in pain and terror. Perhaps a bullet in the stomach was a good idea now. Except that she guessed that the first shot was going to cue the other two into desperate motion and after that there would be nothing for it but the long, destructive burst which would bring the curtain down.

She saw him glance at the woman, the boy's mother, and smile. His hand moved on the table and she came to the brink of action. But it only strayed to cover the woman's and squeeze it. So, there was something between them. Her mind took this in, weighed it. She'd been wondering what to do about the woman, but if she were emotionally involved with Cicero, this gave birth to new refinements of revenge.

She said flatly, 'I'm going to kill you all, you know that. Your only options are to sit quiet till I'm ready, or pick your own time by making a move.'

Now they knew. It wouldn't stop them wriggling, but they knew and that was important.

First wriggle came from Beck.

'Surely killing me's a little outside your brief, Bridie,' he said with complete calm. 'That's not the way to get your money back, and there'll be long faces in Dublin if you go back empty handed.'

'I think you're mistaking the situation, Beck,' said Cicero. His voice was just as calm, but while Beck's had been the calmness of control it seemed to Heighway that his was the calmness of indifference.

She moistened her lips in anticipation of ripping that indifference to tatters. A bullet through his girl friend's breast perhaps . . .

He was still speaking.

'Miss Heighway isn't here out of zeal for a cause. In fact I doubt if the actual cause ever meant all that much to her. No, this is personal business, so you'll need to dredge up something better than money to talk your way out of it.'

'No one's talking their way out,' said Bridie Heighway. 'Nothing anyone can say will change a thing.'

'Good,' said Cicero. 'Accepting that, we can at least check out a few facts without being accused of special pleading.'

He knows I want to spin out the climax, thought Heighway. And he's trying to use it. I'll let him have the first one in mid-sentence, just when he's thinking he's getting somewhere.

But the direction of Cicero's sentence took her by surprise.

'Did Jonty Thrale kill Madeleine Salter?' he asked brusquely.

'Who?' She'd let herself be surprised into answering.

'The woman at the college, whose telephone number you got from Mrs Maguire, which led you to Jane.'

Now she was curious where this was leading.

'No. I didn't even know she was dead. What reason would Jonty have for killing her?'

'I did wonder,' said Dog. 'Then presumably it was you, Beck. That's the first place you'd go when you came down to London hoping to make contact with Jane. She probably told everything she knew to you as Father Blake, but you wanted to be sure, and once you'd moved from confession to inquisition, she had to be permanently silenced. Jane, I'm sorry. I thought it might be him, but I wouldn't have said anything till I was sure.'

Maguire was looking at Beck in horror.

'Is it true, Oliver?' she demanded. 'You murdered Maddy? Oh God! Maddy . . .'

This was fun, thought Bridie Heighway. This trio had pain of their own to spread among themselves, poisoning their last moments more than mere fear could.

Beck's only response to Maguire's accusation was to shrug. A man trying to find a way out of dying didn't waste energy on irrelevancies. Fixing his eyes on the woman with the gun, he said urgently, 'OK, if this is personal, you've got even less reason to kill me. How have I harmed you? It was this bastard here who brought all the trouble to your door. Blow him away by all means. You'd be doing me a favour. After that, well, do whatever you want. If money's a problem, I'd be delighted to help.'

'And the woman?' probed Heighway. 'What shall I do about her?'

Beck considered then shrugged once more.

'Up to her,' he said indifferently. 'They're sitting there holding hands. If they want to be together that much, I don't see why I should stand in their way.'

Suddenly she was tired of them all, tired of their wriggling, tired even of the pain they were inflicting on each other.

Dog saw decision enter her eyes as he'd seen it enter the eyes of hundreds of poker players. Time for one last bet.

He said, 'You think I killed Thrale, don't you? Why?'

She said, 'I know you killed him.'

He nodded and said, 'Of course. Toby Tench told you that, didn't he? I'm sorry to tell you this, Bridie, but it's not personal after all. Whether you like it or not there's only one reason you're here and it's nothing to do with avenging Thrale. You're working for the Brits! Toby Tench has recruited you for Special Branch!'

He began to laugh, recovered, said, 'I'm sorry. Look, what did he tell you? That I got out of the cottage and left you and Jonty to burn? Then the fire brigade turned up, just in time to rescue you, but not Jonty? Is that it? Of course it is. Then he turns you loose. I bet he let slip that I'd gone to America. He was sending you after me, Bridie, don't you see? If the trail happened to lead to Beck, well and good, but his main concern was for you to put me out of the way. No time to explain why, but that's the truth of it. And the rest of the truth is, I didn't kill Jonty. I didn't even leave him to burn. This bastard blew his skull off with his own gun, then he cracked my head open with it and left me to the flames. But I got out, Bridie. I got out and, like an idiot, I dragged you out with me. God help me, I saved your life so that Toby Tench could turn you loose to kill me!'

He spoke with a passion which surprised himself and he saw the force of his outburst had reached the Irish woman. He had almost convinced her. He could see it in her face. But he could also see that it didn't matter.

Oliver Beck saw it too. The time for words was past. Best would have been for Cicero to make the move, draw the fire. But the fellow was all mouth. One last thought, three million – had it been worth it? Maybe. The next couple of seconds would tell him that.

Then he blanked out thought and launched himself forward.

One useful spin-off from the pig's outburst – it concentrated Heighway's attention so there was a fraction of delay in her reaction. But all it meant was that she had to step swiftly sideways to avoid his flailing arms and her first shots caught him high on the right shoulder instead of through his chest.

He screamed in pain. His impetus carried him towards the open patio door and what had been assault became flight. Inside it would be cool and shady with places to hide, weapons to find. All he had to do was reach the shadows.

He passed through the doorway and the second burst of bullets passed through with him, splintering his spine and throwing him face down onto a white leather sofa. For a couple of seconds he thrashed helplessly in a spasm of short-circuiting nerves. Then he was still.

Every sinew in Jane's body was screaming at her to run, to let the sound of the shots explode her into action as the starting pistol had in her athletics days. But Dog Cicero's mind had computed the odds and opted for stillness. His hand closed tight on hers, communicating more than imprisoning, for she could easily have pulled free. Instead she obeyed, and when the smoking muzzle swung round to bear on them, it found a motionless target.

He'd been right. But he'd also been wrong. Because they were so still, Bridie Heighway did not fire immediately as she would certainly have done at a moving target. But in flight, there would have been a faint chance that Dog's broader frame would have protected Jane long enough for her to reach cover. Now all he'd won was a few seconds' respite. Nothing had changed in her face. Their sentence was still written clear there.

'Isn't it enough?' said Dog, gesturing at the corpse of Oliver Beck.

'What could ever be enough?' she hissed.

'But not her! Why kill her?' he demanded desperately.

'Why not?' said Bridie Heighway.

Her finger tightened on the trigger.

Then a voice called, 'Auntie Bridie! Auntie Bridie!'

And running up the steps from the lower terrace came the excited figure of Noll Maguire.

The gunshots had aroused him. Behind him, Maria too had been awoken and was crouching by her lounger, her face slack with doubt and apprehension. But Noll had only the egotistic certainty of the loved child.

'Is that the gun Billy promised me, Auntie Bridie? Have you brought it for me?'

Beneath his hand Dog felt Jane's clench into a fist, hard and cold as a snowball. She wanted to call out to Noll but was terrified he might come running to her, putting himself between the Beretta and its target. So she bit her words back and watched as her son clung to Bridie Heighway's legs and reached up covetously to the unwavering gun.

'Please, Auntie Bridie, is it mine?'

She looked down at the eager, hopeful face of the little boy and he looked up into her pale, ice-sculpted features. There was nothing there but cold, lonely hate. But the world had not yet taught him how to react to that. Funny faces were part of Aunt Bridie's treasure-trove of talents, and this one just made him laugh out loud with uninhibited delight.

For long moments there was no response. Then slowly, miraculously, she began to smile. And finally she stooped and swung him up in the crook of her free arm.

'No, not this one, my little piglet,' she said. 'This one's too big for you. But I'll send you another one, I promise. As soon as I can. Now I've got to go away. Will you step with me a little way and see that I come to no harm?'

313

She set him down and took him by the hand. Jane was on her feet.

'Not again,' she said in a voice full of agony. 'Please. Not again.'

'Just a little way, I promise,' said Bridie Heighway. 'You'll not be wanting him to look in there.'

She nodded towards the open patio door, then she turned to Dog.

'Cicero, they tell me you're a gambling man. I should give it up. Your luck must surely have run out. You can't keep on winning with all the losing hands God keeps dealing you.'

The boy was tugging impatiently at her hand.

'All right, Noll, we'll be off,' she said. 'You remember that song I taught you? "Green grow the rushes oh"? Shall we sing it as we go?'

'Yes!' shouted the boy.

'Right then. *I'll give you one oh. Green grow the rushes oh!* Now it's you.'

*'What is your one oh?'* carolled Noll.

*'One is one and all alone and ever more shall be so.'*

So hand in hand and singing in turn, they set off together down the path to the gate.

Jane Maguire stood and watched them go.

Beside her, Dog said urgently, 'It'll be all right, I know it will.' But he could tell she didn't hear.

He left her and turned to meet Maria who was coming hesitantly up the steps. He stopped her from going any closer to the doorway into the villa and said, 'Senhora Beck, please do not go inside. There has been an accident to your husband, Senhor Beck, a serious accident. Stay down by the pool for a while. I must make arrangements. Rest assured, you and your baby will be looked after as your husband would have wished. Only there must be no fuss, no disturbance, you understand. If there is any disturbance, if the authorities come before we are ready, they will take all this, the villa, all your husband's

314

money, everything. You understand?'

Terrified, she nodded and retreated to the pool.

He turned and looked down the hill. Bridie Heighway and the boy were close to the gate now. Jane was still standing like a statue, watching and willing. He went into the villa, tried Beck's pulse, picked up a telephone and dialled. It was answered almost immediately. He said in Italian, 'I am a colleague of Endo Cicero. He said if I needed any advice or assistance I should contact you . . .'

When he had finished talking he closed the Venetian blinds, then slipped behind them and out of the door which he locked.

He went and stood beside Jane. Bridie Heighway was at the gate now, kneeling and talking to Noll. Then she put her arms round him, hugged him, and passed through the gate without a backward glance up to the villa.

'I bet the bitch takes my taxi,' said Dog.

But Jane was no longer there. She was racing down the pathway towards the gate where her son was waving goodbye to the receding cab.

He started to walk slowly down the track towards them.

Endo's friends would clear up this mess, he had no doubt, extracting their payment from Beck's estate, leaving enough to keep Maria quiet. But the larger mess, the mess of lives and emotions, of pasts and futures, would need a lot more than a network of bribes, favours and fears to tidy up. He tried to look inside himself to see if he had the strength, the staying power, but he quickly gave up the search. Some things you only found out by doing.

He reached Jane, who was kneeling as Bridie Heighway had knelt with her arms around her son. He leaned over them and lightly embraced them both. Then Noll, who clearly found all this hugging a bit of a bore, wriggled free and raced away up the hillside.

Gently he raised Jane to her feet.

She looked into his face and said seriously, 'Dog, have I ever said thank you?'

'Once,' he said with a faint smile. 'At least I think that's what you said.'

'I don't know what's going to happen now,' she said flatly. 'I'm numb. I don't know what I feel about anything, about the future, about you. Except that I . . . that we owe you more than I can ever repay.'

'You owe me nothing,' he said. 'It's a new game. But from now on, I'll collect everything I win.'

'That may not be much,' she said softly. 'She was right. God keeps on dealing you a lot of losing cards.'

'There ain't no such thing as losing cards,' he said. 'Only losing players.'

'Uncle Endo?' she asked.

He considered.

'No,' he said. 'I think that was pure me.'

The sun was slipping fast behind the mountains, sending their shadows racing eastwards across the dark blue reaches of the sea towards the still gleaming horizon.

He took her hand lightly in his and, swinging their arms between them like children, they began to climb the steep and narrow path up to the villa.

# On Beulah Height

## Reginald Hill

They moved everyone out of Dendale that long hot summer fifteen years ago. They needed a new reservoir and an old community seemed a cheap price to pay. They even dug up the dead and moved them too.

But four inhabitants of the valley they couldn't move, for no one knew where they were. Three little girls had gone missing, and the prime suspect in their disappearance, Benny Lightfoot.

This was Andy Dalziel's worst case and now fifteen years on he looks set to relive it. It's another long hot summer. A child goes missing in the next valley, and old fears resurface as someone sprays the deadly message on the walls of Danby: BENNY'S BACK!

Music and myth mingle as the Mid-Yorkshire team delve into their pasts and into their own reserves of experience and endurance in search of answers which threaten to bring more pain than they resolve.

'All Reginald Hill's novels are brilliantly written, but he has excelled himself here: and has, too, put together an intricate narrative with the complex ingenuity of a watch-maker'          T. J. BINYON, *Evening Standard*

ISBN: 978-0-00-731317-4